The Coffee Trader

David Liss

W F HOWES LTD

This large print edition published in 2003 by
W F Howes Ltd
Units 6/7, Victoria Mills, Fowke Street
Rothley, Leicester LE7 7PJ

1 3 5 7 9 10 8 6 4 2

First published in the United Kingdom in 2003
by Abacus

A CIP catalogue record for this book is available
from the British Library

ISBN 1 84197 602 4

Typeset by Palimpsest Book Production Limited,
Polmont, Stirlingshire
Printed and bound in Great Britain
by Antony Rowe Ltd, Chippenham, Wilts.

The Coffee Trader

CHAPTER 1

F irmer than water or wine, it rippled thickly in its bowl, dark and hot and uninviting. Miguel Lienzo picked it up and pulled it so close he almost dipped his nose into the tarry liquid. Holding the vessel still for an instant, he breathed in, pulling the scent deep into his lungs. The sharp odour of earth and rank leaves surprised him, it was like something an apothecary kept in a chipped porcelain jar.

'What is this?' Miguel asked, working through his irritation by pushing at the cuticle of one thumb with the nail of the other. She knew he had no time to waste, so why had she brought him here for this nonsense? One bitter remark after another bubbled up inside him, but Miguel let loose with none of them. It wasn't that he was afraid of her, but he often found himself going to great lengths to avoid her displeasure.

He looked over and saw that Geertruid met his silent cuticle mutilation with a grin. He knew that irresistible smile and what it meant: she was mightily pleased with herself, and when she looked

1

that way it was hard for Miguel not to be mightily pleased with her too.

'It's something extraordinary,' she told him, gesturing towards his bowl. 'Drink it.'

'Drink it?' Miguel squinted into the blackness. 'It looks like the devil's piss, which would certainly be extraordinary, but I've no desire to know what it tastes like.'

Geertruid leaned towards him, almost brushing up against his arm. 'Take a sip and then I'll tell you everything. This devil's piss is going to make both our fortunes.'

It had begun not an hour earlier, when Miguel felt someone take hold of his arm.

In the instant before he turned his head, he ticked off the unpleasant possibilities: rival or creditor, abandoned lover or her angry relative, the Danish fellow to whom he'd sold those Baltic grain futures with too enthusiastic a recommendation. Not so long ago the approach of a stranger had held promise. Merchants and schemers and women had all sought Miguel's company, asking his advice, craving his companionship, bargaining for his guilders. Now he wished only to learn in what new shape disaster would unfold itself.

He never thought to stop walking. He was part of the procession that formed each day when the bells of the Nieuwe Kerk struck two, signalling the end of trading on the Exchange. Hundreds of brokers poured out on to the Dam, the great plaza at Amsterdam's centre. They spread out along the alleys and roads and canal sides. Along the Warmoesstraat, the fastest route to the most popular taverns, shopkeepers stepped outside, donning wide-brimmed leather hats to guard against the damp that rolled in from the North Sea. They set out sacks of spices, rolls of linen, barrels of tobacco. Tailors and shoemakers and milliners waved men inside; sellers of books and pens and exotic trinkets cried out their wares.

The Warmoesstraat became a current of black hats and black suits, speckled only with the white collars, sleeves, and stockings or the flash of silver shoe buckles. Traders pushed past goods from the Orient or the New World, from places of which no one had heard a hundred years before. Excited like schoolboys set free of the classroom, the traders talked of their business in a dozen different languages. They laughed and shouted and pointed; they grabbed at anything young and female that crossed their path. They took out their purses and devoured the shopkeepers' goods, leaving only coins in their wake.

Miguel Lienzo neither laughed nor admired the commodities set out before him nor clutched at the soft parts of willing shop girls. He walked silently, head down against the light rain. Today was, on the Christian calendar, the thirteenth day of May 1659. Accounts on the Exchange closed each month on the twentieth; let a man make what manoeuvres he liked, none of it mattered until the twentieth, when the credits and debits of the month were tallied and money at last changed hands. Today things had gone badly with a matter of brandy futures, and Miguel now had less than a week to pluck his fat from the fire or he would find himself another thousand guilders in debt.

Another thousand. He already owed three thousand. Once he had made double that in a year, but six months ago the sugar market had collapsed, taking Miguel's fortune with it. And then – well, one mistake after another. He wanted to be like the Dutch, who regarded bankruptcy as no shame. He tried to tell himself it did not matter, it was only a little while longer until he undid the damage, but believing that tale required an increasing effort. How long, he wondered, until his wide and boyish face turned pinched? How long until his eyes lost the eager sparkle of a merchant and took on the desperate, hollow gaze of a gambler? He vowed it would not happen to him. He would not become one of those lost souls, the ghosts who haunted the Exchange, living from one reckoning day to the next, toiling to secure just enough profit to keep their accounts afloat for one more month when surely all would be made easy.

Now, with unknown fingers wrapped around his arm, Miguel turned and saw a neatly dressed Dutchman of the middling ranks, hardly more than twenty years of age. He was a muscular wide-shouldered fellow with blond hair and a face almost more pretty than handsome, though

4

his drooping moustache added a masculine flair.

Hendrick. No family name that anyone had ever heard. Geertruid Damhuis's fellow.

'Greetings, Jew Man,' he said, still holding on to Miguel's arm. 'I hope all goes well for you this afternoon.'

'Things always go well with me,' he answered, as he twisted his neck to see if any prattling trouble-maker might lurk behind him. The Ma'amad, the ruling council among the Portuguese Jews, forbade congress between Jews and 'inappropriate' gentiles, and while this designation could prove treacher-ously ambiguous, no one could mistake Hendrick, in his yellow jerkin and red breeches, for anything appropriate.

'Madame Damhuis sent me to fetch you,' he said.

Geertruid had played at this before. She knew Miguel could not risk being seen on so public a street as the Warmoesstraat with a Dutchwoman, particularly a Dutchwoman with whom he did business, so she sent her man instead. There was no less risk to his reputation, but this way she could force his hand without even showing her face.

'Tell her I haven't the time for so lovely a diversion,' he said. 'Not just now.'

'Of course you do.' Hendrick grinned widely. 'What man can say no to Madame Damhuis?'

Not Miguel. At least not easily. He had difficulty saying no to Geertruid or to anyone else – includ-ing himself – who proposed something amusing.

Miguel had no stomach for doom; disaster felt to him like an awkward and loose suit. He had to force himself each day to play the cautious role of a man in the throes of ruin. That, he knew, was his true curse, the curse of all former Conversos: in Portugal he had grown too used to falseness, pretending to worship as a Catholic, pretending to despise Jews and respect the Inquisition. He had thought nothing of being one thing while making the world believe he was another. Deception, even self-deception, came far too easily.

'Thank your mistress but give her my regrets.' With reckoning day soon upon him, and new debts to burden him, he would have to curb his diversions, at least for a while. And there had been another note this morning, a strange anonymous scrawl on a torn piece of paper. *I want my money*. It was one of a half-dozen or so Miguel had received in the last month. *I want my money*. Wait your turn, Miguel would think glumly, as he opened each of these letters, but he was still unnerved by the terse tone and uneven hand. Only a madman would send such a message without a name – for how could Miguel respond even if he had the money and even if he were so inclined to use what little he had for something so foolish as paying debts?

Hendrick stared, as though he couldn't understand Miguel's good, if thickly accented, Dutch.

'Today is not the day,' Miguel said, a bit more forcefully. He avoided speaking too adamantly to Hendrick, whom he had once seen slam a butcher's head into the stones of the Damplatz for selling Geertruid rancid bacon.

Hendrick gazed at Miguel with the special pity men of the middle rank reserved for their superiors. 'Madame Damhuis told me to inform you that today *is* the day. She tells me that she will show you something, and when you set your eyes on it, you will forever after divide your life into the time *before* this afternoon and the time *after*.'

The thought of her disrobing flashed in front of him. That would be a lovely divide between the past and the future and would certainly be worth setting aside his business for the afternoon. However, Geertruid loved to play at these games. There was little chance she meant to take off as much as her cap. But there was no getting rid of Hendrick, and urgent as his troubles might be, Miguel could make no deals with this Dutchman lurking in his shadow. It had happened before. He would trail Miguel from tavern to tavern, from alley to canal side, until Miguel surrendered. Best to have this over with, he decided, so he sighed and said he would go.

With a sharp gesture of his neck, Hendrick led them off the ancient cobbled street and across the steep bridges towards the new part of the city, ringed by the three great canals – the Herengracht, the Keizersgracht, and the Prinsengracht – and then towards the Jordaan, the most rapidly growing part of town, where the air echoed with the ring

7

of hammer on anvil and the chipping of chisel on stone.

Hendrick led him along the waters of the Rozengracht, where barges pierced the thick canal mist as they headed towards the docks to unload their goods. The new houses of the newly wealthy stood on either side of the murky water, facing the oak-and linden-lined waterway. Miguel had once rented the better part of so fine a house, red-brick and steeple-gabled. But then Brazilian production of sugar had far exceeded Miguel's expectations. He'd been gambling on low production for years, but suddenly Brazilian farmers unleashed an unexpected crop, and in an instant prices collapsed. A great man of the Exchange as instantly became a debtor living off his brother's scraps.

Once they departed from the main street, the Jordaan lost its charm. The neighbourhood was new – where they stood had been farmland only thirty years before – but already the alleyways had taken on the decrepit cast of a slum. Dirt replaced the cobblestones. Huts made of thatch and scraps of wood leaned against squat houses black with tar. The alleys vibrated with the hollow clacking of looms, as weavers spun from sunrise until late into the night, all in the hope of earning enough to keep their bellies full for one more day.

In moments of weakness, Miguel feared that poverty would claim him as it had claimed the wretched of the Jordaan, that he would fall into a well of debt so deep he would lose even the dream of recovering himself. Would he be the same man then – himself, yet penniless – or would he become as hollow as the beggars and luckless labourers he passed on the streets?

He assured himself it would not happen. A true merchant never gives in to gloom. A man who has lived as a Secret Jew always has one more trick to save his skin. At least until he fell into the clutches of the Inquisition, he reminded himself, and there was no Inquisition in Amsterdam. Just the Ma'amad.

But what was he doing here with this inscrutable Dutchman? Why had he allowed his will to collapse when he had business, important business, to pursue?

'To what sort of place are you taking me?' Miguel asked, hoping to find a reason to excuse himself.

'A miserable sort of place,' Hendrick said.

Miguel opened his mouth to voice an objection, but it was too late. They had arrived.

Though he was not, like the Dutch, inclined to believe in omens, Miguel would later recall that his venture had begun in a place called the Golden Calf, surely an unpromising name. They climbed down a steep and viciously low-ceilinged stairwell to the cellar, a little room that might comfortably have held thirty souls but now contained perhaps fifty. The choking smoke of cheap West Indian tobacco and musty peat stoves nearly suppressed the scent of spilled beer and wine, old cheese, and the odour of fifty unwashed men – or, rather, forty men and ten whores – whose mouths puffed out onions and beer.

At the bottom of the stairs, an enormous man, shaped remarkably liked a pear, blocked their passage, and sensing that someone wished to get by he moved his bulk backwards to prevent anyone from squeezing past. He held a tankard in one hand and a pipe in another, and he shouted something incomprehensible to his companions.

'Move your monstrous bulk, fellow,' Hendrick said to him.

The man turned his head just enough to register his scowl and then looked away.

'Fellow' – Hendrick tried again – 'you are the hard turd in the arse of my journey. Don't make me apply a purgative to flush you out.'

'Go piss in your breeches,' he answered, and then belched laughter in his friends' faces.

'Fellow,' said Hendrick, 'turn around and see to whom you speak so rudely.'

The man did turn around, and as he saw Hendrick the grin melted from his jowly three-days-unshaved face. 'Begging your pardon,' he said. He pulled his cap down off his head and moved quickly out of the way, knocking clumsily into his friends.

This newfound humility wasn't enough to satisfy Hendrick, who reached out like the lash of a whip and grabbed the man's filthy shirt. The tankard and pipe fell to the floor. 'Tell me,' Hendrick said, 'should I crush your throat or not crush your throat?'

'Not crush,' the drunk suggested eagerly. His hands flapped like bird wings.

'What do you say, Jew Man?' Hendrick asked Miguel. 'Crush or not crush?'

'Oh, let him go,' Miguel answered wearily.

Hendrick released his grip. 'The Jew Man says to let you go. You remember that, fellow, next time you think to toss a dead fish or rotten cabbage at a Jew. A Jew has saved your hide today, and for no good reason, too.' He turned to Miguel. 'This way.'

A nod from Hendrick was enough, and the crowd gave way for them as the Red Sea parted for Moses. Across the tavern, Miguel saw Geertruid, sitting at the bar, pretty as a tulip in a dung heap. When Miguel stepped forward she turned to him and smiled, wide and bright and irresistible. Miguel could not help but return the smile, feeling like a foolish boy, which was how she regularly made him feel. She had an illicit charm about her. Spending time with Geertruid was like bedding a friend's wife (something he had never done, for adultery was a most dreadful sin, and no woman he'd ever met had been tempting enough to lead him down that path) or giving a virgin her first kiss (which was something he *had* done, but only once, and that virgin later became his wife). The air around Geertruid always tingled with forbidden and elusive desire. Perhaps it was because Miguel

11

had never spent so much time with a woman to whom he was unrelated without bedding her.

'Madam, I'm honoured you wished to see me, but I'm afraid I haven't time for these diversions just now.'

'Reckoning day approaches,' she said sympathetically. She shook her head with a sadness that bordered somewhere between maternal and mocking.

'It approaches, and I've a great deal to put in order.' He thought to tell her more, that things had gone badly and, unless he could devise a remarkable scheme, he would be another thousand in debt within a week. But he didn't say that. After six months of brutal, relentless, numbing indebtedness, Miguel had learned a thing or two about how to live as a debtor. He had even considered writing a little tract on the matter. The first rules were that a man must never act like a debtor and he must never announce his troubles to anyone who did not need to know them.

'Come, sit next to me for a moment,' she said.

He thought to say no, he preferred to stand, but sitting next to her was much more delicious than standing near by, so he felt himself nodding before he'd realised he'd made a decision.

It was not that Geertruid was more beautiful than other women, though she certainly had some beauty about her. At first glance she seemed nothing unusual, a prosperous widow in her middle thirties, regally tall, still quite pretty, particularly if a man gazed upon her from the proper distance or with enough beer in his belly. But even though she was past her prime, she yet retained more than her share of charms and had been blessed with one of those smooth and circular northern faces, as creamy as Holland butter. Miguel had seen youths twenty years her junior staring hungrily at Geertruid.

Hendrick appeared from behind Miguel and removed the man sitting next to Geertruid. Miguel moved in as Hendrick led the fellow away.

'I can only spare a few minutes,' he told her.

'I think you'll give me more time than that.' She leaned forward and kissed him, just above the border of his fashionably short beard.

The first time she had kissed him they had been in a tavern, and Miguel, who had never before had a woman for a friend, let alone a Dutchwoman, thought himself obligated to take her to one of the back rooms and lift her skirts. It would not have been the first time a Dutchwoman had made her intentions known to Miguel. They liked his easy manner, his quick smile, his large black eyes. Miguel had a rounded face, soft and youthful without being babyish. Dutchwomen sometimes asked if they could touch his beard. It happened in taverns and musicos and on the streets in the less fashionable parts of town. They claimed they wanted to feel his beard, neatly trimmed and handsome as it was, but Miguel knew better. They liked his face because it was soft like a child's and hard like a man's.

Geertruid, however, never wanted anything more than to press her lips against his beard. She had long since made it clear that she had no interest at all in having her skirts lifted, at least not by Miguel. These Dutchwomen kissed anyone they liked for any reason they liked, and they did so more boldly than the Jewish women of the Portuguese Nation dared to kiss their husbands.

'You see,' she told him as she pulled away, 'even though you've been in this city for years, I still have new sights to show you.'

'I fear your stock of the new may be running thin.'

'At least you needn't worry about that Hebrew council of yours seeing us in this place.'

It was true enough. Jews and gentiles were permitted to conduct business in taverns, but what Jew among the Portuguese would choose this foul pit? Still, a man could never be overly cautious. Miguel took a quick look around for the telltale signs of Ma'amad spies: men who might be Jews dressed as Dutch labourers, conspicuous fellows alone or in pairs, eating none of the food; beards, which hardly anyone but Jews wore, cut close with scissors to resemble clean shaves (the Torah forbade only the use of razors on faces, not the trimming of beards, but beards were so out of fashion in Amsterdam that even the hint of one marked a man as a Jew).

14

Geertruid slid her hand along Miguel's, a gesture that came just short of the amorous. She loved freedom with men above all else. Her husband, whom she spoke of as the cruellest of villains, had been dead some years now, and she'd not yet finished celebrating her liberty. 'That sack of fat behind the bar is my cousin Crispijn,' she said.

Miguel glanced at the man: pale, corpulent, heavy-lidded – no different from ten thousand others in the city. 'Thank you for letting me witness your bloated kinsman. I hope I may at least ask him to bring me a tankard of his least foul beer to drown the stench?'

'No beer. I have something else in mind today.'

Miguel did not try to suppress a smile. 'Something else in mind? And is this where you have decided I might finally know your secret charms?'

'I have secrets aplenty – you may depend on it – but not such as you're thinking.' She waved over to her cousin, who replied with a solemn nod and then disappeared into the kitchen. 'I want you to taste a new drink – a wondrous luxury.'

Miguel stared at her. He might have been in any one of half a dozen other taverns now, speaking of woollens or copper or the lumber trade. He might be working hard to repair his ruined accounts, finding some bargain that he alone could recognise or convincing some drunkard to sign his name to the brandy futures. 'Madam, I thought you understood that my affairs are pressing. I have no time for luxuries.'

She leaned in closer and looked him full in his face, and for an instant Miguel believed she meant to kiss him. Not some sly buss on the cheek but a true kiss, hungry and urgent.

He was mistaken. 'I didn't bring you here idly, and you will find that I offer you nothing ordinary,' she told him, her lips close enough to his face that he could taste her fine breath.

And then her cousin Crispijn brought out something that changed his life.

Two earthen bowls sat steaming with a liquid blacker than the wines of Cahors. In the dim light, Miguel gripped the lightly chipped vessel with both hands and took his first taste.

It had a rich, almost enchanting, bitterness – something Miguel had never before experienced. It bore a resemblance to chocolate, which once he had tasted years ago. Perhaps he thought of chocolate only because the drinks were both hot and dark and served in thick clay bowls. This one had a less voluptuous flavour, sharper and more sparing. Miguel took another taste and set it down. When he had sampled chocolate, he had been intrigued enough to swallow two bowls of the stuff, which so inflamed his spirits that even after visiting two satisfactory whores he had felt it necessary to visit his physician, who restored his unbalanced humours with a sound combination of emetics and purges.

'It's made of coffee fruit,' Geertruid told him,

folding her arms as though she had invented the mixture herself.

Miguel had come across coffee once or twice, but only as a commodity traded by East India merchants. The business of the Exchange did not require a man to know an item's nature, only its demand – and sometimes, in the heat of the trade, not even that.

He reminded himself to say the blessing over wonders of nature. Some Jews would turn away from their gentile friends when they blessed their food or drink, but Miguel took pleasure in the prayers. He loved to utter them in public, and in a land where he could not be prosecuted for speaking the holy tongue. He wished he had more occasions to bless things. Saying the words filled him with giddy defiance; he thought of each openly spoken Hebrew word as a knife in the belly of some Inquisitor somewhere.

'It's a new substance – entirely new,' Geertruid explained, when he was done. 'You take it not to delight the senses but to awaken the intellect. Its advocates drink it at breakfast to regain their senses, and they drink it at night to help them remain awake longer.'

Geertruid's face became as sombre as one of the Calvinist preachers who railed from makeshift pulpits in town plazas. 'This coffee isn't like wine or beer, which we drink to make merry or because it quenches thirst or even because it is delightful. This will only make you thirstier, it will never make you merry, and the taste, let us be honest, may be curious but never pleasing. Coffee is something . . . something far more important.'

Miguel had known Geertruid long enough to be acquainted with her many foolish habits. She might laugh all night and drink as much as any Dutchman alive, she might neglect her affairs and tramp barefoot around the countryside like a girl, but in matters of business she was as serious as any man. A businesswoman such as she would have been an impossibility back in Portugal, but among the Dutch her kind was, if not precisely common, hardly shocking.

'This is what I think,' she said, her voice hardly loud enough to rise above the din of the tavern. 'Beer and wine may make a man sleepy, but coffee will make him awake and clearheaded. Beer and wine may make a man amorous, but coffee will make him lose interest in the flesh. The man who drinks coffee fruit cares only for his business.' She paused for another sip. 'Coffee is the drink of commerce.'

How many times, conducting business in taverns, had Miguel's wits suffered with each tankard of beer? How many times had he wished he had the concentration for another hour's clarity with the week's pricing sheets? A sobering drink was just the thing for a trading man.

An eagerness had begun to wash over Miguel, and he found his foot tapping impatiently. The sounds and sights of the tavern drifted away. There was nothing but Geertruid. And coffee. 'Who now drinks it?' he asked.

'I hardly know,' Geertruid admitted. 'I've heard there is a coffee tavern somewhere in the city – frequented by Turks, they say – but I've never seen it. I know of no Dutchmen who take coffee, unless it be prescribed by a physician, but the word will spread. Already, in England, taverns that serve coffee instead of wine and beer have opened, and men of trade flock to them to talk business. These coffee taverns become like exchanges unto themselves. It can't be too long before those taverns open here as well, for what city loves commerce so well as Amsterdam?'

'Are you suggesting,' Miguel asked, 'that you want to open a tavern?'

'The taverns are nothing. We must put ourselves in a position to supply them.' She took his hand. 'The demand is coming, and if we prepare ourselves for that demand, we can make a great deal of money.'

The coffee's scent began to make him light-headed with something like desire. No, not desire. Greed. Geertruid had stumbled upon something, and Miguel felt her infectious eagerness swelling in his chest. It was like panic or jubilance or something else, but he wanted to leap from his seat. Was this energy from the strength of her idea or the effect of the coffee? If coffee fruit made a man unable to keep from fidgeting, how could it be the drink of commerce?

Still, coffee *was* something marvellous, and if he could dare to hope that no one in Amsterdam plotted to take advantage of this new drink, it could be the very thing to save him from ruin. For six dismal months, Miguel had at times felt himself in a waking dream. His life had been replaced with a sad imitation, with the bloodless life of a lesser man.

He loved the money that came with success, but he loved the power more. He relished the respect he had commanded on the Exchange and in the Vlooyenburg, the island neighbourhood where the Portuguese Jews lived. He loved hosting lavish dinners and never enquiring of the bill. He took pleasure in giving to the charitable boards. Here was money for the poor – let them eat. Here was money for the refugees – let them find homes. Here was money for the scholars in the Holy Land – let them work to bring in the age of the Messiah. The world could be a holier place because Miguel had money to give, and he gave it.

That was Miguel Lienzo, not this wretch at whose failings children and beefy housewives smirked. He could not much longer endure the anxious stares of other traders, who hurried away from him lest his ill fortune spread like plague, or the pitying looks from his brother's pretty wife, whose moist eyes suggested she saw kinship between her misery and his.

Perhaps he had suffered enough, and the Holy One, blessed be He, had put this opportunity before him. Did he dare to believe that? Miguel wanted to agree to anything Geertruid proposed, but he had lost too many times in recent months by acting on foolish hunches. It would be madness to forge ahead, particularly when he would be plunging with a partner whose very existence would make him vulnerable to the Ma'amad.

'How is it that this magic potion has not swept through Europe already?' he asked

'All things must begin somewhere. Must we wait,' she added in a conspiratorial voice, 'until some other ambitious merchant learns its secret?'

Miguel pushed back from the counter and sat up straight. 'Tell me what you propose.' He waited with startling hunger for Geertruid's words; she could not answer quickly enough, and Miguel wanted to reply before the words had even been uttered.

Geertruid rubbed her long hands together. 'I have determined to do some sort of business with coffee, and I have some capital, but I have no idea how to proceed. You are a man of business, and I need your help – and your partnership.'

It was one thing to call this high-spirited widow his friend when they were private together, to drink and gamble with her, to stand for her on the Exchange and make small trades now and again – despite the Ma'amad's having forbidden Jews to broker for gentiles on pain of excommunication. It was another thing to take her as a partner in business. Some Jews might emerge unscathed from

21

so unusual an arrangement, but Miguel could not count on his luck, not without money or influence to protect him.

Once Miguel had scoffed at the council's humourless censures, but the Ma'amad had begun to carry out more of its threats. It sent its spies in pursuit of violators of the Sabbath and eaters of unclean food. It cast out those, like the usurer Alonzo Alferonda, who broke its arbitrary rules. It hounded those like poor Bento Spinoza, who uttered heresies so vague that almost no one even understood that his words were heretical. More than that, Miguel had an enemy on the council who surely only waited for the flimsiest excuse to strike.

So many risks. Miguel bit his lip, forcing back the urge to smirk. He could live with the risks if he could promise himself not to think of them too often.

Miguel began to tap the counter. He wanted to act immediately. He could begin at once to secure contacts and agents upon almost any important exchange in Europe. He could juggle coffee by the barrelful, moving it from this port to that. This was the true essence of Miguel Lienzo; he made deals and connections and arrangements. He was no coward to shrink from an opportunity because bitter and hypocritical men told him that they knew better than the Sages what was right and wrong.

'How shall we do this?' he said at last, suddenly aware he had not spoken for several minutes. 'The coffee-fruit trade belongs to the East India

Company, and we can't hope to take control away from men of their power. I don't understand what you're proposing.'

'Nor do I!' Geertruid threw her hands into the air excitedly. 'But I am proposing *something*. We must do *something*. I won't allow the fact that I do not know what I am proposing to stand in my way. As they say, even the blind may stumble upon Heaven. You worry about the twentieth – you owe money? I am offering you riches. A great new venture with which to rebuild and make your current debt seem trivial.'

'I'll need time to think about it,' he told her, though he needed nothing of the kind. But Geertruid would have to wait. A man does not get many such opportunities in his life, and to ruin his chances out of impatience would be madness. 'We'll discuss these things again after the twentieth. In a week.'

'A week is a long time,' the widow said thoughtfully. 'Fortunes are made in a week. Empires rise and fall in a week.'

'I need a week,' Miguel repeated softly.

'A week, then,' Geertruid said, in her amiable way. She knew not to push further.

Miguel realised he had been fidgeting with the buttons of his coat. 'And now I must leave and tend to my more immediate concerns.'

'Before you go, let me give you something to help you consider the enterprise.' Geertruid signalled to Crispijn, who hurried over and set down before her a rough woollen sack.

'He owes me some money,' she explained, once her cousin had walked away. 'I agreed to take a little of this as payment, and I wanted to give you something to think about.'

Miguel looked in the bag, which contained perhaps a dozen handfuls of brownish berries.

'Coffee,' Geertruid said. 'I've had Crispijn cook the berries for you because I know a Portuguese hidalgo cannot be expected to roast his own fruit. You merely need to grind them to a powder, which you mix with hot milk or sweet water, then filter out the powder if you like, or just let it settle. Don't drink too much of the powder itself, lest you agitate your bowels.'

'You did not mention bowel agitation when you sang its praises.'

'Even nature's greatest glories can harm if taken in the wrong dose. I wouldn't have said anything, but a man with uneasy bowels makes a poor business partner.'

Miguel let her kiss him again, and then he squeezed through the tavern and stepped out into the misty cool of the late afternoon. After the stench of the Golden Calf, the salty air off the IJ felt as wonderfully cleansing as the *mikvah*, and he let the mist fall on his face for a moment until a boy, not six years old, began to pull on his sleeve and weep piteously about his mother. Miguel tossed the boy a half stiver, already relishing the wealth coffee would bring: freedom from debt, his own home, a chance to marry once more, children.

In an instant he chastised himself for indulging in these fancies in light of the day's setbacks. Another thousand guilders in debt. He owed three thousand already throughout the Vlooyenburg, including fifteen hundred to his brother, borrowed after the sugar market collapsed. He'd allowed the Bankruptcy Office at the Town Hall to settle his debts to Christians, but the Jews of his neighbourhood ordered their own accounts.

High tide had begun to move in, and the waters had crept up beyond the Rozengracht to slick the streets. Across town, in his brother's house, the cavernous cellar where Miguel now slept at night would soon begin its own flooding. That was the price of living in a city built in the water upon piles, but Miguel now thought nothing of the discomforts of Amsterdam that had troubled him when he had first arrived. He hardly noticed the dead-fish stench of canal water or the squish of walking on wet ground. Dead fish was the perfume of Amsterdam's riches, the squish of water its melody.

The prudent thing would be to go home at once and write a note to Geertruid explaining that the risks of working with her were too great and might well lead to his ruin. But he would never free himself from debt with prudence, and ruin was already upon him. Only a few months ago his sugar had crammed canal-side warehouses; he had strutted across the Vlooyenburg like a burgher. He had been ready to set the loss of Katarina behind him, to take a new wife and have sons, and the marriage brokers had clawed at one another to gain access to him. But now he was in debt. His standing had collapsed to worse than nothing. He received threatening notes from a man who must be mad. How could he turn his fortune if not by doing something daring?

He had taken risks all his life. Was he to stop because he feared the arbitrary power of the Ma'amad, those men who, entrusted to uphold the Law of Moses, valued their power above God's Word? The Law had nothing to say about Dutch widows. Why should Miguel avoid making his fortune with one?

He might have tried to conduct a little more business that day, but he suspected his agitation would lead to nothing productive, so instead he went to the Talmud Torah synagogue for afternoon and evening prayers. The now-familiar liturgy soothed him like spiced wine, and by the time he left he felt renewed.

As he walked the short distance from the synagogue to his brother's house, keeping close to canal-side houses to elude both thieves and the Night Watch, Miguel listened to the click of rat claws on the wooden planks stretched over the sewers. *Coffee,* he chanted to himself. He hardly needed a week to give Geertruid his answer. He only needed time to convince himself that any scheme he embarked on with her would not complete his ruin.

26

From

The Factual and Revealing Memoirs
of Alonzo Alferonda

My name is Alonzo Rodrigo Tomas de la Alferonda, and I brought the drink called coffee to the Europeans – gave birth to its usage there, one might say. Well, perhaps I phrase that too strongly, for coffee surely would have made its murky way without my efforts. Let us say instead that I was the man-midwife who eased its passage from obscurity into glory. No, you will say, that was not me either, it was Miguel Lienzo who did that. What role, then, could Alonzo Alferonda have played in the triumph of this great fruit? More than is generally believed, I assure you. And for those who say I made nothing but mischief, that I thwarted and hindered and harmed rather than advanced, I can only say I know more than my detractors. I was there – and you, in all likelihood, were not.

My true name is Avraham, as was my father's name and his father's. All first-born Alferonda

27

men have secretly called their first-born sons Avraham for as long as Jews have had secret names, and before that, when the Moors ruled Iberia, they called themselves Avraham openly. For much of my life, I was not permitted to speak my name aloud except in dark rooms, and then only in whispers. Those who would question my actions should remember that. Who would you be today, I ask you who judge me harshly, if your own name was a secret whose revelation could cost your life and the lives of your friends and family?

I was born in the Portuguese city of Lisbon to a family of Jews who were not allowed to pray as Jews. We were called New Christians, or Conversos, for our ancestors had been made to take the Catholic faith or surrender their property – and often their lives. Lest we face torture and ruin and perhaps even death, we prayed publicly as Catholics, but in shadows and in cellars, in secret synagogues that moved from house to house, we prayed as Jews. Prayer books were rare and precious to us. In the light of day a man might measure his wealth in gold, but in the dark of those dark rooms, we measured wealth in pages and in knowledge. Few among our number could read the Hebrew of what few books we had. Few knew the right prayers for the holy days or for Shabbat.

My father knew, or at least he knew some. Having spent the first part of his childhood in the East, he had grown up among Jews unrestrained by the law from practising their religion. He had prayer books that he lent out freely. He owned a few volumes of the Babylonian Talmud, but he knew no Aramaic and could make little sense of its pages. The Secret Jews in Lisbon came to him for instruction in the rudiments of reading the holy tongue, of the prayers for Shabbat, of fasting on fast days and feasting on feast days. He taught them to eat out-of-doors during Succoth, and of course he taught them to drink themselves to a merry stupor on Purim.

Let me be direct: my father was no holy man or sage or saint. Far from it. I admit this freely and think it no insult to his name. My father was a trickster and a cheat; in his hands, trickery and cheating were beautiful and marvellous things.

Because he was schooled in the ways of our faith – no scholar, mind you, but simply a man with an education – my father was tolerated among the Secret Jews of Lisbon in ways he might not have been otherwise, for he brought far more attention upon himself than was wise for any New Christian. Wherever merchants with a few spare coins might find themselves, my father would be there with his potions to lengthen life, improve virility or cure any malady. He knew tricks with cards and balls and dice. He could juggle and rope dance and tumble. He knew how to train dogs to add and subtract simple numbers and how to train cats to dance on their hind legs.

A natural leader of men, my father attracted to him others who made their living through countless deceptive and curious entertainments. He commanded an army of cardsharps and dice cheats, fire-eaters and blade-swallowers. Those who could earn a living simply by displaying the shapes with which nature had burdened them also rallied to my father's banner. Among my earliest childhood companions were dwarfs and giants, the monstrously fat and the horrifically gaunt. I played games with the snake boy and the goat girl. As I grew older I developed an unhealthy curiosity about a person my father knew who had the anatomy of both a man and a woman. For a few coins, this unfortunate would allow anyone to watch it fornicate with itself.

When I was but ten years of age my father received a late-night visit from an older boy,

Miguel Lienzo, whom I recognised from synagogue worship. He was a roguish fellow, as
much drawn to my father's company of tricksters and oddities as he was to my father's
learning. I say he was roguish, for he loved
always to defy one authority or another, and in
the time I knew him in Lisbon those authorities
he loved defying most were his own family and
the Inquisition itself.

This Lienzo came from a line of relatively
sincere New Christians. There was no shortage of these: men who, out of either genuine
belief or merely a desire to avoid persecution,
conformed entirely to the Christian way and
shunned those of us who sought to live as
Jews. Lienzo's father was a successful trader
and had, in his opinion, too much to risk the
ire of the Inquisition. Perhaps for this reason
alone, Miguel came eagerly to our secret prayer
meetings and struggled to learn what my father
could teach him.

More than that, young Miguel used his father's
connections with the Old Christian community
to learn what he could of the Inquisition. He
had a keen ear for rumour, and he delighted
in providing warnings where he could. I knew
of a half-dozen families who had fled the night
before the Inquisitors pounded on their doors

31

– all because Lienzo had known where to lurk and listen. I believe he did these great deeds both from a desire to see justice done in the world and for the pleasure of treading where he had no business. Years later, when I saw him again in Amsterdam, he did not recognise me or even remember what he had done for my family. I have never forgotten his kindness, though some have insisted otherwise.

Miguel came to warn us after he had volunteered to help our priest scrub his private chambers in the church (he always volunteered for these thankless tasks in the hopes of gaining some intelligence) and had then chanced to hear a conversation between that wretch and an Inquisitor who had developed an interest in my father.

And so, in the dark of night, we left the only home I had known, taking many of our friends with us. We were Jew and Christian and Moor and Gypsy all, and we travelled to more cities than I can now enumerate. For years we lived in the East, and I was fortunate to spend many months in the holy city of Jerusalem. It is but a shadow of its former glory, but there were times in my unfortunate life when the memory of those days, of walking the streets of my nation's ancient capital, visiting the place where the holy Temple once stood, have sustained me when I could find meaning in nothing else. If it be the will of the Holy One, blessed be He, I shall return some day to that sacred place and live out my remaining days there.

In our travels we also traversed Europe, and we were in London when my father died of a brain fever. I was then five-and-twenty, grown to a man but not a man of my father's disposition. My younger brother, Mateo, wanted to take command of the army of outcasts, and I knew he had the character to lead them. Though I had wandered for years, I was not myself a wanderer. I could perform card cheats and dice tricks, but not half so well as Mateo. I could get a dog to do nothing but show me its belly and a cat to do nothing but nestle upon my lap. My father had always spoken of the importance of Jews to live as Jews and among Jews, and I recalled from a visit to Amsterdam some years earlier that in that city Jews enjoyed a degree of freedom unrivalled in the rest of Christendom.

So I crossed the North Sea and found myself embraced by the large community of Portuguese Jews who lived there. I was, at any rate, embraced at first. And that is why I write this memoir. I wish to make clear why I was unjustly exiled from a people I loved. I wish to tell the world that I am not the villain it thinks me. And I wish to set on paper the true facts regarding Miguel Lienzo and his dealings in the coffee trade, having been much blamed in that sphere, and blamed very unfairly too. It is my intention to describe my doings in Amsterdam, the conditions of my excommunication, my life in that city afterward, and precisely what role I played in Lienzo's affairs.

It is true that before I knew how to walk I could hide a card in my clothes and make the dice roll the way I wished, but I vow to practise no trickery in these pages. I will be like the Bear Man, a petulant fellow with whom I travelled for years. I will disrobe to show you nature's truth. If you like, reader, you may even pull on the fur to see that it is no deception.

CHAPTER 2

Geertruid could never understand the difficulty Miguel faced in doing business with her. She might smile sympathetically when he spoke of his fears, but in the end she almost certainly believed his resistance was some wilful Hebrew eccentricity, like not eating squid or refusing to talk business on Saturday day, but being happy to talk on Saturday night.

Miguel hated that she should think him foolish or stubborn. When he would violate some small law or other – drink impure wine or labour, just a little, on the Sabbath – she would ask how he could do these things and still purport to care so much for his observance. He did not know how to explain that no one but a *tsadik* – a saint – could hope to obey all the laws; it was the effort that brought a man closer to the Holy One, blessed be He.

Although he had told her about his past, Geertruid still had no understanding of what it had been like to live as a Secret Jew in Lisbon. If it was so truly terrible, she would ask, why do any of you Jews remain?

Why indeed? Because it was where they had

always lived, for hundreds of years. Because their families were there, their businesses. Some stayed because they had no money, others because they had too much. The stories of freedom to worship in Amsterdam or in the East sounded as elusive as the coming of the Messiah.

Many New Christians embraced Catholicism with a slavish fervour, and Miguel's father had been such a man. Not that he believed deeply, but he believed deeply in convincing the world of his sincerity with his regular church attendance, his public denouncement of Jewish 'superstition', his donations to the Church. New Christians, sincere or not, lived in a single community, and Miguel's father wanted his sons to stay away from the backsliders. 'My grandparents chose to convert rather than be exiled,' he had explained, 'and I'll not dishonour their choice.'

Perhaps for the pleasure of defying his father, perhaps because it was dangerous, Miguel had begun secretly attending study groups when he was still a boy. The older men there encouraged him, made him feel special with their praise, and let him know without words that they too thought his father a great boor. Miguel had loved the feeling of being included in something larger than himself and of doing something wicked that was, at the same time, righteous.

Miguel's younger brother, Daniel, understood this division between father and son and exploited it, showing his father every day in a dozen ways that he was not one of those horrible back-sliders who brought nothing but woe to their community. Their father was inclined to favour Daniel at any rate, since he looked far more like his side of the family, Miguel bearing a striking resemblance to his mother's father. Daniel had always been thin, like the elder Lienzo, all hard angles and sharp corners, eyes too large for his face, hands too small for his body. Miguel took after his mother's side – meaty men who commanded attention; just the sort of man the elder Lienzo had always despised.

When his father discovered that Miguel had been attending the secret synagogues, he called him a traitor and a fool. He locked Miguel in a room for a week with nothing but wine, some dried figs, two loaves of bread and a chamber pot far too small for so long a duration. Later Miguel would find this choice of punishment horribly ironic, for it was his father the Inquisition had taken and locked in a prison and tortured – accidentally, they claimed – to death. He had been named by another Converso who, under the Inquisitor's knife, had shouted any names he could recall, whether they be Christian, Jew, or Muhammadan.

Miguel had been three years gone by then, after a rupture with his father over his marrying a woman with an insufficient dowry. Miguel's father had absolutely forbidden the marriage. Not only had Katarina too little money but her family consisted of well-known Judaisers who would bring down trouble on the rest of them. And, he insisted, she was far too pretty. 'I don't like to see you with so beautiful a girl,' he'd said to Miguel. 'It's unseemly for you to marry a better-looking woman than your father did. It makes you appear undutiful.'

Miguel was not so easily swayed by dowries, and he thought it perfectly seemly to marry someone pretty. But more than beauty, Katarina had possessed great understanding. Her family was devout, and she had an uncle who was a great Talmudist in Damascus. She understood Hebrew better than most men in Lisbon. She knew the liturgy and could keep a home in accordance with the holy writings. Miguel's father had spat on the floor when Miguel announced that they had secretly married. 'You'll regret defying me,' he'd said, 'and you'll regret marrying a woman who knows how to read. I won't say another word to you until you come to me and beg my forgiveness.'

Four months later, when Katarina had died of a sudden fever, they spoke for the last time. 'Thank Christ that's over with,' his father had said to Miguel at the conclusion of the funeral. 'Now we can get you married to someone who will do our family some good.' Two weeks later, Miguel boarded a ship bound for the United Provinces.

While he established himself in Amsterdam, Miguel's father and brother continued to export wine and figs and salt, but then the Inquisition arrested the elder Lienzo and everything came to an end. By Portuguese law, the Church could confiscate the material goods of anyone convicted by the Inquisition, so wealthy merchants made particularly popular victims. After suddenly expiring during a questioning session, Miguel's father was found guilty posthumously, and the family business ceased to exist. Left with only a few items in his own name, Daniel had no choice but to leave Lisbon. Following his brother and the mass exodus of Conversos to Amsterdam had seemed the inevitable choice.

The Ma'amad had welcomed Miguel when he came to Amsterdam; its teachers helped him expand his understanding of the holy tongue, taught him the liturgy, and explained the holy days. Though still disorientated with grief for Katarina, those first few weeks had been full of excitement and learning, and though his circumcision was an event best not recollected too often, even that bloody affair had been moving. However, it was not long before he discovered that the council's aid did not come without its price. The *parnassim*, the men who composed the Ma'amad, ruled absolutely, and those who would live in the community lived by their law or were cast out.

Two evenings after his meeting with Geertruid, Miguel had attended a study meeting at the Talmud Torah. Here was where the Ma'amad shone. Study groups met constantly in the synagogue's cloistered chambers. Jews recently escaped from Iberia and the Inquisition, who knew nothing of their faith but that it was in their blood, learned how to conduct themselves, to pray, to live as Jews. In the next chamber wise men, the *chachamim*, argued details from the Talmud that Miguel did not believe he would ever begin to comprehend. He met with a group of men not unlike himself – returned within the past few years but dedicated to embracing the ways of their fathers. They read in Hebrew the weekly Torah portion and worked through its meaning while a *chacham*, who served as their guide, discussed the Talmud commentary.

Miguel loved these meetings. He looked forward to them all week. He had not the luxury to study quite so much Torah at home as he would have liked – though he did try to go to the early morning study sessions at least once or twice a week – and what time he did have he did not always use wisely. These meetings were therefore doubly precious. For the space of a few short hours he was able to forget that reckoning day crept cruelly towards him, and the brandy futures he'd bought so impulsively would make his debts even more hopeless.

In the halls of the Talmud Torah, just after his meeting, Miguel paused with his friend Isaiah Nunes to continue debate on the interpretation of a particularly thorny bit of Hebrew grammar. Nunes traded mostly along the Levant routes but had recently begun to expand into Portuguese wine. Having sampled too many of a buyer's wares before the meeting started, he now argued loudly. His voice echoed off the high ceilings of the nearly empty synagogue as they made their way towards the exit.

Nunes was a large man, bulky without exactly being fat. Not yet thirty years old, he had already managed to establish himself as a man to be reckoned with in the Levant routes. Miguel liked the young trader, but there were limits to how much an indebted widower his age could like someone so young and successful. Almost by accident Nunes stumbled on lucrative deals; he invested cautiously but with obscene success; he had a beautiful and obedient wife who had given him two sons. However, these accomplishments were tempered by Nunes' inability to take pleasure in anything he'd done. Growing up, he'd witnessed one relative after another taken by the Inquisition, and he'd become nervous by disposition. He regarded his success as a mere illusion, a trick of the devil aimed only to raise Nunes' expectations before dashing them.

The two made their way out in the darkness, for only a few candles burned in the common areas. Nunes had been in the midst of a long harangue, half of which was pure nonsense, as he reasoned, backtracked, apologised for making little sense, and then demanded that Miguel agree with him. Then he stopped short and bent over.

'By Christ, I've just broken a toe!' he shouted. Like most Jews from Portugal, he cursed like a Catholic. 'Miguel, help me along!'

Miguel bent to help his friend. 'You drunkard, on what did you break a toe?'

'On nothing,' Nunes whispered. 'It's a ruse. Don't you know a ruse when you see one?'

'Not if it's a good ruse.'

'I'll take that a compliment, I suppose.'

'Now that we have established that you have only pretended to break your toe in order to fool me,' Miguel said quietly, 'perhaps you might tell me why you would do such a thing.'

'By the Virgin,' Nunes cried out, 'it hurts! Help me, Miguel!' In the dim light of sparse candles, Miguel could see Nunes close his eyes in a moment of concentration. 'There's a man lurking in the shadows by the door,' he added more quietly. 'He's been watching you.'

Miguel felt himself tense. A man lurking in the shadows awaiting him could never be good news. More than once he'd been spirited away to some dank tavern cellar by an angry creditor who kept him there as prisoner until he could send for the money he owed or – and this was more likely to happen – he could talk his way out of imprisonment.

Then another thought crossed his mind. Those strange notes he had been receiving. *I want my money.* He felt his skin prickle.

'Did you see who it is?' he asked Nunes.

'I caught a quick glimpse, and unless I miss my guess it is Solomon Parido.'

Miguel stole a look towards the exit and saw a

figure step towards the dark. 'Christ's tabernacle. What does he want?' The *parnass* had been his enemy since an unfortunate incident two years earlier, which had ended with his withdrawing his offer to wed his daughter to Miguel.

'Nothing good, you can depend on that. A *parnass* lying in wait is always bad news, and Parido is worse news than most. And Parido lying in wait for Miguel Lienzo – well, it is hard to think of a more dire situation. To be honest, I would hate him to see us together. I have troubles enough without a *parnass* looking into my affairs too deeply.'

'You have no troubles at all,' Miguel said darkly. 'I should lend you some of mine.'

'Your brother does business with him, doesn't he? Why don't you have him ask Parido to leave you alone?'

'I think my brother encourages him, frankly,' Miguel said bitterly. It was bad enough that he was dependent upon his younger brother, but Daniel's friendship with the *parnass* particularly unnerved him. He could never quite shake the feeling that Daniel reported everything Miguel said or did.

'Let's go back inside,' Nunes suggested. 'We'll wait for him to pass.'

'I won't give him that satisfaction. I'll have to take my chances, but I don't think your performance has fooled anyone. We should break your toe in earnest. If he wants to examine your

43

foot, you'll be found guilty of having lied in the synagogue.'

'I've put myself at risk for your sake. You ought to show some gratitude.'

'You're right. Should he inspect your toe and find it whole, we'll tell him that a great miracle happened here.'

They hobbled out to the courtyard and, though he meant to restrain himself, Miguel couldn't help but look to the corner where he had seen Parido lurking. But the *parnass* was already gone.

'Parido lying in wait for you is bad enough,' Nunes observed, 'but spying on you and disappearing into the shadows – that is something altogether more terrible than I had thought.'

Miguel had fears enough without having his friend fan the flames. 'Soon you will tell me that a quarter-moon makes things worse.'

'A quarter-moon is a bad omen,' Nunes agreed.

Miguel let out a raspy noise, half chortle, half cough. What did the *parnass* want from him? He could think of no religious laws he'd openly violated in the recent past, although he might have been seen on the street with Hendrick. Still, inappropriate contact with gentiles hardly warranted this kind of surveillance. Parido had something else in mind, and while Miguel could not think what it might be, he knew it was nothing good.

From

The Factual and Revealing Memoirs of
Alonzo Alferonda

My relocation to Amsterdam proved, at first, to be all I could have hoped for. After wallowing too many years in the squalid mud of London, that putrid capital of a putrid island, Amsterdam seemed to me the cleanest and most beautiful of places. England had become a disorderly nation, with its revolutions and regicide. While living there I had the chance to meet a man called Menasseh ben Israel, who came from Amsterdam to convince England's warrior-priest king, Cromwell, to allow English Jews to make a home there. Menasseh painted a picture of Amsterdam that made it sound like the Garden of Eden with red-brick houses.

In my early days there, I was inclined to agree. The local Ma'amad, the ruling council of Jews, warmly embraced newcomers. It arranged for kind strangers to take us in until we could find a place of our own. It at once assessed our understanding of the customs and holy laws of our race and began training us in those areas in which we showed ignorance. The Talmud Torah, the great synagogue of the Portuguese Jews, offered the opportunity for study at all levels of understanding.

I arrived in Amsterdam with a few coins in my purse and could afford to establish myself in business, though I did not yet know what business I would make my own. However, I soon discovered something to my liking. On the Exchange a new form of commerce had emerged, that of buying and selling what no one owned and, indeed, what no one ever intended to own. It was a gambling sort of trade called futures, in which a man gambled on whether the price of a commodity would rise or fall. If the trader guessed correctly, he would earn far more money than if he had bought or sold outright. If he guessed incorrectly, the cost could be formidable, for he would not only lose the money he had invested, he would owe for the difference between what he had bought and the final price. I saw at once that this was no trade for the timid or even for the merely brave. This was a trade for the lucky, and I had spent my life learning how to manufacture my own luck.

I was not alone in doing so. Throughout the Exchange were groups called trading combinations, and they would manipulate markets as best they could. A combination might circulate a rumour that it intended to buy, let us say, British woollens. The Exchange, hearing that a large group of men planned to buy, would respond, and the price would rise accordingly. All along, however, the combination intended to sell, and once the woollens reached a rewarding price, the combination would react accordingly. These organisations, my astute reader will see, engage in a tricky business because these men will have to do as they pretend most of the time; otherwise rumours surrounding their movements will never be believed.

I soon found myself something of a purveyor of rumours. I would make commodities do pretty little dances as I saw fit, and I had a knack for disguising my footprints as I did so. Check the dice if you wish, dear sir. You will see that they are but ordinary. A word dropped here, a rumour spread there. Not by me, of course, but done all the same. This commodity bet on, this one bet against. It all proved a handy little trade.

Shortly after my arrival in the city I found

myself passing idle hours in a little gambling establishment owned by a fellow called Juarez. Gambling was strictly forbidden by the Ma'amad, but many forbidden things were, in truth, tolerated, so long as they were done quietly. Juarez ran a tasteful little tavern that catered to Portuguese Jews. It offered food and drink that conformed with our holy laws, and he permitted no whores to ply their trade, so the parnassim chose not to bother him.

I played cards there with, among other men, a merchant some ten years my senior named Solomon Parido; he disliked me and I disliked him. Why should that be? I cannot say for certain. There was no initial slight that began it, no wrong left to be revenged. It is sometimes so simple as two men having natures that cannot stand to be near each other, like magnets that push one another away. I found him too sour; he found me too ebullient. Though our work and worship often threw us together neither was ever happy to see the other. We might be in the same room, and for no reason he would scowl at me and I would smile saucily in return. He might make some reference to cheats, meaning to needle me for my background; I would return a reference to idiots, knowing that his only son had been born deficient of mind.

Perhaps you will say, *Alferonda*, you are cruel to mock a man for his misfortune, and surely you would be right to say so. It is cruel, but Parido brought forth the cruelty in me. Perhaps had he been kinder I would have looked upon him compassionately. I might then have seen his wealth – his massive house full of rugs and paintings and gold trinkets, his indulgent coach-and-four, his manoeuvres on the Exchange that succeeded simply because of the sheer volume of capital propping them up – as some small compensation for his domestic sadness. I might have looked at his expensive clothes as a mask behind which he could hide his melancholy. I might have viewed his lavish banquets – indulgent affairs with dozens of guests, barrels of wine, wheels of cheese, herds of roast cattle – with new eyes, for I would have been a guest at those banquets and seen what satisfaction he took in playing host. But I never received the handsomely inscribed invitations to Parido's house. My friends did, I can assure you, and I listened to the tales of their delight. But Parido could find no place for Alferonda in his magnificent house. Why, then, should Alferonda make room in his equally magnificent heart?

One night fate placed the two of us together

at a game of cards. I'd had more wine than a gambling man ought, and seeing Parido showing a pleasant face to every man at the table but me, I was unable to resist the urge to cheat him, if just a little.

If a man cheats at cards to win for himself, he is bound to raise the suspicions of all. But if he cheats at cards for no reason other than to make another man lose, he is likely to find more allies than enemies. The more Parido regarded me with disdain, the more I saw to it that the cards did not turn the way he wished. The suit or the number he longed for would find its way to another man's hand or, if I was desperate, in my sleeve. Moments when he thought all would go his way burst like flimsy bubbles. More than once he cast a suspicious look in my direction, but I had only modest winnings to show for myself. How could I be responsible?

I suppose this might have come to nothing if it had ended there. He lost a few guilders that night, but nothing of consequence. A man like Parido knows never to bring more to the table than he is prepared to lose as the price of an evening's entertainment. A few months later, however, matters took another turn.

I knew Parido and his trading combination planned a manoeuvre with Setúbal salt. The price had been depressed for some time, so exports had been reduced. They were therefore due to rise, and Parido's men wanted to effect that rise themselves rather than be taken by surprise. I caught wind of this from a tavern keeper – one of the many I paid for such information – and saw an opportunity to profit for myself. I want to be clear that I never engaged in any action simply for the purpose of stinging Parido. I did not much like him, nor he me, but that mattered for little when it came to trade. I did what I did to earn a profit. It was nothing more than that.

Parido's combination began to spread the tale that the latest shipments of Setúbal salt were selling for a much higher price than had been anticipated. By doing so, they hoped to spark a buying frenzy upon the Exchange of those wishing to secure the current low price. Thus they intended to profit from the salt they had themselves acquired and from their puts: wagers that the price would rise. When they began to sell their salt at the new price, I and my agents sold as well, flooding the market in order to capitalise on the price differential. My method enabled me to exploit their scheme for some fair gains. It also had the unavoidable side-effect of making their trade unprofitable, and their puts ended up costing them a slightly more than insignificant amount. But that is the price they had to pay for their trickery.

I was always certain to hide myself behind strange and unknown brokers when I attempted these sorts of manoeuvres, but Parido prided himself on being mightily well connected, and he found me out. The next day he came up behind me on the Exchange. 'You've crossed the wrong man, Alferonda,' he said.

I said I knew nothing of his complaint. My father had always told me to deny everything.

'Your lies don't impress me. You've profited from ruining my scheme and costing me money, and I'll see to it that you get what such a low trickster deserves.'

I laughed off these threats as I had laughed off others. Indeed, as the months and even years passed, I forgot his words. He never much liked me, he spoke ill of me when he could, but never that I knew did he act against me in matters of consequence. It could have been, I realised, that he acted against me in any of a number of trades that went bad, but that might have been fate, and I tended to believe that he would not have been shy about taking credit for any harm he might send my way.

But then he was elected to the Ma'amad.

As both a wealthy merchant and a *parnass*, he possessed as much power as was possible for a man in our community. I had no reason to celebrate his election, but I had no reason to suspect that he would use his new position to attack me so ruthlessly.

CHAPTER 3

Down in the kitchen, Hannah nearly severed her thumb as she chopped asparagus. She'd not been paying attention, and the knife, which had grown dull under months of the maid's inattention, slipped easily from her grasp and dug into her flesh with amputating force. But the same dullness that made the blade dangerous rendered it impotent, and the wet metal barely broke her skin.

Hannah looked up to see if Annetje had noticed. She hadn't. The girl was busy grating cheese, humming some drunken ditty to herself – appropriate enough since she'd been dipping into the wine again. If she'd noticed Hannah's mishap, she'd certainly have said something: *Oh, look how clumsy you are* or *What a fine thing that can't handle a knife*. She would say it with a laugh and a turn of her pretty head, as though a laugh and a turned head made everything amicable. Hannah would let her pretend that it *did* make everything amicable, though she'd be biting back the urge to slam the half wheel of cheese into the girl's face.

Hannah stabbed at the drop of blood with her

rigid tongue and pushed the asparagus into the bowl, where it would be mixed with the cheese and some old bread and baked into a flan like they had eaten in Portugal, except in Lisbon they had used different vegetables and different cheeses. Annetje thought flans were disgusting – unwholesome, she said, a term she used to describe any food she hadn't eaten growing up in Groningen.

'Someday,' she was now observing, 'your husband will notice that you plan elaborate suppers only when his brother dines with you.'

'Two people don't eat much,' Hannah answered, almost successfully willing herself not to blush. 'Three people eat a great deal more.' That was something her mother had taught her, but it was particularly true when her husband was involved. If Daniel had his way, they'd eat nothing but bread and old cheese and pickled fish, anything they could get cheaply. And he was the one who insisted that they make something of the evening meal when his brother joined them, probably so that Miguel wouldn't think Daniel a miser – which he already did.

But she also liked to feed him well. Miguel did not eat properly when left to himself, and she did not like him to go hungry. Also, unlike Daniel, he always appeared to relish his food, to regard it as a pleasure rather than a mere necessity that kept him alive for one more day. He would thank her and praise the quality. He went out of his way to say little meaningless things to her, observing that the

55

added nutmeg in the herring made the dish sparkle or that the prune sauce she served over the eggs was more delicious than ever.

'The carrots need to be stewed in the prunes and raisins,' Annetje said, seeing that Hannah had taken a moment to rest.

'I'm tired.' She sighed to emphasise her point. She hated pleading weakness to the girl, but she *was* with child now, and that ought to be excuse enough. It ought to be, but there was nothing to be gained by thinking about what ought to be. It ought to be, for example, that the wife of a Portuguese hidalgo was not in a hot and nearly windowless kitchen chopping asparagus with her maid. Still, that was what he asked of her, and that is what she would do. She took grim pleasure in keeping his house in order, in making herself blameless in his eyes.

After their move to Amsterdam, Daniel had allowed her to hire a houseful of servants, but within weeks he had learned it was the Dutch custom for wives, even the wives of the greatest *heren*, to share their labours with their maids. A house with no children never had more than one servant. Eager to save his money, Daniel had dismissed nearly everyone, keeping just the girl, whom he favoured because she was a Catholic, to help Hannah with her chores.

'You're tired,' Annetje repeated sourly. Then a shrug.

Hannah knew only a passable amount of Dutch,

and Annetje less Portuguese, so their interactions were often terse and limited. Not limited enough. Hannah – fool, fool, Hannah – had trusted the girl too much in those early days. She'd trusted her pretty smile and her sweet temper and sea-green eyes. In the hours they spent together, toiling like equals – scrubbing floors, washing the stoop, sweating puddles on to the kitchen floor – Hannah had come to like the girl and to confide in her. Annetje taught her as much Dutch as Hannah could learn, and she tried patiently to learn Portuguese. She taught Hannah how to scrub the front stairs of a house (which no one had ever done in Lisbon), how to pick the best produce from the merchants on the Dam and how to tell if a baker added chalk to whiten his bread.

Hannah had come to look on the girl as her only true ally. She found few friends among the other Jewish women of the Vlooyenburg, and she hardly had time for idle friendship with her chores. Floors to scrub, clothes to launder, meals to cook. Breakfast before dawn, dinner when Daniel returned home from the Exchange – anywhere between two and six, so it had always to be ready – and later, depending on when he had his dinner, a light supper. There were the Sabbath meals he hosted, and the havdalah gatherings. Sometimes when he invited friends or colleagues for meals, he would supervise as Hannah and Annetje prepared the food, making foolish suggestions and getting underfoot.

Hannah had never been made to do so much work in her life. In Lisbon she'd been asked to sew and mend and to help cook on the holidays. She'd minded children for older relatives, and she'd cared for the sick and the elderly. Nothing like this. After a week, Annetje had found her huddled in the corner, weeping so hard she could hardly keep from banging her head against the brick behind her. The girl had pleaded for her to say what was wrong, but where to begin? What was wrong? Amsterdam. Jews. Prayer. Synagogue. Cooking. Scrubbing. And Daniel. It was all wrong, but she could say none of it aloud, so she'd let the girl comfort her and bring her hot wine and sing songs to her as though she were an infant.

Then she began to tell Annetje secrets, like how she had, unbeknownst to her husband, gone to see the witch woman who lived outside of town for a charm that would help her get with child. She told her about Daniel's quirks and foibles and coolness. For example, he would never, under any circumstances, take off all his clothing. She told Annetje how after he used his chamber pot he would return, hour after hour, to sniff at it.

And she told the girl other things too, things she now wished she could take back. Even as she'd said them, she knew she had confided too much. Maybe that was even why she'd done it. The thrill of speaking the forbidden, of asking for help in doing what must not be done – it had been all too delicious. And it would most likely be her undoing.

'We'll go tomorrow?' Annetje asked now, as though she sensed Hannah's thoughts.

'Yes,' Hannah said. These furtive trips had been exhilarating at first. Warm and welcoming, but also exciting in the way forbidden things always were. Now it was a terrible duty, one she could not avoid without seeing a little sparkle in the maid's eyes, a sparkle that said *Do as I instruct or I'll tell your husband what you would not want him to know*. She'd only uttered the threat aloud once, when she'd been very angry at Hannah for not wanting to give her more than the secret ten guilders a week above what her husband paid her. That one time had been enough. Now she only hinted. 'I'd hate to say things best left unsaid,' she would tell her mistress or 'I fear sometimes that my tongue is too loose, and if your husband is around – well, we'd best not talk of that.'

Hannah looked again at the dull knife. In Lisbon she might have been tempted – truly tempted – to plunge it into the girl's heart and be done with her. Who would have asked questions if a kitchen girl died in the home of a rich merchant? In Amsterdam, though, with its levelling politics and merchant culture, a housewife would hardly get away with killing a servant. Not that Hannah could really bring herself to murder another human being, no matter how much she might hate her. Still, it was better to have the option.

Daniel's teeth were bothering him today. She could see that when they sat down for dinner.

He had fingers from both hands in his mouth and was fishing around for who knew what. He would do that at night too, digging for hours on end, paying no mind to where his elbow flew or whom it struck.

After months of this she had urged him to see a surgeon – a tricky business, since Daniel took great offence if she suggested anything to him. If his hand were on fire and she suggested that he dunk it in a bucket of water, he'd glare at her and let himself burn. To soften the advice, she'd given it in anecdotal form: 'Jeronimo Javeza's wife tells me her husband had a problem tooth pulled by a skilled dentist who works near the Damrak. She says he hasn't been so comfortable in five years.'

So Daniel had gone but come back with the same troubling teeth with which he'd left the house that morning. 'The thug of a surgeon wanted fifteen guilders to pull five teeth,' he'd said. 'Three guilders a tooth. For fifteen guilders, a man should get new teeth, not lose old ones.'

Now, at the table, Daniel looked almost ready to aid his excavation with a knife while Miguel blessed the wine as the girl poured it. Miguel prayed over everything they ate, over anything that didn't move. He might pray over his own turds, for all she knew. When Daniel ate alone with her, he would mutter the Hebrew words or mutter some of them if he couldn't remember the rest. Often he forgot to pray at all. He would always forget when he ate alone, there being no one to impress or instruct.

Miguel, however, would bless his food whenever he ate. She'd seen other men of the Vlooyenburg with their Hebrew and their blessings, and often they seemed to her angry or frightening or alien. With Miguel there was delight in his utterances, as though he were remembering something wonderful each time he said the prayers. It was hard not to hear these strange words anew each time he spoke them – not mumbled and swallowed, the way some men did, but clearly articulated, like oratory. She heard the poetry of a foreign tongue, its cadences and repetitions complementary sounds. And she knew things would be different if Miguel, instead of Daniel, were her husband.

This wasn't just some idle fancy born from her constant reflection that Miguel was far more handsome and robust than his brother. Where Daniel was thin and looked like a beggar in merchant's clothes, Miguel was round and pink and hearty. Though Miguel was the elder brother, he looked more youthful and healthy. His large black eyes always darted here and there, not nervously like Daniel's, but with delight and wonder. And his face was so round – delicate and somehow still strong. What would it be like, she wondered, to be married to a man who loved laughter instead of resenting it, who embraced life instead of squinting at it with suspicion?

That was fate's little irony. She knew her father had been seeking an alliance with the Lienzos and wanted his daughter to marry the elder son.

Hannah had never met either of them, so it was all one to her, but then the elder son had upped and married a penniless girl without his family's approval, so her father had opted for the next Lienzo in line. By the time Miguel's wife died, only four months later, Hannah was already married to Daniel.

What would these prayers mean to her if she had married Miguel? Daniel knew almost nothing of the liturgy. He went to synagogue because the *parnassim* expected it of him, particularly his friend Solomon Parido (whom Hannah was inclined to dislike because of his sour attitude towards Miguel). He had often enough spared her the tedium of going herself, but now that he had got her with child, he made her come along so the men of the congregation could be reminded of his virility. More than one had wished him a son so he might have someone to say kaddish for him when he died.

He had not even spoken in private to Hannah of Jewish worship until they began their preparations to move to Amsterdam. Her father and three brothers had all been devoted Secret Jews, but no one had told her so before her marriage. On the eve of her wedding, when she was but sixteen years old, her father had explained that because her mother was renowned throughout the land for her loose tongue, he had assumed that Hannah would have the same streak of womanly treachery and had decided not to entrust the truth to his daughter. For the good of the family she had been allowed to think of herself as a Catholic, worship as a Catholic, and hate Jews as a Catholic. Now, as she prepared to marry this stranger who had been selected without even asking her opinion (he had dined with her family twice, and, her father had pointed out, Hannah had politely returned his awkwardly tight-lipped smiles that looked like the grimace of a man in pain), her father had chosen to reveal to her the family secret.

The secret: she was not the person she had always been led to believe she was; even her name had been a lie. 'You are not truly Bernarda,' he told her. 'You are Hannah, which is also the true name of your mother. You must call yourself Hannah from this moment on, but not in public, for that would betray us all, and I hope you are not so stupid as to do that.'

How could she be a Jew? Was it possible that she was of the race of child-killers and well-poisoners? Surely her father had made some mistake which her husband would clarify, so she had merely nodded and tried not to think too much about it.

But how could she not think about it? Her father had kept her own name from her, and now she had to practise strange rituals, which he explained rapidly and impatiently, assuring her that her new husband would clarify any foolish questions she might be imprudent enough to ask. She never asked and it would be years before he explained. Later she heard strange stories: that only the circumcised can enter the Kingdom of Heaven (did that mean women were forever banned from their eternal reward?); that only flattened bread should be eaten in springtime; that blood must be drained from meat before it can be eaten.

Her father, on the eve of her wedding, had cared nothing for Hannah's knowledge or for her ability to keep the laws – only her tongue. 'I suppose your silence will now be your husband's problem,' he had said, 'but if the Inquisition should take you, I hope you'll have the good sense to betray *his* family rather than your own.'

Hannah sometimes regretted that she had never had the opportunity to betray either.

She could tell at once that the meal would go badly. Annetje spilled some of the flan on the table and almost dropped a steaming heap of it into Daniel's lap.

'Learn to conduct yourself, girl,' Daniel snapped, in his nearly incomprehensible Dutch.

'Learn how to put your lips to my plump ass,' Annetje answered.

'What?' Daniel demanded. 'What did the girl say? I can't understand a word of her garbled accent.'

It was true enough that she spoke in the odd manner of Dutch northerners – and exaggerated the accent when she spoke impertinently – but Daniel only used that as an excuse for barely knowing the tongue of a land in which he had lived for more than two years. He had no idea what she'd said, but he saw Miguel's stifled laugh, and that was enough to set the mood.

Miguel, who Hannah was sure had put his own lips to all sorts of places on Annetje's anatomy, tried to avert discomfort by praising the food and the wine, but there was no appealing to his host's pride.

'I've heard,' Daniel said, 'that you're to lose a great deal in the brandy trade.'

Daniel had never shown warm feelings for his brother. There had always been a rivalry between them. She knew that when they were boys their father had told them that the Lienzo brothers had never got along, not since their great-great-grandfather had killed their great-great-great-uncle in an argument over a tavern bill. When he saw the boys playing happily together, he would remind them of this tradition. Miguel wanted only to avoid his brother whenever possible, but Daniel believed in a more aggressive approach, and he had grown even more acrimonious in recent months. Perhaps Daniel had been embarrassed by Miguel's difficulties in trade, perhaps he regretted having loaned his brother so large a sum, and perhaps it had something to do with his friendship with Solomon Parido.

Hannah did not entirely understand the relationship between her husband and the *parnass*, but it had formed almost from the instant they arrived in

Amsterdam. A member of the community always looked after new arrivals (Daniel had been asked to do this but had refused, saying it was well known that refugees always brought strange smells into an established household), and Parido had been the one to look after Daniel. Within a few months they had begun working together, as Parido mined Daniel's Portuguese contacts to trade mostly in wines, but also in figs and salt and olives and sometimes dried lemons. In that first year she had overheard a conversation – really, quite by accident – in which Daniel lamented already having a wife, and thus far a barren wife too, since Parido's daughter was of a marriageable age and an alliance between them would be the most beneficial thing in the world. That was how they had begun to think of linking the family through Miguel.

If that marriage had gone through as planned, perhaps feelings between the brothers would have softened, but things went horribly badly. Not that Hannah minded. She had disliked the girl and thought Miguel might do better. But the disaster had left Daniel feeling he could speak to his brother any way he liked, a feeling only intensified by Miguel's losses in the sugar market.

Miguel, however, at least maintained the appearance of calm. As his brother harassed him about his brandy futures, he only took a sip of his wine and half smiled. 'Reckoning day has not yet come. We'll see how things stand then.'

'As I hear it, you'll stand another thousand or more in debt.'

Daniel had loaned Miguel fifteen hundred guilders when his affairs soured, and while Daniel never referred to the loan directly, he knew a hundred ways to refer to it obliquely.

Miguel attempted the same half smile but said nothing more.

'And what is this I hear,' Daniel pressed on, 'about the coffee trade?'

Miguel kept his smirk, but at once it seemed to turn waxy and false, as though he had tasted bitter meat and needed somewhere discreet to spit it out.

'What makes you think I have an interest in the coffee trade?' he asked.

'Because when you came home last night, you woke me by clattering drunkenly around the house and muttering about coffee.'

'I have no recollection of doing so,' Miguel answered, 'but I suppose that is the nature of drunken mutterings – one never recollects them.'

'What is your interest in coffee?'

'No interest. I was feeling overly wet in my humours, so I took a prescription of coffee to dry myself out. I was most likely merely marvelling at its curative powers.'

'I cannot recommend that you enter into the coffee trade,' Daniel said.

'I have no plans to do so.'

'I think you will find it a less hospitable commodity than you might imagine. After all, it is only a medicine used by a few apothecaries, prescribed by a few physicians. What advantage could you find in trading in so unwanted a thing?'

'I'm sure you're right.'

'Trading in something no one wants can only lead to more ruin.'

Miguel set down his glass of wine too hard, and a few drops rose up to splash him in the face. 'Are you deaf?' He wiped away the wine from his eye. 'Are your ears in your teeth? Have you not heard that I have no interest in the coffee trade?'

'I only wish to make myself clear,' Daniel said sulkily, as he pushed his food around his plate, waiting for it to reach the same temperature as the interior of his mouth so he could eat it without difficulty.

'However,' Miguel added after a moment, 'your resolve makes me curious. Why should a man, whoever he might be, fear to involve himself in the coffee trade?'

But now it was Daniel who wanted to speak no more of it.

They ate the rest of the meal mostly in silence, Daniel staring at his food, Miguel exchanging glances with Hannah when he felt he could do so without her husband noticing. If he ever contemplated that he might well have been married to her, he never showed any signs of it, but he was always kind. Miguel was rarely home except to sleep in his damp cellar, so there were few occasions for them to talk without her husband's presence, but on those occasions he spoke to her warmly, as though they were old friends, as though he valued her opinion.

Once she had even dared to ask him why he slept in the cellar. When he had first moved in, Daniel had placed him in a small windowless room on the third floor – what the Dutch called the priest room – but Miguel had complained that it was too hot and smoky if he burned peat and too cold if he did not. Hannah suspected he'd moved out for other reasons. The priest room was located directly under the room in which she and Daniel slept, and on Saturday mornings, after she and her husband had observed the tradition of conjugal duties (one of the few rules of the Hebrews Daniel showed any interest in adhering to – at least until she had become pregnant), Miguel always seemed embarrassed and uncomfortable.

So now he lived in the damp cellar, sleeping in a cupboard bed that even the shortest man would have to curl up to fit into. At night, when the tides rose, the canal water spilled through the windows and on to the floor, but he still preferred it to the priest room, at least when he wasn't creeping up the stairs to Annetje's garret chamber.

At the conclusion of the cheerless meal, they were rescued from their misery by a pounding at the door. It turned out to be the *parnass*, Senhor Parido, who entered the room and bowed in his overly formal way. Like her husband, Parido dressed like a Portuguese man, and while she had grown up thinking nothing of men who wore bright colours and giant hats, in Amsterdam such clothes appeared to her slightly ridiculous. At least Parido went to a decent tailor, and his suits of reds and golds and bright blues somehow looked more appropriate on him than on her husband. Parido had wide shoulders and a muscular frame, a rugged face with dull eyes.

He radiated a melancholy that Hannah had never fully understood until the day she'd seen him on the street, leading his only son by the hand. The boy was her age but addled in his head and hooted like a monkey she'd once seen in a travelling show. Parido had no other sons, and his wife was too old to bear more.

Parido's sadness meant nothing to Daniel. Hannah would have been surprised if he had even noticed it. Daniel saw only the enormity of Parido's house, the expense of his clothes, the wealth that he gave to the charitable boards. Parido was one of the few men in the city, Jew or Gentile, who owned a coach, and he maintained his own horses in a stable on the fringes of the city. Unlike in Lisbon, horse travel was not generally permitted in Amsterdam, and each venture had to be approved by an office in the Town Hall. And even though the coach had little practical use, Daniel envied its shiny gilding, the padded seats, the envious looks of the pedestrians they passed. That was what Daniel wanted. The envy. He wanted to be the object of everyone's envy, and he had not the first idea how to go about it.

Daniel greeted the *parnass* in the most elaborate terms imaginable. He nearly fell over, getting up from the table so he could return the bow. He then told Hannah that he and Senhor Parido would withdraw to the front room. The maid should bring them some wine – a bottle of his best Portuguese – and then she should get out before she offered any of her tongue.

'Perhaps the elder Senhor Lienzo would like to join us,' Parido suggested. He stroked his beard, which he kept fashionably short and slightly pointy, like a painter's rendition of his namesake.

Miguel looked up from the last of his stewed herring. He had barely responded with a nod to Parido's bow. Now Miguel continued to stare as if he didn't understand his Portuguese.

'I'm sure my brother has other things to do with his time,' Daniel suggested.

'It does seem likely,' Miguel agreed.

'Please, why don't you join us?' Parido suggested again, an unusual softness in his voice. Miguel could not refuse unless he wished to risk utter rudeness, something Hannah was not willing to dismiss.

Instead he nodded sharply, almost as though trying to shake something out of his hair, and the three men disappeared together into the front room.

Hannah had begun eavesdropping, despite her

71

intentions to obey her husband's wishes. A year before she had found Annetje, in the great tradition of Dutch servant girls, pressing her ear against the heavy oak door to the antechamber. Inside, Daniel's nasal voice vibrated, muffled and incomprehensible, through the walls. Now she could no longer recall to what the girl had been listening. Daniel with a tradesman? Daniel with a business partner? It might have been Daniel with that nasty little portrait painter who once, when he had got Hannah alone, tried to kiss her. When she protested, he'd said it was no matter and that she was too plump for his taste anyhow.

Hannah had walked into the hall to find Annetje with her face against the door, her dung-coloured cap pushed askew by the force of her eagerness.

Hannah had placed her hands upon her hips. She screwed her face into a mask of authority. 'You mustn't eavesdrop.'

Annetje had turned from the door for an instant, not even the hint of a smile on her pale Dutch face. 'No,' she'd said. 'I must,' and so resumed her business.

There had been nothing for Hannah to do but to press her ear against the door herself.

Now she could hear Parido's muffled voice on the inside. 'I was hoping I might have a moment to speak with you,' he said.

'You might have taken that moment last night. I surely saw you at the Talmud Torah.'

72

'Why should he not have been at the Talmud Torah?' Daniel asked. 'He is a *parnass*.'

'Please, Daniel,' Parido said quietly.

A moment of silence and then Parido began again. 'Senhor, I have but this to say. Things have been uneasy with us for a long time now. After the business with Antonia, you sent me a note in which you offered an apology, and I was uninterested at the time. I now regret my coolness towards you. Your behaviour was foolish and inconsiderate, but not malicious.'

'I will agree with that assessment,' Miguel said, after a moment.

'I don't expect us to become great friends in an instant, but I would like to see less discomfort between us.'

A brief pause, and sounds like the drinking of wine. Then: 'I have felt particular discomfort when you brought me before the Ma'amad.'

Parido barked out a laugh. 'Do me justice and acknowledge that I never charged you unfairly, nor have you ever faced serious punishment. My duties as a *parnass* require that I guide the behaviour of the community, and in your case I have tried to show mercy out of affection for your brother rather than be cruel out of resentment towards you.'

'It is strange that it never occurred to me.'

'You see?' Daniel said. 'He has no interest in ending animosities.'

Parido seemed to ignore him. 'We have been angry with one another these two years. I cannot expect for us to be friends because I say so. I only ask that you not look to extend hostilities, and I will do the same, and in time we may come to trust each other.'

'I appreciate your words,' Miguel said. 'I'd be happy if things could become easy between us.'

'The next time we see each other,' Parido pressed, 'we will meet if not as friends then at least as countrymen.'

'Agreed,' Miguel said, with a bit more warmth. 'I thank you for this gesture.'

Hannah heard scraping sounds, like feet shuffling towards the door, and dared not risk remaining in the hall any longer.

Women were not made privy to business affairs, but she knew that Parido had long done what he could to harm Miguel's dealings. Could he now trust this offer of friendship, coming as it did so suddenly? It put Hannah in mind of children's stories, of witches who lured children into their homes with promises of sweets, or hobgoblins who tempted greedy travellers with gold and jewels. She thought to warn Miguel, but he scarcely needed her wisdom. Miguel knew a witch or a hobgoblin when he saw one. He would not be easily fooled.

CHAPTER 4

Though he had more pressing things to consider, Miguel visited a bookseller near the Westerkerk and found a translation of an English pamphlet extolling the virtues of coffee. The author wrote with an enthusiasm that dwarfed Geertruid's. Coffee, he insisted, has all but destroyed the plague in England. It preserves health in general and makes those who drink it hearty and fat; it helps the digestion and cures consumption and other maladies of the lung. It is wonderful for fluxes, even the bloody flux, and has been know to cure jaundice and every kind of inflammation. Besides all that, the Englishman wrote, it imparts astonishing powers of reason and concentration. In the years to come, the author said, the man who does not drink coffee may never hope to compete with the man who avails himself of its secrets.

Later, down in his space in Daniel's cellar, Miguel fought back the urge to pick up a pewter pitcher and hurl it against the wall. Should he give his attention to coffee or brandy? Could he separate the two? The brandy business pulled him down like a weight on a drowning man, but coffee could be the very thing to buoy him up.

He turned for comfort, as he increasingly did, to his collection of pamphlets. Since coming to Amsterdam, Miguel had discovered a love of Spanish adventures, translated French romances, marvellous travel stories, and, most of all, salacious tales of crime. Of these accounts of murderers and thieves, Miguel loved best the pamphlets recounting the adventures of Charming Pieter, the clever bandit who had been playing his wily tricks on the foolish rich in and around Amsterdam for years. Geertruid had first introduced him to the adventures of this scoundrel hero who, she said, along with his Goodwife Mary, embodied the very core of Dutch cleverness. She read the pamphlets eagerly, sometimes aloud to her man, Hendrick, and sometimes to an entire tavern of men, who laughed and hooted and toasted this thief. Were the stories true, were they mere fictions like *Don Quixote*, or something in between?

Miguel had resisted the allure of these stories at first. In Lisbon he had never bothered with lurid accounts of murderers and executions, and now he had reading enough with his studies of Torah. Nevertheless, Charming Pieter had won him over; Miguel had become enchanted by the bandit's celebration of his own duplicity. The Conversos of Lisbon had been duplicitous by necessity, even those who fully embraced the Catholic Church. A New Christian could be betrayed at any time by a victim under an Inquisitor's knife. Miguel had habitually lied, hidden facts about himself, eaten pork in public; he had done anything to prevent his name from being the one to come to a prisoner's lips. Deception had always been a burden, but Pieter revelled in his duplicity. Miguel was enchanted by these tales because he longed, like Charming Pieter, to be a trickster instead of a liar.

Tonight he tried to lose himself in one of his favourite stories, that of a rich burgher who, entranced by Goodwife Mary's beauty, had thought to cuckold Pieter. While she provided a distraction with her wit and artful ways, Pieter and his men carried off all of the burgher's possessions. After turning the burgher out of his own home, naked to the world, Pieter and Mary opened up the man's larder to the people of the village and allowed them to feast upon his wealth. And so, in his own way, Charming Pieter carried out the justice of the common folk.

When he closed the little volume, Miguel was still thinking about brandy and about coffee.

That afternoon, he received a letter from the usurer Alonzo Alferonda, with whom he maintained a cautious friendship. Alferonda had a reputation as a man dangerous to neglect – dozens of blinded and lamed debtors in Amsterdam would testify to that – but Miguel found Alferonda's hobbled victims hard to reconcile with the plump and jovial fellow with whom he maintained a now-forbidden friendship. The Ma'amad would have destroyed Miguel for his congress with a man it had expelled, but Alferonda's company was too merry to set aside. Even in his exiled state, he had knowledge and information, and he never hesitated to pass it along.

Some months ago, Miguel had mentioned a rumour he'd heard, and Alferonda volunteered to find out what he could. Now he claimed to have learned something important and requested that they talk – always a tricky business, but usually managed well enough with a bit of caution. Miguel wrote to Alferonda suggesting they meet in the coffee tavern, which he had found by enquiring of a few men he knew in the East India trade.

Miguel knew only that the place was located in the Plantage, which stretched out east of the Vlooyenburg, endless walks cutting through sculpted gardens. Square paths crisscrossed walkways, peopled with the high and the low alike. The burgomasters had ruled that no permanent buildings might stand on its verdant grounds, so all structures here were made of wood, ready to be taken apart should the city so decree. On pleasant evenings, the Plantage became a garden of delights for those who had the coin and the inclination. Strollers could walk among bands of fiddlers and fife players. On the well-lighted paths, entrepreneurs had set up tables and poured beer and served sausage or herring or cheese; in houses hardly more than huts, a man could buy delicacies of a more human kind.

Miguel located the meeting place with difficulty, after asking several other proprietors for directions. Finally he came upon what he suspected was the right building, a poor wooden structure built at crazed angles, hardly looking fit to withstand a rainstorm. Miguel found the door locked, but a nearby brothel keeper assured him that it was the right place, so he knocked loudly.

Almost at once the door opened a crack and Miguel stared at a dark-skinned Turk in a yellow turban. The man said nothing.

'Is this the coffee tavern?' Miguel asked.

'Who are you?' the Turk grunted in muddled Dutch.

'Is the tavern private? I did not know.'

'I did not say it was. I did not say it wasn't. I only asked who you are.'

'I'm not sure my name will mean anything to you. I am Miguel Lienzo.'

The Turk nodded. 'Senhor Alferonda's friend. You may come in. Senhor Alferonda's friends will always find themselves welcome here.'

Senhor Alferonda's friend? Miguel had no idea that Alferonda had even heard of coffee, but apparently he was well known among the Muhammadans. Miguel followed the Turk into the building, hardly more impressive on the inside than the outside. Rough chairs and tables sat on a damp earth floor. At once he was overwhelmed by the scent of coffee, far more intense and pungent that what he had smelled at Geertruid's cousin's tavern. On a half-dozen or so benches sat an odd assortment of men: Turks in turbans, seafaring Dutchmen, a hodgepodge of foreigners – and one Jew. Alonzo Alferonda sat conversing with a tall Turk in faded blue robes. He whispered something as Miguel approached, and the Turk departed.

Alferonda stood to greet Miguel, though standing only emphasised his shortness. He was a rounded fellow with a wide face and large eyes hidden behind a thick beard of slightly graying black. Miguel could scarce believe there were so many men who trembled before this pudgy face. But then one night they had walked together after drinking at a tavern near the docks. A pair of thieves had leapt from an alley, knives brandished, set to take their purses. One look at Alferonda, and they scurried away like frightened cats.

'I was surprised you asked to meet here,' Alferonda said. 'I had no idea you had any taste for coffee.'

'I might say the same of you. I've only just learned of it. I wanted to see what a coffee tavern would be like.'

Alferonda gestured for them to sit. 'It is not much, but they obtain good fruit, and the demand is low enough that they rarely run out.'

'But supplies are sometimes short?'

'They can be.' The usurer studied Miguel. 'Coffee is controlled by the East India Company, and as there is not much demand in Europe, the Company doesn't import a great quantity. It mostly trades the fruit in the East. What do you care about the supplies?'

Miguel ignored the question. 'I'd forgotten you'd lived in Orient. Of course you know coffee.'

He opened his hands wide. 'Alferonda has lived everywhere and has connections everywhere, which is why you seek him out.'

Miguel smiled at the hint. 'You have information?'

'Excellent information.'

Miguel had asked Alferonda to inquire into a rumour he'd overheard regarding Parido's involvement in an impending whale oil trade. He'd been hesitant to pursue this affair; it would be dangerous to oppose the *parnass* in matters of business. Still, Miguel only sought information, he told himself. He needn't act on it.

'You were certainly right about Parido,' Alferonda began. 'He has a spy inside the East India Company.'

Miguel raised his eyebrows. 'I would have thought that beyond even his ambition.'

'The Company is not so powerful as it would have you believe. Gold works for Company men as it does for everyone else. Parido has learned that they plan to buy large quantities of whale oil to sell in the Japans and Cathay, but these Company fellows have the patience to wait for the price to drop since they know production has been climbing steadily of late. Parido has been quietly collecting whale oil on other exchanges – just a little here and there, you understand – and hopes to flood the market slowly enough to lower the price without raising suspicion. Meanwhile, he and his combination are also buying calls, which will allow them to secure the current low prices.'

Miguel let out a breath. 'I am no friend of that man, but I am impressed. At some point the East India Company will decide the price is low enough to buy and stock their own warehouses, and when that happens the price goes up. Meanwhile, Parido's combination has the calls, which allow them to buy at the artificially lowered price and then turn around and sell at the new inflated price.' Trading combinations manipulated the markets all the time, but this plan – buying on other exchanges, creating a market to tempt a buyer – was beyond anything Miguel had ever heard. 'How did you learn all this?'

Alferonda smoothed his beard. 'Anything that is known can be learned. You hear rumours about whale oil, I ask some questions, and soon everything is revealed.'

'When will this trade take place?'

'Sometime next month, between this reckoning day and the next. I need hardly say anything to you, but as your friend I must warn you to proceed carefully. You may hitch a ride on Parido's venture if you like. He'll scowl that you should have profited from his work, but do him no harm that he can see or he'll never forgive you.'

'You must think me addled to lecture me about that,' Miguel said good-naturedly.

'Not addled, but I would hate to see your eagerness undo your ambitions. Now, I've already bought whale oil at its low price, and I suggest you do so too as quickly as you can.'

'It will have to wait until after this reckoning day. I hope to have a few coins to my name then.'

A Turk placed two small bowls before them. They were smaller than any drinking vessels Miguel had ever seen and contained a liquid black and thick as mud.

'What is this?' Miguel asked.

'It's coffee. Have you not tried it yet?'

'I have,' Miguel said, as he picked up the bowl and held it closer to an oil lamp, 'but it seemed a different thing than this altogether.'

'This is how the Turks drink it. They boil it three times in a copper pot to darken and distil it. In their native land, they often serve it with great ceremony. But Amsterdammers have no time for the frivolity of ritual. Be careful. Let the powder rest at the bottom.'

'When I drank it before,' Miguel said, eyeing the drink sceptically, 'it was made with milk. Or sweet wine. I can't recall.'

'The Turks believe that combining milk and coffee causes leprosy.'

Miguel laughed. 'I hope not. You seem to

know a great deal about coffee. What else can you tell me?'

'I can tell you about Kaldi, the Abyssinian goatherd.'

'I don't know that I have any interest in goatherds.'

'You'll find this one interesting. He lived quite some time ago, tending his flock in the hills of Abyssinia. One afternoon he noticed that his goats were much more lively than usual, dancing about, raising up on their hind legs, bleating out their little goat songs. Kaldi spent several days watching them, and they grew increasingly more lively. They ran and played and hopped about when they should have been sleeping. They danced and sang instead of eating.

'Kaldi was certain a demon had possessed the goats, but he summoned his courage and followed the beasts, hoping to catch a glimpse of this fiend. The next day, he saw that the goats had come upon a strange bush. After they ate the fruit of the bush, they once again began to leap about. Kaldi ate some of the berries himself, and soon he could not resist the urge to dance with the goats.

'A holy man happened by at that time and asked Kaldi why he capered with his herd. He explained that he had eaten the fruit of the bush, and it had filled him with untold vigour. So the holy man, who was rather a boring fellow, took some fruit home. He was plagued by the fact that his students would fall asleep while he was lecturing, so he made a drink out of the berries and fed it to his students before he lectured. Soon he was known throughout the world of the Muhammadans as a man who could deliver discourses from sundown to sunrise without his students falling asleep.'

Miguel paused for a moment. 'That is very interesting, but I thought to enquire about the coffee trade as it is now, not among Abyssinian goatherds.'

Alferonda raised one eyebrow. 'There is no vigorous coffee trade outside of the Orient, and the East India company controls that. Not much remains for the rest of us.'

'But you are speaking about the East. Perhaps coffee would be of interest to men here in Europe. I, for one, have no love of sleep. I see it as a waste of time. If I could drink coffee instead, I would be most pleased.'

'You would have to sleep in the end,' Alferonda said, 'but I take your point. Men who drink coffee come to love it beyond all things. I've heard that among the Turks a woman can divorce her husband if he does not provide her with enough coffee. And the coffee taverns of the East are strange places. There the drink is combined with powerful medicines, like poppy extract, and men go to such places in search of pleasures of the flesh.'

Miguel looked around. 'I see nothing so pleasurable here.'

'The Turks don't look kindly upon women in

social places such as a coffee tavern. The pleasures you pay for in those places are the pleasures of boys, not women.'

'That is a strange way to do things,' Miguel said.

'To us, but they enjoy themselves. In any case, you must keep me informed about your interest in coffee. If I can be of any help, you may depend on me. But you must remember to be careful. Coffee is a drink that brings out great passions in men, and you may be unlocking great forces if you trifle with it.'

Miguel drank down the rest of his bowl, swallowing a bit of the powder at the bottom. It coated his mouth uncomfortably. 'You're the second person to warn me off coffee,' he told Alferonda, while he wiped at his mouth with his sleeve.

The usurer cocked his head. 'I hate being second at anything. Who was the first?'

'My brother, if you can believe it.'

'Daniel? Reason enough to pursue it if he warns you off. What did he say?'

'Only that it was dangerous,' Miguel said. 'He somehow knew I'd developed an interest. He told some story about me muttering drunkenly, but I'm not sure I believe him. More likely he's been searching my things again.'

'I would pay his warning no mind. Your brother, if you will excuse me for saying so, has no more brains than the idiot son Parido keeps locked in his garret.'

'I thought it odd,' Miguel said. 'I wonder if he's somehow learned that I have been thinking of the coffee trade and wants to set me off out of spite. He doesn't like that I carry on with his serving girl.'

'Oh, she's a pretty one. Are you fond of her?'

Miguel shrugged. 'I suppose. I'm fond of her looks,' he said absently. In truth, Miguel found her somewhat impertinent, but she was the one who had begun the dalliance, and Miguel had known from an early age that a man never turns away an eager serving girl.

'Not so pretty as the mistress though, eh?' Alferonda said.

'True enough. My brother doesn't much like the way I speak to her.'

'Oh?' A wide grin spread across Alferonda's face. 'What way is that?'

Miguel had the feeling he'd fallen into a trap. 'She's a pleasant girl. A pretty thing, with a quick mind, but Daniel never has a kind word. I think she takes a great deal of pleasure from the occasional bit of congress with me.'

Alferonda was now moving his eyebrows up and down and flaring his nostrils. 'I, for one, thought it was a fine thing when the rabbis revoked the commandment against adultery.'

'Don't be foolish,' Miguel said, turning to hide his blush. 'I only feel sorry for her.'

'I've known Miguel Lienzo to have dealings with pretty girls, and what he feels is generally not sorry.'

'I have no intention of bedding my brother's wife,' he said. 'In any case, she is far too virtuous a woman to allow it.'

'May the Holy One, blessed be He, help you,' Alferonda said. 'When a man starts protesting about a woman's virtue, it means he's either had her already or would kill to do so. I will say that it is one way to get back at your brother for his foul temper.'

Miguel opened his mouth to protest but thought better of it. Justification was for the guilty, and surely he had done nothing wrong.

From

The Factual and Revealing Memoirs of Alonzo Alferonda

I had been plying my trade with a fair amount of success for some time when I was approached by a Tudesco merchant with a proposition that appeared to me both lucrative and rewarding. For some years now the Tudescos, the Jews of Eastern Europe, had been making their presence increasingly felt in Amsterdam, and this development was not at all to the Ma'amad's liking. While we Jews of the Portuguese Nation have no shortage of beggars among our number, we also enjoy our share of wealthy merchants, and these can afford to be charitable. Our community had struck a deal with the Amsterdam burgomasters to remain a city apart, taking care of our own charitable cases and producing no burden on the metropolis itself. Thus we took care of our own, but the Tudescos had few men of significant wealth, and most were desperately poor.

Though with our beards and our bright

colours we looked different from the Dutch, we thought ours a dignified difference. A Hebrew of Portugal could not go anywhere in the city, no matter how neatly trimmed his beard and no matter how dull his clothes, without being recognised for a member of his nation, but the Ma'amad believed the merchants among us were ambassadors. We might say, in the silence of our finery, *Behold us. We are different, but we are worthy people with whom to share your land.* More importantly, they might look on our poor and think, *Ah, those Jews feed and dress their own mendicants, relieving us of the burden. They're not so bad.*

Thus the problem of the Tudescos. They had heard that Amsterdam was a paradise for Jews, so they fled to our city from Poland, Germany, Lithuania, and all manner of other places where they were savagely abused. I had heard that Poland in particular was a land of ghastly torments and scarcely believable cruelties: men made to watch while their wives and daughters were brutalised, children tied in sacks and thrown on burning fires, scholars buried alive with their murdered families.

The *parnassim* surely sympathised with these refugees, but they had grown to depend on the comforts of Amsterdam and, like the fat and rich of all nations and beliefs, they were unwilling to sacrifice their ease for the well-being of others. Their concerns were not unfounded, and they dreaded a future in which the streets of Amsterdam were crawling with Jewish beggars and Jewish hucksters and Jewish whores. The Dutch would then surely rescind their former generosity. The Ma'amad concluded that the Tudesco community would be best handled if kept small.

There were several plans for accomplishing this goal, but they all centred around keeping these troubling people at a distance from Iberian wealth — a manoeuvre they believed would make Amsterdam less appealing than cities where their own kind thrived. Tudescos were therefore forbidden from enrolling their children in schools run by Portuguese Jews. They could have no position of standing in Portuguese synagogues. Their meats were declared unclean and off limits to Portuguese households, so their butchers could not sell to our people. The Ma'amad even declared it a crime, punishable by excommunication, to give charity to any Tudesco except through one of the official charitable boards. These boards believed that the best charity would be passage on ships heading out of Amsterdam, so it could do no good to encourage them to stay by dropping a stiver or two into their greedy little hands.

I knew all this, but I did not have it much in my thoughts when I was approached by a member of the Tudesco community. Many of the refugees, he told me, managed to escape from their oppressive lands with a precious stone or two hidden away on their persons. Would I be willing to broker these stones to Portuguese merchants? He suggested that I would ask for a bit more than the lowest price, explaining that the stones belonged to wretched wanderers who longed to begin anew, and take only a fraction of the usual brokering fee. I might make a few extra guilders and still do a good deed that would win me favour in the eyes of the Holy One, blessed be He.

For several months I went about this business, during what time I could spare for it. A bottle of wine purchased, a smile, a word about the importance of charity, and I soon found most gem merchants willing to pay a few extra guilders for a stone if it would help a poor family enjoy a peaceful Shabbat. So it went until I one day came to my home and found a note for me, composed in florid Spanish, written in a fine hand. I had been summoned to the Ma'amad.

I still thought nothing of the matter. Sooner or later every man found himself standing before that council. A rumour of unclean food eaten or a Dutch slut got with child. The council itself was little better than a pack of old women, wanting only a soothing word to make them calm again. I knew that my old enemy, Solomon Parido, now held a place on the council, but I hardly thought he would use his power for nefarious ends.

Yet that is precisely what he did. He sat there, stiff in his laced suit, glaring at me. 'Senhor Alferonda,' he said, 'you are surely aware of the ruling of the council that no help shall be given to the Tudescos other than through the charitable boards of the synagogue.'

'Of course, senhor,' I said.

'Then why have you ensnared men of our nation, law-abiding men, into your wicked schemes of jewel peddling?'

'My wicked schemes, as you style them, provide aid to the poor. And while you have made it clear that you do not want us throwing our coins to Tudesco beggars, you have said nothing about buying and selling with them.'

'Is it not the same as tossing coins if you intentionally ask merchants to give more than

93

they wish to pay that the seller might take that money and do with it as he will?'

'*As he will*,' I pointed out, 'often means buying bread.'

'That is not your concern,' one of the other members of the council said. 'There are charitable boards to see that these people don't starve.'

The offence was minor enough, but Parido wished to cast it the most dire light possible. He turned the other *parnassim* against me. He prodded me into speaking angrily. And yet, though I saw all that, I could not help but be angry. I had done nothing wrong. I had violated none of the holy laws. Indeed, I upheld the commandment to give charity. Was I now to be punished for doing as the Torah commands? This question, in particular, may have been what set them against me. No one likes to have his hypocrisy exposed.

After much interrogation, the *parnassim* asked me to wait outside. When they called me back in, after more than an hour, they announced their decision. I was to ask the men for whom I had brokered to rescind their sales. They were, in other words, to buy back their stones.

I had seen the men for whom I had

brokered. They were poor, dressed in rags, crushed by hardship and despair. Many had lost parents or children or wives to the cruelty of Poles or Cossacks. To go to them and ask them to return money, which they surely no longer had because they had spent it rather than starve or go naked, seemed to me not only preposterous but depraved. I supposed it was meant to be so. To undo these sales, I would have to buy those stones back with my own money, and surely Parido had known I would refuse to do so.

The council urged me to reconsider, but I swore I would never obey such an unreasonable demand. The *parnassim* then told me I had forced their hand and they had no choice but to put me under *cherem*, the ban – to excommunicate me.

Men fell under the ban frequently. Most times it was but for a day or a week but in some it was permanent. And so they meant it in my case. More than that, Parido made it clear to the Tudescos that if they admitted me into their synagogue they would be made to suffer for their kindness. He wrote to the Ma'amads of every community upon the face of the earth, giving them my name and speaking of my crimes in the most exaggerated terms. I had become an outcast with nowhere to go, the mark of Cain upon me.

They chose to treat me like a villain. What choice did I have but to become one in earnest?

CHAPTER 5

Miguel first met Geertruid nearly a year before she proposed a venture in coffee. It was in the Flyboat, a tavern off the Warmoesstraat, close enough to the Exchange that merchants regarded it as adjunct, a place to continue business when the gates of the bourse closed. Though owned by a Dutchman, it catered to Jewish traders by offering drinks that conformed to the dietary codes. Jewish boys of the Portuguese Nation were hired to keep separate the serving glasses for the Jews and to clean them in accordance with Jewish law, and a rabbi would occasionally come to inspect the kitchens, strolling like a general with his hands behind his back as he peered into cabinets and pried open containers. The owner charged almost twice the going rate for wine and beer, but Jewish merchants gladly paid higher prices in exchange for the chance to conduct business in a Dutch tavern with an easy conscience.

Miguel had been continuing a conversation with a sugar merchant after the close of the Exchange, and the two men had taken a table and talked of their business for hours, all the while drinking with Netherlandish intensity. The sugar merchant was one of those good-natured Dutchmen who found Jews fascinating, as though their alien beliefs and customs made them a puzzle. The Vlooyenburg crawled with these men, who came to learn Hebrew or study Jewish theology, in part because it helped them better to understand their own religion but also because the Dutch were curiously attracted to foreigners. The Ma'amad's strict injunction against religious debate with gentiles made Miguel only more irresistible, and the merchant had bought drink after drink, with the playful intention of breaking Miguel's defences. At last he abandoned the effort, announcing that he must return home to his wife lest he face her fury.

Warm with beer, Miguel had been in no mood to return to the solitude of his own home, so he remained at his table, quietly drinking, while he puffed lazily upon a pipe of good tobacco. Conversations swirled all around him, and he half listened for any useful rumour or tip. Then he heard a fragment of conversation that jolted him out of his stupor.

'. . . a sad end for the *Indian Flower*,' a voice pronounced, with the kind of narrative fervour only to be found on the lips of a drunk Dutchman. 'Cleaned out to her core, until there was nothing left but a pack of unmanned sailors shitting themselves silly.'

Miguel turned slowly. He owned shares in the

Indian Flower – quite a few, in fact. Wading through a swamp of boozy confusion, he tried to recall how much he had invested. Five hundred guilders? Seven hundred? Not enough to ruin a man who stood as he had at the time, but well enough that he could not count the loss insignificant, particularly since he had already invested his anticipated profits.

'What did you say?' Miguel demanded of the speaker. 'The *Indian Flower*?'

He took his first look at the fellow, a grizzled man well into his middle years with the blotchy face of a lifelong sailor. His companions were all the rougher sort of Dutchman who frequented taverns closer to the docks.

'The *Indian Flower*'s been taken by pirates,' the older fellow told Miguel. 'I heard they were pirates, at any rate. They're all in service of the Spanish Crown, if you ask me.'

'How do you know this?' Miguel demanded. His twisted his hands, which felt awkward and spongy from too much drink, but his head had already begun to clear.

'I've got a mate on the *Glory of the Palm*,' the man explained, 'which came into dock late this afternoon. He told me the news.'

This afternoon. No one knew yet. He might yet salvage this wreck.

'Have you a particular interest in that ship?' One of the man's companions spoke. He was younger than the rest, with less of the look of the sea.

'Suppose I have?' He meant no challenge. The two men were testing each other.

'I might be able to offer you my services,' the raggedy trader told him. 'By this time tomorrow, word will be out and those shares of yours won't be good for much more than wiping your arse. But tonight they just might be worth something.'

'Something other than wiping your arse,' one of his friends clarified.

'What are they worth tonight?' Miguel knew a schemer when he saw one, but schemes were the blood flowing through the city's veins, and only a fool would refuse to listen.

'If you want to sell at fifty per cent, I'd be willing to unburden you.'

Miguel had no taste for losing half his investment, but even less for losing all of it. Still, something sat ill with him. 'If the ship has been taken, what good are the shares to you?'

'I'll sell them, of course. Tomorrow the Exchange opens, and I'll unload them at seventy-five or eighty per cent. By the time the news hits the exchange, I'll be rid of them.'

'Then why should I not do the same?' Miguel asked. 'I could have eighty per cent back rather than a mere fifty.'

'You could,' the man said, 'but there's always the chance that the news may beat you to the Exchange. Besides, men know you; if you sell, your reputation might suffer. I'm used to plying my trade in The Hague, so I won't lose for my deeds here.'

Miguel put his hands to his forehead. He could not entirely ignore the moral issue that presented itself: if he sold his shares to this fellow, he would be knowingly allowing an unknown person to buy something that was worthless. Did the sages not say that the man who robs his fellow of even the smallest coin is as sinful as a murderer? On the other hand, all investment was risk. Miguel did not know when he bought the shares that the ship would be taken by pirates, yet it had been; perhaps it had been destined to be so taken. Surely the Most High knew of the boat's fate, but Miguel did not believe that the Holy One, blessed be He, had cheated him. What difference did it make if *someone* knew beforehand?

The trader read Miguel's uncertainty. 'You do what you like, Jew. I'll be here for another hour or so. If you want to do business, it had best be done quickly.'

Before Miguel could respond, a new voice rose up. 'Aye, quick enough that this man not learn the truth.' The woman sounded like a heroine from a stage play. There she stood, hands upon her hips, ample bosom thrust outward, her soft features pointed defiantly at these men.

In her yellows and blacks, she looked like a honeybee and a pretty one at that, if a bit older than Miguel liked his women. He couldn't decide if she were more wench or virago.

'What truth is that?' he asked cautiously, not for the first time suspicious of the old sailor and his friends. Against these grizzled fellows stood this handsome woman, both confident and defiant. Miguel decided in an instant that he trusted her far more than the sailor and his friends.

'That the ship they speak of remains unharmed,' she announced. 'At least it does as best they know.'

The men at the table exchanged glances. 'Have I met you, mother?' the older fellow asked. 'You ought to think carefully before you accuse a man in public, ruining his trade and such. Otherwise,' he added, with a glance to his companion, 'he and those he's friendly with might take some offence and offer your plump bottom a spanking.'

'Aye, you know me. My name is Geertruid Damhuis, and you were the kindly stranger who told me of the wreck of the *Angel's Mercy*, a ship in which I owned shares. You were good enough to take those shares off of me for half price. Then the ship sailed into port a few weeks later, on schedule and bursting with cargo.'

'You've made a mistake,' the older man said, at the same moment that the trader said, 'I cannot guarantee the truth of every rumour I hear.' Seeing that they had undone themselves, the party arose in a single movement and dashed out of the door.

'Should we pursue,' Miguel asked, 'or call the Night Watch?'

Geertruid Damhuis shook her pretty head. 'I'll

not raise my skirts to go running in the dark for a gang of ruffians who would only knock me down.'

Miguel laughed, feeling a sudden rush of friendship and gratitude. 'I thought you valiant enough just this moment.'

She grinned: wide, beautiful, white as pearl. Miguel sucked in his breath, feeling as though he had caught a glimpse of something forbidden. 'It's an easy thing to be valiant when surrounded by a few dozen men who would never stand to see a woman set upon. Quite another to go chasing after thieves in the dark.' She let out a long sigh and pressed her fingers to her chest. 'By Christ, I need a drink. See how I shake?' She held up her trembling hand.

While she drank, Geertruid explained that these men made it their business to learn the names of those who had invested in particular ships and then to track them down and tell stories so the investors might overhear. From there it took only a little trickery to convince even the most sceptical man to part with his shares.

'It is the urgency that undoes their victims,' Geertruid told him. 'I had to make a decision at that moment or suffer the consequences, and I could not endure the thought that I might have avoided total disaster yet lacked the resolve to do so. As they say, the patient dog eats rabbit while the hasty dog goes hungry.'

Miguel was taken at once with Geertruid's

easy demeanour, somehow both mannish and seductive. She explained that her husband, who had never done her a kind turn before he died, had left her comfortable, and though most of her money was bound up in neat little investments, she had some few guilders with which to play.

Though he and Geertruid spoke often and drank and smoked together, there were many things Miguel did not understand about this widow. She kept much about herself quiet – Miguel hardly even knew the part of town she called home. She would ask him to broker for her, but only small quantities, surely far less than she had at her disposal. She would disappear for weeks at a time, neither telling Miguel before she departed nor explaining her absence after her return. She would flirt with Miguel incessantly, leaning in close to speak with him, showing him her deep cleavage, intriguing him with talk both lascivious and vague.

One summer night, after they had both had too much beer and were wet from an unexpected rain shower, Geertruid had leaned in to whisper some silly thing in his ear, and he kissed her hard upon the mouth, knocking his teeth into hers as he attempted to slide a hand between her breasts. Geertruid extricated herself from his clumsy grip and made some little quip, but it was clear that Miguel had crossed a line she would not have him cross again. The next time she saw Miguel, she handed him a tiny volume as a present:

'*t Amsterdamsch Hoerdom,* a guide to the whores and bawdy houses of the city. Miguel had thanked her with good cheer but in truth had felt a humiliation greater than that of his bankruptcy, and he vowed never again to fall victim to her amorous nonsense.

And then there was the matter of Hendrick, a man some fifteen years her junior. Geertruid kept him at her feet almost all the time. He would sit sometimes apart from her at taverns while she chatted with men of business, but he always kept one eye upon her, like a half-sleeping hound. Was he her lover, her servant, or something else Miguel could not quite fathom? She would never say, eluding his questions with graceful ease so that Miguel had long since ceased to ask them.

Often when they met, Hendrick would slink off, glowering at Miguel for a moment before he took himself to wherever such a man might go. Yet he never quite acted with resentment. He called Miguel Jew Man, as though to do so were the height of wit or a sign of their private friendship. He would clap Miguel on the back, always just hard enough to seem something other than amicable. But when the three of them sat together, if Miguel grew quiet or preoccupied with his troubles, it was always Hendrick who tried to draw him out, Hendrick who would burst into a bawdy song or tell some ribald tale, often at his own expense, such as the time he nearly drowned in a trough of horse dung. If such a thing had happened to Miguel, he was sure he'd never recount the tale, not even to bring cheer to the messiah.

Miguel resented Geertruid's refusal to talk about her companionship with Hendrick, but he understood her to be a woman well able to keep a secret, and that was a quality not to be underestimated. She knew their friendship could cause Miguel problems with the Ma'amad and so rarely showed herself at taverns where Jews congregated – or, if she did have business there, she pretended not to know Miguel. Certainly he had been seen speaking to her a little intimately once or twice, but that was the very beauty of her being a woman – she was invisible to the men of the Nation. If they saw her at all, they saw her as Miguel's whore; he had even been teased once or twice for liking his Dutchwomen over-ripe.

CHAPTER 6

Miguel arrived at the Dam a quarter of an hour before noon, when the Exchange gates would open. Already the din of trade had begun to echo off the walls of the surrounding buildings. The burgomasters had limited the hours of trade from noon until two because the guilds complained that the din of commerce disturbed all manner of business across the city. Miguel thought the charges absurd. The sound of trade was a monetary aphrodisiac; it drove men to empty their purses. If the hours of trade were twice as long each day, the city would be twice as rich.

Miguel loved the excitement that spread across the plaza in the moments before the Exchange gates opened. The conversation quietened to a hum. Hundreds of men looked like racers, awaiting the signal to begin their sprint.

All along the Dam, peddlers hawked bread and pies and trinkets in the shadow of the great wonders of the plaza, the monuments of Dutch grandeur: the massive and imposing Town Hall, which stood like a civic cathedral; the Nieuwe Kerk and the Exchange, and, puny by comparison, the Weigh

House. Along the Damrak, fishmongers shouted their wares in the busy market, and whores cast their lines for amorous investors; moneylenders operating outside the law looked for the eager and desperate; fruit and vegetable sellers wheeled their pushcarts through the maze of merchants eager to spend newly got money on anything polished or juicy or bright with colour. Tradesmen joked amiably with fatpursed merchants, and women attempted to shock men into purchases with talk so bawdy that even Miguel blushed to hear it.

Among the brokers and speculators, black suits such as Miguel always wore remained the height of Dutch fashion. Here was perhaps the height of the austere influence of the Calvinist divines. The preachers of the Reformed Church ruled that gaudy fashions and bright colours only indulged vanity, and thus the men of Amsterdam dressed in modest black but spiced their dark ensembles with fine cloth, expensive lace, silk collars, and costly hats. The sea of black occasionally sparkled with an Iberian Jew in red or blue or yellow or perhaps a defiant Dutch Catholic, who dressed in what colours he liked. In other lands the locals would gawk at foreign dress, but there were so many aliens in the city that strange clothes were admired more often than ridiculed. Miguel believed the Dutch the most curious of all races – the perfect blend of Protestant faith and business ambition

As Miguel gazed out at the crowd he noticed a desperate-looking fellow moving directly towards him. He thought the man might be a petty tradesman, perhaps in the midst of a dispute with a customer, but as he stepped aside the ruffian continued to fix his gaze on Miguel.

The fellow stopped and flashed a mouth full of wretched teeth. 'You don't know me, Lienzo?'

The sound of the voice steadied him; Miguel saw that he did indeed know the man: Joachim Waagenaar. Joachim, who had once dressed like a gentleman in velvet suits and fine lace, now wore the close-fitting leather cap of a farmer, a stained doublet of rough cloth, and torn, baggy breeches. Once a man to wear perfume and trim his moustache just so, Joachim now smelled of piss and sweat like a beggar.

'Joachim,' Miguel said after a moment. 'I didn't recall you at first.'

'I suppose not.' Joachim unfurled another strained grimace. He'd always had unhealthy teeth, but several that had been broken before were now gone, and along the bottom they were all cracked and had the rough edges of gravel. 'Times haven't gone well with me.'

'I was sorry to hear of your losses,' Miguel answered, speaking so quickly that his Dutch sounded garbled even to his own ears. 'I lost greatly too,' he added hastily, in answer to unspoken charges. He had, after all, urged Joachim to put his fortune in Miguel's failing sugar futures, believing that if he found enough investors he could keep the price of sugar buoyant, but these efforts were like sandbags set against the force of a flood, and the price had tumbled all the same. Joachim had not lost nearly as much as Miguel, but his fortune had been much smaller, so he had fallen fast and hard.

'Those are fine clothes you have upon your back.' Joachim looked him up and down and ran a hand along his own face, which was rough with a beard that grew in a great diversity of lengths, as though he had taken to shaving by hacking at himself with a dull blade. 'They did not take your clothes,' he said. 'They took my clothes. They forced me to sell them.'

Who might *they* be – creditors, pawnbrokers? Miguel had been abducted and taken to taverns where he was held prisoner until he agreed to pay bills. He had suffered the humiliation of having his hat knocked into the mud by a particularly angry wine merchant. He had been threatened and insulted and angered beyond all reason. But he'd never been made to sell his clothes.

Anything was possible with an odd fellow like Joachim. The son of a fishmonger who had profited in the tulipomania thirty years before, Joachim had come of age believing that only fools laboured for their money when they might buy and sell for it instead. Even so, he seemed to know nothing of the Exchange but which taverns were closest, and he always depended on brokers to do his thinking. But for a man who was little more than a drunk with money, he was remarkably anxious about holdings, and he'd always fretted over a stiver lost here and there, suspicious of the very means by which he chose to make his money.

'The business of the Exchange is like the weather,' Miguel had told him once. 'You might see signs of rain, but then nature delivers sunshine.'

'But what has happened to my guilders?' Joachim had asked him, after losing a trifling fifty guilders in an East India deal that had not gone quite as Miguel had expected.

Miguel forced a laugh. 'Where is the wind after it blows on your face?' He almost added that any man who wonders such things should remove his money from the Exchange and return to selling. Joachim seemed to Miguel ill-suited for this new species of investment, but Miguel did not have so many clients that he could afford to send one away.

Joachim stood there, panting like a dog, letting his breath blow in Miguel's face. In the distance the gates to the Exchange opened, and the traders began to file inside, some of the more eager men shoving like unruly boys.

Although everyone had his own affairs to tend to, Miguel worried that someone might see him with this wretch. The burghers of Amsterdam had forbidden Jewish traders to broker for gentiles, and though the Ma'amad claimed to punish this crime with excommunication, Miguel believed it to be the second most violated law in the city (just after the law prohibiting brokers from trading for their own profit as well as their clients'). Nevertheless, a man in Miguel's situation had to fear being prosecuted for crimes that others could perpetrate with impunity. This conversation with Joachim would have to end quickly.

'I am sorry things have gone hard with you, but I haven't the time to speak of it now.' Miguel took a tentative step back.

Joachim nodded and stepped closer forward. 'I would like to do a little business with you to make up for what I've lost. Perhaps, as you say, everything was unintentional.'

Miguel could not think quite how to respond. *Perhaps everything was unintentional.* Did this man have the audacity to accuse Miguel of deceiving him, of having set some sort of trap, as though Miguel's losses in sugar had been some ruse to get Joachim's five hundred guilders? Not a day goes by that a broker does not give unsound advice, perhaps ruining those he aims to serve. Those who cannot live with risk have no business in trade.

'I want what you owe me,' Joachim insisted.

At once Miguel recognised Joachim's ragged voice. He could see it transposed in his mind into an awkward hand, scratchy and uneven. '*You've been sending me those notes.*'

'I want my money,' Joachim affirmed. 'I want you to help me get back my money. It's no less than what you owe me.'

With no more room in his life for debt, Miguel disliked this talk of what he owed. He'd made an error in judgement, nothing more. They had both suffered; it should end there.

'What manner of business is this when you send such notes? What am I to make of your strange communications?'

Joachim said nothing. He looked at Miguel the way a dog looks at a man who lectures it.

Miguel tried once more. 'We will talk about this when I am at leisure,' he told Joachim, looking about nervously for signs of Ma'amad spies.

'I understand that you are a busy man.' Joachim spread his hands wide. 'I, as you can see, haven't many demands on my time.'

Miguel cast a glance at the Exchange. Every minute here could mean lost money. What if, even now, the man on whom he could unload his brandy futures, at perhaps not too significant a loss, was buying those shares from someone else?

'But I have,' he said to Joachim. 'We'll talk later.' He took another exploratory step backward.

'*When!*' It came out hard, a command more than a question. The word had a power to it, as though he had shouted *stop!* Joachim's face had changed, too. He now gazed at Miguel sternly, like a magistrate issuing a decree. In the butcher stalls, several people halted in their steps and looked over. Miguel's heart began to thump a panicky beat.

Joachim moved along with him in the direction of the Dam. 'How will you contact me when you don't know how to find me?'

'Very true,' Miguel agreed, with a foolish laugh.

'How thoughtless of me. We'll speak on Monday, after the close of the Exchange, at the Singing Carp.' It was a little out-of-the-way tavern that Miguel visited when in need of a quiet spot for drink and contemplation.

'Good, good.' Joachim nodded eagerly. 'I see it will all be made right. What's done can surely be undone, so now we'll shake on it like men of business.'

But Miguel was not about to touch Joachim's flesh if he could help it, so he hurried away pretending he had not heard. After pressing into the crowd outside the Exchange, he risked a look behind him and saw no sign of Joachim, so he took a moment of rest before entering. Merchants filed past him, many shouting a greeting as they headed through the gates. Miguel straightened his hat, caught his breath, and muttered in Hebrew the prayer said upon receiving ill news.

CHAPTER 7

He should have known better than to stand still in the Exchange, for the moment Miguel stopped moving he found himself descended upon by a dozen traders of the lowest sort, each out to test the limits of his indebtedness. 'Senhor Lienzo!' A man he hardly knew stood inches away, nearly shouting. 'Let's take a moment to talk of a shipment of copper from Denmark.' Another edged the first aside. 'Good senhor, you are the only one I would tell this to, but I have reason to believe that the price of cinnamon will shift dramatically in the next few days. But will it go up or down? Come with me to learn more.' A young trader in Portuguese attire, probably not even twenty years of age, tried to pull him from the crowd. 'I want to tell you how the syrup market has expanded these past three months.'

After the unnerving encounter with Joachim, Miguel was in no mood for these scavengers. They were of all nations, the fellowship of desperation requiring no single language or place of origin, only a willingness to survive by leaping from one precipice to the next. Miguel was attempting to force his way past when he saw his brother approach, the *parnass* Solomon Parido by his side. He hated for Daniel and Parido to see him in such low company, but he could hardly run off now that he had been spotted. It is all posture, he told himself. 'Gentlemen, gentlemen,' he told his gathering of unfortunates, 'I think you mistake me for a man who might have interest in doing business with you. Good day.'

He pushed off and nearly collided with his brother, who now stood inches away.

'I've been looking for you,' said Daniel, who, since the sugar collapse, had rarely so much as glanced at Miguel during Exchange hours. Now he stood close, leaning in to avoid having to shout above the clamour of trade. 'I did not, however, expect to see you dealing with miserable men such as these.'

'What is it you gentlemen wish?' he asked, directing his attention in particular to Parido, who had thus far remained silent. The *parnass* had developed a habit of turning up far too frequently for Miguel's taste.

Parido bowed to Miguel. 'Your brother and I have been discussing your affairs.'

'The Holy One has truly blessed me, that two such great men take the time to discuss my dealings,' Miguel said.

Parido blinked. 'Your brother mentioned that you were having difficulties.' He ventured a half smile, but he looked no less sour for it.

Miguel looked at him icily, not quite sure how to respond. If that fool brother of his had been talking about coffee again, he would strangle him in the middle of the Exchange. 'I think,' he said, 'that my brother is not so well-informed of my business as he would like to believe.'

'I know you're still receiving letters from that heretic, Alferonda,' Daniel said blithely, as though unaware that he revealed information that could put Miguel under the *cherem*.

Parido shook his head. 'Your correspondence is of no interest to me, and I think your brother, in his eagerness to help you, speaks of family matters best kept private.'

'We are in agreement there,' Miguel said cautiously. What did this new generosity mean? It was true that Parido's anger seemed to have abated somewhat since Miguel had lost money in the sugar collapse. He no longer approached merchants – even while Miguel stood there speaking to them – to advise them to pursue their affairs with a more honest broker. He no longer left a room simply because Miguel entered it. He no longer refused to speak to Miguel when Daniel invited the *parnass* to dinner.

Even after Miguel's losses, however, Parido would find ways to inflict injury. He would stand with his friends and openly mock Miguel from across the Dam, pointing and smirking as though they were schoolboys. Now he wished to be friends?

Miguel did not bother to conceal his doubt, but Parido only shrugged. 'I think you'll find my actions more convincing than any suspicions. Take a walk with me, Miguel.'

There was nothing to do but agree.

Miguel's difficulties with the *parnass* had begun because he had followed Daniel's advice to take Parido's only daughter, Antonia, as his wife. At that time, nearly two years before, Miguel had been a successful trader, and it had seemed both a good match and a way of solidifying his family's standing in Amsterdam. Already married himself, Daniel could not make himself part of Parido's family, but Miguel could. He had gone too long without remarrying, the wives of the Vlooyenburg said, and he grew weary of matchmakers hounding him. Besides, Antonia came with a handsome portion and with Parido's business connections.

He had no reason to dislike Antonia, but neither did she appeal to him. She was a handsome woman, but he did not find being with her a handsome experience. Miguel had seen a picture of her before they met, and he had been most pleased by the miniature portrait, but though it was a good likeness, the painter had rendered her features far more animated than nature had done herself. Miguel would sit in Parido's front room, taking stabs at conversation with a girl who would not meet his eye, asked no questions not directly related to the food or drink set out by the servants, and could answer no questions with words other than 'Yes, senhor' or 'No, senhor'. Miguel soon became intrigued by the idea of teasing her and began asking her questions touching on theology, philosophy and the political skullduggery of the Vlooyenburg. Such enquiries produced the far more entertaining 'I could not say, senhor.'

He knew he ought not to take such pleasure in torturing his future wife, but there was little else of interest to do with her. He wondered what it would be like to be married to so dull a woman. Surely he could mould her more to his liking; he could teach her to speak her mind, to have opinions, possibly even to read. And in the end, a wife was merely someone to produce sons and keep an orderly house. An alliance with his brother's patron would be good for his own business, and if she was good for nothing more, there were whores enough in Amsterdam.

So, possessed of every intention of following through on his promise, Miguel had been discovered by Antonia in her maid's room – he with his breeches down, she with skirts lifted. The shock of walking into the room and facing Miguel's bare ass aimed in her direction had proved overwhelming, and she had let off a shriek before fainting and knocking her head against the door on her way down.

The planned marriage between the two was certainly ruined, but disgrace could have been avoided, and Miguel considered it entirely Parido's fault that the incident had turned to scandal. Miguel wrote him a long letter, begging forgiveness for having abused his hospitality and unwittingly brought embarrassment upon him:

I cannot ask you to think no more of these events or to put them from your mind (he wrote). I can only ask that you believe I never wished to see either you or your daughter harmed, and I hope the day may come that will provide me with an opportunity to demonstrate the extent of both my respect and my remorse.

Parido had sent back only a few harsh lines:

Make no effort to contact me again. I care nothing for what you imagine as respect or how you scheme to frame your meagre remorse. You and I must be now opposed in all things.

The letter did not mark the end of the conflict, much to the delight of the gossiping wives of the Vlooyenburg. The maid, it was soon discovered, was with child, and Parido publicly insisted that Miguel provide for the bastard once born. With popular sentiment on Parido's side, for he had kept his breeches on through the whole affair, Miguel endured a week in which old women hooted at him and spat in his direction and children tossed rotten eggs at his head. But Miguel would not accept these accusations. Experience had taught him a thing or two about reproductive rhythms, and he knew the child could not be his. He refused to pay.

With a mind set to vengeance rather than justice, Parido insisted that Miguel be brought before the Ma'amad, to which Parido had not yet been elected. The council was well used to these paternity disputes, and its investigators revealed the father to be Parido himself, so finding himself publicly humiliated, he retired to private life for a month, waiting for some new scandal to entertain the neighbourhood. During that month, believing that Antonia could never find a husband in a city that knew she had seen Miguel Lienzo with no breeches, he sent his daughter to marry his sister's son, a merchant of moderate standing in Salonika.

The world knew the story – that Miguel was to have married Antonia Parido, that the engagement had fallen into ruin, and that Parido had made accusations that had come back to haunt him. There was something that the world did not know.

Miguel had been unwilling to sit idly by while the Ma'amad decided the case, for Parido was a powerful man, destined for the council, and Miguel was but an upstart trader. So he had gone to see the little doxy and conducted his own inquiry. After Miguel had prodded her for some time, she finally admitted that she could not name the child's father. She could not name him because there was no child; she only claimed that one grew in her belly because she wanted something for her trouble, being cast out on the street as she was.

Miguel might have tried to convince her to tell the truth, and in doing so perhaps restored himself somewhat in Parido's eyes, but Parido might also have spat upon that gesture. Instead, Miguel explained to the girl that if she convinced the Ma'amad investigators that the child was Parido's, she would profit most handsomely for her trouble.

Parido, in the end, gave the girl a hundred guilders and sent her on her way. Miguel could once more walk the streets of the Vlooyenburg without fear of assault from grandmothers and children. However, a new disquiet had taken the place of the old. If Parido were ever to learn of Miguel's treachery, he would show no mercy.

The great open-air Exchange spread out before them, in structure no different from every other bourse in every trading centre in Europe. Amsterdam's Exchange was an enormous rectangle, three massive red-brick stories in height, with an overhang along the inner perimeter. The centre remained exposed to the elements, such as the misting rain that now fell, so light as to be indistinguishable from fog. Along the interior and beneath the overhang supported by thick and magnificent columns, hundreds of men gathered in dozens of clusters to shout at one another in Dutch or Portuguese or Latin or a dozen other tongues of Europe and beyond, to buy and sell, to trade rumours, and to attempt to predict the future. Each section of the Exchange had, by tradition, its own designated meeting place. Along the walls, men traded in jewels, property, woollens, whale oil, tobacco. A merchant could converse with dealers in goods of the East Indies, the West Indies, the Baltic or the Levant. In the less prestigious roofless centre gathered the wine merchants, paint and drug sellers, traders with England, and, towards the far south end, dealers in brandy and the sugar trade.

Miguel regularly saw Spaniards and Germans and Frenchmen. Less frequently, he might encounter Turks and even East Indians. It was something of a mystery why this city should have emerged in the last fifty years as the centre of the world's trade, attracting merchants from every land of importance. It should hardly have been a city at all; the locals liked to say that God created the world, but the Dutch made Amsterdam. Carved out of swamp, plagued with a port only the most skilful pilot could navigate (and then only with luck on his side), lacking any native wealth except for cheese and butter, Amsterdam rose to its place of greatness because of the sheer determination of its citizens.

Parido walked silently for only a few moments, but Miguel could not shake the feeling that the

123

parnass derived some pleasure from withholding his business.

'I know your debts weigh heavily on you,' Parido began at last, 'and I know you've been trading in brandy futures. You've gambled that the prices will rise. By closing day two days hence, however, they will surely remain as low as they are now. If I calculate correctly, you stand to lose close to fifteen hundred guilders.'

This was about brandy, not coffee, thank the most high. But what did Parido know about it – or care, for that matter? 'It is closer to a thousand,' he said, hoping to keep his tone even. 'I see you're well-informed of my business.'

'The Exchange is little able to hide secrets from the man who wishes to learn them.'

Miguel let out a barking laugh. 'And why should you wish to know my secrets, senhor?'

'As I said, I want to make things more comfortable between us, and if you are to trust me, to believe that I will not use my influence as a *parnass* against you, you must see me act in your benefit. Now, as to the problem at hand, I may know a buyer, a Frenchman, who will relieve you of your futures.'

The irritation dropped away. Here was just the sort of lucky turn for which Miguel had hardly dared to hope. Based on rumours of an impending shortage, received from a very reliable source, he had bought the brandy futures at a 70 per cent margin, paying only 30 per cent of the value of the

124

total quantity up front, and then either losing or gaining as though he had invested the entire sum. Come reckoning day, if brandy increased in value, he would profit as though he had gambled on a much larger amount, but if brandy lost value, as it appeared the shares would, he would owe far more than he had already invested.

An eager buyer was just what he needed, it was like a gift from the heavens. To be rid of this new debt would surely be a sign that the tide of his misfortune had turned. Could he really believe that his enemy had, out of the goodness of his heart, decided to present the solution to Miguel's most pressing problem? Where could he produce a buyer for these futures, futures that the world knew would only bring debt to their owner?

'I cannot imagine that any man, French or otherwise, would be mad enough to buy my brandy holdings when the market has turned against them. The value of brandy won't much change in the few days between now and the monthly reckoning.' Unless, Miguel thought, a trading combination plotted to manipulate the price. More than once Miguel had lost when he thought he saw a new trend in prices and only later learned that he had become the victim of a combination's plot.

'The price may change and it may not.' Parido shrugged. 'It should be enough that he is willing to buy something of which you'd like to be rid.'

Before he could respond to the proposal, Miguel heard his name called out and saw it was a boy with bright orange hair and blotchy skin. The unsightly fellow waved a letter and shouted the name *Lienzo* again, in a voice more loud than shrill. Miguel called him over and offered him a coin for the letter. He recognised the hand at once as Geertruid's. He took a step backward before tearing it open.

Senhor

I hope all fares well with you on the Exchange, but any profits you might make for yourself are but a mere shadow of the wealth that the fruit of the coffee tree can offer you. While you attend to your daily business, let the spirit of this marvellous berry animate your mind and increase your profits. I write these words only in the capacity of one who is your friend.

Geertruid Damhuis

Parido smiled thinly. 'It looked to me like a woman's hand. I hope you aren't allowing yourself to be distracted by intrigues during hours meant for business. You're an amorous fellow, but these gates open for only two hours each day.'

Miguel returned the false smile. 'There's no intrigue here. It is nothing of consequence.'

Parido scratched at his nose. 'Then let's do something that *is* of consequence. We'll find this merchant I know and see if we can't set things right.'

★　　★　　★

They forced their way to the south end of the Exchange, where brandy changed hands. Some traders came to fill orders or to sell what their ships brought into port, but increasingly men bought calls and puts and futures, trading in goods they never sought to own and would never see. It was the new way of doing things, turning the Exchange into a great gaming pit where outcome was determined not by chance but by the needs of the markets around the world.

In his earlier days, Miguel had believed he possessed an uncanny ability to predict those needs. He had enjoyed connections among the most influential West Indian merchants and had been able to acquire sugar at excellent prices and then sell at superior ones. The red-brick warehouses of the Brouwersgracht had been bursting with his acquisitions, and all of the Exchange knew Miguel as the man to see for sugar. But then fortune had taken Miguel by surprise, and now all that sugar was washed away.

Towards the corner where men bought and sold brandy, Parido introduced Miguel to a stunted little Frenchman – no taller than a child – with a sad fleshy face and a nose like a walnut. He wore a high ruffled collar, such as had been popular fifty years earlier, and his reddish coat had turned almost brown with Amsterdam mud.

'Never judge worthiness by the clothes,' Parido whispered, assuming his role of the great sage of the Exchange. 'Fools may be tricked by baubles and bright colours, but who does not know that a chicken makes better eating than a robin?'

This Frenchman, whom Miguel would have taken for a hard-pressed fellow of the middling ranks, croaked out in his clumsy accent an interest in doing business. He thrust forth his hands in Miguel's direction. 'You are the man with the brandy futures to sell,' he said in halting Dutch. 'I'd like to talk about these holdings, but do not think to be grasping with me, monsieur, or you will find you have no sale at all.'

'I always conduct business like a man of honour,' Miguel assured him. His heart knocked eagerly in his chest as he explained to the Frenchman that he was in possession of futures for 170 hogsheads of brandy. He kept his voice free of inflection, not wanting to urge his holdings on the merchant. The situation called for a lighter touch.

'That's what you have!' The Frenchman shouted, as though Miguel had just tipped his hand. 'Ha! Not so much as I thought, nor nearly so good neither. But it is worth a little something to me. Six hundred guilders is more than you can expect, but I shall pay it.'

'That is an absurd offer,' Miguel replied, and indeed it was, though not for the reasons he wished to imply. The Frenchman must be mad to enter into a deal almost guaranteed to lose money. Either that or he knew a great secret from which Miguel might profit. Still, Miguel had invested just over five hundred guilders, so the offer could not be dismissed idly; it would mean a slight profit rather than a significant loss.

'I'll not part with them for less than six fifty,' he said.

'Then you'll not part with them at all. I have no time for your Dutch haggling back and forth, this way and that way. We'll make this trade or I'll find another man and offer him the same, and he will be more grateful than you.'

Miguel smiled by way of excusing himself and led Parido a few feet away.

'Needless to say, you will take his offer,' Parido announced.

Here was the worm dangling so deliciously, and Miguel was the fish. He might well get the worm, but did he want a hook through his cheek for the trouble?

'I'm sceptical,' Miguel said, rolling his thumb and index finger together, as though feeling the air for something suspicious. 'Why should he want these futures so badly? It might be wiser to hold them myself so I can profit from whatever it is he knows.'

'Profits on the Exchange are the treasures of goblins, changing from coal to diamond and back to coal once more. You must take your profits where you can find them.'

'I prefer a bolder approach,' Miguel said drily.

'There are times for boldness and times for prudence. Think a moment. What do we know of this Frenchman? He may want those futures for a scheme of his own that can't possibly benefit you. He may only wish to thwart an enemy by hoarding what another fellow seeks. He may be mad. He may know the price will triple in value. You cannot tell. You can only know that if you sell now you will have saved yourself a debt and even earned a little profit. That is how a fortune is made – in small pieces and with great caution.'

Miguel turned away. Few men were as well-connected on the Exchange as Parido, and if he had decided that he wished to end his animosities with Miguel, this transaction could be the first step in a friendship that would help extricate him from debt. Would Parido attempt to worsen Miguel's affairs in full view of the world? Still, Parido had been sour for nearly two years, and Miguel sensed something sinister in this new altruism.

His instincts told him to reject the offer, to hang on to these futures and see what the market offered him, but dare he follow his instincts? The thrill of being rid of the cursed futures was tempting. He could end this month with a profit. Next month he could trade in whale oil – another guaranteed gain – and begin his coffee venture. He might at this moment be staring at a turning point in his fortune.

Faced with a grave decision, one on which his future might well depend, he asked himself what had become the only question that came to mind in these circumstances: What route would Charming Pieter take? Would he defy Parido and follow his instincts, or would he surrender his will to the man who had once been his enemy but now protested friendship? Pieter, Miguel knew, never foreclosed an opportunity, and it was better to make a man who intended trickery believe he had succeeded than to expose him to his face. Pieter would follow Parido's advice.

'I'll make the trade,' Miguel said at last.

'That is the only thing to do.'

Perhaps it was. Miguel should have been euphoric. Perhaps he would be in a few hours, when the inexpressible relief of being rid of those poisonous shares finally seemed real. He said a prayer of thanks, but even as he recognised his luck he could not quite shake the bitter taste from his mouth. He had liberated himself from these difficulties only with the help of a man who, two weeks before, would have gladly sewn him in a sack and tossed him into the Amstel.

It might be as Parido said – he wished only to mend their rift – so Miguel turned to the *parnass* and bowed in thanks, but his face was dark. Parido could not mistake its meaning. If this turned out to be a trick, Miguel would have his revenge.

From

The Factual and Revealing Memoirs of Alonzo Alferonda

It will be hard to explain to my Christian readers precisely what the cherem excommunication can mean to a Portuguese Jew. To those of us who had lived under the thumb of the Inquisition, or in lands such as England where our religion was outlawed, or in places such as the cities of the Turks where it was barely tolerated, to dwell in a place such as Amsterdam seemed a small taste of the World to Come. We were free to congregate and observe our holidays and our rituals, to study our texts in the light of day. For us who belonged to a small nation, cursed with having no land to call our own, the simple freedom to live as we chose was a kind of bliss that I never, not for a single day I lived with my brothers in Amsterdam, forgot to give my thanks to God.

Of course there were those cast forth from the community who cared not at all. Some were happy to leave what they saw as an overly scrupulous and demanding way of life. They would look at our Christian neighbours, who ate or drank what they liked, for whom the Sabbath, even their Sabbath, was but another day, and they would see those freedoms as a release. Yet most of us knew who we were. We were Jews, and the power of the Ma'amad to take away a man's identity, his sense of self and belonging, was truly terrifying.

Solomon Parido did all he could to make me an outcast, but in truth I might have gone far away and changed my name. No one would have known I was Alonzo Alferonda of Amsterdam. I knew deception the way other men knew their names.

And such was my plan. I would do it, but not quite yet. I had plans for Parido, and I would not leave until I had seen them through.

CHAPTER 8

Hannah believed she knew what coffee was, but she had no guess as to why Daniel would want to keep Miguel from trading in it, or why Miguel would think anyone would want to buy the stuff. Miguel and Daniel had talked suspiciously about coffee, and there, in Miguel's cellar, she found a sack of curiously pungent berries the colour of dead leaves. She put one in her mouth. It was hard and bitter, but she chewed it anyway despite the vague ache in her teeth. Why, she wondered, would anyone care about so foul a substance?

She supposed she probably ought not to be rummaging around in Miguel's things, but it wasn't as though she would let her husband know what she found. In any case, Miguel never told her anything about his life, and how else would she learn if she didn't pursue these things herself? Only through her own guile had she learned about his debts and his troubles with Parido and the strange threatening notes he'd been receiving. Annetje, whom Hannah sometimes sent to follow Miguel at a distance, told her he maintained a curious friendship with a pretty Dutch widow. One time Annetje had even led Hannah to peer through the window of a tavern and she'd seen the woman for herself, so proud and convinced of her own importance. What had this woman ever done that was so significant, other than marry a man with money and then outlive him? Another time, when the two of them had clearly been drinking, he brought her home, believing that she and Daniel were off eating with one of his business associates. The widow had stared at her until Hannah blushed, and the two of them hurried outside, erupting in childish laughter. Hannah thought that if Miguel wanted to be friends with a woman, surely he ought to choose one far less silly, one who lived in the same house.

She opened the bag of coffee again and took out another handful of the berries, letting them run through her fingers. Maybe she should eat more of them, develop a taste for their bitterness. When Miguel someday suggested that she eat coffee, she could laugh and say, 'Oh, coffee, how delightful!' and toss a handful in her mouth as though she had been eating bitter fruit all her life – which, after all, she had. She carefully picked out another berry and crushed it with her back teeth. It would take some time before she could find it delightful.

Still, there was something pleasant about it. By the time she'd eaten her third berry, she'd come to like the way the bits of coffee shards shattered in her mouth. The flavour seemed to her less bitter, even slightly satisfying.

Sneaking through Miguel's things and eating his secret berries left her feeling guilty, which was probably why Annetje caught her by surprise when she went back upstairs. The girl slyly raised her narrow eyebrows.

'It's almost time to go, senhora,' she said.

Hannah had been hoping she'd forgotten. Why should the girl even care if they went or not? Well, Hannah knew why: it made Annetje feel powerful. It gave her something to hold over Hannah, to get from her another few guilders when she wanted them, to get Hannah to look the other way when she found Annetje frittering away her time with some Dutch fellow instead of tending to her chores.

There was a place in their own neighbourhood but Hannah had never dared to visit it, not with the thick crowds that gathered on the Breestraat and wide walkway on their side of the Verversgracht. When they went, they went instead down near the docks, just off the Warmoesstraat, trekking circuitously through crooked streets and over steep bridges. Only when they were far from the Vlooyenburg, a good distance past the Dam, walking along the crumbling narrow alleyways of the oldest part of the city, did Hannah pause to remove her veil and scarf, terrified as she did so of the Ma'amad spies who were known to lurk everywhere.

Covering herself had been one of the most difficult adjustments to life in Amsterdam. In Lisbon her face and her hair had been no more private than her outer coat, but when they'd moved to this city, Daniel had told her no man but he could ever see her hair again, and she must cover her face when in public. She later learned that nothing in Jewish law demanded that women hide their faces. The custom had come from the Jews of North Africa, and it had been adopted here.

Hannah surreptitiously ate a few of the coffee beans on the way, slipping them into her mouth as Annetje forged ahead. By the time she'd eaten more than a dozen, she'd come to find them pleasant, almost reassuring, and she regretted that with each berry she ate there was one less in her little stash.

When they were near, Annetje helped her place a simple white cap upon her head, and in an instant she could hardly be distinguished from any Dutchwoman. With her face and hair exposed, Hannah now walked to the open street, emerging on the Oudezijds Voorburgwal, the canal named for the old city wall. And there it stood. Several houses had been combined to make a space that was handsome, if paltry by Lisbon standards, and though the street was not far from some of the most dangerous parts of Amsterdam, here all seemed quiet and contained. Great oaks lined the canal on either side, and men and women walked along in their Sunday finery. A small cluster of gentlemen had gathered in their bright suits of blues and reds and yellows, unencumbered as they were by the Reformed church's dislike of gaudy colours. Their wives wore jewelled gowns with shimmering silk bodices and sparkling caps; they talked loudly, laughed, and pressed hands to shoulders.

Still following Annetje, Hannah climbed to the fourth floor, a single room, hollowed out and turned into a holy place. The large windows let in the soft cloud-filtered light, but the church was made brighter by the countless smokeless candles flickering on the chandeliers. She glanced at the paintings: Christ upon the cross, Saint Veronica with the burial shroud, Saint John in the wilderness. Once they'd given her some comfort, made her feel familiar, as if she recognised herself, but increasingly they had begun to make her feel uneasy, as though these saints were Annetje's conspirators, winking and smirking as the two women passed.

The burgomasters had not ruled Catholic worship illegal in Amsterdam, but it was condoned only if conducted privately, and churches must be unrecognisable as such from the outside. Inside they could be as opulent as the Catholics liked, and the wealthy merchants of the Catholic community had been generous with their donations. The church served as a sanctuary as well; though Catholic worship enjoyed legal protection, papists were not well loved by the populace, the memory of Spanish oppression running deep as it did. Hannah

138

had once seen Father Hans of this church hounded through the streets by a pack of dung-throwing children.

Hannah found a seat on the first level, for the church was not crowded today, and began to relax a little. She liked the familiar sounds of the organ, and she allowed herself the luxury of letting her mind wander. She thought about her child – a daughter, she decided. She'd had a dream the night before that the child was a beautiful girl. Most dreams were only silly illusions, but this one had the firm substance of prophecy. What a blessing a girl child would be. She wrapped herself in the thought until she could almost feel the baby in her arms, but when the priest began to intone his prayers, her fantasy shattered.

Perhaps it had been wrong to seek comfort in the old religion, but Annetje had sweetly convinced her to go once – and after that she had no more choice in the matter. Besides, all those men who had kept the truth from her or given her sad half versions of it had no right to pull her this way and that. How could she decide for herself if she wanted to be Jew or no? She could not choose her religion any more than she could choose her own face or disposition. As she sat there, only half listening to the prayers echoing through the chamber, Hannah felt her irritation with Daniel gathering force. Who was he to tell her that she had to worship in a new way and then not tell her anything about the new way? Ought she not to complain of this injustice? Other

139

women spoke their minds to their husbands – she could hardly step out on the streets without seeing a Dutch wife scolding her man for drunkenness or sloth. It was wrong, she determined fiercely. She surprised herself by slapping a hand against her thigh.

After the service, the maid chatted amiably as they walked down the stairs, but Hannah was in no mood for idle talk. She wanted to get out, to go home, to go somewhere. She ought to enjoy Annetje's easy mood, she told herself. The girl made herself most companionable when she had her own way, and she was so delighted with having taken Hannah to church that she would now be at her most agreeable. But why, Hannah asked herself, as she slipped a coffee berry into her mouth, should she require the agreeableness of her maid?

This was one injustice she ought not to tolerate. She could hardly rebel against her husband, but her maid was another matter. These threats to report her worship to Daniel were nonsense. Why would Daniel believe the girl? He thought no more of her than of a dog.

After prayers, they emerged from the church and walked along the Oudezijds Voorburgwal with the other worshippers. Hannah allowed herself to enjoy the anonymity of the crowd for a few sweet moments before deciding that the time for playing at freedom had ended.

'My veil and scarf, please,' she said to the maid. She spoke faster than she had intended, so the words sounded like an order. She took several more steps before she realised that Annetje had stopped and stood behind her, grinning.

'Come quickly,' Hannah said. 'Someone might see me.'

'A woman shouldn't have to hide herself from the world,' Annetje told her, taking a step forward. 'Not when she is as pretty as you. Come, we'll take a stroll.'

'I don't want to take a stroll.' Sharp words began to well up inside her, and she was in no mood to restrain them. The girl loved to tease, to take liberties, to push the limits of her power, but that was because Hannah always let her win. What would happen if Hannah refused to let her order everything as she liked? 'Give them to me,' she demanded.

'Don't be a prude. I think we should show the world your great beauties.'

'My beauties,' Hannah said, 'are none of the world's business. Give me my things.'

Annetje took a step back. She reddened, and for a moment Hannah feared she would grow angry. Instead, she burst into a shrill laugh. 'Come and get them, then.' And she lifted her skirts just a bit and ran out of Leidekkerssteeg, the way they had come.

Hannah remained motionless, too stunned to move. Out of the alleyway, the girl turned right and disappeared. And here was Hannah, across town from the Vlooyenburg, alone and unescorted, with no covering for her head and face. What could she say to Daniel: that she had been attacked? That some ruffian had stolen her veil and scarf and sent her on her way?

Maybe the girl only made sport. She would be waiting just outside the alleyway on the Oudezijds Voorburgwal, that impish grin on her face. Should she run and give Annetje the satisfaction of showing terror, or should she stroll slowly and preserve the illusion of dignity?

She walked, but she walked quickly. Outside the alley, crowds of handsome men and women strolled along, a group of children loudly played a game with a ball, and some rag-tag jugglers hoped for spare stivers along the canal side. But no Annetje.

Then she heard the maid's voice, her laughter: across the canal and moving away from her, toward the Zeedijk. She laughed and waved the scarf in the air as though it were a flag of victory; then she began to run again.

Hannah lifted her skirts and ran after her. She hardly ever had cause to exert herself in this way, and her lungs began to ache after only a few steps up the steep canal bridge. Men paused to stare at her, children to call her names she did not understand.

Annetje slowed her pace to let Hannah gain ground and then began to run south on the Zeedijk. What did she mean by running toward the Nieumarkt? In that part of the city they would be attacked for certain. But an attack could be Hannah's salvation. She envisioned herself returning home bloodied and bruised, to be cared for rather than condemned. So she followed the maid, who ran and ran and ran. And then stopped. Hannah stopped too, and turned around to observe Annetje coming toward her, and then she turned to face the Weigh House. At the south end of the Nieumarkt, it marked the divide between the clean and the unclean, the foul and the fair. It was no place for the wife of a Jewish merchant.

Seeing that her mistress had stopped running, Annetje laughed loudly and ran back the way she had come. Hannah thought the clouds had begun to empty themselves of a hot rain but then realised they were tears, moistening her face, and cursed herself for being so weak. It took a moment for her to recognise that these weren't tears of fear or sadness but of rage. Run, she thought, as she watched the little bitch scurry off. You had better run, because if I catch you, I'll strangle you.

For an instant she forgot where she was, so clear was the image in her mind of wrapping her hands around Annetje's slender neck. Then she snapped out of her reverie and realised that a face had caught her eye. Over by the Weigh House was a woman in a red and black dress, cut low to expose her ample bosom. A pert little red cap sat aside her head, showing off to the world the generous pile of nut-brown hair. She stood conversing with a pair of men; they looked most serious, but not the woman. No, the woman hardly knew seriousness.

Hannah looked too long and too hard, and somehow the woman felt her gaze and returned it. And in an instant, Hannah knew. It was Miguel's friend, the widow.

The woman glanced over, and her pretty gaze locked with Hannah's. Her perfect sparkling eyes set upon Hannah's own timid gaze, and recognition washed over the widow's face.

And the widow recognised more than her face; she knew with an understanding beyond words that Hannah was on a secret errand – and Hannah, though she could not say how, understood that the widow was on a secret errand of her own.

The widow smiled at Hannah and then raised a finger to her red lips in a gesture of silence, absolute and unambiguous. Hannah would see it again in her dreams. She would see it whenever she closed her eyes. It was with her when she wandered, dazed as a soldier limping off the battlefield, back towards the secret church, where Annetje returned her clothes and tried to make idle chat as though they had only been teasing each other like little girls.

Hannah had no mind to make chatter, to forgive Annetje – or not to forgive her. She could only think of that finger to those lips. It would be some days before Hannah was to learn whether this gesture had been a command or a promise.

CHAPTER 9

On Monday the Exchange opened once more, and Miguel approached the Dam with an excitement fuelled partly by an eagerness to see how his affairs closed and partly by the three bowls of coffee he'd taken that morning. He deserved a reward for having freed himself of the brandy futures, and he'd been unable to resist any longer the seductive odour that had begun to permeate his chamber. That morning he'd slipped off to the kitchen for a mortar and pestle. Back in the cellar, he'd removed the bag, which seemed not so full as he recollected. No matter, he told himself, and ground the coffee into a coarse grain and mixed it with some sweet wine, stirring constantly, hoping to see the grains dissolve. He then recalled that this was not sugar or salt, so he let the grounds sink to the bottom and drank deep.

It was not as good as what he had taken with Geertruid, or even what he'd tasted at the Turkish tavern, but he nevertheless liked the way the bitterness and the sweetness played off each other. He took a sip and savoured how the coffee washed into his mouth like a kiss. He sniffed at the bowl and looked at it in the light of the oil lamp. And before he finished, he knew he would make another helping before he left his cellar.

As he poured the water, he nearly laughed aloud. He had made himself one bowl, only one bowl, and he had done it badly – this much he knew because he had tasted better – and he still could not resist the urge to drink another. Geertruid had been right. She had latched on to something that would bring them wealth, if only they could find a way to act quickly and decisively. But how? How, how, how? Miguel grew so agitated he kicked one of his shoes across the cellar and watched it fall to the floor with a satisfying thud.

'Coffee,' he muttered to himself. But drinking it would have to be enough for this moment. He still had too much to do.

Miguel stood before the Town Hall, that great palace of white stone built by merchant wealth. Not the smallest chunk of marble could be found in all the United Provinces, yet the interior was lined with marble, countless tons of the stuff – marble and gold and silver everywhere, the finest paintings upon the walls, the finest rugs upon the floor, exquisite woodwork and tiling. Miguel had once taken pleasure in strolling about the Town Hall, with its bank and courts and prisons, exploring the public spaces, dreaming of the opulence hidden in the private chambers of the burghers. Since he had learned first-hand what secrets lie in the private chambers of the Bankruptcy Office, the Town Hall had lost its charms.

Miguel looked up and saw a shadow directly in his path. A few quick blinks of the eyes and the figure came into focus: short, rounded, with long hair and a neat beard. He was dressed in a suit of bright blue, the colour of the sky, and he had an enormous wide-brimmed hat to match, pulled to just above his heavy-lidded eyes: Alonzo Alferonda.

'Lienzo!' he shouted, as though they met only by happenstance. Wrapping one arm around Miguel's shoulder, he continued to walk, dragging Miguel with him.

'By Christ, are you mad to approach me in this place? Anyone might see us together.'

'No, I am not mad, Miguel, I am your most ardent well-wisher. There was no time to risk with notes and errand boys. The business with Parido and whale oil: it is to happen today.'

'Today?' Now it was Miguel who led. He pulled Alferonda down the narrow path behind the Nieuwe Kerk. 'Today?' he said again, when they stopped in the damp darkness of the alley. A rat stared at them defiantly. 'What do you mean today? Why do you say today?'

Alferonda leaned forward and sniffed. 'Have you been drinking coffee?'

'Never mind what I've been drinking.'

Alferonda sniffed again. 'You've been mixing it with wine, haven't you? You waste your berries that way. Mix it with sweet water.'

'What do you care if I mix it with the blood of Christ? Tell me about whale oil.'

The usurer let out a little laugh. 'It's certainly put the devil into you, hasn't it? Don't give me that look. I'll tell you what I know. My contact in the East India Company, a ruddy little fellow who owes me forty guilders – he sent me a note this morning.'

'I don't need every detail of your discovery. Just speak.'

'The thing is, the whale oil trade will happen today.'

Miguel felt a pain build inside his skull and burst like a musket's report. 'Today? I haven't yet bought my whale oil futures. I was waiting for after reckoning day.' He spat on the ground. 'The rottenness of it. All planned as it was, and now for nothing – for want of a single day. I would have bought those futures tomorrow morning.'

'Forget futures for a moment.' Alferonda shook his head. 'You've been trading so long in airy pieces of paper that you neglect simple commerce. Go and buy whale oil – not futures but the thing itself. You may recall that the rest of the world still transacts their business in that quaint manner. Then, before the close of the Exchange today, you may turn around and sell what you've bought at a handsome profit. It's all very simple.'

Miguel let out a laugh and grabbed Alferonda's shoulders. 'You are right. It *is* simple, I suppose. Thank you for the warning.'

'Oh, it's nothing. I'm always happy to lend a hand to my friends.'

'I know you are,' Miguel said, shaking his hand, Dutch style. 'You're a good man, Alonzo. The Ma'amad knew nothing when it treated you so rottenly.' Miguel now wished for nothing so much as to break free and get to work on the Exchange. Geertruid was right: coffee is the drink of commerce, for the coffee he'd swallowed that morning, now combined with greed, proved too powerful a pull to be ignored.

'Before you scurry off,' Alferonda said, 'I wish to ask you something. I heard that Parido helped you broker brandy futures that had been dangling around your neck like a noose.'

'Yes, that's so. What of it?'

'What of it? What of it, you ask? Let me tell you, Miguel, that Solomon Parido does not forget a grudge. If he has helped you, it is because he has some other scheme in mind, and you would be wise to be on your guard.'

'Do you imagine that such thoughts never occurred to me? Parido is from Salonika and I am from Portugal. He grew up a Jew; I grew up pretending to be a Catholic. In a war of deception, he can never hope to defeat me.'

'He defeated me,' Alferonda said bitterly. 'He may not be as sharp as we Secret Jews, but he has the power of the Ma'amad and that counts for a great deal. Before you dismiss him so lightly, you had better think of the bitterness of never being able to enter a synagogue on Yom Kippur, of never again attending a seder for Passover, of never again greeting the Sabbath bride. And what of your business dealings? Would you see them crushed, your colleagues fearing to trade with you? If you plan to trade in coffee, my friend, you had better keep an eye on Parido and make sure he doesn't sour your scheme.'

'Of course you're right,' Miguel said impatiently.

'Believe no pretended gestures of friendship,' Alferonda urged him.

'I understand.'

'Good. Then I wish you luck with your venture today.'

Miguel needed no luck. He had knowledge no one else possessed. And he had coffee.

As he passed through the great arch of the Exchange, he closed his eyes and muttered some half-recalled prayer in an effort to sustain his trading efforts that day. The Holy One, blessed be He, had not yet abandoned him. Miguel was sure of it. He was almost sure of it.

The business with Alferonda had only taken a few minutes, but already the tone of the Exchange had calmed since the riotous opening of the gates. On reckoning days, traders roamed the bourse, checking how their prices stood in order to hedge their accounts against unexpected changes. Within the first quarter-hour, most had already learned what they needed to know.

Miguel hurried to the north-west corner of the Exchange and found a Dutch acquaintance in the Muscovy trade from whom to purchase whale oil. The current price was thirty-seven and a half guilders per quarter ton, and Miguel bought fifty quarters at just under nineteen hundred guilders – an amount he could ill afford to lose, particularly since it was all debt.

Miguel then took a turn around the Exchange, always keeping an eye on the clock and the far end of the plaza. He did a little business, buying some cheap timber that a fellow needed to unload to raise capital, and then chatted with a few friends until he noticed five black-clad Dutchmen approaching the whale oil corner. They were young, round-faced, and clean-shaven and had the confident expression of men who traded in large sums that were not their own. They were East India Company agents, and they wore their affiliation like a uniform. Men halted their conversations to watch them.

All five began at once. They cried out for whale oil, they slapped hands in agreement, and they moved on to the next deal. In almost an instant, Miguel heard someone calling out to buy at 39 a quarter. The cries began in Dutch, Latin, and Portuguese: 'Buying one hundred quarters at forty and a half.' Another voice returned, 'Selling at forty.'

Miguel's heart pounded in the thrill of trade. It was just as Geertruid had said – the coffee was like a spirit that had taken hold of his body. He heard each cry with clarity; he calculated each new price with instant precision. Nothing escaped his notice.

With his receipt clutched in one hand, he read the mood of the crowd more clearly than he had ever done before. He had seen dozens of these frenzies, but never before had he felt he could see its currents in the river of exchange. Each price sent the current in a new direction, and a man who paid close attention, whose wits were sharpened with this marvellous drink, could see everything unfold. Miguel now understood why he had failed before. He had always thought of the future, but he now understood that the future counted for nothing. Only this moment, this instant. The price would peak today in the excitement, tomorrow the price would plummet. Now was all that mattered.

Forty-two guilders per quarter ton. Forty-four guilders. It showed no sign of slowing. Forty-seven.

Always before he had wondered how to know when to make his move. It took skill and luck and clairvoyance to know when prices had peaked. It was better to sell just before the peak than just after, for prices fell much more quickly than they rose, and being off by an instant could mean the difference between profit and loss. Today, he would know the right instant.

Miguel stuck close, watching the faces of the merchants, looking for signs of panic. Then he noticed the five East India agents just beginning to turn away from the chaos they had created. Without their presence, purchasing would now slow down considerably, and the price would soon fall. The cry went out for fifty quarter tons at fifty-three guilders each. It was time to strike.

Now! the coffee screamed. *Do it!*

'Fifty quarters,' Miguel called out loudly, 'for fifty-three and a half guilders.'

A fat little broker named Ricardo, a Jew of the Vlooyenburg, slapped Miguel's hand to acknowledge the trade. And it was done.

His heart pounded. His breathing came in quick rasps as the prices fell around him: fifty guilders, then forty-eight, forty-five. He had sold at precisely the right moment. Seconds later would have cost him hundreds. The doubt that had been plaguing him, the sluggishness, the murky thinking, were all gone now. He had used coffee to banish them the way a great rabbi uses the Torah to banish demons.

Miguel felt as though he had just run all the way from Rotterdam. Everything had happened so quickly, it had all whirled around him in a murky coffee haze, but now it was done. The space of a few frantic moments had yielded a pure profit of eight hundred guilders.

He could barely keep himself from laughing out loud. It was like waking from a nightmare when he would tell himself that the terrors of the dream world were not his; he need not worry any longer. This debt that tormented him might as well disappear in the wind; that was how little it now mattered.

He hadn't planned it, but Miguel grabbed a young broker, a fellow fresh to Amsterdam from Portugal. He took this neophyte by the shoulders. 'Miguel Lienzo has returned!' he shouted. 'Do you understand me? Hide your money in the cellar, fellow. It's not safe on the Exchange – not with Miguel Lienzo here to win it from you!'

By the clock on the tower, he could see that there was scant time left before the Exchange closed for the day. Why flitter about doing little things? It was time to celebrate. The most wretched time of his life had just come to an end. The indebted, struggling Lienzo was banished, and a new era of prosperity was upon him. He let loose a fresh burst of laughter, caring nothing for how the young broker hurried away as though Miguel might hurt him, caring nothing for the cluster of Dutchmen who now stared as though Miguel were a lunatic. They mattered not at all, but lest he forget the author of all good fortune, he called out his thanks to the Holy One, blessed be He, for sustaining him and allowing him to reach this season.

And then, as though in answer, the idea descended upon him all at once.

It came with unexpected force, and even at the time it seemed as though something had fallen from the heavens, for he did not pull it from himself. It came upon him from outside. It was a gift.

Miguel forgot about whale oil profits. He forgot about his debts and Parido. In a glorious instant, he knew, with perfect clarity, how he would make his fortune from coffee.

The idea paralysed him. He understood that if he could truly midwife this idea into the world he would have wealth on an order of which he had only dreamed. Not comfort money, not prosperity money: opulence money. He would be able to marry whoever he wished and at last fill the empty holes in his life; he would be able to bring forth Hebrew children and situate them as he liked; they would not be merchants toiling for their bread as he had been made to do. The descendants of Miguel Lienzo would be gentlemen, rentiers, anything they might choose, and with the leisure to devote their lives to the study of Torah – or, if they were daughters, to marry great scholars. His sons would be dedicated to the Law, they would give money to the charities, sit upon the Ma'amad and give wise rulings, and scatter petty men like Parido to the fringes of Jewish society.

He needed a moment to collect his thoughts, which were jumbled and sluggish. Standing still in the midst of the Exchange, merchants and brokers pushing past him like gusts of wind, he repeated his scheme back to himself to make sure he could fully articulate it in all its glory. He engaged in a silent dialogue, a session of interrogation as intense and merciless as any Ma'amad inquiry. If he were to be struck on the head and lose consciousness and sleep until the next day, he wanted to be certain that he would remember this idea as easily as he remembered his own name.

He had it. He understood it. It was his. Now he had to begin.

With his back straight, his pace measured – Miguel thought of a murderer he had once watched walking to the hanging scaffold erected yearly in the Dam – he pushed his way towards the portion of the Exchange where the East Indian merchants congregated. There, among the group of Jewish traders, he found his friend Isaiah Nunes.

For a man so young, Nunes had already proved himself a remarkably capable factor. He possessed invaluable contacts within the Dutch East India Company, who fed him news and gossip and no doubt profits as well. He obtained goods other merchants could only wish for, and he did so frequently, and in doing so always looked as guilty as a man trapped under his lover's bed while her husband searched the room.

Despite his nervous disposition, Nunes chatted easily with a group of merchants, most more than twenty years his senior. Miguel marvelled at the paradox of his friend, at once anxious and so eager. When the price of sugar had plummeted, Nunes alone of all Miguel's friends had volunteered his help. He had offered a loan of seven hundred guilders unbidden, and Miguel had repaid this money within weeks with funds borrowed from Daniel. Nunes might shrink from attracting Parido's attention, he might do nearly anything in his power to avoid the scrutiny of the Ma'amad, but he had proved himself in an hour of crisis.

Now Miguel approached his friend and asked if they might exchange a few words. Nunes excused himself and the two men moved over to a quiet corner, cool in the shadow of the Exchange.

'Ah, Miguel,' Nunes said. 'I heard you had a bit of luck with whale oil. I'm sure your creditors are already off scribbling notes to you.'

The power of rumour never ceased to amaze him. The trade had only happened moments before. 'Thank you for taking the taste of victory from my mouth,' he said, with a grin.

'You know, that whale oil upheaval was Parido's doing. His trading combination was behind it.'

'Really?' Miguel asked. 'Well, how fortunate for me that I happened to stumble upon his machinations.'

'I hope your stumbling has not hurt his machinations. He hardly needs any excuse to be angry with you.'

'Oh, we're friends now,' Miguel said.

'I heard that too. It is a strange world. Why would Parido go out of his way to help you? If I were you I'd be on your guard.' Nunes' voice trailed off as he looked at the clock on the Exchange tower. 'Have you come to try your fortune in the East for these last few minutes?'

'I have a project I wish to pursue, and I might need someone with your particular contacts.'

'You know you can rely on me,' Nunes told him, though perhaps without the warmth Miguel would have liked. In all likelihood, Nunes would want to avoid doing too much business with Parido's enemy, even if the *parnass* now professed friendship.

Miguel took his time to consider how he wished to begin his enquiry, but he could think of nothing clever, so he began directly. 'What do you know about the coffee fruit?'

Nunes remained silent for a moment as they walked. 'Coffee fruit,' he repeated. 'Some East India men acquire it from Mocha, and much of that is traded in the Orient, where the Turks drink it as their wine. It's not very popular in Europe. Most of what I see traded on this Exchange is sold to factors for London, with a little for men in Marseilles and Venice. It's taken on some appeal at foreign courts as well, now that I think about it.'

Miguel nodded. 'I know of some parties who have shown an interest in coffee, but it is a delicate matter. It is difficult to explain fully, but there are those who would see this trade fail.'

'I understand you,' Nunes said cagily.

'Let me be blunt, then. I wish to know if you can import coffee berries for me – a large quantity – twice what is brought in now during a year's time. And I wish to know if you can keep this transaction secret from all prying eyes.'

'Certainly it can be done. I think about forty-five barrels come in each year, and these are sixty pounds each. Coffee is selling now at just over a half guilder a pound, which is thirty-three guilders a barrel. You're asking for ninety barrels, yes? At just under three thousand guilders?'

Miguel tried not to think about the enormity of the sum. 'Yes, that's right.'

'Quantities are hardly unlimited, but I think I can get ninety barrels. I'll speak to my East India contacts and commission them to bring it in for you.'

'I must emphasise the importance of secrecy. I wouldn't want even the sailors to know what they carried, for how many deals are made and lost owing to their loose lips?'

'Oh, that is nothing. I need only instruct my factors to mislabel the manifest with a more common commodity. I make such manoeuvres more often than not. I would not be in business long if I could not keep such things secret.'

Miguel wished to clap his hands with joy, but he held himself in check. Show nothing but calm, he told himself. Look slightly bored, as though these plans are hardly of interest. 'This sounds promising. Once I place my order, how long will it take for the goods to appear in a warehouse here in Amsterdam?'

Nunes considered the question. 'To be safe, I'll need two months, perhaps three. It may take a little time to collect the amount you want. And

Miguel, I can keep things silent here, but I cannot say how quiet this business will be regarded in the Company. Once my factors start buying coffee in large quantities, someone will notice and the price will go up.'

'I understand.' He almost said *no matter* but stopped himself. Best not to reveal too much. Nunes could be trusted, but that didn't mean he should know more than was necessary. 'My buyer has accounted for that possibility.'

Nunes ran a hand along his close-cut beard. 'It occurs to me that the Company has taken a renewed interest in coffee too. The port of Mocha, where coffee is now bought, is crowded with ships from the East. It can take days for a ship to obtain its consignment.'

'But you say you can get what I require?'

'The Company likes to hoard its supplies. I'll tell you something else: the Turks, you may know, have made it a crime punishable by death for any man to remove a living coffee plant from their empire. They wish no one to grow and sell the fruit but themselves. The world knows what a wily lot they are, but I can tell you they are but lost little lambs compared to the Dutch. A sea captain named van der Brock has managed to smuggle a plant out, and now the Company is beginning its own plantations on Ceylon and Java. It hopes to produce enough to gain leverage with oriental trading partners. But it must have other plans as well.'

Miguel nodded. 'Once the crop begins to yield, the Company will want to build a market in Europe.'

'Precisely. I won't ask you what you are planning, but I think we might make a pact. I'll be happy to let you know what news I hear of the trade if you will think first of me as your supplier here on the Exchange – provided you don't mention this to anyone.'

'I consider it a bargain well struck,' Miguel told him.

They slapped their right hands together, formalising the agreement. Nunes must certainly have felt he would make a little money on this deal and might even hope that his friend's interest signified a shift in the markets he might exploit.

Miguel could not recall when he last felt such excitement, so even when he heard that the price of brandy had improved at the last minute – and if he had held on to his futures he would have made four or five hundred guilders – he hardly cared. What did such petty sums mean to him? In a year's time he should be one of the richest men among the Portuguese in Amsterdam.

From

The Factual and Revealing Memoirs of Alonzo Alferonda

After I had been cast out of the community, most of my friends and associates would have nothing more to say to me. Many shunned me because they feared the power of the Ma'amad, others because they were but cattle who had come to depend on the council and believe in its rulings to so strong a degree that they could not for a moment imagine I would have been put under the cherem unjustly. And, if I am to be honest as I have promised, there were those who believed I had cheated them or used them ill and were delighted to see no more of Alferonda.

Men who owed me money boldly refused to pay, as though the ruling of the Ma'amad somehow superseded all civic law and personal honour. Old business contacts returned my notes unopened. Parido's influence left me without a livelihood, and though I had

162

some money saved, I knew it would not last me long.

I cannot say precisely how I fell into lending money at interest. An enquiry here, a promise there, and one morning I awoke and could not longer deny that I had become a moneylender. The Torah speaks ill of usurers, but the Talmud teaches us that a man may bend the Law in order to live, and how else was I to live if those responsible for upholding the Law unjustly took away my livelihood?

There was no shortage of my kind in Amsterdam. We were as specialised as taverns, each of us serving one particular group or another: this lender serves artisans; that one, merchants; yet another, shopkeepers. I resolved never to lend to fellow Jews, for I did not want to travel down that path. I would not want to have to enforce my will on my countrymen and then have them speak of me as one who had turned against them. Instead, I lent to Dutchmen, and not just any Dutchmen. I found myself again and again lending to Dutchmen of the most unsavoury variety: thieves and bandits, outlaws and renegades. I would not have chosen so vile a bunch, but a man has to earn his bread, and I had been thrust in this situation against my will.

I knew at once that I would have to be something of a villain if I were to see my money returned, for I lent to those who earned their bread by taking what did not belong to them, and I had no reason to believe my capital would be any more sacrosanct than a traveller's purse or shopkeeper's strongbox. The only way to force these men to make good on their promises was to let them fear the consequences of not doing so.

Sadly, Alfonzo Alferonda is not a villain. He cannot find it in his heart to be harsh and cruel and violent to his fellow man, but what he lacks in cruelty he compensates for in guile.

I let it be known, therefore, that I was not a man with whom to trifle. When the body of a nameless mendicant was found floating in a canal, it was no hard thing to circulate a story that there floats a fool who thought he could avoid paying Alferonda. When an impoverished fellow broke his arm or lost an eye in some unfortunate accident, a few coins in his hand easily persuaded him to tell the world that he wished he had paid Alferonda in a timely fashion.

Though I believe the Holy One, blessed be He, has granted me a warm face, one full of kindness, it was not long before the thieves of Amsterdam trembled at my countenance. A scowl or a raised eyebrow was enough to make the gold flow.

When I confronted a debtor who truly could not pay me, I made him believe that here, for the first time in his life, Alferonda had decided to show a measure of mercy, a mercy so tentative and fragile that even to think of abusing it would the greatest madness in the world. This thief would pay me before he would put food into his own mouth.

These small deceptions fooled my audience easily. Thieves are, by nature, simple and easily duped, inclined to believe in monsters and ogres. Some, when they paid me, even believed I knew the contents of their purses, the locations of their paltry stashes, as though I were more witch than moneylender. I did nothing to make them believe otherwise. Alferonda is no fool.

I knew my name was spoken in the most unflattering terms among my fellow Jews in the Vlooyenburg, but I also knew I was blameless in the sight of the Lord – at least as blameless as a man who lends money to thieves can ever hope to be.

CHAPTER 10

Miguel met Geertruid in the Three Dirty Dogs, a tavern near the docks where great ships lay at anchor, packed with goods desired the world over. The day was warm and uncharacteristically sunny, and Miguel paused to look at the ships glimmering in the light reflecting off the harbour. Some of the vessels were great monsters from ports around the world, ships whose captains knelt in prayer while their pilots manoeuvred the treacherous waters of the Amsterdam port. These giants were awesome to behold, but not nearly so awesome to Dutch eyes as the smaller *vlieboots* – flyboats – sleek little vessels that were handled with far more agility by a smaller crew and yet held more cargo than the massive ships of other nations. Thanks in part to these maritime miracles, the Dutch now stood supreme not only in trade but in transport, for who would not want his goods shipped in Dutch bottoms when such conveyances reduced costs by as much as a third?

The Three Dirty Dogs was infrequently visited by Jews – its patronage consisted of warehouse workers and owners – and Miguel knew any man of the Nation who saw him there would have his own secrets to keep. It had become a regular habitation for Geertruid, whose husband had been part-owner of one of those great buildings along the Brouwersgracht.

The windows of the tavern had been placed strangely towards the ceiling, and bright sharp-angled shafts of sunlight criss-crossed the dusky interior. Most of the tables were occupied, but the space was not crowded; groups of men sat in small clusters. Near the door someone read a news-sheet aloud in a booming voice while a dozen men listened and drank.

Geertruid sat at the back, dressed in grey skirts and a blue bodice, modest and nondescript. She did not go to the tavern to make merry today but to do business, and she wore no bright colours with which to attract attention. She puffed at a pipe and sat in close quarters with her man, Hendrick, who whispered something conspiratorial when he saw Miguel.

'Good afternoon, Jew Man,' the Dutchman said with what might have been genuine warmth. He was a tricky one; he might present himself as a villain one instant and the grandest man in the world the next. 'Join us. How have we managed all this time without you? We have been as parched as the desert without your company.'

Miguel sat. The knowledge of his impending wealth vied in his heart with the chafing impression that Hendrick mocked him.

'You look cheerful,' Geertruid told him. 'I hope your month closed well.'

'Marvellously well, madam.' Miguel could not contain his grin.

'Ah, I'd been hoping that smile on your face meant you have some firm plans to do business with me.'

'It might mean that too,' Miguel answered. He hardly liked to give his name or the time of day with Hendrick around. 'But we need not discuss these things at this moment.'

'What sound is this?' Hendrick grinned and leaned to the side with a hand cupped to his ear. 'Someone calls my name? Well, then, I'll let you get on with your chatter, for I have no interest in things of business. That's a Jew's affair, and I've Christian matters to look after.'

'Whoring or drinking?' Geertruid enquired.

He laughed. 'That's between me and my Maker.'

'Then I shall see you on the morrow,' Geertruid told him, squeezing his hand gently.

Hendrick pushed himself to his feet and swayed violently towards Geertruid. He snatched the side of the table to steady himself. 'Rot these crooked floors, eh, Jew Man? Rot them, I say. Rot them.' He paused for a moment, as though waiting for Miguel to rot the floors.

A woman who saw her servant or lover in such a state might have shouted in anger or blushed in embarrassment, but Geertruid had already turned away, her attention arrested by some story read by the man with the news-sheet. Therefore she did not see that after Hendrick had taken a few uneasy steps towards the door, he spun around, almost so quickly that he fell over but, instead, caught himself on Miguel's shoulder.

The brawny man's breath smelled remarkably sweet for a man who had been drinking beer and feasting upon onions, but his moustache was slick with grease, and Miguel shrank back from the disquieting intimacy.

'Last time I saw you,' he said directly into Miguel's ear, his voice hardly more than a whisper, 'a man asked me as I left if I might be your acquaintance. Some Jew fellow, I believe. Asked me if I'd be interested in helping him out a bit.'

Miguel looked at Geertruid, but she paid them no attention at all. She was laughing aloud at something in the news-sheet, and much of the tavern laughed with her.

'I think this fellow must have been some rogue, out to trick both you and me,' lied Miguel. Who could this Jew fellow be, Parido? One of his spies? Daniel? Joachim, somehow pretending to be a Jew?

'Just as I thought. Besides, I won't squeeze a friend's friend. It's not my way.'

'I am glad to know it,' Miguel murmured.

Hendrick patted his shoulder once more, this time a bit harder, something just short of a blow, and then swayed off, knocking one table and then another on his way out.

Miguel wondered if perhaps he should have thanked the fellow, both for the information and for not, as he had so menacingly phrased it, putting the squeeze on him. But Miguel had no mind to go about thanking men such as Hendrick for the harm they didn't do.

'Well, now, beautiful madam,' Miguel said, to summon Geertruid's attention. 'We have much to discuss, haven't we?'

She turned to face Miguel, flashing something like surprise, as though she had forgotten that anyone sat at her table. 'Oh, senhor. I long to hear what you have to say.' Geertruid pressed her hands together. Her left eye showed a sudden twitch. 'With any luck you have been thinking about coffee as much as I have.'

Miguel called for a beer while Geertruid brought out a small leather pouch containing the sweet tobacco she favoured. 'I have,' he told her. 'You have seduced me with your proposal.'

She beamed at him. 'Have I now?'

'I've been lying awake thinking of it.'

'I never knew my ideas had such an effect on you.'

The serving boy placed a tankard before Miguel. 'So, let us discuss particulars.'

Geertruid finished refilling her pipe, lit it with the oil lamp on the table, and leaned forward. 'I love to talk of particulars,' she said, in a breathy voice. She puffed at her pipe, sending forth clouds of smoke. 'I won't pretend to be surprised to hear you are with me, however. I knew from the beginning that you were my man.'

Miguel laughed. 'Well, before we proceed, I thought we should work out a few details. If I am to enter into trade with you, I should like to know the conditions.'

'The conditions will depend on your plan. You do have a plan, don't you? Without a sound idea, my capital will hardly be put to good use.'

A genuine laugh escaped Miguel's throat, but his emotions ran somewhat higher than he demonstrated. Geertruid had the capital. That was the very thing he needed to hear.

'Madam, I've devised a plan so clever you will think you've gone mad. This idea of mine.' He shook his head. 'Even I can scarcely believe it.'

Geertruid set aside her pipe. She pressed both palms upon the table and leaned in towards Miguel. 'Tell me everything.'

So Miguel told her everything. He spoke of his idea with a kind of clarity he had not known he possessed – from the earliest details of the planning, to the many layers of execution, to the final vastly complicated and yet elegantly simple conclusion. His tongue flowed easily, perhaps because of the beer, yet he never stammered or slurred or stumbled. He spoke like an orator, and before he was halfway through his explanation he knew he had her.

Geertruid remained silent for a moment after he had finished. Finally she sat back. 'Remarkable.'

She ventured to take a sip of beer. She took another sip and looked up with the appearance of a woman who has just been awakened from an unplanned nap. 'You have taken my most optimistic hopes and rendered them laughable. Do you think such a thing can work? Why, the very size of it – I can hardly take it all in.'

Miguel felt himself grinning like an imbecile. His life was changing before him. How many times does a man stand by foolishly while his life changes form, with no idea that anything out of the ordinary transpires? But for a man to rise to greatness by his own plan and to know the moment that this greatness begins – that was a glorious thing to be savoured.

'We've a great deal to do, it's true. We'll have to plan this business down to the minute. We'll have to hire agents – at least a dozen of them – to act for us where we cannot act ourselves. It is all coordination, orchestration. But, once done, the business will take care of itself.'

She slapped the table with her hand – not hard, but hard enough to send Miguel's nearly empty tankard rattling. 'By the grace of God, this scheme of yours is – well, I cannot even say.'

'However.' Miguel cleared his throat before beginning anew, trying hard to get the smile off his face. This was, after all, a serious topic. 'However, it will take money. We must clarify that part of the arrangement.' This was the moment he had dreaded. Had Geertruid merely been talking to sound impressive, or did she have access to sufficient capital, as she had hinted? Without money, they could do nothing.

She picked his hand up gently, as though fearing it might fall and shatter were she to drop it. 'I have been my own mistress long enough to understand that capital is but one element of the business. Do not think because I put forth the money that you will suffer for it. I propose a split of fifty percent. With all the capital in the world I could not do this thing without you. Is that not the way in Amsterdam, the way that has made this city great? We rule the world because we have devised joint stock companies and corporations and trading combinations to share the danger.' She gave his hand a good squeeze. 'And the wealth.'

'The thing of it is,' Miguel said hesitantly, 'I cannot make any moves in my own name – owing to some small debts. If these niggling creditors were to learn of the business, they might make demands on me that could prove disruptive.'

'Then we'll use my name, virginal as an infant's. It hardly matters what name we use.'

'Of course,' he agreed. 'We should perhaps be clear on the degree of the togetherness and determine to keep our business from everyone, including our nearest friends.'

'You mean Hendrick.' Geertruid laughed. 'He hardly understands the nature of a transaction as complex as buying a prune pie. I would never tax his brain with such a thing as this, even if it were not a secret. You needn't worry there. And even if he were to catch some wind of our plan, and even if he were to understand it, he would never tell a soul. There is nowhere to be found a man with more loyalty.'

He paused to consider how he wished to word his next concern. 'We have not yet discussed the requirements of this plan or the scope of your resources.'

'My resources have their limits,' Geertruid agreed. 'How much do we require?'

Miguel spoke quickly, wanting this most difficult part resolved. 'I believe that, in order to perform these tasks, I'll require of you no more than three thousand guilders.'

He waited. A man could live in great comfort for a year on three thousand guilders. Could Geertruid have so much at her disposal? Her husband had left her an estate of some value, but did she live the life of a woman who could summon three thousand guilders upon command?

'It's not easy,' Geertruid answered, after a thoughtful pause, 'but it can be done. When will you need it?'

Miguel shrugged, trying hard to contain his glee. 'A month?' Best to act as though three thousand guilders were of no importance. In fact, seeing how easily she agreed to the sum, he at once regretted not having asked for more. Had he requested four thousand, he might have used the extra money to pay off some debts and provide a little room to breathe – surely a legitimate business expense.

Geertruid nodded with great seriousness. 'I'll arrange for the funds to be transferred to your account at the Exchange Bank, so you may proceed without the world knowing that my hand is thrust in with yours.'

'I know we don't like to look into each other's affairs, but now that we are business partners, not merely friends, you will understand if I am curious about a thing or two.'

'I would be surprised if you were not,' Geertruid answered happily. 'You wonder how I can produce so great a sum so easily.' She remained cheerful, careful that Miguel not even suspect a hint of bitterness. The question, after all, was certainly proper.

'As you've brought it up, I must admit curiosity.'

'I haven't buried it in my cellar,' Geertruid said. 'I propose to sell off some holdings. It may take a few weeks to be certain that I obtain the best prices, but I can raise the funds without undoing myself.'

'Would you like me to broker these matters for you?'

She clapped her hands together. 'I should be delighted if you would do so. It would relieve me of a great burden.' Then her eyes narrowed. 'Yet I wonder if you should. I know you fear your evil council. Do you wish to do anything in public that might announce our partnership more than necessary?'

'The council is not evil, only over-zealous, but I take your point. Have you other men to whom to turn?'

'I'll take care of everything.' Geertruid rolled her head back, looked towards the ceiling, and then turned to Miguel. 'It must have been the will of God that brought us together, senhor. I am in awe of you.'

'Soon the world will be in awe of us both,' he told her.

This plan, this child of Miguel's mind, seemed to him so simple he could not believe that no one had thought of such a thing before. Of course, it required certain conditions. A man had to make his move at just the right time in the life of a commodity, and this was the time, he knew with ferocious certainty, for coffee.

First, Miguel would arrange to bring a large shipment of coffee into Amsterdam – a shipment so large it would flood the market, which was now very small and specialised – in this case, ninety barrels. No one would know of this consignment, so the first stage of making money involved the element of surprise. To take advantage of this secret, Miguel would purchase a large quantity of puts, guaranteeing him the right to sell at the predetermined price of approximately thirty-three guilders per barrel.

When news of the shipment spread, the price of coffee would drop and Miguel would profit handsomely from the difference in price, as dictated by the puts, but these profits would only whet his appetite, a small first course in the larger feast ahead. By that time, Miguel and Geertruid would have hired agents to do their bidding on the dozen or so most active import commodity exchanges in Europe: Hamburg, London, Madrid, Lisbon, Marseilles and several others he would carefully select. Each agent would know his own task but not that he was part of a larger scheme.

A few weeks after their shipment arrived in Amsterdam, once the rest of Europe had learned that the coffee market was flooded and the price had now dropped at every exchange, these agents would move. Every man would buy all the coffee upon the market at its now artificially lowered price. They would act at a single time – this was the part so brilliant it made Miguel need to empty his bladder just to think of it – if word were to reach London that a man sought to buy all the coffee in Amsterdam, the price in London would soar, making the acquisition unprofitably expensive. It was the simultaneity that Miguel embraced as his most clever stroke. Before anyone knew what had happened, he would own all the coffee in Europe. The price would be his to dictate as he pleased, and they would be in a position to give the law to the importers. They would have that most sought-after of powers, a rare thing upon which unimaginable fortunes are built: a monopoly.

Maintaining the monopoly would require some skill, but it should be possible to manage it, at least for a while. The East India Company, which imported the coffee, would find itself in a position to break Miguel's control of the prices, but only if it could dramatically increase the amount of coffee on the European market. True, the Company had plantations in Ceylon and Java, but it would be many seasons before those crops yielded significant quantities, and to deplete its warehouses in the East would mean sacrificing a trade of far more importance. The Company would have no motive to act for some time; it would be content to watch and wait. It would plant and it would hoard. Only when the Company had enough coffee to break his hold would it strike.

Let it strike, Miguel thought. Five, ten, perhaps even fifteen years will go by first. The Company had the patience of a spider; by the time it moved, Miguel and Geertruid would be immeasurably wealthy.

Perhaps long before that time the Ma'amad would learn of Miguel's partnership with Geertruid. What could it say once he had donated tens of thousands of guilders to charity? Miguel was only a few months away from the kind of wealth that most men only dream of, but already he could hold it in his hand and know its taste. It tasted savoury indeed.

So great was his enthusiasm that later that night

as he lay in bed, when he recollected that he had utterly forgotten to meet Joachim Waagenaar as planned, Miguel felt only the slightest twinge of regret.

From

The Factual and Revealing Memoirs of Alonzo Alferonda

I talk about myself too much. I know that. I've looked over the pages I've penned, and what do I see but *Alferonda* and *Alferonda*? To this objection my readers will surely say, 'But my dear Alonzo, what more interesting subject can there be but your life and your opinions?' Fair enough, dear readers. You have swayed me with your gentle arguments. But there are other things to write about, reasons why I began this memoir in the first place.

For one thing, there is coffee.

Not so long ago, in the time of my boyhood, coffee was like any other exotic powder or dried berry you might find in an apothecary's musty cabinet. It was given in small doses for diseases of the blood and bowels. Too much is poison, they would say. Even now, as this elixir spreads like a murky tide across Europe, the apothecaries cry out to drinkers to stay their hands. Great quantities of this medicine will make you weak, they say. It dries out the blood; it leads to impotence and infertility. Coffee leads to nothing of the sort, I promise you. I consume it in great quantities, and my blood is as robust as that of a man half my age.

It has always been looked on with some suspicion, this poor drink that only wants to improve us, to make us more than we are. It first became known among the men of the Orient, who were suspicious of its marvellous effects. Those of the Muhammadan faith shun alcohol, so they had no experience of drinks that change a man's disposition. Over a hundred years ago, in the land of Egypt, the viceroy summoned the great imams to debate whether coffee was permitted or forbidden by the dietary code of their sacred teachings. Coffee is like wine, one imam declared, and is therefore forbidden. But who could agree or disagree, these all being righteous men who had never themselves tasted wine and could only guess. They knew wine makes a man sleepy, yet coffee makes him alert. Therefore coffee could not be like wine.

Another shouted that coffee is black, and the beans, when roasted, are like dirt. The eating of dirt was forbidden by Muhammad and therefore coffee is forbidden. But another argued that since fire purifies, the process of roasting the berries makes them not unclean but rather cleanses away that which was once unclean in them. In the end they could only say that coffee was neither forbidden nor permitted, but was mekruh, undesirable.

Of course they were mistaken. Coffee is nothing if not desirable. All men desire its power, and when it first emerged there were those who desired the wealth it might bring. One such man, of course, was Miguel Lienzo, the benefactor of my youth. How good he had been to my family, providing us with warning about the Inquisition when no one else thought to save us! Did he do this for profit? No, there could be none. Did he act out of love? He barely knew us. He did it, I believe, because he is a righteous man and delights in thwarting the plans of evil-doers.

I had no desire to make him uncomfortable, so when I formed a friendship with Lienzo in Amsterdam, I did not embarrass him by recollecting the kindness he had done my family. Instead, I did some small business with him, joined him at taverns and eateries, and studied with him at the Talmud Torah.

When I saw him we talked of little of consequence. Then one day he informed me that he wanted to enter into the coffee trade. I knew about coffee from the years I had sojourned in the East. I knew that a man who drinks coffee is twice as strong, twice as wise, and twice as cunning as the man who abstains. I knew that coffee unlocks doors in the mind.

And I knew other things too. I knew things I was not quite prepared to tell my friend Senhor Lienzo. Not because I wanted him to fail, oh, no. Nothing of the sort. I held on to my secrets because I wanted him to succeed, and I had every reason to believe that this new coffee venture could be just the thing I needed.

CHAPTER 11

C offee. It was a fire that fed on itself.

Miguel sat in his cellar, his feet cold from canal water, as he drank bowl after bowl of coffee and wrote to brokers and traders on every exchange he knew. It would be weeks, of course, before he would get responses, but soon they would come. He urged quick replies. He promised generous commissions.

It was as Alferonda had said. He remained awake half the night, reading through his letters, tearing them up, and rewriting them. He studied the week's Torah portion and knew he would dazzle his study group at the synagogue. He reread eight tales of Charming Pieter.

The next day he felt weary, but if that was the price of productivity he was willing to pay. In any case, morning coffee paid the debts incurred by the coffee of the previous night.

Miguel heard that Parido and his trading combination had lost a great deal – that is to say, they had not profited as handsomely as they had intended – because of Miguel's interference in whale oil. When the two men saw each other

184

on the Exchange, however, Parido showed no ill will.

'I hear your month ended well,' the *parnass* said. He might have been discussing the death of a friend for all the cheer in his voice.

Miguel smiled brightly. 'It might have been better.'

'I could say the same for my own. Did you know your machinations in whale oil caused me to incur some unpleasant losses?'

'I'm terribly sorry to learn that,' Miguel said. 'I had no idea you were involved, or I would never have ventured there myself.'

'So you tell me, but things appear somewhat dubious,' Parido said. 'There are those who whisper in my ear to tell me your whale oil scheme was a slap in the face.'

'I would not let my brother whisper in your ear if I were you. His breath would fell a horse. If you don't have faith in my honesty, at least have faith in my caution. Why would I risk your displeasure by trading knowingly against your interests?'

'I cannot say what compels a man to act as he acts.'

'Nor can I. You know, brandy surged at the last moment. Some Dutch fellows bought a massive quantity and sent the price soaring. You had no knowledge of that, I suppose, though men might whisper a thing or two in my ear if I let them.'

Parido frowned. 'You don't think I would trick you out of your futures, do you?'

'Things appear somewhat dubious,' Miguel said.

Parido let out a sour little laugh. 'Perhaps we are on an equal footing. You lost far less in brandy than I did in whale oil, but your losses are surely more significant to you than mine are to me.'

'Surely,' Miguel agreed.

'Let me ask you one thing, however. How is it that you just happened upon whale oil? It is an odd coincidence, don't you think?'

Miguel could think of no answer, but Parido spoke again before the silence became too conspicuous.

'Did someone advise you to trade in whale oil?'

It was as though Charming Pieter whispered the name. Of course. Why not say so?

To implicate this man could not be counted as a betrayal, because the man was out of Parido's grasp. 'I did receive a note – unsolicited, of course – from that fellow Alferonda. He advised me to buy into whale oil.'

'And you believed him, this man we had cast out of the community?'

'I thought he had no reason to lie, and when I examined the commodity for myself and asked around the Exchange, I concluded that the advice had been good.'

Parido scratched at his beard thoughtfully. 'I had supposed it might come to this. I would advise you to have no more dealings with him, Lienzo. Pay him a broker's fee if you must, but be rid of him. The man is a danger to anyone he touches.'

Miguel could hardly believe his luck, having so easily escaped Parido's anger. Certainly he seemed irritated that he had lost money, but he was too eager to blame Alferonda to waste his anger upon Miguel. Meanwhile, Miguel had begun to realise that obtaining his whale oil profits might be more difficult than he thought. After reckoning day, when no money had been deposited into his account at the Exchange Bank and he began receiving letters from his Muscovy agent regarding his nineteen hundred guilders, Miguel thought it was time to hunt his money. He found Ricardo, the broker to whom he'd sold his shares, at a tavern popular with Portuguese Jews. He was already slightly drunk and looking like he wanted, more than anything else, to be in his own bed – or, at the very least, away from Miguel.

'How are you, Lienzo?' he asked, and then walked off without waiting for an answer.

'Oh, I've been a busy man, Ricardo,' Miguel said, hurrying after him. 'I've made a few trades here and there and earned a few guilders. The thing of it is, when a man earns a few guilders, he expects to have those guilders appear in his account at the Exchange Bank.'

Ricardo turned. 'I've heard your creditors say much the same thing.'

'Oh, ho!' Miguel shouted back. 'You've a sharp tongue today. Well, you may sharpen your tongue all you like so long as you also sharpen your pen before signing over my money.'

'As you've only been in Amsterdam five years,' Ricardo said quietly, 'and you clearly haven't mastered the art of doing business here, let me make bold by explaining something to you. The flow of money is like the flow of water in a river. You may stand by the shore and urge it on, but doing so won't earn you much advantage. You'll get your money in due time.'

'In due time? The fellow I borrowed from in order to buy that whale oil isn't talking about due time.'

'Maybe you should not have extended credit when you had none to extend. I would have thought you might have learned that lesson before now.'

'You're in no position to lecture me about extending credit when you won't pay me. Who is your blackguard client anyhow who holds back?'

Ricardo sneered under his unkempt moustache. 'You know I won't tell you that,' the broker explained. 'I won't have you making trouble for my clients, or for me either. If you don't like the way I do business, you know what you may do about it.'

Here was something of a bind. Had Ricardo been a Dutchman, Miguel could have taken the matter to the Exchange board or to the courts, but the Ma'amad discouraged Jews from resolving their differences so publicly. Instead, it preferred to resolve these things itself, but Miguel was disinclined to bring a matter before the council.

Parido might choose to lead the Ma'amad against Miguel out of spite, and then he would have no recourse.

'I don't much like the tone you've taken with me, Ricardo,' Miguel said, 'and I promise you that this incident will not shine favourably on your reputation.'

'You're a fine fellow to talk about reputations,' the broker answered, as he turned away.

Later that week, Miguel left his brother's house early and strolled along the Herengracht, whose handsome wide streets were bursting with linden trees newly rich with foliage. Grand houses rose upwards on either side of the canal, glories of the prosperity that the Dutch had built for themselves in the last half-century. These were enormous red-brick dwellings – too well constructed to require the sealing black tar that covered so many houses in the city – grand structures with ornate angles and dazzling flourishes. Miguel loved to study the gable stones above the doorways, coats of arms or symbols of the source the household's wealth: a bound bundle of wheat, a tall-masted ship, an African brute in chains.

Just ahead, a beggar wound his way through the street, stumbling like a drunkard. He was filthy, covered in rags, and missing most of his left arm from an accident still new enough to leave the wound raw and rancid. Miguel, who was kind, sometimes too kind, with the city's mendicants, felt the pull of generosity. Why should he not be munificent? Charity was a *mitzvah*, and in a few months' time he would hardly miss a handful of stivers.

As he reached for his purse, something stayed his hand. Miguel felt the burn of eyes on him and turned. Not fifteen feet behind him, Joachim Waagenaar flashed his wincing smile.

'Don't let me stop you,' he said as he approached. 'If you, in your goodness, meant to give a few coins to that unfortunate, I would hate to think I stood in your way. A man with money to spare must never be shy in giving charity.'

'Joachim!' Miguel called out, with all the semblance of cheer he could muster. 'Well met.'

'Keep your false kindness,' Joachim said, 'after you so rudely spurned our meeting.'

Miguel deployed the easy voice with which he convinced men to buy what they did not want. 'An unfortunate turn of events prevented me from arriving. It was all very disagreeable, and I assure you I would rather have been with you than those unpleasant gentlemen.'

'Oh, such dreaded circumstances can only be imagined,' Joachim said, raising his voice like a mountebank. 'Such horrible circumstances as would prevent you not only from fulfilling a promise but from sending along word to tell me that you could not make it as we had agreed.'

It occurred to Miguel that he ought to be worried about this public encounter. Should he be spotted by a Ma'amad spy, Parido might well undertake an official investigation. A quick glance revealed only housewives, maids and a few artisans. He had walked a route not generally frequented by those of his neighbourhood, and he believed he might continue this conversation, at least for a few more minutes, without risk of exposure.

'I must tell you that I don't believe any business arrangement between us is possible at this time,' he said, making an attempt to keep a kindly tone in his voice. 'My resources are limited, and, if I may speak frankly, I am encumbered by a great deal of debt.' It pained him to say the words aloud to this wretch, but at the moment the truth struck him as the best strategy.

'I too have debts – with the baker and the butcher – and both have threatened action if I do not pay what I owe at once. Therefore, let's go to the Exchange,' Joachim suggested. 'We can put some money into a likely trading ship or some other scheme you devise.'

'What manner of investment is this,' Miguel asked, 'when you cannot pay for bread?'

'You'll lend me the money,' he answered confidently. 'I'll repay you from my portion of the profits, which ought to motivate you to invest more wisely than you have sometimes done in the past – when you invested someone else's money.'

Miguel stopped walking. 'I am sorry you believe yourself wronged, but you must understand that I too lost a great deal in that unfortunate affair.'

He took a breath. Better to say it than to endure Joachim's fantastical notions. 'You speak of your debts, but I have debts that would buy your baker and butcher outright. I'm sorry for your need, but I don't know what I can do for you.'

'You were going to give to that beggar. Why give to him if you will not give to me? Are you not being merely wilful?'

'Will a handful of stivers make a difference to you, Joachim? If so, you may have them with all my heart. I would have suspected that such an amount would only insult you.'

'It would,' he snapped. 'A few stivers against the five hundred you took from me?'

Miguel sighed. How could life hold such promise and such tedium all in the same morning. 'My finances are a bit disordered just now, but in half a year I'll be able to offer you something – I'll be able to help you in this plan as you've suggested, and I'll do it gladly.'

'Half a year?' Joachim's voice had begun to grow shrill. 'Would you lie in shit-smeared straw and dine on piss gruel for half a year? My wife, Clara, whom I promised to make comfortable and content, now sells pies in the alleys behind the Oude Kerk. She'll turn whore in half a year. I tried to take her to live with relations in Antwerp, but she wouldn't stay in that wretched city. You think you can make things easy for us by telling me about half a year?'

Miguel thought about Joachim's wife, Clara. He

had met her once or twice, and she had proved to be a spirited woman with more sense – and certainly more beauty – than her husband.

Thinking about Joachim's pretty wife left Miguel feeling more generous than he might otherwise have been. 'I don't have very much on me,' he said. 'Nor have I much elsewhere. But I can give you two guilders if that will help your immediate needs.'

'Two guilders is but a paltry beginning,' Joachim said. 'I'll consider it but the first payment of the five hundred I lost.'

'I'm sorry you believe yourself injured, but I have business to attend to. I can hear no more.'

'What business is this?' Joachim asked, stepping in front of Miguel, blocking his exit. 'Business without money, is it?'

'Yes, so you may find it in your best interest not to hinder my efforts.'

'You should not be so unkind to me,' Joachim said, shifting to heavily accentuated Portuguese. 'A man who has lost everything can lose nothing more.'

Some time ago, when they had been on far more pleasant terms, Miguel had muttered something to himself in Portuguese, and Joachim had astonished him by answering back in that language. Then he had laughed and told Miguel that in a city like Amsterdam one must never assume that a man does not understand the language you speak. Joachim used Portuguese now perhaps to suggest a dangerous intimacy, a familiarity with the ways of the Portuguese nation, including the power of the Ma'amad. Was the Portuguese a threat, an indication that, if he did not get what he wanted, Joachim would tell the council that Miguel had been brokering for gentiles?

'I'll not be menaced,' he said in Dutch. He held himself straight.

Joachim held out his hand and pushed Miguel. The gesture lacked power; it was almost contemptuous – just a little shove, enough to make Miguel take a step and a half backwards. 'I think,' he said, mocking Miguel's accent, 'that you will be menaced.'

Miguel had no idea what to say. He hated Joachim well enough for threatening him with the Ma'amad, but to threaten him with violence was more than he could endure. But what could he do; strike at him? The dangers of striking a madman aside, Miguel could not risk a violent confrontation with a Dutchman. The Ma'amad would expel him without a moment of hesitation. Back in Lisbon, he hardly would have scrupled to beat this wretch bloody, but here he could only stand impotently.

Sensing Miguel's hesitation, Joachim flashed his broken teeth with animal menace.

Around him Miguel noticed the glances of passing strangers: a neatly dressed Jew locked in uncomfortable conversation with a beggar. Among the openly curious Catholic Portuguese, this strange pair would have been surrounded by a crowd of curious maids and peasant housewives, staring with open amusement as they wiped their floured hands on their aprons, laughing and heckling as though this conflict were a puppet show staged for their pleasure. Here, among the Dutch, who had taken to heart the introspective doctrine of their Reformed Church, the curious looked away politely, as if to cast their eyes upon someone else's business was shameful. Surely they had troubles of their own that needed tending.

'We understand each other,' Joachim said. 'I'll take those two guilders.'

Miguel took a step back, but he considered it a defiant retreat. 'You'll get nothing from me now. I offered you kindness, and you repay me with impudence. Keep your distance from me, or shit-smeared straw and piss gruel will seemed to you the greatest luxuries in the world.'

Miguel turned in the other direction and headed towards the Exchange, pushing his legs, now heavy and stiff, as quickly as he could, trying to erase the discomfort of the encounter by doing something decisive. He replayed the incident again and again in his mind. He should have given the fellow his two guilders. He should have given him ten. Anything to make him go away.

'Damn my pride,' he murmured. A madman might say anything to anyone, including the Ma'amad. If Parido should learn that Miguel had been brokering for a gentile, all his protests of goodwill would be like smoke in the air.

A few weeks before, Miguel might have even struck Joachim and allowed the consequences to come as they may. Now he had too much to lose. He would not put his new expectations at risk for a disgruntled vagabond. He would see Joachim at the bottom of a canal first.

CHAPTER 12

Hannah loved to visit the fish market during Exchange hours because she had to pass along the Dam and would occasionally catch sight of Miguel. He would be oblivious to her presence, locked in conversation with some great merchant or other, his confidence radiating, one hand contemplatively rubbing his bristly beard. He would laugh and slap his friend upon the back. She had never seen him so at ease as when he was upon the Dam, and she liked to believe that this agreeable happy man was Miguel's secret self, at home in the shadow of the palatial Town Hall and the glorious Exchange, the self he would become once he cleared himself of his debt and his brother's yoke.

Daniel had grown particularly fond of herring, since their arrival in Amsterdam, and wanted to eat it three times a week, prepared in stews, or in sauces with raisins and nutmeg, and sometimes smothered in butter and parsley. The stall keepers down at the fish market had a hundred ways to sell bad herring, but Annetje knew all their tricks and made herself useful in testing the most handsome

197

specimens for signs of being slicked with oil, dyed, or salted to hide the smell of rot. After the women bought their fish, they crossed the Dam to seek out sellers of vegetables and, as Daniel had been generous with money that morning, fruit for after the meal. As she went about her purchases, Hannah kept her eyes on the Exchange, never knowing when she might be treated to a glimpse of Miguel, aglow in his pecuniary glory.

Annetje had been unusually kind to her since their church outing. She knew nothing of Hannah's fleeting encounter with the widow, so she knew nothing of why Hannah had returned to her care so sullen. The girl had brought her home and given her hot wine with extra cloves. She had cooked leafy cabbage for her to improve her blood, but if her blood had improved, Hannah showed no signs of it. Annetje joked with her, snapped at her, coddled her, poked fingers in her sides, and by turns kissed and pinched her cheeks, but nothing worked. The girl eventually settled in with Hannah's new moodiness and declared she would not waste her time attempting to coax so sad a mope into better spirits.

Hannah had thought to tell her. She wanted to tell someone, but she had been in no mind to share more secrets with the girl, so she said nothing. She lay in bed at night thinking of that wicked stare, and once or twice she had thought to awaken Daniel – or merely shove him, for he was often enough awake with aching teeth – and confess all to him. He would never cast her out, not while she carried his child. Still, she kept her tongue. She thought about telling Miguel. The widow was his friend, after all, but she could not even dream of explaining to him what she had been doing in that part of town.

No one need know, she repeated to herself during those long nights. No one would find out, and there would be no consequences if she just kept silent.

Only the coffee berries comforted her now. She had slipped down to Miguel's cellar once more and slid a handful into her apron. One handful. How long would that last? So she took another, and then a half-handful to be sure she need not come again so soon. Inside the sack, the beans appeared diminished, but Miguel would hardly notice. If he traded in the fruit, he might get more as easily as he pleased. For all she knew, this was a new sack entirely.

Now, as she and Annetje returned to the Vlooyenburg, their baskets heavy with fish and carrots, she chewed on her berries, working them slowly so they might last longer. But even though she had eaten a dozen berries or more, the fear pulled at her, and she began to wonder if the effect of the fruit was no match for the terrors that now lurked everywhere.

She hardly noticed where they walked, so Annetje, observing her absent frame of mind, led her through the narrow and ancient Hoogstraat, where the stones were red with blood from the hog butchers that lined either side. She took obvious pleasure in the idea of trailing pig blood into a Jew's house. Hannah snapped alert to avoid the congealing puddles, but when they were halfway through the isle she was distracted by the burn of eyes upon her like the hot breath of a predator. She dared not turn around, so with her free hand she gripped Annetje's arm, hoping her intent would be clear: let us hurry. It was not. Annetje sensed something was amiss, so she stopped and turned to look. There was nothing left for Hannah but to turn around too.

Pretty as a portrait, the widow approached her, smiling her wide irresistible smile. She hardly looked where she walked, but her natural grace steered her past the puddles of blood and offal. A few paces behind lagged her man, young, fair-haired, and handsome in the most menacing way imaginable. He held back, to keep a watchful eye on her.

'My dear,' the widow said to Hannah, 'do you understand my language?' She turned to Annetje.' Girl, does the senhora understand?'

Hannah was too frightened to lie or even to answer. Her head clouded with the pungent scent of pigs' blood. Surely the widow now wanted something for her silence, and if Hannah could not provide it, she would find herself, her husband, her child destroyed. To save himself, Daniel would surely divorce her. He might be able to repair his reputation in the community by acting cruelly to the wife who had defiled his name. And then what would Hannah do, throw herself and her child upon the mercy of some convent?

'She understands well enough,' Annetje said, making no effort to hide her confusion. She knew who the widow was and could not imagine her business with Hannah. 'But her tongue is too ill-made to form the sounds of Dutch.'

Wicked though she might be, Annetje proved her worth now. If Hannah could not speak, it would shorten their conversation, force the widow to be clear and direct.

'Very well, sweetheart, you just nod if you understand me and shake your head if you do not. Can you do that, my dear?'

Hannah nodded.

'You are a stout girl, you know, and a pretty one too, under those cruel clothes. How sad such beauty must be hidden. Senhor Lienzo has often spoken of how pretty you are, and of his brother's good fortune to have such a pretty wife.'

Hannah did not know if she should nod. It seemed to her immodest to affirm her own beauty. But Miguel thought her pretty, and that was something.

Unable to resist, she reached into her apron and grabbed one of the last coffee berries, dirty with lint and street dust. With it clutched in her fingers, she lifted her hand, as though holding it to her mouth in fear, and slipped the hard fruit inside. It was too soon to chew, she told herself, and took comfort in clenching the berry with her molars. A little too much pressure, and the bean split. It would be fine if she just chewed it carefully.

'On Sunday.' Annetje was repeating some words Hannah had missed. The girl's mind churned through possibilities. 'Near the Weigh House?'

'Near the Weigh House,' the widow agreed affably. 'The senhora and I saw each other. Is that not right, my dear?'

Hannah nodded again: a fine opportunity to work at some of the larger pieces of the berry.

'I saw you chasing after your girl. I can hardly imagine what she had done to make her mistress chase after her, but I suppose that is none of my concern.'

Annetje clucked her tongue. 'I am certain the antics of youth are a distant memory to you, and so they appear puzzling.'

'Such a witty slut. I'll indulge you your barbs, so I may sooner get to the heart of my meaning.' She looked at Hannah. 'I only want you to know that I happened to be near the Weigh House all morning. Indeed, I saw you as I came by way of the Oudezijds Voorburgwal, and I saw from which house you came. I know what it would mean if the world were to know you were inside it.' She reached out and pressed her fingers ever so gently on Hannah's belly. Just for an instant. 'I only wanted to beg you to be more careful. Do you understand?'

Hannah nodded once more.

'What does she care for your concern, old woman?' Annetje demanded.

The widow smiled thinly. 'You probably know nothing of who I am. I cannot imagine dear Senhor Lienzo speaks of me to you, so I must think you concerned about this knowledge I now possess. I only wanted to tell you that you needn't fear anything from me. I have many talents, dear senhora, but none so precious to me as that of keeping secrets. You may sleep at night knowing I will never speak of what I saw to a living soul – not to Senhor Lienzo, though he is a great friend of mine; not even to my dear Hendrick.'

Hendrick bowed at Hannah.

'All I ask in exchange,' began Geertruid, but she stopped herself. 'No, not in exchange. I won't make a bargain with you, I won't have you believe my silence some precious thing, easily broken. I will keep your secret, yet I would ask a favour of you, lamb. May I do so?'

Hannah nodded and swallowed the last of her coffee.

'I'm so very glad. You see, I only ask that you not speak of what *you* saw – not to Senhor Lienzo or your husband or your friends or even to this sweet girl here, upon whom you depend. I think it best we both forget we saw each other that day. Do you not think so?'

Another nod.

'I'm so glad. May I kiss you?' This time

Geertruid did not wait for a nod. She leaned in and put her soft lips against Hannah's veil, pressing through so she could feel the warmth the widow's mouth. 'Were things ordered differently, I'm sure we could be friends. It's sad that it cannot be, but know that I always wish you well. Goodbye, my dear.'

Geertruid turned and walked toward Hendrick, who offered the ladies another bow.

'Christ,' Annetje said loudly. 'I hope the senhor doesn't fuck anything that withered.'

Hannah began walking quickly. Annetje remained a moment, watching them depart, and then hurried after her mistress.

'By Jesus,' Annetje swore, 'you had better tell me what that was about.'

Hannah kept her eyes straight ahead. A group of women, thick-waisted matrons, passed them by, glancing at Hannah's veil.

'You may speak now,' Annetje urged. 'There's no harm in it.'

'I won't speak of it,' Hannah said. She felt as though the widow had been some kind of witch, that a spell had been cast, and that to defy the widow's wishes would bring down her curses. How could she be sure the widow was *not* a witch?

'Don't be a silly,' Annetje urged quietly. 'Because that old whore says it doesn't mean it must be so. She can't know of what we speak.'

'If I'm to hope she keeps her silence, I must keep mine.'

'A peculiar sort of logic.' Annetje clicked her tongue. 'I want to know her secret.'

Hannah stopped. She looked Annetje full in the face. 'My child is in danger. I beg of you not to speak a word of this to anyone. You must promise me.'

Annetje laughed airily. 'I will not,' she said. 'I can ruin you more easily than that widow can, and I'll not make any vow because you tell me.'

Hannah did not turn away. She would not be intimidated, not about this. 'You will promise me, and honour your word too.'

Annetje's laugh ended, and her smile retracted into her face like a cat's claws. 'You want my promise? I promise that if you keep secrets from me, I'll tell what I know of them to your husband. There is my promise. Keep your affairs hidden from me again, and you'll have cause to regret it,' she said. 'Now stop staring at me like a puppy and let's go.'

Hannah nodded helplessly. Still, she had won, hadn't she? Annetje had demanded that she not keep *more* secrets, not that she reveal this one. The girl had backed down.

Perhaps her will was worth something after all. But what to do about the widow? She hated to hold something back from Miguel, but what choice had she been given? In any case, the widow was his friend. Perhaps she planned something for him as a surprise. Perhaps she secretly helped him with some business. Yes, that made a great deal of sense. She helped Miguel behind his back and did not want him to know lest his pride be injured. All would be well, she told herself again and again, each time hoping to believe it.

CHAPTER 13

After a disappointing afternoon, nothing would have been so welcome as the cool isolation of his brother's cellar. Sad home though it was, it offered some retreat from the world.

It had been more than two weeks, and still no word from any of his prospective agents. True, it was still early, but after two weeks it was now within the realm of the possible that he might have word. That was what he had told himself. *Don't look for answers before two weeks had passed*, though he had secretly hoped to receive word sooner.

Now all that might comfort him would be a few struck candles, a glass of wine – or perhaps even some coffee. Miguel had stopped by the bookseller that afternoon and found a new tale of Charming Pieter and his Goodwife Mary. It was only eighteen pages long, so he took no more than a glance at it in the shop, not wanting to spoil the pleasure of the discovery.

Miguel had received yet another note from his Muscovy agent that day. The fellow had too many debts and too many creditors pressing for them.

He needed to call in his own loans, and if Miguel could not comply there would certainly be consequences.

There were always consequences, he told himself, and he'd ignored his share of similar communications, but not with Dutchmen who might well drag him before the courts – something he could little afford now that he was beginning to order his affairs. So he spent the day in search of Ricardo, but no luck. Instead he ended up at the Flyboat, drinking with Isaiah Nunes.

'What do you know about Ricardo?' Miguel asked his friend.

'Nothing more than you know. He's just a broker of middling skills.'

'You have no idea who his clients are?'

'That is one thing Ricardo does well: he keeps quiet. He's very popular among men who don't want to pay a moment before they choose to pay. I don't think Ricardo would risk tricking you outright, but it could be another month or even more before he pays. I heard he once sheltered a client for more than a year.'

Miguel had no intention of waiting a year. 'I would blacken his eye, if I thought he wouldn't go running to the Ma'amad. Trouble from the council is the last thing I need while I work out this business with coffee.'

'Are you still committed to that project?' Nunes let his eyes wander around the room.

Miguel felt the hair on the back of his neck tingle. 'Of course.'

'Maybe now is not the best time,' Nunes suggested, half swallowing his words.

Miguel leaned forward. 'What are you telling me – that you can't get what you promised? By Christ, if you can't, you had better tell me who can.'

'Of course I can get what I promise,' he answered hastily. 'I'll not promise what I can't do. Even the East India Company would not cross me.' An idle boast, of course.

'I am utterly certain that the East India Company would not hesitate to cross me,' Miguel said, 'but I hope *you* would.'

Nunes let out a nervous sigh. 'I only wondered if perhaps, now that you have made a little money in whale oil and are feeling confident, it might be a poor time to invest in something so full of risk. Why not make yourself safe?'

'My brother tried to warn me off coffee too,' Miguel said.

'I'm not trying to warn you off,' Nunes assured him. 'If you suggest your brother put me up to this, you are wrong. You know how little I value him. If Parido did not befriend him, he'd be without two stivers to buy bread. I just don't want to see you lose in a risky venture.'

'Just do what I pay you to do,' Miguel said, loud enough to make his friend cringe.

On the walk home, he'd begun to regret his words to Nunes. Miguel had lost a great deal of money, and the loss had hit him hard. His friends were right to worry about him, and he had not exactly told Nunes the truth about his coffee venture. He would find Nunes tomorrow, apologise by buying him a few tankards, and the matter would be forgotten.

On entering his brother's house, Miguel found his plans for a quiet retreat quickly dashed. Daniel sat smoking a pipe in the front room with Hannah, who appeared lost in thought, oblivious to her husband.

'A word, please,' Daniel said, with a little more urgency than his brother liked. 'I must speak to you for a moment. Leave the room, wife.'

Hannah picked up her glass of mulled wine and retreated to the kitchen, stealing a glance at Miguel. Their eyes locked for an instant, but she turned away first. She always did.

Daniel rose to meet his brother. He held up a few pieces of paper, which looked very much like letters. 'You received these today.'

Miguel took them. The letters appeared on the surface nothing special, but Miguel already recognised the hand on one of them: Joachim.

'That's the one,' Daniel said, noticing Miguel's frown. 'I can see, just from the handwriting, that the letter is written by a Dutchman. I wonder at your receiving such communications, and receiving them in my house as well. Is this some man for whom you broker? You know that these transactions with gentiles are illegal.'

Miguel checked to make certain that letter was unopened, but the seal was of simple wax. It could easily have been broken and sealed again.

'I see nothing wrong with receiving any letter at my place of lodging.' He would soon control all the coffee in Europe; even having this conversation was beneath him. 'Do you suggest that you never have need to communicate with Dutchmen? All your affairs, from your banking to the acquisition of wall paintings, are transacted only with Jews?'

'Of course not. Please don't bombard me with absurdities. But I don't think this letter is of such a nature, and I wish to know what it contains.'

'So do I, but I have not read it.' He leaned forward. 'I wonder if you can say the same. I might remind you that we're no longer in Lisbon,' Miguel said after a moment. 'Here a man need not keep so suspicious an eye on his brother.'

'That's not the point. I charge you to open that letter in my presence, so its contents may be revealed before the community.'

Revealed before the community? Had Daniel grown mad and come to believe that Parido had steered him to a seat on the Ma'amad?

'Shall I translate it for you as well?' Miguel asked. 'Would Portuguese or Spanish be more to your liking?'

'Am I to be upbraided for not speaking the language of gentiles?'

'Of course not. Let us continue our conversation

in Hebrew. I'm sure your mastery of the tongue is superior to mine.'

Daniel began to turn red. 'I think you forget yourself. Now open the letter, if you please, unless you have something to hide.'

'I've nothing more to hide than any man of business,' Miguel returned, unable to choke back the words he knew he could not afford to utter. 'My letters are my own concern.'

'My wife is with child. I won't have strange Dutch letters plaguing her quiet.'

'Of course.' Miguel looked downwards to hide his mirth. His wife's quiet surely existed independent of any Dutch letters that came to the house. 'If you like,' he proposed, knowing he was now being provoking, 'I'll have all my letters directed to a tavern, where it will be the barkeeper's task to protect his own wife's quiet.'

'No,' Daniel answered, too quickly. 'No, perhaps I shouldn't interfere with your business. A man has a right to order his own affairs.'

'You are very kind.' Miguel had not meant for his words to sound quite so bitter.

'I only enquire into your business out of curiosity. Brotherly curiosity, you know. For example, I should love to learn more of this coffee trade you mentioned.'

Miguel felt the tingle of panic. 'I told you, I have no such trade.'

'Let's be open with each other. I'm certain it must be a safe topic within these walls.'

'I have no plans,' Miguel said as he walked away, 'but if you think the coffee trade so promising, I'll be certain to look into it.'

Miguel passed through the kitchen, where Hannah and Annetje busied themselves with moving carrots and leeks from this place to that in an effort to appear as though they had been tending to the meal and not listening at the door.

Once in his cellar, he struck a few candles and then ground some beans with the mortar and pestle he had not yet returned to the kitchen, and which had not yet been missed, and heated some wine. Only once he had poured the mixture into a bowl and allowed it to settle did he break open the letter from Joachim.

Senhor Lienzo,

When we spoke earlier, I may have grown unnecessarily heated. Nevertheless, I think you will agree that my anger is well justified and that you indeed owe me more than you have been willing to admit. Therefore, please accept my regrets. I wish you to know I am glad that we may enter into a matter of business that will serve our mutual interests.
I remain your servant
Joachim Waagenaar

He took a sip of his drink, though he might have been drinking beer for all he noticed the bitterness. Surely this man was far madder than Miguel had imagined. Had Joachim understood nothing of their conversation, even his own part?

After folding the letter and placing it upon the fire, Miguel went through the rest of his correspondence, which included more troubling lines from the Muscovy trader, who, it seemed, had taken to writing twice a day now. Miguel had not the heart to reply to these meddlesome words and, instead, took out his new pamphlet, but the tricks of Charming Pieter held no allure for him.

He set down both pipe and bowl, however, when he heard footsteps upon the stairs. He thought he might have to face Annetje, whose silliness would only irritate him, but instead he saw that Hannah had descended halfway down to the cellar. She held a smoky candle in her hand, and she peered with seeming difficulty into the dimly lit room.

'Are you there, senhor?' she called softly.

Miguel could not think how to reply. Hannah had never before come into the cellar, and that she did so without knocking seemed to him unthinkable. He might have been undressed. He recalled that he had not closed the door, so perhaps Hannah believed that to be a sign of his willingness to receive guests. Such a mistake, he determined, must never again be permitted.

'I'm here, senhora.' He set down his bowl of coffee and moved towards the foot of the stairwell. 'Do you require me?'

'I smelled something strange,' she told him,

taking a few more steps down. 'I wanted to make certain all was well.'

No odour, other than fire or vomit, ought to provoke such a response. The coffee was certainly the culprit. Since he had received the beans of Geertruid, Miguel had grown accustomed to the aroma but recognised that it might smell alien to someone unfamiliar with it.

'Oh, the floor is all wet,' Hannah observed. 'Have you spilled something?'

'It is the canal, senhora. It floods at night.'

'I know,' she said quietly. 'I worry that you'll grow ill.'

'I do well enough, senhora. And it is better to sleep in the damp than in a heated room with no windows. I enquired of a physician.'

'I wanted to see about the odour.' She sounded confused, as though she had taken too much wine. Now that he thought about it, her voice did have a loose, unformed quality. She seemed to be making an effort to say something more, as though she could not bring herself to her topic. He knew she took undue pleasure in his company, that she loved to look upon him and make idle chatter with him, but to descend to the cellar – had she discovered some new boldness?

'There is no need to so trouble yourself, senhora. The smell is nothing but a new kind of tea. I am sorry it disturbed you.'

'A new kind of tea!' she nearly shouted, as though this had been what she had longed to

215

hear. Miguel, however, did not quite believe it. It was more, he thought, as though she had latched on to some opportunity. Hannah now ventured another step, until she hovered only a few inches above the wet. 'Daniel thinks tea a waste of money, but I love it.'

Miguel noticed that Hannah's scarf had come askew and he could see a thick lock of her black hair dangling across her forehead. As a woman who had returned to the Jewish faith only recently, she perhaps did not feel to the depth of her soul the force of the Law that prohibited a married woman from showing her hair to any man but her husband. Miguel had found the injunction strange when he had first arrived in Amsterdam, but he had absorbed its urgency to such a degree that he would hardly have been more shocked had she exposed to him her bare breasts – which were large and of significant interest to him.

As it was, he found this lock of hair strangely exciting. 'Perhaps you might taste it some day,' Miguel said, in rapid words that betrayed his discomfort. His face grew hot, and his pulse quickened. His eyes fixed upon this lock of hair. In an instant, he knew what it must feel like to the touch – smooth and brittle at once – and he could smell its musty aroma. Did she know she so exposed herself? Miguel could hardly think so. He wanted to say something so she might undo the error before Daniel discovered it, but if he were to tell her that she had so disrobed herself, mortification might overwhelm her.

'I'll be happy to share the tea with you some other time,' he told her. 'I hope you will close the door to the room when you depart.'

Hannah could not mistake his meaning. 'I am sorry to have bothered you, senhor.' She retreated up the stairs.

He thought to call out, to say she had not bothered him. He could not let her walk away feeling foolish. But he knew that was precisely what he ought to do. Let her feel foolish. Let her come down here no more. No good could come of it.

Miguel returned to his writing table and finished his drink. He would not allow himself to think about her, having trouble enough without letting thoughts of his brother's wife confuse him. Better he should think of how to extract Joachim Waagenaar from his affairs.

Miguel stumbled upon no solutions though the problem kept him awake. Many hours after the household had fallen into quiet, he slipped up to the attic to awaken Annetje, and only after he had spent himself with her did he find any rest.

From

The Factual and Revealing Memoirs of Alonzo Alferonda

Since Miguel Lienzo developed an interest in the wondrous fruit, I had been meeting him in a little coffee tavern in the Plantage run by a Turk I called Mustafa. This may have been his true name or it may not; I have no way of knowing. It was the name of the Turk in a play I had seen once, and this fellow reminded me of that fictional Muhammadan. If he objected to my calling him by that name, he never told me so.

One afternoon when I met Lienzo I had been fortunate enough to be served a most unusual delicacy by Mustafa. I was sitting and enjoying the drink when Lienzo showed himself most eagerly. He had enlisted my aid in a matter of whale oil, and it had turned out rather well for him.

'I hear you've done well,' I said, as I signalled Mustafa to bring a cup of the strange mixture he'd been brewing. 'How lucky you are to have Alferonda as a friend.'

'I may have done well, but I haven't yet got that money,' Miguel said. 'The broker who bought it, that fellow Ricardo, is refusing to pay me.'

I knew Ricardo, probably better than Miguel did, and I could not have been less surprised. 'What? He's paid you nothing?'

'Nothing. He's promised in a month or so, and meanwhile my Muscovy agent is demanding I pay in full what I borrowed of him.'

'I, for one, advise that a man should always pay his debts, but I have a proprietary interest in these matters.'

Mustafa now set the drink before Miguel. It was served in a little white bowl, not much bigger than a hollowed-out eggshell. The drink inside had a yellow, almost metallic-gold colour, and there was not much of it, for it was very expensive and very rare. Of course, I would not say as much to Miguel. I would pay for his drink.

'What is this?' he asked me.

'You think there is only one kind of coffee? Coffee is like wine: a hundred varieties and flavours. A hundred nations around the world drink it, each with its own preferences, and each has pleasures for the discriminating drinker. My Turkish friend managed to get

219

a small quantity of this treasure from the East Indies, and I convinced him to share it with us.'

Miguel sniffed as cautiously as a cat, and, after saying a blessing, raised the little bowl to his lips. His forehead wrinkled at once. 'Curious,' he said. 'It is muskier than the other coffees I've had, but at the same time thinner. What is it?'

'It's called monkey coffee,' I said. 'There is a particular kind of beast in those tropical forests that eats the coffee fruit. Indeed, it eats only the most perfect berries, and so the locals have learned that a flavourful drink can be made from this creature's droppings.'

Miguel set down the bowl. 'This is made from monkey turds?'

'I would not have put it so boldly, but yes.'

'Alonzo, how can you have fed me this abomination? Besides being disgusting, surely it violates the dietary laws.'

'How so?'

'It comes from a monkey, and monkey flesh may not be eaten.'

'But can monkey turds be eaten? I have never heard of them being forbidden.'

'If we may not eat its flesh, how can we eat its turds?'

'I don't know,' I said with a shrug. 'However, I do know that a chicken is flesh, but its eggs are neither flesh nor dairy. Thus we can conclude that the sages believed that what comes out of a creature's guts may not be of the same quality as the creature itself.'

Miguel pushed the bowl away from him. 'You make a convincing case, but I don't think I'll drink any more shit brew.'

I smiled and sipped at my own bowl. 'I hear that Parido's help is not so valuable as one might hope.'

'Yes,' he said, 'the brandy. There's no way of knowing if he intended for me to lose out or if the change in price caught him by surprise.'

'Of course he intended it. Parido has been your enemy these two years, and when he suddenly declares himself your friend and acts on your behalf, it costs you money. I don't believe in mere happenstance, Miguel. He's shown his colours.'

'I took at least as much from his pocket when I traded on whale oil.'

'That may be,' I observed, 'but if you took that money from his pocket, it has not shown up in yours.'

'Are you saying that Ricardo's client is Parido, that it's he who refuses to pay me?'

221

'It needn't be that direct. Parido could simply be using his influence to keep that money from you. I suggest you press Ricardo a little more forcefully. You can't bring him before the Ma'amad, but you may be able to find other ways to make him yield.'

'Have you any suggestions?'

I shrugged. 'If I think of something. I will be certain to inform you.'

'That's not very helpful. I feel like everything is getting away from me. I earned money in whale oil, but I cannot get it. I begin a trade in coffee, but the world warns me off it.'

'Who has warned you?'

'Isaiah Nunes. And my brother.'

'Nunes trembles at the sound of his shit falling in his chamber pot. You oughtn't let his cowardice affect you. And as for your brother, he is Parido's creature before he is your kin.'

'What are you saying?'

'I'm saying that Parido may know of your trade in coffee and want you to stay away from something that will make you successful. You must remain fast and cling to your purpose.'

'I have no intention of doing otherwise,' he said.

That was precisely what I wanted to hear.

CHAPTER 14

In the kitchen, Annetje chopped onions while Hannah cleaned the sour-smelling fish. She slid the knife into its soft greyish belly, fighting the fish's fibrous resistance, and pushed up with more force than necessary. The fish slid apart easily, and she scraped its innards into a wooden bowl. Annetje would use the guts for a *hutsepot* she made out of ingredients permitted by Jews – *Joodspot*, she called it.

'I've been thinking about your encounter with that old widow,' Annetje said.

Hannah didn't look up from the offal. She had a few coffee beans in her apron, but she did not want to touch them with her fishy fingers. Still, the fruit called out to her. She hadn't eaten one for hours now. Hours. Her supply had been running low, and after her embarrassing visit to Miguel's cellar the night before, she thought she had better make do with what little she had.

'You must not say anything to Senhor Lienzo – Senhor Miguel Lienzo, I mean. Of course you know you should not say anything to your husband.'

'I've been thinking of it as well,' Hannah

223

confessed, 'and I'm not certain I should remain quiet. That woman claims to be his friend. He ought to know she's keeping secrets.'

'People must be permitted their secrets,' Annetje said, this time more generously. She sprinkled a pinch of cinnamon into a bowl of onions. 'You have your secrets, and you are better, your husband is better, and the world is better for your keeping them. Who is to say that the same is not true of the widow?'

There had been a time when these words would have silenced her, but now things were somehow different. 'But we don't *know* that it is true.' Her finger probed the meat under the fish's skin. 'What if she means him harm?'

'I am sure it is nothing we need concern ourselves with, and even if it were, there's nothing to do about it. You don't want her speaking of your secrets, after all.'

Hannah thought about it for a moment. 'But Senhor Miguel is not my husband. He can be trusted to keep silent.'

'You don't know that. You don't know the senhor like I do.'

She closed her eyes. 'Perhaps not.'

Annetje bit into an onion as though it were an apple and chewed with her mouth wide open. Hannah had many times asked her not to eat onions. If Daniel learned that she helped herself so freely to their food, he would lose himself in wrath. 'He's found your behaviour curious. He told me you came to him in the cellar last night with your scarf askew and your hair exposed.'

The girl would see a scarf askew if Hannah used it to strangle her. 'I didn't know it was loose until after I left him.'

'I think he found it exciting,' she said, her mouth full of onion.

'I smelled something in the cellar,' she said.

'And I smell something now, and it's foul. You cannot tell him. He will betray you. He cares more about his devil's religion than he does you, I can promise you that. He thinks you are only a fool girl, and if you speak to him he'll discover how right he is.'

'Why would he think me a fool for trying to help him?'

'Help him nothing. He'll betray you for the pleasure of it. I tell you that you must not trust him. If you do speak to him, I will consider myself betrayed. Do you understand me?'

'I understand you,' Hannah said quietly, thinking only of the coffee in her apron.

The letters started coming in all at once. Miguel had sat in the cellar, lighted two oil lamps, and opened the day's correspondence, hardly daring to hope. But there it was: a letter from a cousin of a friend who now lived in Copenhagen. He didn't understand why Miguel needed to buy at a particular moment on a particular day, but he was none the less willing to comply based on the commission proposed.

Miguel made a celebratory bowl of coffee and read the rest of his letters. Nothing from prospective agents, but the next day he heard from an old acquaintance in Marseilles and a distant cousin's husband in Hamburg. By the middle of the next week he'd heard from three more. A week later produced another four, and surely more on the way. The thing was nearly done. There remained only one major problem to discuss with Geertruid.

She suggested they walk to the Plantage. Miguel thought a visit to the coffee tavern might be in order, but Geertruid had no interest. 'There are things in life besides coffee,' she said. 'You must not forget that I am a Dutchwoman and like to drink great quantities of beer. Staying up all night to look at ledgers and books – that's for Jews.'

They walked along tree-lined paths where bright torches blazed to turn night into day. Handsomely attired couples passed by, wealthy burghers with their beautiful or plain wives, young couples out to gaze upon the fashionable life, cleverly disguised thieves. Back in Lisbon, these happy pleasure-seekers would have been well born and of old families, but these were new men, merchants of the Exchange and their pretty wives, the daughters of merchants.

Miguel took Geertruid's arm in his, and they strolled as though they were married. But even if he had a wife, could he take her to the verdant paths of the Plantage? No, she would remain at home with the children, and Geertruid would still be the woman upon his arm.

Geertruid raised her eyes and smiled at her friend; she seemed to like nothing more than to stroll with him on such nights. She had worn one of her most handsome gowns, all dark blues and reds. 'Where do things stand?' she asked. 'Tell me all the wonderful tidings. Delight me with tales of our impending wealth.'

'Things stand quite well,' Miguel told her. 'As soon as you have transferred the money to my account, dear woman, I'll be able to pay my East Indian merchant for the coffee. From that time on, we have to make certain we've contacted our agents and orchestrated the plan perfectly before the goods arrive. I estimate two months.'

'Two months,' she repeated dreamily. 'Two months, and we'll have accomplished all you say? You speak of it as though you anticipated trout for your dinner.'

'Well, I like trout.' He looked at her, her face aglow in the torchlight, dim enough to hide the imperfections of age.

They stopped to look at a sloppily erected stage where the players performed some adventures of the Sea Beggars, maritime rebels who fought off the Spanish tyrants to win the United Provinces their freedom. Miguel had never bothered to learn the names of the celebrated heroes or the pivotal battles, but Geertruid became absorbed instantly. They watched for a quarter-hour, and

Geertruid clapped and cheered with the crowd, losing herself in girlish glee as the players spoke of the miraculous storm that saved the town of Leiden from the Spanish. Then she decided she'd seen enough and began to walk again.

'I must still coordinate with our agents for the exchanges,' he continued, after a moment.

'And do you have your agents selected?'

Miguel nodded. 'I have contacts at this very moment in Marseilles, Hamburg, Vienna, Antwerp, Paris and Copenhagen. A cousin of a friend of mine at this moment is in Rotterdam, but he plans to return to London, and I'll make arrangements with him soon enough. I can handle the business in Amsterdam myself. Still, I foresee a few problems.'

'Only a few problems,' Geertruid said thoughtfully. 'That's wonderful. It is utterly wonderful. I should have thought there might be countless problems, but you have managed things so handsomely. It is a great comfort to me.'

Miguel smiled at her. He looked at her lips, wondering if he saw a vaguely ironic smirk. 'Nevertheless, you might wish to hear the nature of those problems.'

'I have every confidence in you, but if you wish to speak of problems, I'll certainly listen.'

Miguel cleared his throat. 'I am concerned about my ability to establish agents in the Iberian exchanges: Lisbon, Madrid and perhaps Oporto. I have not continued to trade there, and many of my former contacts there have fled to places of safety. Indeed, the contacts I have in Marseilles, Hamburg and Antwerp are all refugees as I am – men I knew in Lisbon.'

'Can't you make new contacts? You're an amicable enough fellow.'

'I'm still exploring that possibility, but doing so is difficult. When dealing with those nations, a man such as myself must conceal his true name and not let it be known that he is of the Hebrew faith. To reveal that would invite rejection, for any man, whether a Secret Jew or no, would fear to do business with a known Jew. Should the Inquisition learn of his activities, it wouldn't hesitate to punish him for suspicion of being a Judaiser.'

'That sounds like a rotten business.'

'The Inquisition funds itself by confiscating the property of those they convict. That makes merchants especially attractive to evil Inquisitors.'

'Can we proceed without those exchanges? After all, how many do we need?'

'We might perhaps fare well without Oporto, and even Lisbon, though I should hate to risk it. We must, however, have Madrid. Coffee has gained some small favour in the Spanish court, which acquires its fruit through the Madrid bourse. If we lose Madrid, the project fails.'

'Whatever shall we do?' Her voice was high and youthful, as though she tested Miguel to learn the depth of his concern.

'There are always manoeuvres and schemes in

the world of trade. It is all thrust and parry, and it's not such an impossible thing to perform a little alchemy and make leaden problems turn to golden opportunities.'

'I know you know your business, so I'll not worry unless you tell me to worry.'

Miguel began to turn left upon the path, but Geertruid pulled him right. She had some destination in mind but offered no more hint than the slightest of smirks. 'How soon do you think you can have the money transferred to my account?' he asked her.

'Should we not wait? If this situation with Madrid does not resolve itself, and we have purchased the goods, shall we not be the losers for it?'

'It cannot happen,' he assured her – and himself.

They had now arrived at a wooden house, far more handsomely put together than most. Geertruid led him inside to a well-lit space decorated with sturdy wooden furniture. Drunken Dutchmen, perhaps a dozen of them, staggered about, and almost as many pretty girls in close-fitting dresses served tankards and whispered into ears. Geertruid had taken him to a brothel.

'What do we here?' he asked her.

'Oh, I thought you a little lonely, and I have heard such tales about a lass at this place – they made me quite blush – and I wanted you to sample the goods for yourself.'

'I thought,' he said, with a mockingly stern

voice, 'that we were to spend the evening together, discussing our business concerns.'

'You may pretend you are with me if you like,' she told him. 'But as to business, I think we have concluded our talk.'

An eager-looking woman now appeared at Miguel's side and took his other arm. She was small in height, and slightly built, but with a charmingly round face and full lips. 'This must be the gentleman you spoke of,' she said to Geertruid. 'He is a fine one indeed.'

'Senhor, this charming creature is called Agatha, and I hope you will treat her as kindly as I would want to be treated myself.'

Miguel laughed. 'If only I knew how kind that was.'

Geertruid tossed her head, a sort of shrug.

'I think we should conclude our conversation first, before I take your generous gift.' He smiled at the girl so she would not feel unappreciated.

'You are a mighty man to keep your mind upon business with two beauties on your arm,' Agatha observed.

'You need only tell me when I can expect the money to be transferred, and we may forget the matter for tonight.'

'Very well.' Geertruid sighed. 'I see you are not to be put off. All the more lucky for our friend Agatha, who they say likes a determined fellow. I can transfer the money before the end of the week if need be.'

Miguel had been sneaking a gaze at Agatha's lively brown eyes, but he turned quickly to Geertruid. 'So soon? You already have it?'

Geertruid pressed her lips together in a smile. 'Surely you don't think my words have been all wind. You asked me to raise the money, and I have done so.'

'If you have raised it, why did you not tell me? I should think after securing that kind of capital – no easy trick – would you not feel more celebratory?'

'Indeed I do. Are we not celebrating here tonight?'

Miguel had been in trade long enough to know when someone lied to him, and badly too. He held himself absolutely still, afraid to move until he had thought this thing through. Why would Geertruid lie? Two reasons: she did not truly have the money, or she did have the money, but its source was not what she had earlier said.

Miguel had not realised he had been quiet for so long until he saw both women staring at him. 'You can transfer this week?'

'That's what I say. Why have you turned so dour? You have your money and you have a woman. What more could any man desire?'

'Not a thing,' he said, breaking free of their hold and placing a hand on both of their soft rumps. It was a freedom he would not have normally taken with Geertruid, but she had taken one with him, so why not return the favour? As for her lie, he would think no more of it tonight. Geertruid had her reasons, and she had her secrets. Miguel was content to live with them.

'I think the senhor would rather you than me,' Agatha said to Geertruid.

Something flashed across the widow's face. 'I think you'll soon discover what the senhor likes, my dear. He has something of a reputation.'

Agatha led him to a back room, where Miguel soon found he hardly thought at all about Geertruid's lies and what she might wish to conceal from so great a friend.

Among his letters the next day, Miguel found a favourable note from his prospective agent in Frankfurt. He read the letter through with satisfaction and then tore open the next, this one from the Muscovy trader. He politely explained that Miguel still owed him a sum approaching nineteen hundred guilders and that, as he knew of Miguel's past difficulties, he could not let the matter rest. 'I must demand immediate payment of half this debt, or I am afraid I shall have no choice but to allow the courts to decide how I might most effectively see my money.' *The courts* meant another public humiliation before the Bankruptcy Board, which would mean exposing both his connection to Geertruid and his coffee scheme.

Miguel swore, drank a bowl of coffee, and began his search of the most likely taverns. Luck was on

233

his side that day, for he found Ricardo in the third place he looked, sitting alone, sullenly drinking a tankard of beer.

'No business today?' Miguel asked.

'As to business,' Ricardo answered, without looking up, 'you should mind your own.'

Miguel sat across from him. 'Make no mistake. This *is* my business, senhor. You owe me a great deal of money, and if you think I'm content to do nothing you are mistaken.'

Ricardo, at last, deigned to look up. 'Don't threaten me, Lienzo. You dare not go to the Dutch courts without risking the anger of the Ma'amad, and we both know that if you go to the Ma'amad you run the risk of a ruling against you, a ruling that could tie up your money for months or years. You have no choice but to be patient, so get you gone before you anger me and I obstruct you even further.'

Miguel swallowed hard. What had he been thinking, coming here? Ricardo was right: he had nothing with which to threaten him – except, maybe, a public airing. 'Perhaps I'll take my chances with the Ma'amad,' he said. 'If I don't get my money, I'll be no worse off than I am now, and I can use a hearing as a public forum to expose you for the blackguard you are. More than that, I can expose your master. Indeed, the more I think about it, the more appealing this becomes to me. The other *parnassim* are only swayed by him because they think him scrupulous. If they learn about his tricks, he'll lose power.'

'I don't know what you are talking about,' Ricardo said, but he looked worried. 'I am my own master.'

'You work for Solomon Parido. He is the only one who might arrange this outrage, and I intend to expose it. If the money you owe me is not in my account by the close of business tomorrow, you can be sure I will seek justice.'

Miguel left without waiting for a reply, certain he had done what could be done, but by the end of business the next day, no money had been deposited in his account. Miguel realised he had no choice. He could not risk a court appearance that would look into his funds, so he transferred just over nine hundred guilders of Geertruid's money into the agent's accounts. He would worry about how to make up the money some other time.

CHAPTER 15

The Exchange heaved and pulsated around Miguel as he sought out an East India Company broker. Only half an hour ago a rumour had come sweeping through with the might of a collapsing building: a powerful trading combination plotted to sell off a large portion of its East India shares. Often enough, when a combination wished to buy, it would circulate rumours that it wished to do just the opposite, and the force of those rumours would drive prices down. Those who had invested with the idea of very short turnarounds would dump their stock at once.

Miguel had been plying his trade on the Exchange long enough to know how to use these rumours to his advantage. Whether or not they were based on truth, whether the combination intended to buy or sell, made no difference. Such were the riches of the Orient that East India Company stock always – always – rebounded from a dip, and only a fool refrained from buying during a frenzy. Miguel had fortified himself that morning with three bowls of coffee. Rarely had he felt so awake, so eager.

This madness could not have come at a more propitious time.

Buyers and sellers pushed through the crowd frantically, each screaming for his contacts as the usual cacophony of the Exchange rose to near-maddening levels. A rotund little Dutchman had his hat knocked off in the fray and, after watching it trampled, hurried away, content to lose something worth a few guilders rather than risk losing thousands. The men who dealt in diamonds, tobacco, grain and other such items, and who shunned speculative trade, stood by, shaking their heads at the disruption of their business.

The value of East India shares were traded based on the percentage of their original value. The shares had opened that morning at just over 400 per cent. Miguel found a broker and laid out five hundred guilders he did not have, buying when the price dropped to 378. He assured his agent that the money could be found in his Exchange bank account, though he knew that he could afford to spend no more of that money on his own trade.

Once he had his shares in hand, Miguel moved towards the edge of the trading cluster to monitor the change in prices. He then noticed Solomon Parido, who also appeared to be buying company stock. Upon seeing Miguel, he sauntered over.

'These combinations,' the *parnass* said loudly, to make himself heard above the noise. 'Without them there would be no market. They keep commerce moving in and out like the tides.'

Miguel nodded, paying less attention to the *parnass* than to the sellers calling out their prices. The shares had dropped again and were now selling at 374.

Parido put a hand upon Miguel's shoulder. 'I hear rumours, Senhor Lienzo, that things are on a new footing with you – that you have something planned.'

'Sometimes a man may not desire to be the subject of rumours,' Miguel told him, with a smile he hoped looked genuine. 'And now may not be such a good time to talk of this.' He gestured towards the crowd of East India stock dealers. He heard a cry of 376.

'Pay that no mind. East India stocks go up and down so fast it hardly matters what a man buys or sells this day or that. Surely you wouldn't want to insult a *parnass* by refusing to speak with him because of this mayhem.'

Miguel heard a call to buy for 381, more than he had paid, but not enough to think about selling. 'I must be able to conduct my affairs,' he said, trying to keep his voice calm.

'I find it odd that you don't want to know the subject of these rumours. On the Ma'amad I've learned that when a man does not ask with what he is charged, he is invariably guilty.'

'That's in the Ma'amad's chamber, not on the Exchange, when that man is attempting to conduct his business. And I've not been charged with anything.'

'Even so,' Parido said.

The price dipped once more to 379, and Miguel felt the tug of panic. Not to worry, he assured himself. He had seen these dips before in moments of frenzy, and they would last only a few minutes. He had a moment to spare for this nonsense with Parido, but just a moment. Yet he could not quite stay calm. 'Then tell me what you have heard,' Miguel said.

'That you are upon some new venture. Something in the coffee-fruit trade.'

Miguel waved a hand dismissively. 'This coffee rumour plagues me. Maybe I should involve myself lest I disappoint so many eager devourers of rumour.'

Miguel heard new calls to sell. 378. 376.

'You're not trading in coffee?'

'I wish I were, senhor. I long to undertake a trade of so much interest to men like you – and my brother.'

Parido frowned. 'It is a terrible sin, punishable by the *cherem*, to lie to a *parnass*.'

Before he could check himself, the indignation, fed by coffee, became his master. 'Do you threaten me, senhor?'

'We have a history filled with mistrust, have we not, Lienzo? I have spoken ill of you in the past, but remember that you have spoken ill of me as well. You must know that I have been more than willing to forgive your actions with my daughter and with the maid and her child.'

'The child wasn't mine and you know it,' Miguel blurted out.

'Nor mine,' Parido said, with a thin smile. 'Nor anyone else's either. I know about your little trick with the whore. A few coins pressed in her hand, and she told me everything. I've known it for more than a year. And yet I have never brought forward that information. I've never used it to harm you, and now I never can, for how could I explain knowing something of such importance and keeping it secret all this time? Is that not proof enough that I am not the enemy you think I am?'

Miguel could think of nothing clever to say. 'You have been very judicious, senhor,' he managed, in a croaking voice.

'I believe *kind* is more the word, but I would hate for my kindness to be misunderstood. It hasn't been misunderstood, has it?'

What in the devil was he talking about? 'No.'

'Good.' Parido patted Miguel on the back. 'I see you're upset, so we'll continue this conversation another time. If you have no interest in coffee, that is the end of it. But if I learn that you have lied to me in this, that you have turned me away when I offer you friendship, you'll discover you have angered the wrong man.'

Miguel spun around and heard a buyer call for shares at 402. What had happened since 378? Miguel had no choice other than to sell what he had rather than risk a sudden dip and lose everything.

Within two days the price rose to 423, but Miguel had done little more with his shares than break even.

Isaiah Nunes looked half drunk. More than half drunk, Miguel decided. He looked fully drunk and half asleep. They sat in the Flyboat drinking thin Provençal wine, and Miguel began to get the feeling that he was boring his friend.

'He comes to me and speaks of friendship, but he does all in his power to confuse me and prevent me from going about my trade.'

Nunes raised one eyebrow. 'Perhaps you had best keep your distance from Parido.'

'That is sound advice,' Miguel said, 'but I have hardly been chasing after him. Both he and my brother hound me about coffee, yet they seem to know nothing of my plans.'

'I told you to stay away from coffee.'

'I don't need to stay away from coffee. I need to stay away from Parido and my brother. And I need a man or two in Iberia.'

'Well, they're hard to come by these days, I hear.'

'You must have contacts,' Miguel suggested.

Nunes raised his head slightly. 'What do you mean, precisely?'

'What I mean is that if you know someone who can act as my agent in Iberia, I would be grateful if you would write to this person and tell him to expect to hear from me.'

Nunes began to shake his head. 'What are you doing, Miguel? You tell me that Parido is troubling you, looking to pry into your business, and you want to involve me? I won't risk Parido's anger, or even his notice. He hardly recognises me when he sees me on the street, and I prefer it that way.'

'You already are involved,' Miguel reminded him. 'You're the one who is bringing my coffee into Amsterdam.'

'And I regret having agreed to do it,' he said. 'Ask no more of me.'

'You won't put me in touch with your man in Lisbon?'

'I have no man in Lisbon.' Nunes drained his glass.

Four days later, Miguel found himself in need of a piss on a horsedrawn barge heading to Rotterdam. Geertruid had not lied when she said that coffee would provoke urine. And here he was, his bladder full, and nowhere to piss but in the canal. There were women on this boat, and though a Dutchman would do his business without a second thought, Miguel could not bring himself to expose his alien member so freely. He did not need a group of strange Dutch women staring and pointing at his circumcised anatomy.

Just another hour to Rotterdam, he told himself. His old associate Fernando de la Monez would be soon leaving that city and heading back to London, where he lived, as he had in Lisbon, as a Secret Jew.

No amount of money would ever serve as incentive for Miguel to once more take to worshipping in darkened rooms, groping in ignorance for some semblance of Jewish ritual, all the while knowing that the world outside would see you dead before permitting this hidden and undignified exercise of faith. In his letters Fernando had insisted that things were not quite so bad in London. There, he said, men of business knew him and his compatriots to be Jews, but they didn't mind so long as they were discreet in their practice.

There were perhaps a dozen or so other people on the long bright-red boat, drawn steadily along by a team of horses that clopped steadily on the side of the canal. It was of a flat design, more like a raft than a boat, but it was sturdy and included a hut-like structure in the centre where passengers might take shelter during the rains. Miguel had been on larger horse-drawn boats, some so large that a tap man sold the passengers beer and pastries, but this conveyance was too small for such amenities.

Miguel paid the other travellers no mind; he hid from the mist in the muted light of the enclosed area and attempted to distract himself from his bladder with a tale of Charming Pieter. It was one he had read many times, concerning the cruel owners of a country estate who had robbed their tenants of their crops. Pieter and Mary pretend to be regents interested in purchasing the land, and once they gain the owners' trust, they rob them in the night, stopping on their way out of the village to return to the peasants what belongs to them.

Miguel had already looked through his pamphlet twice by the time the boat arrived, and he wasted no time in finding a private spot to take care of his pressing concerns. Once relieved of distractions, he felt free to take in the city. In many ways, Rotterdam was like a smaller, neater version of Amsterdam. He had visited there often enough to know how to navigate, and he found the tavern Fernando had specified with little difficulty. There, he and his friend met and discussed the particulars of Fernando's duties in London's exchange. Fernando seemed puzzled by Miguel's insistence that the trades take place at a particular time, but he agreed none the less, once Miguel assured him that nothing he did would in any way bring suspicion upon him or the fragile community of Jews in London.

It grew late by the time they had finished, and Miguel accepted Fernando's offer to remain in Rotterdam, where he attended evening prayers at the small synagogue and then took the morning boat to Amsterdam. He settled into his wooden bench on the boat and closed his eyes, thinking of what tasks remained to him before he could consider the coffee-fruit scheme in hand. In the cool of the morning he fell asleep, he knew not how long, and awoke from a hazy dream with a loud mutter. Embarrassed, he looked around to see who had heard him. A quick glance told him he recognised no one, and he almost turned back to his thoughts before something caught his eye. He looked again. In the back of the boat, quietly engaged in private conversation, he saw a pair of finely dressed gentlemen. Miguel dared take only a passing glance, but it was enough for him to see they wore beards. True, they were cut very short, but beards all the same. One man was particularly dark, and his closely shorn facial hair crept like a black fungus halfway down his throat. Any Dutchman would shave such a thing away. The only man who would wear his beard thus was a Jew – one trying hard not to look Jewish.

There could be no mistake about it. These were Ma'amad spies.

CHAPTER 16

When the boat reached Amsterdam, Miguel walked a short distance out of his way to see if the two men would follow him, but after huddling together in a brief meeting of bobbing heads they both walked off towards the Exchange. Miguel stood for a few minutes by the canal and gazed at the overcast sky before buying a pear from an old woman with a pushcart. It tasted mealy, like parsley root, and after one bite he threw it down on the road. The woman urged her wobbling cart along, determined not to notice Miguel's displeasure, while two filthy boys lunged for the remains. Rolling the taste of bad pear around in his mouth for a moment, Miguel decided that the day was too far gone for there to be much to do on the Exchange, so he headed home.

The spies had disordered him, and he kept turning around, searching for signs of treachery in beggars and servants and burghers as they strolled along the streets. This is no way to live, he told himself; he could not spend his days jumping at every shadow. But just when he had convinced himself to be calm, he crossed the bridge into the Vlooyenburg and saw Hannah in the middle of the street – despite the veil, Miguel recognised her instantly – and, alongside her, Annetje. And Joachim Waagenaar.

Joachim had backed them into a corner. There was nothing threatening in his gestures, and he appeared calm. A passing stranger might not have noticed anything odd – although it would have been unusual for a veiled woman to speak casually with so low a man.

Annetje saw Miguel first. Her face brightened and she sucked in her breath; her bosoms heaved in the pretty blue bodice that matched her handsome cap.

'Oh, Senhor Lienzo!' she exclaimed. 'Save us from this madman!'

Miguel answered in Portuguese, addressing Hannah. 'Has he harmed you?'

Speechless, she shook her head no.

Then the stench hit him. The wind must have shifted, for the smell drifted in his direction. Miguel felt himself overwhelmed. The Dutch were a fastidiously, even recklessly, clean people, washing themselves far more frequently than was healthy for the body. Joachim had clearly abandoned the practice; he smelled more foul than the least washed Portuguese peasant. It was more than odours of the body, too, but smells of urine and vomit and – it took Miguel an instant – rotted meat. How does a man smell of rotten meat?

He shook his head, trying to break the numbing

effect of the stench. 'Hurry home,' he told Hannah. 'Speak of this to no one. And keep the girl quiet.' They began to ease away from Joachim. 'Be sure she knows to hold her tongue,' he said to Hannah, 'or I'll turn her out.'

He turned to Joachim. 'Step back.'

To Miguel's relief, he did so. The women slipped past him, pressing their backs against the wall to increase as much as they could the distance between themselves and the Dutchman. As soon as they had cleared him, they hurried into a brisk walk.

'Let's go,' Miguel demanded. 'Across the bridge. Now.'

Again Joachim obeyed, like a servant who has been caught by his master at something naughty. Miguel looked around to see if anyone he knew had witnessed the encounter and muttered a prayer in thanks to the Holy One, blessed be He, that the spies had not followed him home and that this disaster had happened during the hours of the Exchange, when any man who might wish him ill was off attending to business.

Once they had crossed the bridge over the Houtgracht, Miguel led Joachim to a little thicket of trees by the canal where they could speak unobserved.

'Have you nothing left of your former self? How dare you approach my brother's wife?' Miguel shifted his position to put himself downwind of Joachim, lessening the stench a bit.

Joachim hardly looked at him. Instead he watched a duck that pecked at the ground near their feet, oblivious to the two men. 'Why do you go on about your brother's wife? I approached your whore too, don't forget,' he said. 'She is a luscious one, senhor. Do you think she'd have me? She seems to me the sort who'd take to just about anyone.'

Miguel sucked in a breath. 'Don't let me see you bother anyone of my family again. Don't let me see you in the Vlooyenburg.'

As if he had never existed, the soft-spoken compliant Joachim was replaced by the angry one. 'Or what should happen? Tell me what you will do, senhor, if you find me upon your streets, talking with your neighbours, telling tales. Tell me, what will you do?'

Miguel let out a sigh. 'Surely you want something. You didn't come to the Vlooyenburg because you have nothing better to do with your time.'

'As it happens, I have nothing better to do with my time. I have proposed that we engage together in some business or other, but you've rejected my proposals and made sport of me.'

'No one has made sport of you,' Miguel said, after a moment. 'And as to this matter of business, I hardly know what you mean. You wish me to set you up in some project, but I know not what that would be. I can't even think of what I might do to satisfy you, and I have far too much to do to take the time to puzzle out your meaning.'

'But that's my very point. You have much to do, but I have so little. I thought perhaps your brother's wife or her pretty servant might feel the same way – a little too much time, which our preachers tell us is the source of much evil in the world. People take their time, and they use it to think and do evil instead of using it to think and do good. It occurred to me that I might help you by giving your family a chance to do good works through charity.'

'I was under the impression that salvation through works was a Catholic principle, not one of the Reformed Church.'

'Oh, you Jews are so clever. You know every-thing. But, still, there's value in charity, senhor. I begin to believe that you have not acted in good faith in our plans to engage upon a business venture, and so my mind must, in the absence of other options, turn to charity. Ten guilders would go a long way towards removing me from the Vlooyenburg.'

Miguel pulled back, disgusted. Joachim's stench hovered thick in the air. 'And if I haven't ten guil-ders to give you?' He folded his arms, determined to be put upon no longer.

'If you haven't the money, senhor, anything might happen.' He flashed his hideous grin.

Bravery and prudence might not always appear to be compatible virtues, Miguel told himself as he opened his purse, and a wise man knows when to bow to circumstance. Charming Pieter himself might have preferred to take his revenge another time. But Miguel did not know if his pride could stomach Pieter's philosophy in this instance.

He briefly considered giving him more than ten guilders. The funds Geertruid had given him had already diminished significantly, what mattered if they diminished more? What if he were to pay Joachim a hundred guilders right now, even two hundred? When offered the coin, Joachim might think himself content with so little. A hundred guilders and no more, Joachim. Surely a man in his condition would not turn away a hundred guilders.

Maybe the reasonable man Miguel had once known was truly lost, but was it not possible that money could be the thing to restore him? Perhaps he was like the woman in an old tale who needed only a magical shoe or ring to return her to her former beauty. Give Joachim a bath, a good meal and a soft bed to sleep on, and hope for the future, and would he wake up himself?

'If you came to me like a decent man,' Miguel said at last, 'and only asked me for the money in a humble way, I would help you. But these tricks of yours make me disinclined. Go away. The next time I see you here, I'll beat you senseless.'

'Do you know what makes me smell so wretched?' Joachim demanded, his voice growing loud and shrill. Without waiting for an answer, he reached into his pocket and pulled out a lump of something grey and slick and – it took Miguel a moment to see that it was not merely a trick of his eyes – moving. 'It's rotten chicken flesh. I put it in my pocket to offend you and your ladies.' He laughed and threw the meat upon the ground.

Miguel stepped back.

'You would be surprised how quickly a poor man learns where to buy maggoty flesh and sour milk. Empty bellies must be filled with something, though my dainty goodwife has no love of rancid victuals. Come.' Joachim took a step closer. He held out his right hand, which was still slick from the meat. 'Let us shake upon our new friendship.'

'Get gone.' Miguel hated to cringe but he would not touch the man's flesh.

'I'll go when I choose. If you don't shake my hand like a man of honour, I'll be insulted. And if I'm insulted, I may have to do something that will harm you for ever.'

Miguel clenched his teeth until they began to ache. He hadn't the energy to spare in wondering when Joachim, in his madness, might decide to tell his story before the Ma'amad. But giving the fool money would not help. He'd drink it and then demand more. Miguel's only choice was to give him nothing and hope for the best.

'Go now,' Miguel said quietly, 'before I lose hold of my anger.'

Miguel turned, wanting to hear no reply, but Joachim's quiet parting words echoed in his ears as he walked home. 'I've only just begun to take hold of mine.'

Miguel slammed the door upon his return, sending a ripple through the house and through Hannah's body. She had been sitting in the drawing room, drinking hot wine. Annetje had tried to comfort her by insisting that she calm herself – though Hannah had shown no signs of agitation – and by assuring her that she did not want to have to slap her.

She knew he would come for her. He would come for her and calm her, attempt to placate her, silence her as the widow had. That was all they wanted from her, and at least, she thought, silence was something she knew how to provide.

After a moment, he entered the room. He offered her a hapless smile in an effort to appear at ease. His black suit was disordered, as though he had been exerting himself, and his hat sat askew on his head. What was more, his eyes had turned reddish, almost as though he had been crying, which Hannah considered unlikely. She knew that sometimes, when he grew intensely angry, a redness spread across his eyes like blood poured into a bucket of milk.

Miguel then turned to Annetje, his expression hard, silently asking her to leave. Hannah tried to hide her smile. At least someone dared to be harsh to the girl.

The moment Annetje stood, however, Miguel went after her. Outside the drawing room, in the front hall, Hannah could hear Miguel whispering to her in rapid Dutch. She couldn't understand the muffled words, but she sensed that he was giving her instructions, explaining something very carefully, listening to the girl repeat everything back to him.

Miguel returned, sat down in a chair across from Hannah, and leaned forward, hands pressing on his thighs. He appeared somewhat more orderly now. Perhaps he had straightened his clothes in the hall or corrected his hat in the mirror. The buoyant handsomeness that had drained from his appearance had been restored.

'I trust you are unharmed, senhora.'

'Yes, I am unharmed,' she said quietly. Her voice sounded strange in her own mouth. So long had she been thinking about what he would say, and what she would answer, that speaking at all had an unreal quality.

He leaned forward. 'Did the fellow say anything to you?'

She shook her head as she spoke. 'Nothing of consequence.' It was true enough. He had talked to her softly in thickly accented Portuguese, but his words had been nonsensical, hard to understand. They were about his suffering, much like any beggar might speak, and it had been hard to concentrate, with the wretched odour wafting from his body.

Miguel leaned back now in an effort to appear at ease. 'Do you have a question for me?'

Yes, she thought. *May I have more coffee berries?* Her supply had run out that morning, and she had meant to raid Miguel's secret sack before he returned, but the girl had not let her alone, and then came the business with the beggar on the street. She'd eaten no coffee in more than a day, and her desire for it made her head ache.

'I don't understand,' she said, after a moment.

'Would you like to know who he is?'

'I assumed,' she said cautiously, 'he was some beggar or other, senhor. I have no need to learn more.' Had she not secrets enough already?

'Yes, that's right,' he told her. 'He *is* a beggar of sorts.'

Something unspoken remained in the air. 'But you know him?'

'He is no one of consequence,' Miguel said rapidly.

She remained silent for a moment, to prove to him that she was calm. 'I do not wish to pry. I know how my husband hates it when I pry, but I wonder if I have anything to fear from him.' And then, because she found his silence frustrating, 'Should we tell my husband?'

'No,' Miguel said. He stood and began to pace about the room. 'You must not tell your husband or anyone else. Do not make more of this incident than is necessary.'

'I don't understand you, senhor,' she said, studying the tiles upon the floor.

'He is but a madman.' Miguel waved his arms about. 'The city has an endless store of these wretches. You'll never see him again, and so there is no need to alarm your husband.'

'I pray you are right.' Her voice sounded whiny and weak, and she hated herself for it.

Just then Annetje returned with a platter in her hands upon which she had balanced two bowls of a dark liquid. Steam poured off from them like twin chimneys. The maid set down the tray and paused to glare at Miguel before departing.

Miguel laughed after she had left. 'She thinks I'm poisoning you.'

What would the widow say? 'There are two bowls, senhor. You are too wise a man to poison yourself as well.'

Miguel cocked his head slightly. 'This is the new tea you smelled the other night. It is made of a medicinal fruit from the Orient.' He took his seat once more. 'It will enhance your understanding.'

Hannah did not think she wanted her understanding enhanced. She felt she understood well enough, all she was capable of understanding. Unless the drink imparted knowledge and wisdom also, it would hardly do her any service. 'You drink as well, but I don't believe senhor needs his understanding enhanced.'

He laughed. 'The drink has its own pleasures.' He handed her a bowl.

Hannah gripped it in both hands and smelled it. It was familiar, like something from a dream. Then she took a sip, and knowledge flowed into her. This was coffee – glorious, glorious coffee – here before her, like a gift from the heavens.

She understood so much now. It was a tea, not

a food. She had been eating what she should have been drinking. In its liquid state it filled her with a glowing warmth, a comfort she had not known for years. 'It's wonderful,' she breathed. And it was. It filled an emptiness inside her, the way she had imagined love would when she'd been younger. 'It's wonderful,' she murmured again, and took another sip to hide the moisture in her eyes.

Miguel laughed again, but this time he seemed less superior. 'The first time I tasted it, I almost spat it out from the bitterness. How strange that you should like it so. I hope you are not only saying so to be polite.'

She shook her head no and took another cautious sip, lest he see her gulp it. She wanted to drink the entire bowl at once and demand more, but she could not let him see how much she loved this thing that she should not know at all.

'I am not being polite,' she said.

They sat together in silence for some time, sipping and not quite looking at each other, until Hannah felt the urge to speak. It was as though something had broken inside of her, some kind of restraint. She wanted to stand up and walk around the room and speak. She did not stand, but she did at last decide to say something.

'I believe you are trying to distract me, senhor. Do you treat me to this new tea so I shall forget the strange man who spoke to me?'

She almost put a hand to her mouth. She ought never to have said such a thing. It was precisely the kind of sauciness her father would have answered with a slap. But it was said, and there was nothing to do but see what happened now.

Miguel looked at her and something flashed across his face, something Hannah found pleasing. 'I did not mean to distract you. I only wished to – to share this with you.'

'You are generous,' she said, astonished by her own boldness before the words had even passed her lips. Could she not control herself now? Had some demon taken her body from her?

'You think me elusive,' he said, looking upon her as though she were some new discovery of natural science, 'but I'll tell you all. You see, that man is a terrible villain. He has a daughter whom he wishes to marry to a very old and mean merchant, a miser of the worst sort. He arranged that her true love should be abducted by pirates, but he learned of the incident and fled. The daughter has fled too, so the miser, knowing that I am friends with the lovers, came to try to force me to give him their location.'

Hannah laughed, loud enough that this time she felt obliged to place a hand over her mouth. 'This tragedy of yours would play prettily upon the stage.'

For a moment she wished her father – or anyone else – was there to slap her. How could she have spoken so pertly? Nevertheless, it was true. Miguel's lie sounded like the stage plays she had seen, with some regularity, back in Lisbon. Some men took their wives to the Jewish theatre here in Amsterdam, but Daniel thought it improper for a woman.

Her foot rotated back and forth like a pigeon by a baker's stall searching for crumbs. This coffee is not a drink of the mind, she realised, it is a drink of the body. And the mouth. And it made her want to say all sorts of things: *I find you remarkably attractive. How I wish I could have married you instead of your cold brother.*

She said none of them. She still could censor herself.

'You don't believe me, senhora?'

'I believe you must imagine me to be remarkably foolish to accept your tale.' The words seemed to come out on their own. Her parents had always taught her to be mild. Her husband had indicated with a thousand unsaid words that he would tolerate only mildness from her. Yet she did not feel mild. She had never felt mild, but she had never before forgotten to act mild.

The coffee, she told herself. Miguel has, knowingly or not, bewitched me and perhaps himself. How long until they began to shout insults at each other or fell into an unrestrained embrace?

There was no point putting the blame on coffee. The drink had not bewitched her, no more than a glass of wine could cast a magic spell. It made her eager, in the same way wine rendered her calm. This sauciness, this pertness that grew inside her mouth came not from witchery but from herself.

259

The coffee drink only let her bad behaviour out.

In recognising the truth, in admitting it to herself, much became clear to her, but nothing so much as a resolution: she would be pert and saucy every chance she had.

For the nonce, however, she had her most distressing encounter to contend with, and no amount of coffee or wine or any other tea she could think of would make the true terror she had felt any less real. She found Miguel's efforts to deceive her both charming and infuriating. 'I know that the world does not work the way it does in plays, and that misers do not send their daughter's lovers into the hands of pirates.' She paused. 'Nevertheless, you can depend on me to keep your secret.'

Miguel leaned back and looked at Hannah as though seeing her for the first time. He glanced at her face, her neck; his eyes lingered at the swell of her breasts concealed in her high-necked gown. Men often thought women had no idea of what their eyes studied, but a woman knew, as surely as though a glance left a handprint.

He had looked at her before, of course. She had sensed that he admired her face and her shape, but this glance was something different. Miguel and men like him rarely thought much of the women they admired and bedded. A woman was an object, sometimes to be consumed like food, other times to be admired like a painting. Miguel now saw her as something more, and the idea thrilled her.

'I trust and believe your promise of silence,' he told her, 'so I'll tell you the truth. The man you saw has an old grudge against me for a wrong that was none of my doing, and he wishes to ruin me. He understands the ways of our community well enough to know how to ruin with whispers as easily as with deeds, and that is why you must not speak of what happened.'

He had entrusted her with the truth, and she still betrayed him with her silence. 'Then I won't speak of it,' she said, her voice hardly above a whisper.

'Senhora.' Miguel shifted uneasily. 'I beg that your silence extends to your husband. I know that such vows of secrecy often include an implicit exception for the special bonds of matrimony, but in this case it is very important that your good husband know nothing.'

Hannah sipped at her coffee. A black mulch had formed at the bottom, and not knowing if she should drink it and thinking it would be rude to ask, she set the bowl back down. 'I, of all people, know what my good husband should and should not hear. I'll not tell him. But you must promise me something.'

He raised an eyebrow. 'Of course.'

'That you will let me drink coffee again,' she said. 'Soon.'

'I would consider drinking coffee with you a great pleasure,' he said warmly.

She studied his face. *Were I a servant or a tavern girl, he would kiss me at this moment. But I am* his brother's wife. He won't kiss me ever. He has too much honour. Unless, of course, she thought, I kiss him first. But that was unthinkable, and she blushed at her own boldness.

'Well, then,' she said with a sigh, 'I'll call the girl to clear away the dishes, lest my husband come home and find that we've been secreted together, drinking forbidden things.'

Her own words astonished her, but she dared not show ill ease. Instead, she enjoyed the look of wonder upon Miguel's face for a moment before relieving him of his discomfort by ringing for the maid.

CHAPTER 17

Miguel believed he had learned a great deal that day, about women and about Hannah. He could never have imagined what spirit lurked beneath her quiet exterior. He had feared the worst of her, that she would repeat all she knew to every wife in the Vlooyenburg. It seemed inevitable that a silly woman would run off with this bit of gossip like a dog who snatched a piece of meat from the kitchen counter. Now he believed he could depend upon her to be quiet. He couldn't explain why he had given her the coffee, why he had confessed to her what he wanted to hide from Daniel. It had been an impulse to give her something, a new secret, to make her feel the bond of trust between them. Perhaps it had been sound reasoning and perhaps not, but the thrill of trusting her had been impossible to resist. And he knew with absolute certainty that she would not betray him.

Miguel shook his head and cursed himself. Did he not have enough trouble without looking for unspeakable intrigues? If something were to happen to Daniel, he thought, he would happily take a closer look at Hannah. And a man might die in many ways: disease, accident, murder. Miguel took a moment to indulge in thoughts of Daniel's body being dragged from a canal, his eyes openly staring at death, his skin somewhere between blue and white. He felt remorse at his pleasure in such thoughts, but they left him less agitated than thoughts of removing Hannah from the unhappy bondage of her clothing.

Wasn't coffee supposed to inhibit such thoughts? But even coffee was no match for the thrill of Hannah's conversation. He had always thought the girl no more than a simple and pretty thing, charming but empty. Now he knew it had all been for show, an act to placate her husband. Give the woman a bowl of coffee, and her true self blossomed. How many other women, he wondered, merely played the fool to escape the notice of their men?

The thought of a world peopled with cunning and duplicitous women did nothing to calm his spirits, so he said his afternoon prayers, adding his silent thanks to the Holy One, blessed be He for having disposed of Joachim without all of the Vlooyenburg knowing of his business.

Miguel soon learned his thanks were premature.

He had thought it fortunate that Joachim had pulled his impudent prank while the men of the Vlooyenburg were scattered about the city in pursuit of their business, but he had forgotten to account for the women, women who sat in their parlour chairs and stood in their kitchens with their eyes upon the streets, praying that this day heaven would release them from their tedium by manifesting the miracle of scandal. Joachim's crude behaviour had been witnessed: from doorways and windows and side streets. Wives and daughters and grandmothers and widows had seen it all, and they had talked eagerly, to one another and to their husbands. By the time Miguel saw Daniel that evening, there was hardly a Jew in Amsterdam who did not know that a strange man had threatened Hannah and her maid and that Miguel had driven him off. Supper creaked under the weight of the incident. Miguel's brother hardly spoke a word, and Hannah's weak attempts at conversation failed utterly.

Later, Daniel crept down to the cellar. He took a seat in one of the old chairs, his feet slightly lifted out of the damp, and remained silent long enough to expand the discomfort that already crept over them. His eyes half focused on Miguel while he poked at a back tooth, all the while making sucking noises.

Finally he extracted his finger. 'What do you know of this man?'

'It does not concern you.' The words sounded feeble even in Miguel's own ears.

'Of course it concerns me!' Only rarely did Daniel lose his temper with Miguel. He might condescend and lecture and express his disappointment, but he shied away from anything like anger. 'Do you know that this encounter is so upsetting to Hannah that she will not even speak of it? What horrors have befallen my wife that she will not gossip?'

Miguel felt some of his own anger subside. He had asked Hannah to protect a secret, and she had done so. He could not let himself worry about what damage he had done to his brother's domestic quiet. Daniel, after all, only believed his wife upset.

'I'm sorry Hannah had a scare, but you know I would never let her come to harm.'

'And that foolish maid. Every time I try to enquire of her what happened, she pretends not to be able to understand what I say. The girl understands my Dutch well enough when I go to pay her wages.'

'You are more practised with those words,' Miguel suggested.

'Don't play the fool, Miguel.'

'And don't play the father with me, my younger brother,' Miguel boomed.

'I assure you, I am not playing your father,' Daniel replied tartly, 'I am playing the father to an unborn son and I am playing the husband, a role that would have taught you much had you not botched your agreement with Senhor Parido.'

Miguel almost lashed out with some hateful words, but he checked his tongue. In this case, he knew, his brother's grievance had merit. 'I am truly sorry that anyone unpleasant should have had contact with the senhora. You know I would never consciously expose her to any danger. This matter was nothing of my doing.'

'Everyone is full of this, Miguel. I cannot tell you how many conversations broke into harsh whispers at my approach today. I hate hearing people talking of my business, of how my own wife had to be saved from a madman set upon her by your doings.'

Perhaps that was the source of Daniel's anger. He did not like that it was Miguel who had saved Hannah from the madman. 'I had always believed you had larger concerns than what wives and widows say about you.'

'Make sport if you like, but this kind of behaviour is a danger to us all. You have threatened the safety not only of my family but of our entire Nation.'

'What madness is this?' Miguel demanded. 'Of what threat to our Nation do you speak? Your wife and Annetje were accosted by a madman. I fended him off. I hardly understand why that should be fodder for scandal.'

'We both know there is more to it. First I hear you have dealings with the heretic Alferonda. Now I have heard that this man who accosted Hannah was seen speaking to you two weeks ago. I have heard he is a Dutchman with whom you have an irresponsible familiarity. And now he lashes out at my wife and my unborn child.'

'You have heard a great deal,' Miguel answered.

267

'I might even go so far as to say it hardly matters if it is true – the harm may be the same either way. I have no doubt the Ma'amad would regard these transgressions very seriously.'

'You speak very authoritatively for the Ma'amad and its outdated policies.'

Daniel looked worried, as though they were in public. 'Miguel, you go too far.'

'I go too far?' he snapped. 'Because I disagree with the Ma'amad in private? I think you have lost your ability to judge the difference between power and wisdom.'

'You mustn't criticise the council. Without its guidance, this community would be lost.'

'The Ma'amad was instrumental in creating this community, but now it rules without account-ability or mercy. It threatens excommunication for the slightest offence, even the act of questioning its wisdom. Shouldn't we be Jews in freedom rather than in fear?'

Daniel's eyes widened in the flickering candle-light. 'We are foreigners in a land that despises us and needs only an excuse to cast us out. The council stands between us and another exile. Is that what you wish? To bring ruin upon on us?'

'This is Amsterdam, Daniel, not Portugal or Spain or Poland. How long must we live here before the Ma'amad understands that the Dutch are not like these others?'

'Do not their clergy condemn us?'

'Their clergy condemn us, but they condemn

paved streets, and lighted rooms, and food with flavour, and sleeping while lying down, and anything else that might bring pleasure or comfort or profit. The people mock their preachers.'

'You are naive if you think we cannot be expelled here as we have been elsewhere.'

Miguel sucked his teeth in frustration. 'You hide in this neighbourhood with your countrymen, knowing nothing of the Dutch, and so you think them evil because you cannot trouble yourself to learn otherwise. This land rebelled against its Catholic conquerors, and then allowed the Catholics to continue to live among them. What other nation has done such a thing? Amsterdam is a stew of foreigners. The people thrive on having aliens around them.'

Daniel shook his head. 'I'll not say you are wrong about these things, but you are not going to change the Ma'amad. It will continue to act as though we are in danger at every moment, and it is better for it to do so than grow complacent. Particularly when Solomon Parido is a *parnass*, you must treat the Ma'amad's power with respect.'

'Thank you for your advice,' Miguel said icily.

'I've not yet given you advice. My advice is that you do nothing to endanger my family. You are my brother, and I'll do what I can to shield you from the council, even if I think you're deserving of its anger, but I'll not place you before my own wife and unborn son.'

Miguel could say nothing.

'There is more,' Daniel said. He paused to play with a tooth for a moment. 'I have not said anything of this to you before,' he mumbled, one finger still in his mouth, 'because I knew you to be in a great deal of difficulty, but I have heard that things have changed with you. There is the matter of the money I lent you – some fifteen hundred guilders.'

Miguel nearly gasped. The loan had been like a fart at Shabbat meal: everyone notices, but no one says a word. After all these months, Daniel now finally spoke of the money, and the spell of silence was broken.

'We have all heard about your success in the whale oil trade – which came, I might add, at the expense of other men. In any case, now that you have some guilders in your account, I thought you might repay me at least a portion of what you owe. I should very much like to see a thousand guilders transferred into my account tomorrow.'

Miguel swallowed hard. 'Daniel, you were very good to lend me that money, and of course I will repay it when I can, but I have not yet received the funds due to me from that trade. You know that broker, Ricardo? He won't pay me or disclose his client.'

'I know Ricardo. I've always found him a reasonable man.'

'Then perhaps you might reason with him. If he pays me what he owes, I will be happy to lighten my debt to you.'

'I have heard,' Daniel said, now staring at the

floor, 'that you have more than two thousand guilders in your Exchange account right now. I must conclude that the rumours you have been spreading about Ricardo are an abuse of a good man's name meant to help you avoid paying your debts.'

Geertruid's money. How had he learned of it? 'That is not money from Ricardo, it is money from a partner for a business transaction. And accounts at the Exchange Bank are supposed to be private.'

'Nothing is private in Amsterdam, Miguel. You should know that by now.'

Nothing was so infuriating as Daniel playing the great merchant with him. 'I cannot give you any of that money; it is not mine to give.'

'Whose is it?'

'That's a private matter, though I'm sure no such private matters are beyond your reach.'

'Why private? Are you brokering for gentiles again? Do you dare to risk the wrath of the Ma'amad after you have so angered Senhor Parido?'

'I never said I was brokering for gentiles.'

'But you don't deny it either. I suppose all this is related to your coffee dealings. I told you to stay away from coffee, that it would ruin you, but you would not listen.'

'No one has been ruined. Why do you jump to these absurd conclusions?'

'I'll have at least part of that money before you

lose it,' Daniel assured him. 'I must insist that you transfer a thousand guilders to me. If you are unwilling to pay a portion of your debt to me when you have money,' he said, 'you insult the charity I have offered you, and your continuing to live here will no longer be acceptable.'

For a fleeting instant, Miguel seriously considered murdering his brother. He imagined himself running Daniel through with a blade, of beating his head in with a candlestick, strangling him with a rag. The outrage of it all. Daniel knew that if Miguel moved out, took his own lodgings, the world would see it as a sign of his solvency, and his creditors would descend and pick away with their ravenous beaks until there was nothing left. There would be demands and challenges and hearings before the Ma'amad. It would be only a matter of days before his dealings with Geertruid were exposed.

'I might consider an alternative, however,' Daniel said after a moment.

'What alternative?'

'I might withhold my demand for the money you have long owed me in exchange for information about your coffee dealings and perhaps the opportunity to invest in your project.'

'Why will you not believe that I have no dealings in coffee?' Miguel demanded.

Daniel stared at him for a moment and then looked away. 'I've given you your options, Miguel. You may do as you like.'

Daniel had given him no choice: surrender a thousand guilders now or lose everything in a matter of days.

'I'll transfer the funds to you,' Miguel said, 'but you must know that I resent your demands, which harm my business and make it all the more difficult for me to extricate myself from my debts. But I promise you this: I will not allow your pettiness to undermine my affairs. I'll be out of debt in a matter of months, and it is you who will come begging to me for scraps.'

Daniel smiled thinly. 'We'll see,' he said.

The next morning Miguel swallowed the bitter medicine of transferring the funds to his brother. He nearly choked as he gave the order to the clerk at the Exchange Bank, but it had to be done.

As he went about his business that day, he tried hard not recollect that of the three thousand guilders Geertruid had entrusted to him, little more than a thousand remained.

From

The Factual and Revealing Memoirs of Alonzo Alferonda

I believe I may have mentioned that Miguel Lienzo was some years my senior and I did not know him well when I was a boy. I knew his brother, however, and if I had not heard from my father that Miguel was a superior and wily boy, I would have had no interest in knowing more of the family.

Daniel Lienzo was a child who knew his assets and shortcomings from an early age. He had not nearly the physical strength of the other boys we played with, but he was much faster. Understanding how to manage his assets, he would have nothing to do with games of wrestling but insisted we race all day. He only wanted to play at a sport in which he could win.

Though he was known to be his father's favourite, he complained bitterly about his older brother, unable to accept the unfairness that Miguel should be older, larger, and further along in the world. 'My brother wastes his time studying Jewish books,' he would tell us in conspiratorial whispers, as if the rest of us were not secreted away by our fathers and taught forbidden things by candlelight. 'My brother thinks himself a man already,' Daniel complained. 'He is always after the serving girls.'

Daniel would have studied Torah if only to prove himself his brother's master. He would have chased girls though he knew not what to do with them, if only to prove he could catch where his brother could not. The idea was absurd. Miguel had a quicker mind than Daniel, and his appearance was far more pleasing to the ladies. Still, Daniel could never forgive the slight of being born second.

I can recall that when I was but twelve years of age, only a few months before we fled Lisbon, Daniel came to us and said he had a trick he wanted to play. His older brother had spirited a kitchen girl away into a quiet closet in their house, and he thought it would be amusing to expose them.

Of course it was a foolish thing to do, but we were children and doing foolish things had a great deal of appeal. We followed Daniel into his father's house and then up three flights of stairs until we stopped outside an old door that sat crooked on its hinges. Daniel signalled for us to be quiet and then threw open the door.

There we saw Miguel sitting on a cushion with a serving girl no more than his own age. Her dress was in a state of disrepair, and it was clear she had been behaving as no good girl ought. The two of them reacted to our presence with utter confusion, and in truth we reacted in utter confusion too. The girl attempted to lower her skirts and close her bodice in a single gesture and, frustrated at her efforts, broke into tears. She called upon the Virgin's mercy. She was undone.

Miguel reddened, not from embarrassment but indignation. 'Leave us!' he hissed. 'You may tease a man, but only a coward teases a young woman.' Before, we had been only eager and curious and full of childish giggles over we knew not what. Now were shamed, by our curiosity and his hard glare. We'd committed a crime we were too young to understand, and our lack of understanding made it all the more terrible.

We all backed away and raced down the stairs, but I paused because I saw that Daniel did not move. He stood in the doorway, preventing Miguel from closing it. I could not see his eyes, but I somehow knew he stared hard. At Miguel? The girl? I don't know, but he was utterly unmoved by Miguel's majestic wrath or the girl's tears.

'Go!' Miguel told him. 'Can't you see the girl is distressed?'

But Daniel stood there staring, listening to the girl's muted sobbing. He never moved for as long as I dared to remain.

For what reason do I mention this? my reader may wonder. Well, it is to help explain some of the animosity between these two men, which went back many years and was, as near as I could tell, utterly senseless.

But such was the way with these brothers. Thus the reader may not be entirely surprised to learn that it was Daniel Lienzo himself who owed Miguel more than two thousand guilders in whale oil debt. Far from being in debt to his brother, Miguel was his creditor and never once suspected it.

CHAPTER 18

The letters had been coming in at the rate of two or three a week, and Miguel stayed up late, straining his eyes against the thin light of a single oil lamp, to answer them. Animated by coffee and the thrill of impending wealth, he worked with jubilant determination, making sure his agents understood precisely what he required of them.

Miguel had not seen Geertruid since his return from Rotterdam, which made it easy to avoid dwelling on having lost most of her capital. He knew of men who had lost their partner's money, and they invariably broke down in confession immediately, as though the burden of living in falseness was too much to endure. Miguel felt he could live with the falseness as long as the world let him get away with it.

Nevertheless, he wanted to see Geertruid and tell her of his progress, and he had other things to say too, but Geertruid was nowhere to be found. It was a cursed time for her to hide herself. Miguel sent messages to all the most likely taverns and paid visits to those places at even the most unlikely hours, but he found no sign of her.

Once, by coincidence, he ran into Hendrick, who stood idly near the Damrak. He leaned against a wall, and busied himself with his pipe, watching as men and women paraded past him.

'Ho, Jew Man,' he called out. He puffed his pipe cordially in Miguel's direction.

Miguel hesitated a moment, wondering if he could pretend to have neither seen or heard Hendrick, but it was no good. 'What news of Madame Damhuis?' he asked.

'What?' Hendrick asked. 'You don't ask after my health? You injure me.'

'I am sorry for the injury,' Miguel said. He had, over time, learned to defuse Hendrick's bombast by pretending to take it seriously.

'As long as you're sorry, that's the important thing. But it's Madame Damhuis you want, and I can't hope to serve as Madame Damhuis serves. I haven't her charms.'

Was he jealous? 'Do you know where I might find her?'

'I haven't seen her.' Hendrick turned his head and blew a long cloud of smoke.

'Perhaps at her home,' Miguel began hopefully.

'Oh, no. Not at her home.'

'Still, I should not mind looking for myself,' Miguel pressed, wishing he could be more clever and subtle. 'Where might I find her home?'

'It's not for me to say,' Hendrick explained.

'You foreigners are perhaps not so clear about our customs. If Madame Damhuis has not told you, it would not be my place to do so.'

'Thank you, then,' Miguel said as he hurried off, eager to waste no more time.

'If I see her,' Hendrick called after him, 'I'll be sure to give her your regards.'

Such was his luck that day. He decided, on a whim, to visit the coffee tavern in the Plantage, but when Turk Mustafa opened the door – only a crack – he stared suspiciously at Miguel.

'I'm Senhor Lienzo,' he said. 'I've been here before.'

'This is not the time for you,' the Turk said.

'I don't understand. I thought this was a public tavern.'

'Go away,' the Turk said, and closed the door hard.

Hannah sat in the dining room, eating her breakfast of white-flour bread with good butter and some yellow apples that an old woman had been peddling door to door the previous evening. Her wine was more heavily spiced and not nearly so watered down as usual. Annetje knew how to be parsimonious with the wine and generous with the water – more wine for herself that way – so Hannah understood what the strength of her drink meant. The maid wanted to talk with her and so tried to loosen her tongue.

Miguel had given her coffee, and now Annetje

gave her wine. The world plied her with drink in order to make her do its bidding. This thought saddened her, but even so, Hannah could not quite forget the thrill of having consumed Miguel's coffee. She loved learning the true nature of that fruit; she loved the way it made her feel animated and alive. It was not as though she discovered a new self; rather, coffee reordered the self she already had. Things at the top drifted to the bottom, and the parts of herself she had chained down rose buoyantly. She had forgotten to be demure and modest, and she loved casting off those constraints.

She now recognised, perhaps for the first time, how Miguel had always seen her: quiet, foolish, stupid. Those Iberian virtues of femininity held no allure for him. He enjoyed connivers like Annetje and his wicked widow. Well, she could be wicked too. The thought almost made her laugh aloud. Of course she could not *be* wicked, but she could *want* to be wicked.

Annetje came up from the kitchen and stood in the doorway, eyeing, as Hannah had suspected she would, the now-empty goblet. Daniel and Miguel had both left to attend to their business, so the girl took a seat at the table, which she loved to do when they were alone together, poured herself some wine from the decanter, and drank it down quickly, apparently unconcerned with how loose her own tongue became.

'Did you and the senhor have a pleasant talk yesterday?' she began.

Hannah smiled. 'You didn't listen at the door?'

Something violent flickered across Annetje's face. 'You spoke too rapidly in your language. I could hardly understand a word of it.'

'He asked me not to talk of what had happened. I am sure he told you the same thing.'

'He did, but he did not give me any special potions to make me obey. Perhaps he has more faith in my silence.'

'Perhaps he does,' Hannah agreed. 'And perhaps you've no faith in mine. That's what you want to know about, yes? If I spoke to him about the widow.'

'Well, I would know if you spoke about the widow. You may count on that. Just as I know from your face now that you haven't, but that you've done something else.'

Hannah said nothing. She cast her eyes downwards, feeling the familiar rush of shame that gripped her when she spoke out of turn or made eye contact with a guest of her husband's.

Annetje arose and took a seat next to her. She took Hannah's right hand in both of hers. 'Are you ashamed of talking so intimately with the senhor?' she asked sweetly, her pretty green eyes locking on to Hannah's. 'I don't think it so wrong that you should enjoy a little innocent congress. The women of my nation do so every day, and no harm comes to them.'

She squeezed Hannah's hand between hers. Here was the Annetje who had first shown herself, who had lured Hannah into revealing her secrets.

Hannah would have no more of it. 'I don't see anything evil in speaking with him. I may say what I like to whom I like.'

'Of course, you are right,' Annetje cooed. 'Let's forget this incident altogether. Shall we go this afternoon?'

'Go?'

'Has it been so long that you do not recall?' Both had understand from the beginning that the name of the place must never be spoken aloud, not in the house, not in the Vlooyenburg, not anywhere Jews or Ma'amad spies might lurk.

Hannah swallowed. She had know this conversation must come, and she had done all she could to brace herself. Even so, she felt unprepared and perhaps even surprised. 'I cannot go.'

'You cannot go?' Annetje asked. 'Are you afraid because of that silly widow?'

'It's not that,' Hannah told her. 'I won't risk it. My child.'

'The child again,' she snapped. 'You act like no one has ever been with child before.'

'I won't take any more chances. God has shown me, he has warned me of the dangers. I was almost caught once, and I would be a fool to ignore His mercy.'

'God did not save you,' Annetje told her. 'I did. I am the one who saved you from being discovered. God will damn you to hell if you do not go today, and your child too.'

Hannah shook her head. 'I don't believe it.'

'You know it's true,' the maid said petulantly. 'We'll see how many nights you can endure, lying awake, knowing that if you are to die in your sleep, you are destined for hell's torments. Then you will change your mind.'

'Perhaps,' Hannah said ambivalently.

'In any case,' Annetje announced more cheerfully, 'you must remember to say nothing to Senhor Miguel. You must keep silence. Will you promise me to do so?'

'I promise.' As she said the words, she knew she lied and felt a strange new pleasure in how easily the lie came. She knew she would tell Miguel, though she could not say when or why or what would be the consequence of an act that could well mean her ruin.

A week after his conversation with Hendrick, Miguel sat with Geertruid in the Singing Carp. She had sent him a note announcing that she wished to see him, and Miguel had hurried over. He found Hendrick in the midst of telling a story when Miguel arrived, and though Geertruid stretched her pretty neck to kiss Miguel, she made no effort to interrupt.

Hendrick spoke in a rapid rural Dutch, and Miguel had a hard time following the circuitous narrative, which had something to do with a childhood friend and a stolen barrel of pickled beef. When he finished, he laughed in appreciation of himself. 'That's some story, eh, Jew Man?'

'I like it very much,' answered Miguel.

'He likes it very much,' Hendrick said to Geertruid. 'He is kind to say so.'

Why did Geertruid not send away this clown? But Miguel could tell that she had been drinking a little too much. Hendrick had been drinking too. 'Now it is your turn,' he said to Miguel. He grinned broadly, but his eyes had a kind of cruelty in them. 'You tell a story.'

This was a test of some sort, but Miguel had no idea how to proceed. 'I have no story to tell,' he answered, 'or none that can compete with your pickled beef tale.' In truth, Miguel could not make himself calm. He had only a third of Geertruid's money remaining, and when the time came, he would have no way of paying Nunes. He'd been able to put the lost money out of his mind, but here with Geertruid he could not bring himself to forget it.

'I have no story to tell,' Hendrick repeated, imitating Miguel's accent. 'Come now, Jew Man. Show yourself to be game for once. You enjoy my generous entertainment, and I would so like you to give something in return. Would you not like to hear a story, madam?'

'I'd love to hear a story,' Geertruid agreed. 'The senhor is so witty.'

'I see I'm outnumbered,' he said, making a show of good nature. 'What sort of story should I tell?'

'That's for you to say. Something that tells of your mighty adventures. You can tell us a story of

285

your amorous victories or the strangeness of your race or some incomprehensible plan to conquer the Exchange.'

Miguel had no time to respond, for a man had come behind Hendrick with a tankard in his hand and swung hard, aiming to hit Hendrick in the head. It was his good fortune that Hendrick had leaned in a few inches to make some comment to Geertruid. The pewter tankard came down hard, but it struck the Dutchman in the shoulder and then flew from the assailant's hand, spraying beer into Miguel's face before it clattered upon the wooden floor.

'God's fucking whore,' Hendrick said, with surprising calm. He leapt from his seat in an instant and turned to face his attacker, a man at least a head shorter than Hendrick and thin – almost shockingly so – but for an enormous belly. His face had turned red with the exertion of his blow and the failure to bring it home.

'You rotten bastard!' the man shouted. 'I know who you are, and I'll kill you!'

'Christ,' Hendrick said petulantly, as though had been asked to perform an unpleasant chore. He let out a puff of breath and struck the man hard in the face. The blow came fast, and his assailant went down on the floor to the cheers of the patrons.

In an instant the keeper came out and, with the help of a servant, dragged the attacker towards the kitchens. Miguel guessed he would be thrown into the alley out the back.

Hendrick smiled sheepishly. 'I'd wager that fellow doesn't much like me.'

Miguel nodded as he wiped the beer from his face.

'I don't think there will be any trouble.' Geertruid said, 'but you may wish to get gone.'

Hendrick nodded. 'I take your meaning. Good day to you, Jew Man.'

The pair sat in silence for a few minutes once Hendrick had left, and Miguel pondered the unanswerable question of how Geertruid understood what had passed.

'Tell me once more why you associate with him,' Miguel said, after a moment.

'Anyone can make enemies,' Geertruid said unconvincingly. 'He is a rough man with rough friends, and they sometimes settle their differences uncouthly.'

It was true enough. Miguel found himself secretly hoping that Joachim might someday confront him with Hendrick near by.

'In any case,' Geertruid said, still sounding a little drunk, 'I am sorry you had to witness such trouble.'

He shook his head. 'Where have you been these past days?'

'I never stay in one place for long,' she told him. She set a hand on top of his. 'I like to visit my relatives in the countryside. It is a sad bird who never leaves her nest.'

'I wish you would inform me of when you plan to

go away and when you plan to return. If we are to do business together, I must be able to find you.'

She patted his hand and looked directly into his eyes. 'Of course. I'll be good to you.'

Miguel took his hand away. He was in no mood for her nonsense. 'It is not a matter of being good to me, but of being good to our business. This is not some silly woman's game.'

'And I am not some silly woman,' she answered, her voice now hard as steel. 'I may be soft, but I am not a fool to be lectured.'

Miguel felt himself go pale. He could not recall her ever having spoken to him thus. Like a Dutch husband, he wanted nothing so much as to placate her. 'Madam, I of all men would never call you a fool. I only wished to say that I must be able to speak to you.'

She turned to him, her head at an angle, her thin lips spread in a warm smile, her eyes wide and inviting. 'Of course, senhor. I have been at fault.'

'It doesn't matter,' Miguel muttered. 'And we have more important business to discuss. I have received several letters from our agents, and I'm optimistic that we'll receive more good news within the next few weeks.'

She took a drink from her tankard. 'Have we all the agents we require?'

'Not quite. We still lack Madrid, Lisbon and Oporto.' He made every effort to sound unconcerned, but the truth was that there could be no control of the market without Iberia. 'It is a problem,' Miguel added.

Geertruid studied him. 'How will you solve this problem?' Her voice sounded icy.

'If I could answer that question I would have already solved it.'

'I put forth the money. I've done my part. Your part is to make it work – otherwise I should hardly need you.'

Miguel shook his head. 'If you have no faith in this project, you must tell me now. There is still time to cancel the sale, though we lose the premium.'

Geertruid shook her head. 'I don't want to cancel the sale. I want the problem solved, and if it cannot be solved, I want to know that I can trust you to tell me so.'

'Very well,' he said sullenly. He had hardly been prepared for her to take this posture. 'If I have not resolved the question of the Iberian agents in two weeks, we'll cancel.'

Miguel showed no emotion, but even the thought of abandoning the deal filled him with misery. Perhaps he could find someone else, someone in the Jewish community to fund him. But that idea presented its own host of problems. He would have to discuss the plan in order to try and bring someone on board. Once he discussed it, it would no longer be a secret. His brother might have put up the money if they were upon better terms, but Daniel had no faith that Miguel could manage his own affairs. No, if he lost Geertruid's money, he could never proceed.

Then there was the matter of cancelling the sale. Geertruid had been concerned about her money, and her lack of trust irritated Miguel. Though he had lost two-thirds of her investment, he wasn't the sort of person who handled money irresponsibly. He had only been unlucky.

Guessing that Geertruid had no idea how such sales were actually ordered, Miguel had simply invented his two-week estimate. He doubted he could get Nunes to cancel the deal in two weeks or even right now. But that difficulty could be dealt with another time. Now Miguel had no concern greater than regaining Geertruid's confidence.

She nodded. 'Two weeks is a goodly amount of time.'

'I had better redouble my efforts.' Miguel stood up. 'I should hate to disappoint you.'

'Don't think I've lost faith.' She reached out and took his hand in both of hers. 'It is a great deal of money I've put forth, and I must protect my investment.'

'Of course, madam,' Miguel said. 'I understand your heart in all things.'

Miguel stopped next at the Flyboat, where he found Isaiah Nunes engaged in conversation with a few other merchants of Miguel's acquaintance. Nunes knew well how to read the expressions on a man's face, and understanding that Miguel needed to speak to him he pushed his muscular form upward. The tavern was far too noisy, so they stepped outside into the cool of the late afternoon. Both men looked around carefully to make sure their conversation could not be overheard.

'If I choose to cancel the sale,' Miguel began abruptly, 'by what date must I do so?'

'Cancel?' Nunes demanded. His face darkened. 'What's gone wrong?'

'Nothing,' Miguel told him warily. 'I have no real plans to cancel, but one of my partners is nervous and asked me to make an enquiry. Besides, you were the one who advised me to be rid of coffee.'

'But not to be rid of our contract. You may tell this partner of yours it is far too late to back out. We don't deal here with some friend of our Nation, you know. We deal with the East India Company, and the Company does not allow a buyer to change his mind no matter how politely one might ask.' Nunes paused for a moment. 'I know you understand how things stand. I would hate for you to put me in an awkward position, Miguel.'

Miguel forced a smile. 'Of course.'

Nunes shrugged. 'In any case, I had actually been planning on sending you a little note tomorrow. I have made all the arrangements, and I now require a portion of the payment.'

'I had thought I would pay upon delivery,' said Miguel, who had thought no such thing.

'You know better than that,' Nunes said, his brow wrinkled in obvious displeasure.

'Shall we say a quarter up front?'

Nunes laughed and put a hand on Miguel's shoulder. 'You're making me laugh now. You know how these things are done. If you'll transfer half the amount to my account by the end of next week, I'd be most appreciative.'

Miguel cleared his throat. 'Sadly, one of my partners has suffered a small – and temporary, I assure you – setback. We cannot come up with the entire sum by next week.'

The smile dropped from Nunes's face.

'I can pay you a thousand by next week,' Miguel suggested. 'No small sum, and certainly an indication of our seriousness.'

Nunes' hand had remained on Miguel's shoulder, but it now pressed so hard he pushed Miguel up against the tavern wall. 'Have you lost your wits?' he asked in a husky whisper. 'There is no manoeuvring with the Company. If I say I need fifteen hundred, I need that sum, not some token. I've contracted with them, you've contracted with me, and the deal is to be done. If you don't give me that money, I will have to pay it out of my own account. You're my friend, Miguel, but you have put me in a terrible position.'

'I know, I know.' Miguel held up his hands up like a supplicant. 'It's these partners of mine – good for the money but slow with payment. But I'll have the funds – by the end of next week, as

292

you say.' Miguel would have told him anything to end the talk of courts and contracts. 'Perhaps,' he suggested, 'you could say a word or two to Ricardo on my behalf.'

'I'll not fight your battle for you, Miguel, nor get between you and Parido.'

He'd had enough disquiet for one day, but when he walked into his brother's house, he knew at once that something terrible had happened. Daniel sat in the front room with a strange look on his face, disappointment and satisfaction all at once.

'What is it?' Miguel asked him. 'Have you been searching . . .' He stopped. It was a line of enquiry that could lead to no good.

Daniel stretched out his arm to present a sealed letter. A sealed letter. How many times would Daniel confront him about his correspondence? But even as he thought the words, Miguel knew this letter was different – and Daniel already knew its contents.

Miguel numbly broke the seal and opened the triple folded paper. He did not have to read the ornate handwriting or the carefully chosen words in formal Spanish. He knew what it said. Miguel had been summoned to appear the next morning before the Ma'amad.

CHAPTER 19

There were only a few hours of daylight remaining, and Miguel wished to use them to his advantage. He could feel the hot breath of ruin upon the back of his neck, but he might still arm himself against the battle and prevail. For all his grievances with the Ma'amad – and he had many – he believed it did possess one quirk that might work in his favour. The council did not condemn on mere principle. Parido might speak against him, might try to persuade the council to act, but the *parnassim* would listen to reason. They wanted the community to thrive so they were inclined to accept apologies and consider particular circumstances. Many a man had pulled his fat out of the Ma'amad's fire by having a careful argument at the ready.

To prepare such an argument, Miguel would have to learn precisely why the Ma'amad wished to see him. Miguel felt almost certain he knew. Surely Joachim had spoken ill of him to the council. Now he needed to know what he had said and what kinds of charges were to be brought against him, and that presented a terrible irony. He had wanted nothing so much as to avoid that madman, but now he must seek him out.

Before Miguel had even begun to formulate a plan whereby he might find Joachim, he recalled something else, something Hendrick had said before he had been attacked in the tavern. *You can tell us a story of your amorous victories or the strangeness of your race or some incomprehensible plan to conquer the Exchange.* Geertruid had sworn to keep their business a secret from her dog, so why was he barking on about it? And what was the true source of her money? Could she and her loose lips be the source of this summons?

Without taking a moment to explain himself to Daniel, Miguel rushed out of the house and returned to the Singing Carp, muttering hopeful half-prayers that Geertruid would still be there. She was not. Miguel asked the tapman, who let it be known he may very well have heard something of her destination, and a coin might help his memory; for two stivers, the fellow recalled that she attended a banquet at the far end of the Bloemstraat.

Miguel found the entrance to the banquet hall in the upper portion of an unpretentious red-brick house. He climbed the stairs and pounded; when a servant boy answered the door, Miguel only said he had come for the feast and the boy ushered him up the stairs to a wide room with six or seven dark wood tables spread out on a series of mismatched Eastern rugs. Sconces with good smokeless candles reached out of the doorposts and along the walls, and great chandeliers descended from the ceiling. Dozens of paintings had been hung without regard to spacing or ease of viewing. Two large fireplaces on the far sides of the room blasted out oppressive heat, and in the corner a pair of fiddlers played madly to make their music audible above the din of drunken chatter.

On the tables, at each of which sat ten or twelve banqueters, were piles and pots of food: oysters, boiled fowl, a steaming vessel of *hutsepot* with the leg of some unclean animal thrust outward like the desperate grasp of a drowning man. There were enormous wheels of cheese and plates of herring, pickled, baked and stewed. There were bowls of hot milk with melted butter floating at the top; also white breads, figs and dates, roast parsnips and Dutch *sla*, made of chopped raw cabbage and carrot. While Miguel struggled to preserve himself, Geertruid feasted.

Buxom girls moved from table to table, pouring drink into cunning goblets with no stems. Miguel had seen, and fallen victim to these vessels himself; they could not be set down, and so they encouraged drinking far beyond one's limit. This merry crowd consisted mostly of men, but there was a woman or two at each table, as red and drunk and merry as the assortment of black-clad tall-hatted gentleman diners, who managed to drink, smoke and eat all at once.

At the table nearest the entrance, a man with one eye and one arm took notice of Miguel. In his remaining hand, his left, he clutched his goblet tight, unable to let go, even to dine. 'Ho, there,' he shouted above the din. 'Who called for a Jew?'

Miguel had not noticed Geertruid until that moment. Even from a distance, the length of two or three men, he could see the gracelessness of her movements and the unfocused wandering of her eyes. With one hand, she pushed herself from her chair and walked unsteadily to meet him by the door.

'Sober yourself,' Miguel snapped. 'I must have words with you. What is this, anyhow? With whom do you feast?'

'It is the Brewer's Guild,' she said.

'What business have you with these men?' he demanded.

'Oh, Miguel, I may have friends and acquaintances outside your approval, you know. Now tell me what has happened.' Her eyes went as wide as a child's.

'It is the Ma'amad. It has summoned me to appear before it tomorrow morning.'

She let out a loud laugh that pierced through the clamour of drunken revelry. 'You and your Muhammad. Are you a Jew or a Turk?'

He took a deep breath. 'Geertruid, I must have some answers.' He hardly ever called her by her first name. He recalled that he had done so the night he had tried to kiss her, and the memory still left him mortified. 'Have you spoken of our business to anyone?'

'Of course not.' She shook her head rapidly, and then reached up with one exploratory hand to make sure her prim little cap, beaded with rubies, had not been knocked out of place.

'Ho, Jew,' one of the men from her table called. 'Send us back our merry friend.'

Geertruid waved them off: a quick, gawky gesture with the back of her hand.

'You haven't told Hendrick?'

'Hendrick,' she repeated. 'That ox. I would not trouble him with the secret of making rocks sink in a canal.'

Miguel swallowed hard. 'What about the money? I know you were not honest with me. How did you get it?'

'Who said I was not honest with you? Who said that? I am very angry.' She lost her balance and held on to the wall, though her gentle swaying continued.

Miguel took her arm, to steady her. 'I haven't time for your anger. I have to know where the money comes from. If it wasn't left to you by your husband, whence does it come?'

She laughed a little and then covered her mouth. 'Oh, it comes from my husband, sure enough. That bastard knew only how to take his fill of me, never thinking of my pleasure. Even in death, that's how he fucks me.' Her eyes narrowed, and something dark passed across her face. 'He left me some little money, but not nearly so much as he should have for what I endured.'

Something twisted in Miguel's guts. 'Where did you get the capital?'

'From the wretched children of his foul first wife. They live with their aunt, his sister, but the bastard left me to guard the funds. He gave me the work of ordering their trust and instructed them that, when they came of age, they should reward me as they saw fit. Can you imagine such treachery?'

Guardians and children from other marriages – none of it made sense. 'Tell me the rest.'

'I have some freedom in what I may do with their wealth, though in order to have such freedom, I must convince a wretched old lawyer in Antwerp that I invest for the good of those evil children. Not so easy to do, but I have been known to charm a man or two in my time.'

A lawyer in Antwerp. Now, at least, Miguel could guess to what place she disappeared. She was off lifting her skirts for this pettifogger.

'So, you have used money meant to be held in trust for your late husband's children. You have done this before.'

She nodded. 'Sometimes I have invested it, and sometimes I have simply spent it. There is a matter of a few thousand guilders I should like to replace.'

She had stolen from her husband's children, and when they came of age there would be a reckoning. 'When do they collect their inheritance?'

'The eldest is not of age for another three years, so I have time to set things right.' She reached out and put her arms around his neck. 'You must help me, Miguel. You are my only true friend.' She laughed again, her yeasty breath blasting his face. 'Not my only friend, but my only true friend, and that is something. Do you not think so?'

'Careful,' a Dutch reveller shouted, 'lest you become entangled in Hebrew scripture!'

Geertruid only pulled him closer, but Miguel worked his way out of the embrace, which now only made him uneasy.

He sucked in air until his lungs hurt, and then took her hand and held it in both of his, ignoring the jeers of the drunken Dutchmen. 'Please understand that everything I value is at risk. You must tell me who knows of this.'

She shook her head. 'No one. Only you and, of course, my lawyer. But he won't tell, for I have secrets of my own, and he's afraid to cross me.'

Miguel nodded. His fortunes, he now understood, would be built upon stolen money. It troubled him, but not so much as next morning's meeting with the Ma'amad, and he now believed that meeting had nothing to do with Geertruid or her trickery.

He cursed himself for the time he had wasted. Night would soon be upon him. It was time to begin his hunt for Joachim.

CHAPTER 20

Because Miguel had no precise knowledge of where Joachim lived, finding him would be time-consuming but yet possible. The fellow said he and his wife had been forced to move to one of the worst parts of the city, the run-down hovels in the shadow of the Oude Kerk where seedy musicos attracted whores and sailors and thieves. Someone in the area would know Joachim; so disorderly a man is always conspicuous.

Before entering the most unsavoury part of town, he took out his purse and counted his money. He had more on him than a man in those neighbourhoods would like, so he separated his coins, leaving some in his purse, some in his pocket, and some wrapped in a nose cloth.

As he walked towards the Oude Kerk, buildings began to take on a gloomy, dilapidated cast. The people in the street seemed to belong almost to a different race of man than those in the rest of the city. Foreigners often wrote that one of the great marvels of Amsterdam was its absence of beggars. That was untrue, though Miguel knew well enough that compared to most cities in Europe, the beggars were few indeed, at least in most parts of town. Those foreigners had no doubt not crossed into this district, where they would have found enough of the legless and leprous tribe to satisfy anyone's requirements.

Miguel walked quickly among the poor, among the whores who slouched in doorways, dangling to one side or the other like hanged men, until they spotted a fellow to their liking. More than once in his short walk, Miguel pushed away some greedy she-devil or other who sprang from her lair and attempted to drag him inside.

He was about to ask a man pushing a cart of root vegetables if he knew of Joachim Waagenaar when he saw a woman with a tray of pies round the corner, calling out her goods. Though dressed in stained and loose clothes and somewhat dirty in the face, Miguel was sure he knew this woman. And then at once he understood where he had seen her before: she was Joachim's wife, Clara. No longer quite the beauty he remembered, she remained pretty enough for the sailors to shout out to her with their cheerful obscenities. One approached her, staggering and lecherous, and Miguel thought to step forward, but Clara spoke a couple of pleasant words to the man, who then doffed his cap and wandered off.

Miguel then stepped forward. 'Have you pies with no meat?' he asked. He thought it unlikely that she would recollect his face, so he said nothing to her to give himself away.

Her neck linen was torn and stained yellow, but the cap that covered the crown of her head appeared new. Where could she have acquired such a thing? Miguel recalled Joachim's fears that his wife would turn whore.

'I have an onion and radish pie, sir,' she told him, watching him with evident caution.

Her caution was well-founded, Miguel thought. What business had a Jew looking for his evening meal in this part of the city? 'I'll be glad of it.'

He ought not to eat such a thing. He had no knowledge of its preparation, and it had certainly sat upon her tray in close proximity to pork and other unclean meats. But there was no Ma'amad here. If this pie allowed him to obtain wealth and thereby become a better Jew, its preparation hardly mattered. He bit into it and discovered that he was ravenous. He liked his crust flakier, his vegetables less cooked – the Dutch did not consider vegetables done until they were almost turned to liquid.

'Did you bake these yourself?' he asked.

She eyed him while pretending to look upon the dirt. 'Yes, sir.'

Miguel smiled. 'What is your name, my dear?'

'My name,' she said, holding her hand forward that he might see her little pewter ring, 'is Another Man's Wife.'

'It's not so pretty a name,' Miguel told her, 'but you misunderstand me. If I wished for that sort of companionship, I might easily find it without buying a pie for my troubles.'

'Some men like the sport.' She smiled at him, and her eyes widened slightly. 'Yet I take your point. My name is Clara, and I'd be curious to know what your business is, sir. You appear to buy your pie as a means and not an end.'

Miguel felt an unexpected tingle of interest. Were he on a different kind of business it might be no difficult thing to convince her to continue this conversation in the private room of a tavern. But what kind of a man would that make him? Regardless of Joachim's current treachery, he had – however unintentionally – wronged the poor fellow, and he was hesitant to make matters worse by cuckolding a madman.

'Perhaps I hardly know my business myself,' he told her. 'It is only that – well, if I may be so bold – you have not the look, nor the sound either, of a woman I might expect to find selling pies near the Oude Kerk.'

'And you have not the look of the sort of man I might expect to buy one.'

Miguel bowed 'I speak to you in earnest. You're a beautiful woman who I think is used to better things. How does your husband permit you to ply such a trade?'

Some of the humour drained from Clara's face. 'My husband has fallen on hard times,' she said at last. 'We once had a fine place to live and fine clothes, but he lost his money, alas, to the trickery of one of your race. Now he has nothing but debts, senhor.'

Miguel smiled. 'You know something of our forms of address. I like that. How long has it been since your husband lost his money?'

'Several months, senhor.' This time the honorific was missing its touch of irony. She began to see something of value in this conversation.

'And you still have debts?'

'Yes, senhor.'

'How much do you owe?'

'Three hundred guilders, Senhor. Not so very much money as what we used to have, but now it is enough.'

'I hope you will at least accept my charity.' Miguel took out his nose cloth, heavy with coin. 'Here are five guilders.'

She smiled when he pressed the handkerchief into her hands. Without taking her eyes off her benefactor, she slid the little package into her own purse. 'I cannot thank you enough.'

'Tell me,' he said brightly, 'where I can find this husband of yours.'

'Find him?' Her eyes narrowed and her brow folded upon itself.

'You say he was done wrong by one of my race; perhaps I can do right by him. I might be able to find him some employment or introduce him to someone who could.'

'You're very kind, but I don't know that he would want to speak to you, and I know not in what way you might help. He is beyond such simple charity.'

'Beyond? What say you?'

Clara turned away. 'He has been taken, senhor, for refusing to work and for lying in a drunken state in the street. He is now at the Rasphuis.'

Miguel felt a vague elation, the thrill of revenge, when he thought of the Rasphuis, that place of cruel discipline from which few emerged and none emerged unbroken. But he was not here for revenge, and Joachim's suffering brought him nothing of value.

'I must find him there,' Miguel said more loudly than he should have, and his hands beginning to twitch with excitement. 'I'll see him at once.'

'See him at once,' Clara repeated back. 'What care you if you see him never?'

'That's no matter,' he answered. Miguel began to hurry off, but Clara grabbed him by the wrist. He could feel her jagged nails scrape along his flesh.

'You've not told me the truth, senhor. I think I know you after all. You are the man who ruined my husband.'

Miguel shook his head. 'No, not ruined, but shared in his ruin. His affairs and my own suffered together.'

She cast an eye upon his clothes, perhaps a bit soiled but finely wrought. 'And what do you want with him now?' Her tone seemed to Miguel not one of protective feeling, or even concern – more of curiosity, and an eager curiosity too. She moved closer to Miguel and let him take in her sweaty and feminine scent.

'I have business of the most urgent sort – it cannot wait until the morrow.'

'I think you will find that the Rasphuis does not offer such liberal hours as our musicos,' she told him, with a little laugh.

'And I think,' Miguel said, with a bravado he did not himself believe, 'you will find that any building is open at any time if a man has but the right key.'

Clara turned her head just so and her eyes widened just enough to let Miguel know that she took some pleasure in his firm resolve. She liked a strong man; he could tell that at once. Joachim, if he had ever been such a one, had long since relinquished his strength, allowing his losses to undo his manhood. More the pity for a woman so fine as she.

'I must go,' Miguel said, gently prying loose his hand. 'I hope I'll see you more,' he said, if only for the pleasure of flirtation.

'Who can say what the future holds?' Clara lowered her eyes. Miguel walked away with the confident stride of a man who could have taken a woman but chose not to. Still, if Joachim persisted in incurring Miguel's ire, if he continued in his absurd programme of abuse and revenge, Miguel thought he might have no choice but to seek out Clara again. Were he to plant a cuckoo in Joachim's unhappy nest, one would then see who had revenge and who looked the fool.

*   *   *

Located in the narrow Heiligeweg, an alley just north of the Singel in the old centre of the city, the Rasphuis stood as a monument to the reverence with which the Dutch viewed labour. From the old cobbled streets outside, it appeared no different from any other great house, a heavy wooden door, above which stood a gable stone depicting a blind effigy of justice presiding over two bound prisoners. Miguel studied the image for a moment in the fading light. It would be dark soon, and he had no desire to be caught on the street without a lantern, nor did he wish to be alone in an ancient ghost-ridden street like the Heiligeweg.

Miguel rapped on the door three or four times before a surly-looking fellow with a grease-slicked face opened the upper portion. Streaked with the light of a candle he had set down on a bench behind him, the guard stood offering his studied scowl to Miguel. He was a short man, but broad and thick-necked. The better part of his nose had been cut off in what looked like the not too distant past, and the inflamed skin glistened in the thin light of dusk.

'What do you want?' he asked, with boredom so intense he could hardly bring himself to move his mouth.

'I must have a word with one of the prisoners within these walls.'

The fellow let out a snorting and gurgling sound. The tip of his nose became even more reflective in the candlelight. 'They're not prisoners. They're penitents. And there are hours to visit the penitents, and there aren't hours. These aren't them.'

Miguel had no time for nonsense. What, he asked himself, would Charming Pieter do?

'Those hours ought to be considered flexible,' he suggested, holding up a coin between his thumb and index finger.

'I suppose you've a point.' The guard took the coin and opened the door to let Miguel enter.

The front hall indicated nothing of the horrors below. The floor was of a chequered heavy tile, and a series of arches on either side separated the entrance hall from a handsome open-air courtyard. Miguel might have thought this the outer garden to some great man's home rather than the entrance to a workhouse famed for its torments.

He had heard little of what actually took place inside these walls, but what he had heard bespoke of cruelty: vagabonds and beggars, the lazy and the criminal, all thrust together and made to do labours of the cruellest sort. The most incorrigible of these men were given the task of rasping Brazilwood, sawing it down to extract the reddish dye. And those who would not do this work, who steadfastly refused to labour, found a worse fate awaited them.

The Rasphuis was said to contain a chamber down below called the drowning cell, into which were thrown those who would not work. Water flooded the room, which contained pumps, that the inmates might save their lives through their toil. Those who failed to pump would meet their end. Those who learned the value of hard work would live.

The Dutchman led Miguel, who strained his ears for the sound of sloshing water, down a set of cold and stony stairs and into a chamber, none the most pleasant but hardly a dungeon of terrors. After they left the courtyard, the floor turned from tile to dirt, and the only furniture included a few wooden chairs and an old table missing one of its four legs.

'Who's the fellow you're looking for.'

'His name is Joachim Waagenaar.'

'Waagenaar.' The Dutchman laughed. 'Your friend's made a reputation for himself in as short a time as any. They got him rasping away even after most have finished for the night, and if he don't meet the demands they've set, he'll find his way to the drowning cell soon enough.'

'I'm sure he's difficult enough, but I must speak to him.' Miguel pressed another coin into the Dutchman's palm. Best to keep the wheels greased.

The fellow set down his candle upon a rough wooden table. 'Speak with him?' he asked. 'That cannot be. There are hours for visiting and there are hours for not visiting. Begging your pardon, I had meant to mention that before, but I must have forgotten myself.'

Miguel sighed. The money, he reminded himself, was nothing. In a few months' time, he would laugh at these little expenses.

He reached into his pocket and withdrew the last coin he had tucked there: five guilders. The noseless Dutchman pocketed it and disappeared from the room, locking it from the outside. A cold panic spread though Miguel, and when no one had returned for nearly a quarter of an hour, he began to wonder if perhaps he had become the victim of some horrible trick, but then he heard it unlatch, and the Dutchman entered, pushing Joachim before him.

Each time Miguel saw Joachim, the fellow was the worse for it. He had lost weight since their last meeting and had now grown sickly gaunt. His hands and arms and much of his face were stained red from sawing at Brazilwood, so that he looked more like a murderer than a penitent in a house of correction.

'You don't mind that I'll listen to your conversation,' the Dutchman said. 'I have to make certain nothing improper happens here.'

Miguel did mind, but he sensed at once that he would have little success removing the fellow, so he simply nodded.

'To what do I owe the pleasure of this visit, senhor?' Joachim's voice sounded even, devoid of sarcasm. He wished to play at formality.

'I must know what you have said to the Ma'amad. Have you sent a note? Is that how you communicated from these walls? I must know.'

Joachim's lips curled just slightly. 'How badly would you like to know?'

'I must have the answer. Tell me precisely what you revealed to them, every word. I have no time to play games.'

'No games. You'll not have the answer of me in here. They have cast me in, and I may not even know the length of time I am to be a prisoner, nor even my crime, other than I did not wish to work as their slave. So I say that if you can get me from this prison, I'll tell you all I know.'

'Get you out?' Miguel nearly shouted. 'I am no magistrate to get you out. How do you propose I do such a thing?'

The noseless Dutchman coughed into his fist. 'These things may be ordered, if one but knows how. Not for every man, but for those thrown here without a crime save only vagrancy.'

Miguel sighed. 'Very well,' he said. 'Speak plainly.'

'Oh, I think twenty guilders should do the business.'

Miguel could scarce believe that he was now prepared to bribe a guard twenty guilders to free from the Rasphuis an enemy he very recently would have paid a much larger a sum to have cast in. But Joachim knew why the Ma'amad had summoned him, and he would consider such information acquired cheap at twenty guilders.

Miguel peered into his purse, embarrassed that the guard now discovered he had apportioned out his money into different piles. He had only a little more than what was required.

The guard counted out the coins. 'What is this? Twenty guilders? I said forty. Do you think me a fool?'

'Surely one of us is a fool,' Miguel replied.

The guard shrugged. 'I'll just take this fellow away, then, and we'll say no harm done.'

Miguel opened his purse once more. 'I have only three and half guilders remaining to me. You must take that or nothing.' He handed it to the guard, hoping that by so doing he would seal the bargain.

'Are you sure you have no more purses or pockets or piles about you?'

'This is all I have, I promise you.'

His words must have conveyed an element of truth, for the Dutchman nodded. 'Get on with you,' he said. 'I won't have you loitering in front of the premises.'

They took a few steps in silence. 'I can't thank you enough,' Joachim then began, 'for this kindness.'

'I should have been happy to see you rot there,' Miguel murmured, as they passed through the courtyard, 'but I must know what you said to the Ma'amad.'

They stepped into the Heiligeweg, the guard closed the door behind them, and the series of locks and bolts echoed into the street. 'I must first ask you a question,' Joachim said.

'Please, I have little patience. It had better be relevant to these matters.'

'Oh, it is. It could not be more relevant. My question is this.' He cleared his throat. 'What the Christ is a Ma'amad?'

Miguel felt an ache in his skull gathering force, and his face grew hot. 'Don't play the fool with me. It is the council of Portuguese Jews.'

'And why should I have ever spoken to so august a body?'

'Did you not tell me before that you would tell me what you know?'

'I did promise, and I have kept my promise. I know nothing of your ruling council, though I believe I now know something of it. I know that you fear I should speak to it.'

'Damn you, you scurvy devil,' Miguel spat. He felt his fist clench and his arm tighten.

'It is all the more shame to you that you should need to be tricked to rescue an old associate from so horrible a fate as the Rasphuis. But you will find me not without gratitude. I'll thank you now and be on my way.' Joachim bowed deeply and then ran into the night.

It took a moment before Miguel could began to collect his thoughts. He could not even allow himself to consider how he had just humiliated himself before his mad enemy. It was of far more importance that the Ma'amad had called him forward and he did not yet know why. If it had not been Joachim who had reported him, this appearance must be the work of Parido. The spies he sent to Rotterdam had seen nothing they could use. Was it the matter of Joachim in the street with Hannah and Annetje? Perhaps, but they could hardly excommunicate him if he had a good explanation. He was certain he could think of one before morning.

CHAPTER 21

Miguel was out of bed before first light. After urinating furiously from the coffee he'd taken before bed – to keep his thoughts active in his sleep – he washed and said his morning prayers with a kind of pleading enthusiasm. He dressed, ate a breakfast of bread and dried cheese, and hastily drank a large bowl of coffee.

Last night, he had been driven by a desperate need to do something to further his cause, but in the silence of his room he could not escape the hard ball of fear that tightened in his belly. This was no ordinary summoning. There would be no indulgent lectures on the importance of the dietary laws or on resisting the charms of Dutch girls.

Could he really turn his back on everything as Alferonda had done? Instead of remaining in Amsterdam, a usurer and a known villain, Alonzo could easily have gone elsewhere, changed his name, settled into another community. There were other Jews in the world besides those in Amsterdam, and Miguel need not remain here. But the *cherem* would mean more than having to choose between being a Jew elsewhere or an outcast in Amsterdam. To leave the city would mean abandoning his plans in the coffee trade, abandoning the money Ricardo owed him. If he stayed, his creditors, no doubt including his sanctimonious brother, would descend upon him and pick his bones clean. Even if he did move to a city where no one knew him, how would he live there? A merchant without connections was no merchant at all. Was he to be a pushcart pedlar?

Miguel made his way to the Talmud Torah unobserved by anyone from the community. At this hour the Vlooyenburg had just begun to stir, and though he heard the early morning cries of the milkmen and bakers, he crossed the bridge unheeded by all except a pair of beggars, who sat eating a loaf of stale and mud-splattered bread while eyeing Miguel suspiciously.

The Ma'amad held its meetings in the same building as the synagogue, but a separate entrance led to the chambers. At the top of a winding stairwell, Miguel stepped into the small familiar room where supplicants awaited their summons. A few chairs had been set along the wall with semicircular windows behind them, allowing the early morning light to filter into a room smelling strongly of mildew and tobacco.

No one else awaited the call that morning but Miguel, and that was something of a relief. He hated making conversation with other penitents, whispering resentments and laughing off accusations. Better to wait alone. He paced back and forth and played out in his mind fantasy after fantasy: complete exoneration, excommunication and all imaginable variations.

The worst would not happen, he told himself. He had always extricated himself from the council's anger. And there was Parido – Parido who was surely not Miguel's friend but who wanted something from him. Parido, who had long known enough to have Miguel cast out and yet had not. There was no reason to believe he would let Miguel be cast out now.

He waited for nearly an hour before at last the door opened and he was ushered into the chamber. At a table at the far end of the room sat the seven men who would pass judgement. On the wall behind them was mounted the great marble symbol of the Talmud Torah: an immense pelican feeding its three young, the congregation having been formed of smaller synagogues some years before. The room reflected the wealth of the community's elite with its lush India rug, handsome portraits of former *parnassim*, and an ivory cabinet in which records were stored. The men sat behind a massive dark table and looked both solemn and princely in their rich attire. To be a *parnass* a man must have the wealth to dress like a *parnass*.

'Senhor Lienzo, thank you for answering the summons.' Aaron Desinea, who led the council, spoke with a kind of arch seriousness. 'Please.' He gestured to the narrow too-short chair that sat in the centre of the room where Miguel would sit while in discussion with the council. One of the legs was shorter than the rest. It took far more concentration than Miguel could spare to keep from wobbling.

In the middle of his seventh decade, Desinea was the oldest of the *parnassim* and had begun to display signs of the ravages of age. His hair had gone from a stately grey to a sickly white and now had the coarse quality of dead leaves. His beard had grown spotty and molten, and it was generally known that his eyes were failing. Even now he stared beyond Miguel, as though looking for a friend in the distance. But Desinea had sat on the council many times, serving his three-year limit, standing down for the required three years, and then finding himself always re-elected.

'You know everyone here, so I'll dispense with introductions. I shall read the charges against you, and you will have an opportunity to answer them. Do you have any questions?'

'No, senhor.' Miguel felt himself longing for another bowl of coffee to sharpen his senses. Already he had become distracted, and he had to fight the childish urge to fidget.

'Of course.' Desinea allowed himself the vaguest hint of a smile. 'By now you know the procedure well.' He held out a piece of paper, but his eyes made no contact with it. He must have memorised it earlier. 'Senhor Miguel Lienzo – who is also known by and does business under the names Mikael Lienzo, Marcus Lentus, and Michael Weaver – you are charged with irresponsible conduct bringing shame before the Nation. You are accused of consorting with dangerous, disreputable, and inappropriate gentiles and bringing such gentiles into our own neighbourhood, where they have behaved disruptively. Do you wish to respond to these charges?'

Miguel suppressed a smile, though he succumbed to the urge to breathe in the sweetness of the air. The meeting might be brought to its conclusion now, for the council would do him no harm. They did not know Joachim's name or Miguel's relationship with him. All the *parnassim* wanted was to hear an explanation and to issue a warning.

'Senhors, I should like to begin by offering my sincere apologies to this council and to the Nation. The man you mention is a Dutch unfortunate with whom, I admit, I have been friendly, but I can assure you that my intentions were always good.' He disliked lying in so holy a place, for it is written that a liar is no better than one who worships idols. But it is also written that the Holy One, blessed be He, hates a man who speaks one thing with his mouth and another with his heart. Therefore it seemed to Miguel that if he believed in his heart that his lie was justified, it was not so sinful after all.

'He is a sad man, ruined in a business misadventure,' he continued, 'and seeing him begging upon the street, I gave him a few stivers. Some days later, he engaged me in conversation, and not wishing to be rude, I made small chatter with him. The next time I saw him, he became aggressive and began to follow me, shouting things. Finally, he came into our own neighbourhood and accosted members of my brother's household. I then spoke to him harshly, warning him that if he continued to behave thus I would be forced to report him to the city authorities. I believe he won't disturb our quiet again.'

'The giving of charity is one of our most important *mitzvot*,' said Joseph ben Yerushalieem. He was a wealthy merchant who had come to Amsterdam some months after Miguel and had been elected to the council after fulfilling (by a matter of weeks) the requirement that a *parnass* must have been living as a Jew for at least three years. Miguel knew he interpreted his duties as sourly as the Law would allow, showing no mercy to new arrivals who refused to embrace an equally strict adherence. 'I commend you on your generosity, senhor, for charity exalts the Holy Name. This council is aware that you have suffered in business, but the rabbis say that a beggar must be treated kindly, for the Lord is with him.'

'Thank you, senhor,' said Miguel, who refused to believe that the Lord could possibly be with Joachim.

'However,' ben Yerushalieem continued, 'this incident demonstrates something that this body has warned you of many times in the past. Your easy interactions with the Dutch, your fluency in their language, and your comfort with their companionship can lead only to difficulties between our two peoples. This community has thrived because it has kept its distance from our Dutch hosts. This incident with the beggar may seem small, and you have been guiltless of any ill intent, but it suggests that you are unwilling to follow this council's advice that you keep a more formal distance from these people.'

'This problem has been brought to our attention before,' Desinea chimed in. 'You are a man who habitually breaks the laws of this council because he believes he knows better than we do what is right for the Nation.'

'Precisely.' Ben Yerushalieem pressed on. 'You have broken the rules of the Ma'amad because you thought yourself the best judge of right and wrong. It makes no difference, senhor, if you are seeking the affections of a pretty Dutch girl or giving alms to an inappropriate gentile. Both are forbidden, and forbidden for good reasons.'

Miguel found the pressure more intense than he had at first anticipated. 'I thank you for taking the time to discuss these matters with me and allowing me the opportunity to improve my behaviour. I shall redouble my efforts to be more vigilant in considering my actions in light of the larger good of this community.'

'I can only hope that you will,' Desinea told him sternly. 'You are a grown man, Senhor Lienzo, not a boy whose transgressions can be overlooked.'

Desinea's words stung furiously, but Miguel knew his pride would recover. The tide had begun to recede, after all. The Ma'amad had made its point. He had been warned.

'I wonder if that is enough.' Solomon Parido leaned forward as though scrutinising something on Miguel's face. Though animated by his expectation of triumph, he appeared, if anything, more morose than ever. Even the taste of victory brought him no joy. 'Such warnings can be effective, I grant you, but I am not convinced they will suffice in this case. I am a friend of Senhor Lienzo's family, so I speak with genuine concern when I say he has been issued many warnings in the past. Now we must ask, Have they led him to change his ways? Have they ever inspired in his heart a new love of the Law? Forgiveness is a blessing in the eyes of the Most High, but we must not forgive too easily or too often without damaging the community.'

Miguel swallowed hard. Perhaps, he thought, Parido only meant to appear harsh that he might better disguise his true intentions of protecting Miguel. Why would he have pretended friendship this past month only now to turn on him? If he sought to impose the *cherem*, why had he not made use of his knowledge that Miguel had bribed a servant girl into fingering Parido as the father of her child? None of it made sense.

'We cannot know how those warnings have shaped the senhor,' ben Yerushalieem commented. 'Is it therefore not pure speculation to say that warnings have done no good? We may have changed Senhor Lienzo's behaviour greatly and rescued him from his own worst self.'

'Senhors, I must commend your generosity, but I wonder if generosity may not do our community more harm than good.'

Miguel felt himself wobble in the chair. This was no mere pretence at harshness. Parido was after blood.

'Really, senhor,' ben Yerushalieem said, 'this denunciation is unbecoming. You and Senhor Lienzo have had disagreements, but Holy Torah commands us not to hold a grudge.'

'This is no matter of grudges. All Amsterdam knows that I've set aside our former differences, but that does not mean that I must hold my tongue when I see evil. I have it on good authority,' Parido pressed on, 'that this man is engaged in a matter of business that presents a direct threat to this community.'

So this is his move, Miguel thought, as he tried to keep his face from twitching. He could not yet see the whole of the plan, but he recognised the pieces. The gestures of friendship now allowed Parido to claim only the best motives.

'Is this true?' Desinea asked.

'By no means,' Miguel managed to answer, though his mouth had grown painfully dry. 'Senhor Parido might wish to re-examine his source of information.'

'Can you tell us more, Senhor Parido?' ben Yerushalieem asked.

'I believe it is Lienzo who must tell us more.'

'*Senhor* Lienzo,' Miguel corrected.

'The members of this council need no lessons in etiquette,' Parido explained softly. 'You are here to answer our questions.'

'Senhor Parido is right,' another *parnass*, Gideon Carvoeiro, announced. 'True, these two men have had words, but that means nothing. The senhor has set forth a question. We cannot bring a man before us and allow him to choose which questions are to his liking.'

Parido made a half-hearted effort to hide a smile. 'Precisely. You must tell us the nature of your new venture.'

And there it was. Parido had sought Miguel's friendship to learn about his plans in the coffee trade. When that had not worked, he had deftly use his position on the Ma'amad not to arrange Miguel's excommunication but to use their old animosity as an excuse to discover the nature of his business. Now Parido surely thought that Miguel had no choice but to divulge his secrets – otherwise he would almost certainly face the *cherem*, for defiance of the council was among the

325

most serious of crimes in its eyes. Parido had set his trap brilliantly: Miguel must give up his secrets or be destroyed.

But Miguel would not be so easily ruined; a Jew from Salonika could not hope to scheme like a former Converso. Miguel believed he might still teach Parido a few things about deviousness.

'Senhors,' he began, after taking a moment to formulate his reply, 'I hope you will consider that a man of business is not always at liberty to answer questions concerning his affairs. I have agreements with other merchants who depend on my silence. I need not explain to you the role of rumour on the Exchange and the importance of keeping some dealings quiet.'

'Quiet is not a luxury you possess right now,' Parido said. 'The Ma'amad's need to protect the Nation must take precedence over your inclination towards secrecy.'

Miguel swallowed hard. He might ruin himself if he spoke with too much arrogance, but the right tone would win the day. 'Then I must respectfully refuse to answer, senhors.'

Desinea leaned forward. 'I must remind you that our Nation knows no greater crime than refusal to cooperate with the Ma'amad. Any business scheme upon which you have embarked, lawful or no, may prove itself difficult to execute if you earn the enmity of our Nation.'

'Senhors,' he repeated, careful to keep his tone modest and respectful, for everything hinged on their response to what he now said. 'I beg you consider what it is you ask of me, whether answers must be pursued regardless of costs. There is no one in this room who does not have a relation or friend who was destroyed by the Inquisition in Portugal. This council has established itself in the hopes that our people may never have to face those horrors again, but I fear that in truly understanding our enemy we may have become too much like him.'

Ben Yerushalieem slammed his palm down on the table. 'I advise you to think before you speak further.' Veins bulged out in his neck. 'You dare liken this council to the Inquisition?'

'I only suggest that we must think about the cost of inquiry, and if the answers are worth the price of the asking.'

'Particularly if those costs are yours,' Parido quipped.

The council laughed, Parido's comment having eased some of the tension, but Miguel clenched his teeth in frustration. 'Yes,' he shot back. 'Particularly if they are mine. This council is designed to protect the well-being of the Nation as a whole. It wants nothing so much as to see the Nation flourish. Yet that nation is composed of people. I believe it wrong that you ask one of those people to sacrifice his well-being to satisfy the vague curiosity of the community. Must I give up my chance of regaining some small portion of my fortune so that you may know I have done nothing wrong? Perhaps if there were specific charges; but to force me to reveal secrets that protect my business interests in order that you might learn if they may prove dangerous to the community – this is an injustice.'

No one spoke for a moment. Parido opened his mouth but understood that Miguel's spirited outburst had changed the council's tone. He could not push too hard here.

'I believe that Senhor Lienzo has argued an important point,' Desinea said at last. 'We need not ask him to expose himself without just cause. Such a pursuit could send a chill throughout the city and discourage others of the Nation from seeking refuge here or embracing their ancestral faith. Moreover, if by speaking here the senhor does any damage to Dutch businessmen, the results could do us greater harm than we can endure.'

'What sort of Dutch businessmen?' Parido demanded. 'That is what we must find out. We have already established his unappealing connections.'

'Please, senhor.' Ben Yerushalieem shook his head slightly. 'We all know there is a subtle divide between business and improper relations.'

The other *parnassim* nodded in agreement, all but Parido. 'How can we learn the truth if we may not enquire into it?'

'You would smash a vessel, Senhor Parido, to learn its contents, thinking nothing of the value of the vessel itself?' ben Yerishalieem asked.

'Perhaps the vessel has no value.'

Desinea stared at Parido. 'You assured this council that you would not allow your personal feelings concerning Senhor Lienzo to affect your judgement.'

'And they have not,' he answered. 'I defy him to tell this council how the revelation of his plans will harm him.'

'Can you do so?' Desinea asked. 'Particularly since you know well that we of the Ma'amad know how to keep secret the inner workings of this chamber?'

Miguel surrendered to the urge to smile. Parido had trapped himself within his own scheme, and the world would now see who was the cleverer man. Miguel would win this battle in a manner worthy of Charming Pieter.

'Senhors,' Miguel began, 'not very long ago Senhor Parido stopped me on the Exchange and demanded to know, for the sake of his business, the nature of my trades. I refused to tell him at the time, believing silence to best serve the ends of myself and my partners. Now, as a *parnass*, he demands the same information, claiming that he enquires not for the sake of his own affairs but for the sake of the Nation. You tell me that the workings of this chamber remain in this chamber, but I hope I do not seem overly suspicious if I wonder if every member of this body will honour the tradition of secrecy.'

A chill quiet fell upon the room. Several members of the council glared at Parido. Others looked away in discomfort. Desenea studied a spot on the table.

'Please step outside,' ben Yerushalieem said, after a moment.

Miguel waited, clearing his mind of all expectations while the members of the Ma'amad talked privately among themselves. Occasionally Parido's voice would pulse through the walls, but Miguel could not discern the words. At last he was summoned to reappear.

'It is the opinion of this council,' Desinea announced, 'that you have ignored the laws of our Nation without malice but to ill effect. We have therefore decided to invoke the *cherem*, to place you under the ban, for a period of one day, beginning with sunset tonight. During that period you may not attend the synagogue, consort with Jews, or involve yourself in any way with the community. At the conclusion of that period, your place among us will be as it was.'

Miguel nodded. He had not escaped unscathed, as he had wished, but he had escaped.

'Let me add,' ben Yerushalieem said, 'that should this council learn that you have misrepresented your affairs, you will find it far less lenient. If your relationship with this beggar is other than what you have said, or if your business is improper, you will find us unwilling to listen to excuses. Have you anything to add, senhor?'

Miguel told those gathered that he was sorry for his offence and deserving of their punishment, and after thanking the *parnassim* for their wisdom he silently withdrew.

To be placed under the *cherem* even for a single day was a great disgrace. It would be the topic of gossip for weeks to come. Men had fled Amsterdam in disgust after being so punished, but Miguel would not be one of them.

He walked home hurriedly, repeating over and over again the prayer of thanks. He had prevailed. Parido had revealed himself, he had sprung his trap, but Miguel had outmanoeuvred him. He paused to hug himself and then regained his stride. He had won.

Yet, it was necessarily a temporary victory. Parido had struck and failed, and the signs of his former kindness would dry up, leaving only ashes. More than that, now Miguel knew he had an enemy, an angry enemy, one who no longer needed to act with subtly or with subterfuge but would attack boldly and surely fiercely.

But why? Why did Parido care so much about Miguel's coffee trade? If he did not want Miguel excommunicated, his scheme somehow depended upon Miguel's scheme, which the *cherem* would ruin. But since Parido could not get what he wanted through the Ma'amad, he surely would in some other way. If he had not thought himself wronged before, he would surely be stinging after Miguel's victory today. There could be no doubt that Parido was now far more dangerous than ever before.

From

The Factual and Revealing Memoirs of Alonzo Alferonda

I made it a habit to employ a few Dutchmen of the lower sort to perform little tasks for me. They were rough fellows, as inclined to steal as the men to whom I lent, but there was no helping that. These ruffians, Claes or Caspar or Cornelis – who can remember these odd Dutch names? – would help me terrify the wretches who had borrowed money from me and were disinclined to pay me back. I'm sure a few of my guilders found their way into those Dutch purses, but what could a man do? I hadn't the inclination to order my business with the iron fist of a tyrant, and I discovered that a little laxity in such matters promoted an odd sort of loyalty.

One afternoon I sat in the basement of a dank tavern sipping thin beer. Across from me sat an ageing thief, and a pair of my men lurked menacingly behind me. I always had them peeling apples with sharp blades or carving pieces of wood at these moments. It saved me the tedium of uttering threats aloud.

This thief presented a bit of a problem. He was perhaps fifty years of age and looked ancient from his time of toiling upon the earth. His hair was long and clumped together in thin strands, his clothes stained, his skin a web of ruptured veins. He had borrowed some ten guilders of me, at a very unreasonable rate of interest I should add, to pay for the expenses surrounding the death of his wife. Now, nearly a year later, he had given me nothing and, what was more, announced he could give me nothing. Here was not one of those men who claimed he could pay nothing while his ringed fingers stroked a belly big with bread and fish. No, he truly had nothing, but though I pitied him, I could not forgive the debt. Where then would I be?

'Surely you must have some article of value you can pawn,' I suggested. 'Some clothes you have failed to mention, old jewels perhaps. A cat? I know a pawnbroker who will give a fair price for a proven mouser.'

'I have nothing,' he told me.

'You are a thief,' I reminded him. 'You can steal it. Or have I, in some way, misunderstood the nature of thievery?'

'I am not much of a thief any more.' He held up his hands. 'My fingers are no longer nimble, and my feet are no longer swift. I dare not make the attempt.'

'Hmm.' I scratched at my beard. 'How long has this been going on – this clumsy finger and leaden-foot difficulty? A while?'

'Yes,' he admitted.

'A long while? Let us say, more than a year?'

'I would say so, yes.'

'So when you borrowed this money of me, you knew you would not be able to repay? Am I a charitable board to hand out alms? Do you come to me because you have heard of my generosity? You must tell me, because I am confused.'

I admit this harangue served no function but to buy myself time as I decided what course of action to follow. Rarely did I find someone who could pay me nothing and who had no skills I could put into service for myself.

'What,' I asked him, 'do you think I should do with one such as you?'

He gave this some long consideration. 'I think,' he said at last, 'that you should cut off the little fingers from each of my hands. I haven't the skill of a cutpurse any longer, so I won't much miss them except as any man would miss parts of his body. And in doing this, you can let the world know that you are determined not to be cheated. I think that would be the merciful thing.'

Here was a handsome situation. How could I avoid cutting off his little fingers – fingers he volunteered for their severing – without revealing myself to be the sort of man who simply refrained from those kinds of cruelties? I truly believed he had forced my hand and I had no choice but to cut off the man's fingers – though, being merciful, I was prepared to cut off only one. How else could I save my fierce reputation? I know not what dark path I might have followed if I had not been rescued by the most unlikely of men.

As I stared at the old fellow and contemplated his fate, I heard the slap of metal on wood. I and my Dutchmen turned and saw a figure standing in the dim light, erect as a royal guard. It was none other than Solomon Parido.

'Here is the ten guilders he owes you,' he said coolly. 'I won't allow this thing to transpire.'

'I had no idea you possessed such charity in your heart,' I said.

'I cannot stand by and see a man mutilated by so cruel a beast. This display sickens me, but

I am at least gratified to know that the moral judgement I made of you has proven sound.'

'Senhor, the air circulates poorly in this room, and I fear your sanctimoniousness will suffocate us all. Nevertheless, I'm sure our friend here is grateful for your intervention.'

The old thief, knowing an opportunity when he saw one, chimed in, 'Ten guilders is but the principal. You have neglected the interest.'

Claes and Caspar looked at me, awaiting orders. I did not want this farce witnessed, so I sent them all out of the room. I told the Dutchmen to free the thief with a slap or two for good measure, and they were gone. I sat facing my old enemy in the thin light of a musky closet. I had not had private words with Parido since my exile. There had been a few barbs exchanged on the street or in taverns where we crossed paths, but nothing like this.

It occurred to me that here was a fine opportunity for revenge. Why could I not have Claes and Caspar remove his little fingers or give him a slap or two for good measure? But that was not the sort of revenge I craved.

'Have you come to apologise to me?' I asked. I gestured for him to sit on one of the old stools in the room and lit my pipe by dipping a large splinter into the oil lamp and then into the packed bowl.

Parido remained standing, too great a man to place his arse on a stool that one such as I might use. 'You know I haven't.'

'I know you haven't,' I agreed. 'Well, then. It must be something for you to come here. I believe it to have worked this way: you had your Ma'amad spies track me to this place and you thought it perfect, for surely no one would see you enter or leave. You were willing to tear open your purse for that old thief because you could not imagine a more private meeting than this, and you were willing to take the opportunity when it presented itself. So now that we know all that, let us move on.' I blew smoke at him. 'What do you want, Parido?'

His dignity would not permit him to swat at the smoke, but I could see him struggling not to gag. 'I have questions for you to answer,' he said.

'I suppose then we'll see if I feel like answering, but I can promise you nothing. You see, Parido, I can't think of any reason why I should want to help you or provide you with answers about anything. You treated me as no Jew should treat another. This is not the Ma'amad chamber of the Talmud Torah, this is the belly of Amsterdam, and if I decide you are never vomited out, no one will hear from you more.'

'Don't threaten me,' he said evenly.

I admired his courage and laughed at his stupidity – perhaps I had not secured my villainous reputation as carefully as I ought. He had every reason to be frightened yet did not seem to know or care. I only shrugged in return. 'I suppose we'll see what's a threat and what isn't. In the meantime, I am nothing short of astonished at your pluck, showing up as you have, as though I might be happy to forgive your wrongs.'

'I won't defend my actions. I have only come to ask you if you encouraged Miguel Lienzo to pursue a trade in whale oil, knowing that his trade would harm me while keeping that possibility hidden from Lienzo himself. In other words, did you use him as your pawn?'

Quite the contrary: I had gone so far as to warn Miguel Lienzo about just this sort of thing, but I was not about to tell Parido that much. 'Why should you ask me that?'

'Because that is what Lienzo says.'

Ah, Lienzo, I thought. Using my name to his advantage. Well, why should he not? Surely Parido cornered him and, rather than risking himself, he blamed the souring of Parido's finances on Alferonda the way peasants blame the souring of milk on imps. The parnass could do me no more harm than he already had. I was in no danger. I therefore did not feel any anger towards Miguel, who had only been behaving prudently.

I shook my head. 'I would have done so if I could have, but I will not commit the sin of lying to protect any man. I had nothing to do with any whale oil futures of yours. I suspect Lienzo is protecting himself or protecting another man by suggesting that it was me.'

But, you may wonder, if I did not resent Miguel for taking liberties with my name, why did I not protect him? Why did I expose him to Parido's anger when I might so easily have absorbed that anger myself?

I did so because I could not risk a rapprochement between the two. Far better that Miguel should face Parido's wrath.

CHAPTER 22

During his brief period of exile, Miguel thought it best to avoid other Jews of the neighbourhood. Their stares and whispers would only sour his victory. Men who had suffered temporary bans always hid themselves away in their homes until they were again free to go about their business. They lurked about like thieves, they closed their shutters, they ate their food cold.

Miguel had too much to do and hadn't the luxury of hiding in his cellar for the day. He sent a note to Geertruid, telling her he wished to meet the next afternoon. He suggested the Golden Calf. That disgusting little place where they had first discussed coffee might not suit his taste, but at least he knew Geertruid's cousin did not serve other Jews, and on the day of his *cherem* he wished for secrecy. Geertruid wrote back and suggested instead another tavern, one near the warehouses. As it promised to be equally obscure, Miguel sent his agreement.

After sending out letters to his agents, Miguel prepared a bowl of coffee and took a moment to think about his most pressing needs: how to raise five hundred guilders to complete the amount Isaiah Nunes required. Instead of obtaining the missing money, he might instead transfer to Nunes the thousand that remained to him at the very end of the week. Nunes would not notice, or he would not be able to speak of it until the beginning of next week. Being too cowardly to face Miguel directly when it came to such awkward things as debt, he would send a letter requesting the remaining amount, and then – since Miguel planned to ignore the request – he would send another note a few days later. Miguel would return a vague reply that would give Nunes some hope that the money was forthcoming at any moment. So long as he avoided running into his friend, he could extend the payment date for weeks before Nunes grew angry enough to threaten him with courts or the Ma'amad. Clearly this matter of five hundred guilders was not nearly so dire as he had led himself to believe.

In a much brighter mood, he indulged himself with a Charming Pieter pamphlet he had read only twice before. He had not even set the water for his coffee to boiling before Annetje appeared from around the winding staircase, her head cocked at an impish angle Miguel mistook for lust. He had not been feeling amorous, but with a free morning before him, there was no reason why he could not summon some enthusiasm. Annetje, however, only wished to tell him that the senhora awaited him in the drawing room.

★　　★　　★

Why should she not summon Miguel to speak with her? She had never done so before, but Hannah could not see that there was anything improper in having friendly relations with her husband's brother. Daniel would be at the Exchange, and he needn't know anything of it, even if it were improper, which it was not. And of course she could count on Annetje's silence. The maid, if she had betrayal on her mind, had far deeper wells from which to draw.

Miguel entered, dressed in his austere Dutch attire, and bowed slightly. His eyes were sunken and the skin below them dark, as though he hadn't slept in days.

'Yes, senhora?' he said, in a voice that managed to be both weary and charming. 'You honoured me with a summons?'

Annetje stood behind him and grinned like a bawd.

'Girl,' Hannah said to her, 'fetch me my yellow cap. The one with the blue stones.'

'Senhora, you have not worn that cap in a year's time. I cannot say where it is.'

'Then you had better start looking,' she answered. She would hear about that later. Annetje would lecture her, tell her mistress it was wrong to speak to her so, threaten and tease her. But Hannah would face those problems when they arose. For now, Annetje would not dare disobey in front of Miguel.

'Yes, senhora,' she replied, in a convincingly

342

subservient tone, before meekly removing herself from the room.

'It is best to give her a task so she does not spend her time at keyholes,' Hannah said.

Miguel took a seat. 'She is a well enough girl,' he answered absently.

'I'm sure you know best.' Hannah felt herself redden. 'I must thank you for taking the time to sit with me, senhor.'

'It is I who should thank you. Conversation with a charming lady will pass the time far more amiably than will books and papers.'

'I had forgotten that you have those things available to you. I had thought you must be sitting alone and in silence, but your learning frees you from dullness.'

'I've thought it must be terrible not to read,' he said. 'Is it a loss you feel?'

Hannah nodded. She liked the softness in his voice. 'My father thought learning improper for me and my sisters, and I know Daniel thinks the same, should we have a girl child, even though I have heard the rabbi, Senhor Mortera, say that a daughter may engage in learning for which the wife has no time.' She lifted her hand, to place it upon her abdomen, but then changed her mind. She had become conscious of growing big, of the swelling pressing against her gown, and while it was a sensation that usually comforted her, she did not want Miguel to think of her as nothing more than a woman growing big with child.

'They say it is not so among the Tudescos,' she continued, half afraid that she prattled like a fool. 'Their women learn to read, and they are given holy books translated into the common tongue. I think that way is better.'

A strange thrill shot through her body, as though she had just thrown herself off a bridge or before a speeding cart. Never before had she dared to say such things aloud. Miguel was not her husband, of course, but he was her husband's brother, and for now that seemed to her dangerous enough.

He stared at her. At first she thought she saw anger, and she pressed herself into her chair in preparation for the sting of rebuke, but she had misread him. His eyebrows raised slightly, a little smile upon his lips. She saw surprise, amusement too, and maybe even delight.

'I had never thought you had such opinions. Have you discussed them with your husband? He might very well permit some learning.'

'I have tried,' she told him, 'but your brother does not wish to hear me speak on matters of which I know nothing. He asked how I can have an opinion on something of which I am entirely ignorant.'

Miguel erupted into a raspy laugh. 'You cannot fault him for his logic.'

Hannah reddened, but after an instant she realised that Miguel mocked not her but Daniel, and so she joined him, and together they laughed at her husband.

'May I ask a favour of you?' she said, and then squirmed uncomfortably at the sound of her own words. She had thought to wait longer before mentioning it but found she grew impatient and nervous. Best to have it said.

'Of course, senhora.'

'May I once again try that coffee-tea you let me drink before?' What else could she do? She dared not steal any more of Miguel's diminishing supply, and she had eaten all the fruit she'd taken. Besides, now that she knew that it was supposed to be a drink and not a food, she did not think there would be as much pleasure in grinding down the berries with her teeth.

Miguel smiled. 'It would be my great pleasure, so long as you recall my request of your silence.' Then, without waiting for her reply, he rang the bell for Annetje, who appeared more rapidly than anyone who had been searching through Hannah's trunks might have hoped. She allowed her eyes to lock with Hannah's, but Miguel alone spoke to her, reminding her of how to prepare the drink. When the girl left, Hannah could feel her face turn hot, but she was almost certain that Miguel did not notice – or that he was most adept at pretending not to notice, which was nearly as good.

Hannah burned in the heat of his attention. He smiled at her, he met her eyes; he listened when she spoke. This is what it would be like to have a husband who loved her, she thought. The women in stage plays must feel thus when they talked to their loves.

Still, she knew it was but fantasy. How long could she talk with him? How long before a clever man like Miguel recovered from his stumble and moved into his own house, leaving Hannah alone with her husband? Not alone, of course. There would, God willing, be her child, and her child – her daughter – would be her salvation.

'Were you to marry again and have children,' she asked, 'would you allow your daughters to learn?'

'I must be honest with you, senhora, and tell you that I have never thought about it. I always assumed your sex cared nothing for learning and was happy to be spared the pains of study, but now that you tell me otherwise I would look at the matter with new eyes.'

'Then you and I are of a mind.'

After moving to Amsterdam, Daniel had been busy with his studies, learning the ancient tongue and the Law, and Hannah thought she should do the same. If she was a Jew, she should know what it meant to be a Jew. She could not know how her husband might respond to such a thing, but she had hoped he would warm to her display of interest. She considered the wording for days, playing out conversations in her mind. Finally, one Shabbat night, after they had engaged in the *mitzvah* of marital relations, she decided she should never find her sleepy and sated husband in a more receptive mood.

'Why have I not been taught the Law, senhor?' she asked.

There was only a vague hastening of his breath.

'I have thought,' she continued, speaking hardly above a whisper, 'that I too might learn to read and understand Hebrew. And perhaps I might learn to read Portuguese too.'

'Perhaps you might learn to transform rods into serpents and to part the waters of the sea,' he had answered, rolling away from her.

Hannah lay there, afraid to move, gritting her teeth with anger and shame. He must have felt some remorse for dismissing her, for a few days later, when he returned home in the evening, he pressed into her hands two silver bracelets.

'You are a good wife,' he said to her, 'but you must not wish for more than what belongs to a wife. Learning is for men.'

'It must be,' she now said to Miguel, 'that learning is not forbidden to women, else the Tudescos would not allow it, for they have the same Law, do they not?'

'It is not forbidden,' Miguel explained. 'I am told that there have even been great Talmudists among the ladies in times past. Some things belong to Law, and some things belong to custom. It is written that a woman may be called to the Law, but her modesty ought to forbid her from answering. But what is modesty?' he asked, as though puzzling out the question himself. 'These Dutch women know nothing of it, and yet they do not feel immodest.'

Annetje now arrived with the bowls of coffee. Hannah breathed in the scent and salivated at the thought of drinking. More than its flavour, she loved how it made her feel. If she had been a scholar, she would have been able to unravel any point of Law. Had she been a merchant, she could have outwitted any man upon the Exchange. Now, she again lifted the bowl to her lips and tasted the engaging bitterness, a taste, she realised, that made her think of Miguel. This is the taste of Miguel, she told herself: bitter and inviting.

She waited for Annetje, who flashed all sorts of knowing looks, to leave before she began to speak again. 'May I ask you what happened between you and the council?'

Miguel opened his mouth in surprise, as though she had spoken of something forbidden, but he also appeared pleased. Perhaps he found her boldness exciting. How bold should she be?

'It is nothing of substance. There were some questions about business partners. Some on the council do not like the people with whom I trade, so they placed me under this *cherem* for a day as a warning. These are pretty questions from so pretty a woman.'

Hannah turned away so that he would not see

her blush. 'Do you suggest that a woman should not ask such questions?'

'Not at all. I delight in an inquisitive woman.'

'Perhaps,' she suggested, 'you delight in an inquisitive woman in the same way you delight in defying the council.'

Miguel smiled warmly. 'I think you may be right, senhora. I have never much cared for authority, and I love to see it challenged – be it the authority of a husband or the Ma'amad.'

Hannah felt herself redden again, but met his gaze all the same. 'When you were married,' she asked, 'did you love to see your wife challenge you?'

He laughed. 'Most times,' he said. 'If I am to be honest, I must say that I am as prone to grow comfortable in authority as any man. That is no reason why I should not be questioned, however. I might have followed my father's example and never studied the ways of our race had I not thought this way, for it is what I love best about the teachings of the rabbis. Everything must be questioned and disputed, looked at from all angles, examined and held up to the light. The *parnassim* and men like – well, like many men I know – forget that. They wish to see things always as they are and never ask how they might be.'

'And is this reason, your delight in challenge, why you were called before the Ma'amad? My husband tells me you have defiled Holy Law.'

'As I say, senhora, there is law and there is

custom, and custom is often little more than a fable. So long as I tell the *parnassim* what they want to hear, all is well.'

'What they want to hear?' Hannah asked, permitting herself the slightest of smiles. 'You lied to them?'

He laughed. 'Only little lies. They do not want to hear important lies.'

'But is it not a sin to lie?'

'You tease me, senhora. I suppose it is a sin, but an insignificant one. A man of business lies all the time. He lies to put trades to his advantage or to construct circumstances just so. A man may lie to make his position look better than it is, or weaker than it is, depending on his goals. None of these are the same as lying in a way that may harm another man. These lies are merely the rules of business, and such rules surely apply when dealing with the Ma'amad.'

'But those rules would not apply to a woman speaking to her husband?' Hannah had meant only to clarify, but she realised that the moment she spoke the words they carried weight she had not intended.

'It depends on the husband,' Miguel answered pointedly.

Her stomach flipped in fear. She was going too far. 'This difference between law and custom is very confusing,' she said quickly, hoping to return the conversation to safer matters.

'The Ma'amad is a political body,' he said.

'Among the Tudescos, there are rabbis who give the Law to the politicians, but among us it is the other way. Sometimes they forget the glory of the Holy Torah; they forget why we are here, the miracle of our being living Jews rather than dead ones or living Papists.' He took a final sip of his coffee and then set down the bowl. 'I thank you for your company,' he told her, 'but I must now go. I have an appointment to keep.'

'How can you have appointments while under the ban?'

He smiled warmly. 'I am full of secrets,' he said. 'Just as you are.'

Maybe he knew everything after all – the church, the widow, everything. As she watched him go, she thought she must tell him. Regardless of the consequences, she must tell him. Then she could tell him about the widow too, and her life would be in his hands. As she sipped her drink, she considered that to have her life in his hands would not be so very terrible at all.

The first thing Miguel saw when he walked into the Singing Carp was Alonzo Alferonda, his squat form spread out toadlike on a bench, speaking quietly to a pair of low Dutchmen. He rose upon seeing Miguel and hurried over on his short legs. 'Senhor,' he called out eagerly, 'I am delighted to hear of your victory.'

Miguel looked around, though he was inclined not to worry about Ma'amad spies on a day when technically he was not a member of the community. 'I hardly expected to see you here.'

'I should like to buy you a drink to celebrate your victory over the Pharisees.'

'Another time, perhaps. I've a meeting just now.'

'You run some errand of the coffee trade?' Alferonda asked.

'This coffee trade will be my undoing. Parido cornered me on the Exchange and demanded to know my dealings in coffee. I refused, and before I could turn my head I stood before the Ma'amad.'

'Oh, he's a tricky one, but the greatest way to foil him will be for you to succeed in your business.'

Miguel nodded. 'Let me ask you something, Alonzo. You know more about coffee than I do; you've been drinking it for years. I read in a pamphlet written by an Englishman that coffee suppresses the urges of the flesh, but I have been feeding some to my brother's wife, and she seems rather animated by it.'

'Your brother's wife, you say? Ho, Miguel, you are more of a rascal than I had thought. And I commend you, for she is a pretty thing, and now plump with child too, so you needn't worry about unfortunate results.'

'I have no plans to cuckold my brother. I have problems enough. I only wonder if the coffee may be the difficulty with her.'

'You cannot cuckold a man whose wife you cannot get with child, but we'll set that aside for

352

the moment. I'd advise you not put too much faith in those English pamphlets. Those people will write anything to sell their scribblings. Here is something I do know, however. When the Queen of Sheba came to visit the court of Solomon, among the gifts she brought him was a great chest full of the most exotic spices of the East. That night, after the palace had gone to bed, King Solomon was so full of desire he forced himself on her.'

'I have heard the story,' Miguel said.

'Among the Turks it is said that the chest of spices included coffee berries, and it was this fruit that spurred his lust. I would feed your brother's pretty wife no more coffee fruit unless you want to follow Solomon's path.'

'Only in wisdom.'

'It is always wise to take a handsome woman when there will be no consequences.'

'I don't know if I would say that it is wise to do so. Only desirable.'

'Then you admit it,' Alferonda said, poking his finger gleefully in Miguel's chest.

Miguel shrugged. 'I admit only in seeing beauty where there is beauty and finding it a sad thing when it is neglected.'

'Merciful Christ,' Alferonda shouted. 'You're in love.'

'Alonzo, you're no more than a gossipy grand-mother with a beard. Now, if you're done inventing tales, I've business to tend to.'

'Ah, his other love, the Dutch widow.' Alferonda

said. 'I understand your haste, Lienzo. I would surely rebuff myself for her sake.'

Geertruid made her way through the crowd and smiled at Miguel as though she were hosting him at her own table. Miguel winced. Somehow he did not like the idea of introducing Geertruid to Alferonda; one illicit presence ought not to consort with another. 'Good day, senhor,' he said, and started to pull away.

'Ho, ho!' Alferonda shouted after them. 'Are you not going to introduce me to this lady?' He pranced forward to stand by Geertruid's side. In a sweeping move, he lifted his wide hat from his head and bowed deeply. 'Alonzo Alferonda at your service, madam. Should you find yourself in need of any assistance a gentleman can provide, I hope you will do no more than to summon your humble servant.'

'I thank you.' She smiled warmly.

'I'm sure the lady will sleep better tonight for having had the offer,' Miguel said, pulling her away.

'I should love to know more of her sleeping,' Alferonda shouted, but he didn't follow.

'What charming friends you have,' she said as they took a seat. If she felt any embarrassment about her revelation of the previous night at the Brewer's Guild feast, she did not show it.

'None more so than you.' He looked across the tavern and saw that Alferonda had left.

Geertruid took a small pipe from a leather sack

and began to stuff it with tobacco. Now,' she said, 'on to business. Have you looked into getting our money returned?'

Miguel could hardly believe her. 'I have hardly had time to tend to that matter. Have you no questions of how I fared before the council?'

She lit her pipe with the flame of the oil lamp. 'I am sure you prevailed. I have faith in you. And you would not be in such good spirits had you not won the day. Now, on to the matter of my investments.'

Miguel sighed, angry that she was souring his victory with this peevishness about money. Why had he ever involved himself with this Dutchwoman with her secrets and stolen capital?

'I know we agreed to wait two weeks,' she told him, 'but if you have no solution to our Iberian problems, we must get the money returned.'

Miguel was determined not to show his concern. 'Madam, where is your adventurous spirit? I begin to suspect that you would rather see your money returned than you would the fortune it will bring you. You must have faith that I will sort out these small difficulties.'

'I don't believe you will sort them out.' She shook her head slowly. With her face turned downwards and her hair dang ling just dangling over her eyes, she looked like a mournful Madonna in a painting. Then she lifted her gaze and grinned. 'I don't believe you will sort them out,' she explained, 'because *I*, silly woman that I am, have found our solution.'

Too much had happened in one day, and Miguel's head had begun to ache. He put one hand to his brow. 'I don't understand you,' he moaned.

'Did I not love you so well, I would demand another five per cent for doing your work, but I do love you, and we'll let the matter pass. As they say, the good farmer makes his own rain. So while you were playing cat and bird with your foolish council, I found an agent of my own to work for our cause in Iberia.'

'You? You have sent an agent into the most pernicious nation on earth? Where did you find this person? How can we be certain he won't betray us?'

'You needn't fear.' She puffed on her pipe with obvious satisfaction. 'I found him through my lawyer in Antwerp, a city, you know, that retains many ties to Spain. I'm assured he can be trusted with my very life.'

'Your life is in no danger, but you had better hope he can be entrusted with your wealth. If the Inquisition suspects he is a Jew's agent, he'll be tortured until he reveals all.'

'That's the very beauty of it. He has no knowledge that he works for a Jew, only that he works for a delightful Amsterdam widow. He can't betray what he doesn't know, and his motions shall attract no suspicion, for even in his own mind he does nothing worthy of notice.'

She had been reckless to embark upon this plan without consulting him, but he could find no fault with her actions. Only a moment ago he had lamented his connection with her, but now he recalled well why he so loved this remarkable woman.

'You trust this man?'

'I've never seen him, but I trust my lawyer, and he says we may depend on him.'

'And what are his instructions?'

'The same as you have given the others.' She licked her lips slowly, as though paused in thought. 'To secure agents in Lisbon, Oporto and Madrid – men who will do our bidding to the letter, though in this case it will only be my bidding. These agents are to await my instructions and then purchase as directed at a particular time and place.' She studied Miguel's face, attempting to register his mood. 'You cannot object.'

He could not object. And yet, somehow, he did. 'Of course not. I am only surprised. We had discussed that these plans were to be mine.'

Geertruid placed a hand on top of his. 'Don't feel unmanned,' she said softly. 'I promise I think you as great as ever, but an opportunity arose that I had to seize.'

He nodded. 'You were right to do it.' He continued to nod. 'Yes, this is all very good.' Perhaps he had reacted too strongly. What did it matter whence the agent came? Geertruid, for all her faults, was no fool. Miguel sighed, tasting the cheap tobacco in the air and savouring it as though it were perfume. A though suddenly flashed before him, and he stood up very straight. 'Do you realise what has happened to us this moment?'

'What has happened?' Geertruid asked. She lounged lazily upon the bench like a satisfied whore waiting to be paid.

'We faced one obstacle, the one thing that stood between us and our riches, and we have just removed that obstacle.'

Geertruid blinked. 'We must still set our agents in place and count upon them to do our bidding,' she said, as though she understood not the first thing of his own scheme.

'A mere formality,' Miguel assured her. 'The Exchange Bank may as well give us unlimited credit, for we are already wealthy. We now only wait for the rest of the world to recognize what we now know.' He leaned over to her and placed his lips as close to hers as he had dared since the night she had rejected his kiss. He didn't care about the *cherem* or Joachim or even that he had lost her money. Those were only details, and details can be managed. 'We are already wealthy, madam. We have already won.'

CHAPTER 23

Though he had been avoiding the East Indies corner of the bourse all week, Miguel had only finished a small trade in pepper when he felt a hard tap on the shoulder. More like a jab. There stood an impatient and sheepish Isaiah Nunes.

'Nunes,' Miguel shouted cheerfully and grabbed his arm. 'You are looking well, my friend. I trust all is on schedule with our little business and we may expect the shipment as planned?'

Nunes could never resist the blunt force of Miguel's cheer. 'Yes, all is on schedule. You know, the price of coffee has been going up, but I secured our price before the price rose. You will still pay shipment at thirty-three guilders per barrel.' He swallowed. 'Some of us honour our words.'

Miguel ignored the jibe. 'And the contents remain a secret.'

'Just as I promised. My agents have assured me that the crates will be marked as you have instructed. No one will know their true contents.' He looked away for an instant. 'Now I must raise another matter.'

'I know what you are going to say' – Miguel held up a hand – 'and do you think I would come seek you out like this if I had no intention of paying you? I promise you the money will be there in two days. Three at the latest.'

Nunes sighed. 'You did not seek me out. I came to you. And you've made promises before.'

'I expect any moment to receive the money I need,' he lied. 'All will be made easy.'

It was Miguel who had not a thing to worry about. The business had been contracted with the East India Company, and it could not be cancelled. Nunes would simply have to float the five hundred guilders for a little while. He had the money; it was no hardship for him.

Miguel decided it was time to set the next phase of his plan in motion. He visited a broker, with whom he had done business before, and bought coffee puts to be due in ten weeks' time, thereby guaranteeing himself the right to sell at the current high price. Miguel wanted to buy a thousand guilders' worth of puts, but the broker seemed reluctant to advance Miguel so large a loan. Having no other choice, he used his brother's name as security. There could be no harm in doing so; Miguel would profit from his puts and pay the broker without Daniel ever learning what his brother had done.

'I'll need to send a letter to your brother confirming his agreement,' the broker said.

'Of course. My brother, however, has a tendency to let his correspondence sit for days. Mark the outside of the note, if you would, with a circle, and I will see he addresses your concerns immediately.' Miguel would have Annetje keep an eye out for the note. It should be easy to keep it from attracting Daniel's notice.

Once the transaction had been completed, Miguel fought off the queasy remorse. Certainly it was tricky, putting his brother's money at risk, but everything was in hand. He would not have been so desperate if his brother hadn't demanded payment on the loan at so rotten a time. It would be one thing if Miguel had been struggling, but never before had he known the market so well as he did now. And with coffee he would be creating and shaping the market, not merely responding to it. The price of coffee would go down because he would make it go down. Daniel's money could not be safer.

He expected the news of his puts to travel fast, but he did not expect it to travel quite so quickly as it did. One hour later, as Miguel shuffled out of the Exchange and on to the Dam, Solomon Parido appeared by his side. He smiled politely, with no signs of resentment over what had happened before the council.

'I hope I have not violated any rules today,' Miguel said. 'Appearing on the Exchange without properly greeting you, perhaps. I expect I'll receive another summons before long.'

'I expect the same.' Parido laughed softly, as though making light with a friend. 'You must not think there was anything of a personal nature in what transpired in that room with the Ma'amad. I merely acted in accordance with what I believed to be right and proper.'

'Of course,' Miguel agreed flatly.

'However, your likening the Ma'amad to the Inquisition – that will make you no friends. There are too many in this city who have lost loved ones to the Inquisition.'

'You forget that the Inquisition took my father; I know what it is, and so does my brother. If he ever sees things as I do, he may not be so quick to follow you blindly.'

'You judge him too harshly. He only wishes to do what is best for his family, and that family includes you. I suspect he will be very proud of you when he learns of your brilliant scheme in the East Indies trade.'

'My scheme?' Miguel studied his face for some sign of what might be coming.

'Yes. I had no idea how clever you were, but now I see in its fullness your plan. Wait until the price of coffee rises because of the growth of demand, and then gamble a large sum of money you do not have on the price falling. Yes, very clever indeed.'

Miguel smiled back. Parido knew nothing but what Miguel had intended the world to learn, though he had learned it with disturbing speed. 'I'm glad you approve.'

'I hope nothing happens to make the price rise again in ten weeks' time.'

'I hope so too,' Miguel told him. He would not appear too clever or too confident. Let Parido believe he knew Miguel's plan, rather than look for more. 'You think the price will rise, but I've heard that since I wagered, others have followed suit and more will follow. We'll see what sort of momentum has begun.'

'I suppose we will,' Parido agreed, clearly thinking about something else already.

There was another note from Joachim when he returned home. Another note in that uneven, drunken hand.

If you speak to my wife again, I will kill you, it said. *I will creep up behind you so you won't know I'm there and slit your throat. I'll do it if you again approach Clara.* There were two lines that had been crossed out, and then underneath he wrote, *In fact, I may just kill you anyway for the pleasure of revenge.*

The note had a kind of manic sincerity. Had Miguel's silly banter with Clara (how could she have been so stupid as to tell him about it?) pushed her husband over the edge? He cursed Joachim and he cursed himself. It would be a long time before he would again feel at ease.

CHAPTER 24

In the deceptive shadows of twilight, a figure crept up behind him but slipped back into the dust before Miguel could spin around to face it. An indeterminate shape lurked behind a tree just out of his vision. Something splashed into the canal a few paces behind his hurried steps. Each street brought Miguel closer to some deadly confrontation with Joachim. Out of the corner of his eye he saw a madman's foul grin, the glimmer of a knife blade, a pair of lunging hands.

Miguel was no stranger to death. In Lisbon he had lived in terror of the arbitrary power of the Inquisition and of the bands of bloodthirsty villains that had roamed the streets almost with impunity. In recent years, Amsterdam had been subject to horrible visitations of plague: men and women turned purplish-black in the face, developed rashes and died within days. Thanks to the Holy One, blessed be He, people now smoked so much tobacco, for it alone prevented the spread of that disease. Still, death lurked everywhere. Miguel knew as well as anyone how to live with its random assaults on the living; he did not know how to live while being hunted.

And so Joachim began to win his war upon his enemy's quiet. Miguel found his concentration wandering, even upon the Exchange. He watched helplessly as Parido made his way through the crowds of merchants, buying coffee futures, betting that the price would continue to rise.

If something should happen to make Miguel unable to control the price of the coffee, he would lose money on his puts, and then Daniel would learn that Miguel had abused his name and his funds. What if Nunes refused to deliver the goods until Miguel paid his debts? It all struck him as futile, when he might be dead at any moment of an assassin's blade.

Miguel knew he could not live with that possibility. Even if Joachim never intended to draw blood, he had already done great harm. No one could doubt Miguel's need to put an end to it. He needed to live his life without fear of some madman stalking him.

It took him a few more days to determine how to proceed, but once he had his idea firmly in mind it seemed to him both sordid and clever. It would involve some unpleasantness, but he could not expect to deal with a person like Joachim without confronting the unsavoury. Certainly that had been his problem all along. He had tried to engage with Joachim as though he were a sound man, as though he might be convinced by reason, but time and time again Joachim had shown himself unable or unwilling to act as a man of sense. He recalled a tale of Charming Pieter in which a ruffian sought revenge against the trickster. Outmatched by an enemy's physical prowess, Pieter had hired an even more dangerous ruffian to protect himself.

At the Singing Carp they told him Geertruid had not been seen for a few days, and that meant she might be gone for a few days more. Often Hendrick would go with her, but not always, and Miguel had no need to wait for her return. In fact, he thought, this might be the better way. Why should Geertruid know all his business?

He spent the better part of the day scouring the taverns where he might expect to see Hendrick, but it was not until late afternoon that he found his man, sitting at a table with a few of his rough friends, smoking a long pipe that smelled like a mixture of old tobacco and dung. Hendrick had mentioned the tavern in passing before, but Miguel had never imagined that anything would lead him to enter such a place. He could taste in his mouth the scent of rotten wood from the tables; the floor had been covered with filthy straw. In the back, a crowd of men made a game of watching two rats fight each other.

Seeing Miguel, Hendrick let out a barking laugh and then whispered something to his friends, who joined in the cackling. 'Why, speak of the devil, it is the very Jew Man.' Hendrick puffed furiously at his pipe, as though the clouds of smoke might engulf Miguel.

'I've been looking for you,' Miguel said. 'I need to talk with you for a moment.'

'Drink up, boys,' Hendrick shouted to his companions. 'I must take my leave for a time. I have a meeting of importance, as you can see.'

Outside the tavern, the dead-fish smell of the canal coated Miguel's throat. The summer heat had begun to settle upon the city, and the stink with it. He breathed in deep through his mouth and led Hendrick towards the alley, which had a slightly more pleasant odour of soil and old beer. A distressed cat with filthy white fur and a mangled ear opened its pink mouth and hissed at them, but Hendrick hissed back and the cat fled into the shadows.

'My lady has gone away for the nonce, and I am used to it being that where there is no Madame Damhuis, there is no senhor either.'

'Has she gone to her lawyer in Antwerp again?'

'So you've come in search of her after all?' He punched Miguel congenially in the arm.

'I've not come for her.' Miguel offered a knowing look of his own. 'But I'm curious.'

'Ha!' Hendrick barked. 'You've kept that curiosity in check, haven't you, good Jew Man? She's a lady with many secrets: from you, from me, from the world. Some say she's as ordinary as buttered bread, but she keeps secrets to seem otherwise.'

'But you know the truth?'

He nodded. 'I know the truth.'

Miguel had so many questions about his partner

367

that he had thought to never have answered. Now Hendrick hinted he might learn them all. But could he trust the Dutchman not to talk of Miguel's questioning? The man liked to drink, and his tongue was known to wag. This conversation was proof enough.

'Tell me only what the lady herself would tell me,' Miguel said at last. 'I'll not pry into any secrets she wishes to keep.'

Hendrick nodded. 'You are a cautious man, aren't you? I respect that. You like the lady and won't have her not liking you. And I think you'd like her all the same if you knew the truth – which is, at best, a dull sort of truth – for she might just as easily tell the world where she goes when she goes. A visit to her lawyer or his sister or her brother's widow need not be a great secret.'

'I've not asked to be told all this.'

'But I've chosen to tell you,' Hendrick said, the levity draining from his voice, 'because I love Madame Damhuis with all my heart, but she can be cruel. She likes to torment men. She loves to drive them mad with desire and then send them on their way. And she likes to drive them mad with curiosity too. She keeps the mundane a secret, and all whisper her name.'

'It's no crime,' Miguel volunteered, feeling the need to defend her.

Hendrick nodded. 'Jew Man, if you said otherwise, I'd slit your throat. No one would insult that lady while I stand by, for I owe her my life and

368

more. But I tell you these things because I know you love her, and you would not love her less for the knowing.'

Miguel held out his hand in the Dutch style. 'I thank you for your trust.'

Hendrick grinned and shook firmly. 'There's been too long an uneasiness between us. I want only to see it end. You and madam are friends, and I would be your friend too.'

Miguel could not but rejoice at his good luck. 'I am glad to hear you say this, for I've come to you with a most delicate problem, and I had hoped you would be able to assist me.'

'You need but name it.'

Miguel took a deep breath. 'I've been bothered by a madman. This fellow believes I owe him money, which is not the case, for we both suffered in the same transaction, which was managed both fairly and legally. Now he follows me and has begun to threaten my life. I've been unable to deter him with reason, and I can't go to the law, because he has not done me or my property any real harm.'

'I shit on the law. The law won't help you,' Hendrick said, still puffing merrily. 'Once he slices you open, then you may seek your redress with the law. What good is that? You need but tell me his name, and I'll see to it that he never does another man harm again.'

'I have seen that you are a man who knows something of how to defend himself,' Miguel explained with some difficulty; it pained him to offer Hendrick even this brutal flattery. 'I recall how well you reacted in the tavern.'

'Make no excuses, my friend. I understand that you cannot risk yourself by engaging in a scrape with a low fellow. Were you Jews not watched, I know a man such as you are could tend to this matter without help. Now, you need only tell me who he is.'

'His name is Joachim Waagenaar, and he lives by the Oude Kerk.'

'If he lives by the Oude Kerk, I suppose any number of accidents might befall a fellow in that part of town without the world taking notice. Of course, good feelings between us being what they are, such things cost money. Fifty guilders should do nicely.'

Miguel blinked several times, as though this price had poked him in his eye. Just what did he hope Hendrick might do? Joachim was a madman, so why did Miguel feel so uneasy about this trans-action. 'That's rather more than I thought.'

'We may be friends enough now, but I still take a risk, you understand.'

'Of course, of course,' Miguel said. 'I did not say I absolutely would not pay it. Only that it was more than I thought.'

'Think as much as you like. When you've made up your mind, come see me.'

'I will do so. And in the meantime . . .'

Hendrick grinned. 'Of course I'll say nothing

to the lady. I understand you well enough, and now that we have each other's secrets, you need not wonder if you can trust me or no.'

Miguel took his hand once more. 'I offer you my thanks. Knowing that I may depend upon you has put my mind at ease.'

'I'm happy to serve you.' He blew out a cloud of smoke and returned to the tavern.

A light mist had begun to fall; it was just the sort of weather for a villain who might hide himself in fog and dark. The rain mixed with his perspiration, making him feel heavy and encumbered in his clothing. Nevertheless, having spoken to Hendrick made him more comfortable already. He had options; he could concoct a strategy of his own. Joachim had not outmatched him.

Perhaps, he considered, it was not necessary to have Hendrick give Joachim a thorough beating. Now that he had almost commissioned the job, he winced at its brutality. If there was a way to avoid it, it would be best avoided. After all, he had not sought out Hendrick to harm Joachim but to make himself feel safer, and the simple act of having discussed the option of the beating rid him of many concerns. He might see that Joachim came to harm at any time he wished; having that power, the righteous thing would be to spare the creature. Mercy, after all, was one of the seven highest qualities of the Holy One, blessed be He. Miguel, too, could aim to be merciful.

He would wait. Joachim surely never meant to

actually kill Miguel, but should he again make these threats, he would learn that Miguel understood justice as well as mercy.

Before he reached the Vlooyenburg, the mist had turned to rain.

Miguel wanted nothing so much as to change his clothes and sit before a fire, and perhaps read a little Torah – all this contemplation of mercy left him longing to feel closer to the holiness of the Most High. First he might review the story of how Charming Pieter had tricked the greedy horse-trader, a tale always certain to cheer him.

Once inside, he removed his shoes, after the Dutch fashion, so as to avoid tracking mud through the house, though his stockings had soaked through, and he left wet footprints upon the tiled floor. He had only gone a little way towards the entrance to the cellar when he saw Hannah hovering in the doorway, the shadows accentuating the swelling of her belly.

'Good afternoon, senhora,' he said, too hastily. There could no longer be any doubt of her intentions. Her eyes, wide and moist under her black scarf, fixed on him greedily.

'I must speak with you,' she said, in a quiet voice.

He replied without thinking. 'You wish another taste of my drink?'

She shook her head. 'Not now. I must say something else.'

'May we go to the drawing room?' he asked.

She shook her head again. 'No, we mustn't. I can't have my husband finding us there together. He will suspect.'

He will suspect what? Miguel almost blurted out. Did she believe them already lovers? Had she so lively an imagination that it did not end with women scholars? Miguel too had indulged in the delicious crime of flirtation, but he did not believe he could take it to the next stage, that of secret meetings, of hiding from her husband, of revelling in one of the worst of sins. No one cherished the delights of a fanciful mind more than Miguel, but a man – a person – must know where fancy ends and truth begins. He might hold Hannah in a new esteem, find her winsome as well as pretty. He might even love her for all he knew, but he would not act on those feelings.

'We must speak here,' she said, 'but quietly. We cannot be overheard.'

'Perhaps you've made a mistake,' Miguel offered, 'and we needn't speak quietly at all.'

Hannah offered a smile, slight and sweet, as though *she* were humouring *him*, as though he were too simple to understand her words. May the Holy One, blessed be He, forgive me for unleashing coffee upon mankind, he thought. This drink will turn the world upside down.

'I am not mistaken, senhor. I have something to tell you. Something that concerns you very nearly.'

She took a deep breath. 'It is about your friend, senhor. The widow.'

Miguel felt a sudden dizziness. He leaned against the wall. 'Geertruid Damhuis,' he breathed. 'What of her? What could *you* have to tell me of *her*?'

Hannah shook her head. 'I don't know precisely. Oh, forgive me, senhor, for I hardly even know how to say what I wish to say, and I fear to do so will put my very life in your hands, but I also fear your betrayal if I do not speak.'

'Betrayal? What do you say?'

'Please, senhor. I am trying. Not very long ago, only a few weeks really, I saw the Dutch widow on the street, and she saw me. We both had something to hide. I don't know what she had to hide, but she seemed to think I did, and she threatened me to keep silent. I thought it could do no harm, but now I am not so certain.'

Miguel took a step backward. Geertruid. What could she have to hide, and what did it mean to him? It could be anything: a lover, a deal, an embarrassment. Or it could be a matter of business. It made no sense. 'What did you have to hide, senhora?'

She shook her head. 'I wish I didn't have to tell you, but I have made up my mind to do so. I know I can trust you, senhor, and if you must confront her, and you make it clear you already know my secret, perhaps she won't tell others, and the worst may be spared. Can I tell you and trust that you will tell no one else?'

'Of course,' Miguel said hastily, though he wished desperately that he could somehow avoid this entire conversation.

'I am ashamed,' she said, 'and yet not ashamed to tell you this, but I saw the widow on my way from a sacred place. A church of holy Catholic worship, senhor.'

Miguel stared at her with unfocused eyes until she blended into the dark wall. He hardly knew what to think. His own brother's wife, a woman for whom he had cared and felt desire, had revealed herself a secret Catholic.

'You have betrayed your husband?' he asked quietly.

She swallowed hard. The tears had not yet come, but they would come soon. They filled the air like a coming rain. 'How can you speak of betrayal? I was never told until the eve of my wedding that I was a Jew. Have *I* not been betrayed?'

'You betrayed?' Miguel demanded, once again forgetting to keep his voice quiet. 'How can you say so? You live in the new Jerusalem.'

'Have you or your brother or the rabbis spoken to me of what is in your Torah or Talmud other than to tell me what I must do to serve you? When I go to your synagogue, the prayers are in Hebrew and the talk is in Spanish, yet I may not learn these tongues. If I have a daughter, must I raise her to serve an arbitrary God who will not even show His face only because she is a girl? It is well for you to talk of betrayal when the world hands you all you desire. I am offered nothing, and if I wish to take for myself some comfort, am I to be condemned?'

'Yes,' Miguel said, though he did not believe it and instantly regretted having said so. But he was angry. He could not have said why, but he felt wounded, as though she had violated some trust between them.

He had not seen the tears start, but there they were, glistening upon her face. He fought the urge to pull her to his body, to feel her breasts against his chest, but he couldn't, so instead he pressed on. 'I have nothing more to say to you. Now leave me so I may think on what to do with this knowledge that I wish I had never heard.'

The cruelty of his words stuck in his throat; he knew what they would mean to her. She would wonder if Miguel might keep quiet. He now knew his brother's wife was a papist, and that information could destroy Daniel. Miguel might reveal this information to usurp his brother's place in the community, or he could use it to threaten Daniel into forgiving his debts.

Miguel would do none of these things. No matter how repulsive her sin, he would not betray Hannah. Even so, he felt such sudden rage that he had to punish her, and his words were the only way he knew how.

'I heard voices. Is something wrong?'

Daniel appeared at the doorway of the kitchen, looking pale. His little eyes focused on his wife, standing far too close to a retreating Miguel.

'It is only your silly brother,' Hannah said, hiding her face in the poor light. 'I saw him come in wearing these wet clothes, but he refuses to change out of them.'

'It is not for a woman to decide if a man is silly,' Daniel pointed out, not unkindly. He merely illuminated information she may have forgotten. 'Nevertheless,' he said to Miguel, 'she may be right. I won't have you catch plague and kill us all.'

'The entire household has an opinion on my clothes.' Miguel affected as best he could an easy manner. 'I'll go change at once before the maid is summoned to speak her piece.'

Hannah took a hurried step back, and Miguel turned instinctively towards the stairwell. Daniel had seen nothing, Miguel could be almost certain of that. What, after all, had there been for him to see? Yet he must know the full vocabulary of his wife's expressions, and surely he had seen one upon her face that could not be a simple matter of housewifely advice.

His confusion about Hannah's Romish inclinations was so intense that he did not even consider what she had said about Geertruid for several hours. Once he recalled her words, however, he found himself awake much of the night, regretting his cruelty and wishing there were a way to go to Hannah and ask her questions. And perhaps apologise.

★   ★   ★

Hannah was first out of the house the next morning, stepping on to the porch to look for the bread man, whose cries she heard through windows hazy with morning cool. Before her husband had opened his eyes, before Annetje had even washed and begun to prepare breakfast for the house, Hannah had dressed herself, put her veil firmly in place and stepped outside.

She found the pig's head. It sat upon the steps just inches from the door, angled in a congealed pool of blood. Already ants had begun to crawl upon it in such numbers that at first it appeared to Hannah black and writhing.

Her shriek roused the house and the closest neighbours. Miguel had slept badly and had already risen, prayed and dressed. He sat struggling with the weekly Torah portion when her shrill voice penetrated the tiny windows of the cellar, and he was the first to find Hannah upon the steps, a hand clasped over her mouth. She turned to him and fell into his arms, burying her head in his shirt as she wept.

They called immediately for the doctor, who gave her potions to help her sleep and explained that if she could be kept calm for a day, the danger to her life would pass. Hannah had insisted that she needed no potions, she had been only startled, but the doctor would not believe a woman could receive so great a shock without its disordering her humours and, more importantly, he explained, the humours of the unborn baby. Daniel shot Miguel hard looks but said nothing, made no accusations. Nevertheless, Miguel could no longer ignore the simple truth that things between himself and his brother would never be the same.

From

The Factual and Revealing Memoirs of Alonzo Alferonda

I returned home one night from evening prayers (yes, evening prayers – there were still, thank God, a few small synagogues that defied the Ma'amad and permitted me to worship among their number so long as I was careful not to be seen), when I felt a hand grip my shoulder. I looked up and saw not some desperate debtor who, fearing for his life, thought to strike at Alferonda before he could be struck, but Solomon Parido.

'Senhor,' I said, swallowing my relief, 'I hardly thought to see you again so soon.'

Parido appeared hesitant. He no more liked coming to see me than I liked seeing him. Perhaps he liked it less. I had nothing to lose from these encounters, but he had his pride. 'I had not thought to seek you out.'

'And yet,' I observed, 'here you are, lurking in the streets, waiting for me.' I had cause to be anxious that he knew I had been at worship,

380

but he said nothing, and I could only conclude that he would not have failed to play so valuable a card. My friends at the small synagogue were safe.

Parido set his jaw as though bracing himself and turned to me. 'I want to know more of what you have planned with Miguel Lienzo.'

I picked up my pace, if only a little. It was a trick I learned so long ago I hardly even notice doing it most times. Varying your pace of walking sets your companion on edge. He has to think more about trivial things than he ought, and that takes his concentration from where it needs to be. 'I marvel at your presumption,' I said. 'What makes you think, if I had anything planned, I would tell my enemy?'

'I may be your enemy, as you style it, but Lienzo is not. You are manipulating him?'

I let out a laugh. 'If you think so, why not tell him?'

'Things have gone too far now; he'd never believe me. I've asked his brother to warn him off you, but I doubt that will do much good.'

'I doubt it too. A better strategy might have been to have his brother encourage him to do business with me.' I winked at him. 'I heard someone left the head of a pig on his brother's doorstep. Have you heard?'

'How dare you accuse me of so wretched a crime? Listen to me, Alferonda. If you bear any friendship for Lienzo, you'll stop this. If he crosses me, I'll destroy him.'

I shook my head. 'You think you can destroy anyone you like. You think you can work miracles of destruction. Your power as parnass has corrupted you utterly, Parido, and you cannot even see it. You've become a distortion of the man you once were. You threaten me, you threaten Lienzo – you see plots everywhere. I pity you. You can no longer tell what is true and what is your own fancy.'

He stared at me for a moment, and I could tell by his face that I had struck something. This was the oldest trick of them all, but I knew it well. I had practised it often. The appearance of sincerity can truly unman even the most stalwart foe.

'Think,' I said, eager to press the advantage, 'of what you have accused me, of what you have accused Miguel. Do you really think it plausible that men engage themselves in these wild plots? Is it not far more likely that your suspicion and greed have misled you not only to suspect things that are untrue but to do real harm to others?'

'I see I've wasted my time,' he said, and turned away.

I was not one, however, to let the fish go, once hooked. 'You haven't wasted your time,' I called after him, 'if you will only think of what I have said. You are wrong, Parido. You are wrong about me and wrong about Lienzo, and it is not too late for you to atone for your sins.'

He began to walk faster and hunched his shoulders as if to protect himself from whatever I might hurl at him. And I did hurl: I hurled lies, powerful lies that fell like stones because they so clearly resembled the truth.

In the same way you can make a simple peasant who has given you his last coin think that a mere lout with too much hair on his back is a werewolf. He fears it may be a werewolf, so all you need do is point and whisper a suggestion, and the peasant will hear the howling for himself.

CHAPTER 25

Though still in bed, Hannah ate her soup that evening and chatted calmly with her husband. Miguel and Daniel both showed their relief, though the storm had not yet passed. Miguel had been doing his best to stay out of Daniel's path, but that night Annetje brought him word that his brother wished to see him in his study. Miguel found him hunched over his writing table, scribbling in the light of a good candle. Three or four more flickered in the breeze of the open window. Daniel had been smoking an acrid tobacco, and Miguel felt a headache gathering its forces.

'How does your wife?' Miguel asked.

'The worst has passed, and I no longer fear for her life. These frights, you know, can be fatal to a woman's delicate humours, particularly one in her condition. But the doctor tells me there is no risk to the child.'

'I'm glad. It's a terrible thing.'

Daniel paused for a moment. He picked up a pen and then set it down again. 'It *is* a terrible thing. What do you know of it, Miguel?'

Though he had considered how he might respond

to this line of questioning for the better part of the day, Miguel still had no clear idea of what he could say to put matters at ease. Did Daniel want a confession, or did he want to be comforted?

'I can't say for certain,' he told his brother at last.

'But you have ideas.' It was a statement, not a question.

'I can't say that I have no guess, but I have no way of knowing for certain.'

'Perhaps you should tell me about your guess.'

Miguel shook his head. 'It would be inappropriate for me to speculate. It is wrong to make accusations where I can prove nothing.'

'Prove nothing?' Daniel slammed his hand down on the table. 'Is not the head of a pig proof? Recollect that you are staying in my house, and your actions have endangered my family. I nearly lost my wife and child today. I insist you tell me what you *suspect*.'

Miguel sighed. He had not wanted to speculate too wildly, but who could deny that his hand had been forced? 'Very well. I suspect Solomon Parido.'

'What?' Daniel stared incredulously. He forgot to finish puffing on his pipe, and smoke drifted lazily from his mouth. 'You must be mad.'

'No, it is precisely the sort of scheme to hatch from Parido's vile mind, and I believe you suspect him as much as I do. He has been plotting against me, and what better way to sully my name than to

385

leave this thing at my door as though I have brought it upon myself?'

'Preposterous. Your conclusions require a contortion of logic. Why would Senhor Parido do such a thing? Where would so righteous a man acquire an unclean animal?'

'Have you some better way to explain this madness?'

'Yes,' Daniel said, with the solemn nod of a judge 'I think you owe someone a great deal of money. I think this money may be the result of a gambling debt or some criminal doing, which is why the person you owe can't go to the courts. This abomination upon the stoop of my house is meant to warn you to pay or face the most unpleasant of consequences.'

Miguel concentrated to keep his face from revealing anything. 'How did you reach this fanciful conclusion?'

'Quite inevitably,' Daniel said. 'Hannah found a note rolled up and slipped through the ear of the pig.' He paused for a moment, that he might study his brother's response. 'She tucked it away in her pocket for reasons I cannot guess, but the doctor found it and presented it to me with the greatest concern.' He reached to the bookshelf behind him for a small piece of paper, which he presented to Miguel. The paper was old and torn – clearly ripped from a document used for another purpose – and it was badly stained with blood. Miguel could not make out much of the writing except a few words in Dutch – *I want my money* – and, a few lines down, *my wife.*

Miguel handed it back. 'I have no idea of its meaning.'

'You have no idea?'

'None.'

'I will have to report this incident to the Ma'amad, which will no doubt investigate. We can't keep the matter quiet, at any rate. Too many neighbours witnessed Hannah's distress.'

'You would sacrifice your own brother to lend a hand to Parido while he carries out his petty vengeance?' Miguel spoke so urgently that for a moment he forgot that circumstance suggested no more likely culprit than Joachim. 'I've wondered about your loyalties, and I always chastised myself for suspecting that you might favour this man over your own flesh and blood, but now I see you're nothing but a player in his puppet show. He pulls your strings, and you dance.'

'My friendship with Senhor Parido is no breach of loyalty,' Daniel snapped back.

'Yet you value him over your own brother,' Miguel said.

'It need not be a contest. Why must I choose one over the other?'

'Because he has made it so that you must. You would sacrifice me for this man, and you would do so in an instant.'

'You know nothing of me, then.'

'I think I do,' Miguel said. 'Answer truly. If you

were asked to choose between the two of us, to make a choice in which you had to definitively side with one or the other, would you even for a moment entertain siding with me?'

'I refuse to answer your question. It is madness.'

'Then don't answer it,' Miguel said. 'You need not bother.'

'That is right. I need not bother. Why even speak of such choices. Senhor Parido has shown his goodness in the kindness he's shown to our family, particularly after the harm you did his daughter.'

'It was no harm. It was but a silly affair and would have been of no lasting consequence if he had not allowed himself to lose all reason. I had a dalliance with his maid, and his daughter saw. Why must he make all this thunder over nothing?'

'There *was* harm, and permanent harm too,' Daniel replied harshly, 'and if Senhor Parido feels anger over the damage done to his daughter, I for one cannot blame him, for you came close to doing the same harm to my unborn child.'

Miguel began to reply, but checked himself. There was something more to this affair than he knew. 'What damage?' he asked. 'She had a fright. It is nothing.'

'I should not have said anything.' Daniel looked away.

'If you know something, you must tell me. I'll ask Parido himself if need be.'

Daniel put a hand to his forehead. 'No, don't do that,' he insisted. 'I'll tell you, but you must not let him know that you know, or that you learned from me.'

Despite his fear, Miguel could have smiled. Daniel would betray Parido if only to save his own flesh from the fire.

'More happened to Antonia than the senhor wanted the world to know. When she came into the room and saw you in your unspeakable act with her maid, she fainted.'

'I know that,' Miguel said testily. 'I was there.'

'You know she struck her head. What you don't know is that she and her husband in Salonika have since had an idiot child, and the doctors say it is the result of this injury. She can have nothing but idiot children.'

Miguel ran a hand along his beard and inhaled sharply through his nostrils. Antonia rendered unable to bear healthy children? He could not fathom the connection between her injury and its consequence, but he was not a medical man to solve such riddles. He knew enough, however, to figure out the rest. Parido's own idiot boy was a shame to him, and Antonia had been his only hope of perpetuating the family, particularly since he had wed her to a cousin also named Parido. The *parnass* was a wrathful man by nature. What anger would he reserve for the man he believed had destroyed the future of his line?

'How long has he known this?'

'No more than a year. And I beg you to recall that you must not tell him I spoke of it.'

Miguel waved a hand at him. 'No one told me.' He rose from his chair. 'No one told me!' he repeated, this time far more loudly. 'Parido had more reason to hate me than I could have known, and yet you said nothing. And now you doubt that he has sent this vile message to injure me? Your loyalties are as preposterous as your beliefs.'

'I won't listen to any such lies about Solomon Parido.'

'Then we have no more to discuss.' Miguel hurried down the narrow staircase, almost stumbling as he did so. In his rage, he had nearly convinced himself that there was no more likely explanation for the pig's head than Parido. Could there be any doubt that, in his rage and twisted sense of rectitude, he would do all he could to harm Miguel? Damn his brother for thinking otherwise.

In the damp of the cellar, he listened to the familiar scrape of floorboards as Daniel dressed and left the house. He had not been gone for more than a quarter-hour when Annetje came down the stairs and handed Miguel a letter. It was addressed to Daniel and contained a circle in the upper corner.

The note was from the broker, asking confirmation of Daniel's willingness to support Miguel's

390

trade. The letter was standard, nothing of consequence, but there was a line at the end that intrigued Miguel.

> You have always been a respected man on the Exchange, and your friendship with Solomon Parido is more surety than any man could wish. Nevertheless, owing to your recent reversals and the rumours of insolvency, I hesitated before considering your guarantee solid enough to back your brother's trade. Nevertheless, I shall gamble on Miguel Lienzo's cleverness and your honour.

So Daniel was in debt. That explained why he insisted on receiving Miguel's money right away. Well, it was no matter. Miguel forged a reply, which he gave to the girl to send off. She hesitated a moment, and only when pressed did she explain that the senhora had requested his company.

Hannah lay propped up, her head wrapped in a bluish cloth and her skin pale and wet with perspiration, but she appeared to be in no great danger. She was stretched out comfortably on that proper bed of hers, long enough that she could lie flat on her back, unlike the cupboard bed that tortured Miguel. This one had been built of an elaborate oak frame that rose above her. Among the wealthy Dutch, these new beds had become the fashion, and Miguel vowed he would buy one for himself the moment he left his brother's house.

The bed had no curtains to part, so she lay there for him to see, her eyes wide and sorrowful. 'We should talk quickly,' she said, her face grave but without accusation. 'I don't know where your brother has gone, so I don't know when he will return.'

'I suspect I know where he has gone,' Miguel observed. 'He's gone to see Parido.'

'That may be,' she said.

Miguel took a step closer. 'I only want to say that I am sorry for what happened to you, and for your distress. I never meant for you to be hurt. I promised you would not.'

She smiled slightly. 'Your brother made more of it than was necessary. I was frightened for a moment, but I soon recovered. I have felt the baby moving all day as she always does. I have no fears there.'

She, Miguel noticed. Would she dare speculate on a girl child in front of Daniel? Did her speaking of it in front of Miguel constitute an intimacy?

'I am very happy to hear there are no lasting consequences.'

'I'm only sorry I couldn't do more. I found a note, and I don't know what it said, but I hid it thinking it might do you harm. Your brother took it from me.'

'I know. It was of no importance.'

'Do you know who left that vile thing there?'

Miguel shook his head. 'I wish I did, but still, I thank you for your efforts. I'm sorry,' he said, taking a sharp breath, 'that I behaved so poorly. I wish to discuss this matter with you again. Perhaps another time. When you are rested.' He had not planned to, but he took her hand in his and held it tight, feeling its coolness, the contours of her smooth skin.

He expected her to pull away, to chastise him for his unforgivable presumption, but she looked up at him as though this gesture of devotion were the most natural thing in the world. 'I am sorry too – that I was so weak – but I knew nothing else.'

'Then we shall have to teach you what you want to know,' he told her kindly.

Hannah turned her head away for a moment, burrowing into her pillow.

'I must ask you something else,' he said, rubbing her hand with his, 'and then I'll let you rest. You mentioned Madame Damhuis. What more did you wish to tell me?'

Hannah remained motionless, as if she might pretend not to have heard him. Finally she turned back to face him with her reddened eyes. 'I hardly even know. She was speaking to some men when I saw her, and I scarcely looked at all. But she thought I had seen something I ought not to have.'

Miguel nodded. 'Did you know the men? Did they appear to you of the Nation or Dutch or something else?'

She shook her head. 'I can't even say that. I think

393

they were Dutch, but one might have been of the Nation. I am not certain.'

'You did not know them? You had never seen them?'

'I think one was her servant man, but I can't be certain.' She shook her head. 'Senhor, I was too frightened to see them.'

Miguel knew the feeling well. 'I'll let you sleep,' he said. He knew he should not do it, he told himself not to, that he would regret it, that it would only bring trouble. But he did it anyway. Before gently setting her hand down upon the bed, he raised it to his lips and softly kissed her warm skin. 'And thank you, senhora.'

He didn't wait for a reply but hurried out of the room, fearing he might cross paths with his brother on the stairwell, but no such thing happened.

Hannah closed her eyes, not knowing what to think, or even how. Miguel had forgiven her. He understood her. He had taken her hand and kissed it. Could she dare to hope for more than that? Oh, what had she done to deserve such mercy? She slid a hand down to the comforting bulge of her belly, caressing this unborn child, this daughter, whom she would protect from all the evil that threatened them both.

When she opened her eyes, Annetje stood before her. Her face was immobile, jaw thrust outwards, eyes little more than slits. Where had she come from? Hannah had heard no one climb the stairs.

The girl could do that; she went in and out of rooms like a ghost.

'You told him,' Annetje said, so quietly Hannah could hardly hear her.

She briefly considered lying, but what good would it do? 'Yes,' she said. 'I thought it important he know.'

'You foolish bitch,' she hissed. 'I told you to keep quiet.'

'You must not be angry with me,' Hannah said, hating the tone of pleading in her voice, but there were things far more important than that tiny shrivelled thing she called her pride. 'The doctor said that I must not grow warm in temper, lest I risk the child.'

'The devil take your child,' Annetje said. 'I hope he does, along with the rest of you heathen Jews.' She took a step closer.

Hannah pulled the duvet up to protect herself. 'He won't betray us.'

Annetje now stood over her, looking down with her cold eyes, green as the eyes of an evil spirit. 'Even if he does not, do you think the widow will honour his silence? And do you think he is so clever that he can avoid betraying you, even without so meaning? You're a fool, and you ought never to be allowed to have a child in your care. I came here with the intention of thrusting a knife up your quim and killing that wretched child of yours.'

Hannah gasped and pushed herself backward.

'Oh, calm yourself. You are as timid as a rabbit.

I said I came up here with that intention, but I have since changed my mind, so you needn't move about like that. I only hope you are grateful that I am not seeking a more fitting punishment. And you'd better hope that the senhor is as good at keeping secrets as he is at learning them, because if you are betrayed you can be sure I'll not help you. If need be, I'll tell your husband all I know, and the lot of you may go to the devil.'

Annetje hurried out of the room. Hannah listened to her feet slap clumsily against the stairs and then, in the distance, the slam of a door.

Hannah took a deep breath. She felt her pulse pound in her temples and she concentrated on soothing her anguish. But even more than fear she felt confusion. Why did Annetje care so much if Miguel knew about the widow? What did it matter to her?

Hannah shuddered. Why had she not seen it before? Annetje was in the widow's service.

Within two days the doctor permitted Hannah to rise from her bed, but things had grown uncomfortably tense in the house. No one spoke more than a few words at a time, and Miguel remained out of the house as much as he could. On Shabbat he invited himself to the home of a West Indian merchant with whom he maintained a friendly acquaintance.

Not all had turned sour, however. He had received a message from Geertruid saying that

396

she had gone to visit relatives in Friesland. She would be back in Amsterdam any day, but in the meantime she had heard that her man in Iberia had secured agents in Oporto and Lisbon and had now travelled to Madrid, where he felt sure of success. The news was good, but nevertheless troubling in light of Hannah's story. What secret could Geertruid have that she wanted kept from her partner? Did he dare trust her? Did he dare do otherwise?

He had received a few notes from Isaiah Nunes, who was finding it difficult to conjure up language that sufficiently expressed his irritation. He wanted his five hundred guilders, and the bonds of friendship that restrained him were growing increasingly frayed. Miguel had no difficulties penning his replies, which made vague promises of immediate action.

Meanwhile, the price of coffee continued to go up, stemming, Miguel believed, from Solomon Parido's influence. He bought calls in anticipation of an increase, and he made it known that he bought them. On the Amsterdam bourse, that was enough to alter the price. Merchants who had hardly ever noticed coffee now began to gamble on its continued rise.

But Miguel still had no idea what Parido planned. Would he entice his trading combination to exercise the calls and buy large quantities, making a monopoly even harder to obtain? Further, such a move would destroy the value of Miguel's puts, ruining his chance to erase his debts and putting him further in debt to his brother. But Parido's strategy would have to be approved by all members of his combination, and most were not content to make business plans based on the desire to shame a rival. Buying calls would cause the price to rise even further, and since the market would become artificially inflated, the combination would have a hard time selling at a profit. Parido might not have the strength of his combination behind him, but he might happily content himself with the thought that Miguel would lose on his investments.

At the Flyboat that afternoon, Miguel turned and nearly collided with Isaiah Nunes, who smiled in the awkward manner of a guilty child. Miguel had been drinking coffee almost constantly that day, and he felt equal to anything, so he approached the merchant and embraced him warmly. 'How are you, my friend?'

'Just the man I've been looking for,' Nunes said, without a hint of irritation.

'Oh? Whatever for?'

Nunes laughed. 'I wish I had your easy way about you, Miguel. But come with me for a moment, I need to show you something.' He led Miguel to the back of the tavern near a window, and in the muted light he spread out a piece of paper he removed from his coat. It was his contract with Miguel.

'I hate to be so particular with you,' he said,

'but I must bring some of the wording to your attention.'

Miguel had felt full of optimism as he strolled along the canal sides, his puts bought (though illicitly, with his brother's money), Joachim no longer a problem (if he wished to unleash Hendrick), his agents in place (if he could trust his partner) – but now, confined in the dark tavern, the energy of the coffee began to work against him. He wanted to move, but it was hard to breathe. The quick words came not so easily as they once had. 'I know what you have to say, my friend, and if you will but –'

'Hear me out, and then I will hear you. It is only fair, yes?' Nunes did not wait for an answer. 'You see what it says here, of course.' He smoothed out the contract and pointed to a few neat and closely written lines. 'It says that you will pay half the delivery cost upon demand of the agent – being myself – when such a price is demanded by the provider – being the East India Company.'

Miguel nodded eagerly. 'I understand the terms –'

'Please. Let me speak.' Nunes took a breath. 'You see the wording. It says here that the money must be paid when the Company demands it, not on the date of delivery. The Company may demand payment when it agrees to sell the goods and deliver them by the earliest date convenient. You understand that, yes?'

'Of course I understand that,' Miguel said, 'and

I have every intention of getting you that remaining five hundred guilders. I know you have had to advance the money out of pocket, but I assure you it will be forthcoming.'

'I am sure it will. I only wanted you to understand the terms of the contract because there has been some rather troubling news.'

This contract business had been irritating, but he now realised that Nunes had been building up to something. 'How troubling?'

'I hope not too troubling. These things can always be resolved, I think.' He kept his voice steady, his back erect, like a man awaiting a blow. 'I fear your shipment will be delayed.'

Miguel pounded the table. 'Delayed? Why? By how long?'

Nunes let out a sigh. 'It is an unfortunate business, but you know I can only factor out my requests to men on East India Company vessels. The ship that had been promised changed its plans in accordance with the will of the Company. It's not going to Mocha at all, and it cannot therefore obtain coffee. What can one do with such bad luck?'

Miguel put his head in his hands. For a moment he thought he might faint. 'Delayed,' he whispered, and then released his face and held on to the side of the table. He looked up at Nunes and forced a broken grin. 'Delayed, is it?'

'I know this seems as though it bodes ill for you, but all is not so bad as you think,' Nunes said quickly. 'My man at the Company promises to obtain the goods for us. It will only take a little bit longer. I asked for a delay of the payment, but the contract, as I showed you, only requires them to send the shipment upon the first convenient vessel, and it is for the Company to determine its own convenience.'

'How much time?' His voice cracked, and he had to repeat the question, again with a forced smile. He dared not display any fear, yet a tingling panic radiated out to his extremities. His fingers went numb, and he flexed his hands as though they had fallen asleep.

Nunes bobbed his head as if to encourage a calculation. 'It's hard to say precisely. There are so many details to consider when trying to organise a shipment. They must find a ship that sails the route in question and then make certain it has room in the hold. You had concerns about secrecy that I assume you still wish honoured, which is something that cannot be accommodated on every ship. Each detail must be planned with the greatest care.'

'Of course, I understand that.' He lifted his hat and ran a clumsy hand across his head. 'But you can speculate, can't you?' The hat fell on the floor, and Miguel stooped to retrieve it.

'Speculate,' Nunes repeated, trying not to be made anxious by Miguel's jittery antics. 'Under these conditions, sometimes it can take a year to set things right, but I've already written some letters and called in some favours. I hope to have your shipment within two or three months of the original date. Perhaps a bit longer.'

Two or three months. He might yet avert disaster. With their agents in place, surely they could delay that long. Yes, there was no good reason why they could not delay. A few months meant nothing in the grand scheme of things, not if they had their coffee in the end. A year from now, they would laugh at those two or three months.

Then there was the matter of his investments, the puts that depended on the arrival of that shipment. The puts he had bought with his brother's money.

Miguel had bet a thousand guilders on the price of coffee going down, and with no coffee to flood the market he had no way of manipulating the price. If he lost that money on coffee months before the shipment arrived, he could face a new ruin to make his last look like a mere inconvenience. Once the world knew that Miguel had committed Daniel without his brother's permission, his name would be a byword for deception. Even if he avoided prosecution, he might never do business on the Exchange again.

'There is something else.' Nunes sighed. 'The price of coffee, as you are aware, has gone up since we struck our first deal. Coffee has risen to .65 guilders per pound, which makes it thirty-nine guilders per barrel. Of course you knew that; you bought puts and such. In any case, you'll have to pay another five hundred and ten guilders, half of which I'll need immediately along with the five hundred you now owe, or you must reduce your order from ninety to seventy-seven barrels to cover the price difference.'

Miguel waved his hand in the air. 'Very well,' he said. He had nothing to lose now by risking more debt. 'I must have the ninety barrels, cost what they may.'

'And the money? I hate to be so insistent, but I am, myself, somewhat extended, if you take my meaning. Had I but a little room for my own affairs, I would not so trouble you, but right now seven hundred and fifty-five guilders signify quite a lot to me.'

'I've just now spoken to my partners.' The words sounded like gibberish to him, but he had told such lies so many times he knew he could tell them again, and tell them convincingly, in his sleep if he had to. He slapped his hands together and rubbed vigorously. 'I'll have to speak to them again, of course. They will be disappointed, but they love a challenge as much as I do.'

'And the money?'

Miguel put a hand on Nunes' shoulder. 'They promise to put the money in my account no later than tomorrow. Or the next day. I promise you will be paid by then.'

'Very good.' Nunes twisted out of Miguel's embrace. 'I am sorry about the delay. This sort of thing was always a possibility, you understand.

Surely you considered a delayed shipment in your plans.'

'Absolutely. Please keep me informed of any news. I have a great deal to tend to.'

Miguel suddenly found the tavern unbearably hot, and he hurried outside, charging into the street – and without seeing Joachim until the man stood only a few feet away. If anything, the fellow looked worse than when they had last met. He wore the same clothes, which had grown more filthy, the sleeve of his outer coat had a rip from the wrist almost up to the shoulder, and his collar was streaked with blood.

'I'm sorry I haven't had much time for you of late,' Joachim said, 'but I've been occupied.' He swayed back and forth a little, and his face flushed red.

Miguel did not pause to consider or contemplate or measure. Black swirls of hatred clouded his vision. He could feel nothing but all the rage in his guts, spurred on by the coffee, turning his humours black and evil. In an instant he was no longer himself but a beast, beyond all thought. He came towards Joachim and shoved him hard, using both hands and without breaking his stride.

The pressure against his flesh felt good and right. There was a momentary sensation of a fragile body against his hands – and then Joachim was gone, blasted out of existence. Miguel felt joy. Elation. He felt like a man. With a simple push he had banished Joachim from his life.

Only Joachim did not stay banished for long. Miguel had intended to continue walking, but he saw from the corner of his eyes that his enemy landed somewhat harder than he had intended. He went down on his side, sliding like a fish tossed along a slick dock.

Miguel froze in his tracks. Joachim was dead. Only a dead man would lie like that, limp and motionless and defeated.

He struggled to break free from the haze of dreamlike disbelief. All his hopes had been dashed in a single act. What might he now expect? Trial and execution, scandal and shame. He, a Jew, had struck down a Dutchman; the Dutchman's lowness would not matter.

Then Joachim moved. He stirred briefly, and with his back to Miguel, pushed himself to his feet. A crowd had gathered and there was a gasp as the onlookers saw his face, which had been scraped hard against the brick of the road. He turned slowly to show the injury to Miguel.

The skin on his right cheek looked all but torn away, as did the very tip of his nose. Neither wound bled very much, but both bled steadily, and the image of blood and dirt sickened Miguel. Joachim looked straight ahead and remained motionless, as though on display before a body of judges. Then, after a moment, he spat out a mouthful of blood and what looked like the better part of one of his precious remaining teeth.

'The Jew attacked that poor beggar, and without

cause too,' he heard a woman say. 'I'll call the constable's men.'

The relief vanished. Were he to be arrested for attacking a Dutchman for no reason – and there were witnesses aplenty to testify that the attack had been unprovoked – the Ma'amad would have no choice but to issue the *cherem*, and no temporary one either. All lay in ruins.

Except that Joachim saved him. Joachim had the power to destroy him in his hands, and he held back. Miguel had no illusions. He knew that Joachim had saved him only that he might continue his torments. A destroyed Miguel served no purpose.

'No need to send for anyone,' Joachim called out, his words slow and syrupy. He was surely drunk, though it seemed likely that the injury to his mouth also made speaking difficult. 'I am content to settle this matter privately.' He took a halting step forward and spat another thick mass of blood. 'I think we should make a hasty departure,' he said to Miguel, 'before someone chooses to send for the law despite my best efforts to protect you.' He put one arm around Miguel's shoulder, as though they were wounded comrades fresh from the field of battle.

Joachim stank of vomit and shit and piss and beer, but Miguel ignored it all. He dared not show his disgust as he helped the poor fellow limp away from the crowd.

They walked toward the Oude Kerk with a slow

and deliberate pace. Miguel couldn't spare the energy to worry about who might see them. He only wanted to keep moving.

Once they were in the shadow of the church, Joachim pulled himself free of Miguel and leaned himself against a building, settling into the grooves in the stone. 'You needn't have attacked me,' he said. He put his free hand up to his cheek and then examined the blood.

'Have you not threatened me to kill many times?' Miguel answered blankly.

'I only greeted you, and you knocked me down upon the street. I wonder what this Ma'amad of yours would think, were I to report this incident.'

Miguel looked around, as though something might offer him inspiration. There were only thieves and whores and labourers. 'I've grown weary of your threats,' he said weakly.

'Maybe so, but what does that matter now? You tried to fuck my wife. You have attacked me. Perhaps I should go right away to that fellow you mentioned, Solomon Parido.'

'I have no heart for this,' Miguel said wearily. 'I never touched your wife. Tell me what you want so we may end our conversation the sooner.'

'I want what I've always wanted – my five hundred guilders. You might have given it to me because it was the just thing to do, but now that I have something you want, I am willing to take the money in exchange.'

'And what do you have that I want?'

Joachim wiped away some of his blood with the sleeve of his shirt. 'My silence. You have brokered for a gentile and you've attempted to commit adultery with a Christian woman. And even more, I've seen you with your friend. I know where she gets her money, and I wonder if this Ma'amad of yours would be interested to learn.'

Joachim could have seen Miguel with Geertruid, but how could he know about Geertruid taking money from her husband's children? It made no sense, but Miguel hadn't the heart to find out how Joachim knew what he knew – he only wished to end the conversation. 'I won't discuss this with you.'

'With so much hanging in the balance,' Joachim said evenly, 'I think you'll find a way to get that money. You'll borrow it, steal it – I don't care, just so long as you get it to me.'

'Your threats are worth nothing, and they won't change what is.'

Miguel turned away and began walking very quickly, sensing somehow that Joachim would not follow. His hands shook and he had to concentrate to make sure he walked properly. His luck this day could not have been worse, but nevertheless he believed with absolutely certainty that Joachim would not go to the Ma'amad. If he had wanted to ruin Miguel, he would have allowed the woman to call the Watch. But once Miguel was punished, the game would be over, and it now appeared that Joachim had become attached to playing it. He fed off of his injuries, blossomed with the issuing of new warnings. It was all he had left.

CHAPTER 26

Miguel needed Geertruid. It hardly mattered now what secrets she kept from him – let her have her secrets, just as he had his. He needed her capital, not her honesty. If he could get another thousand guilders from her, it might be enough to save himself. He could pay off Nunes, and he could buy more puts to counter Parido's calls. With a little luck, he could yet turn the tide on the price of coffee. Then he would use those profits, not to pay off his debts as he had planned, but to restore Geertruid's original investment. It was not all he had hoped, but with another thousand guilders, or fifteen hundred if he dared hope, he might make everything easy.

Even though there had been some sort of falling out, Miguel thought that the foul Golden Calf might be his best opportunity. Miguel hurried over and found the fat barman, Crispijn, nearly alone in the tavern, sitting on a stool behind the bar, slurping at a bowl of beer soup and washing it down with a redundant tankard of beer.

'Good morning, Crispijn,' Miguel shouted cheerfully, as though they were old friends. 'How does the day find you?'

'Who in Christ are you?' Crispijn studied Miguel for a moment and then lost interest, wrapping his large hands once more around the soup bowl.

'We met many weeks earlier,' Miguel explained, attempting to keep his cheer intact. 'I was with Geertruid Damhuis.'

Crispijn's forehead wrinkled. 'Were you now?' He spat, inexplicably, into his own soup. 'Well, I'll have no more to do with that devil's bitch if I can help it.'

'Let's be civil.' Miguel took a step forward. 'I don't know what has happened between the two of you, but I must contact Madame Damhuis, and I thought you might know how I could do so, or know someone who would.'

'How should I know how to contact that she-wolf? I have heard she's gone south, and while that is not nearly so good as her going to the devil, I'll take it as good enough.'

'Differences aside' – Miguel pressed on – 'you are still family.'

Crispijn laughed hard enough to make his large body undulate. 'She's no kin of mine, nor would I want any such. I have better family than that come out my arse each morning.'

Miguel put his index finger and thumb to his forehead. 'You are not her kinsman?'

Another laugh, but not nearly so forceful. Now the barman showed something like compassion. 'You seem to be confused. I know nothing of either my father or my mother. I haven't a relative

411

in the world I can call my own, and no cousins neither. Maybe she would be kinder to a man if she were his relative, but I've no luck to call her that.'

More than once she had called Crispijn her cousin. Perhaps the term was some new cant she used freely. It hardly mattered, and Miguel lacked the energy to sort out the confusion.

He might again try Hendrick. The Dutchman had made it clear he could reach Geertruid, even if he seemed unwilling to reveal how. 'Do you know where I can find her man?' he asked.

'Hendrick? You'll do better to run from him than seek him,' the barman said. 'I don't understand you, friend. You're no ruffian to be seeking out someone of Hendrick's sort, and you don't seem to understand that you're plunging into deep water. What want you with such filth?'

'I've dealt with Hendrick before. Do you know where I can find him or no?'

Crispijn shrugged his heavy shoulders.

Miguel understood perfectly, though in his mood he would have preferred a simple request. He handed the tavern-keeper a half guilder.

Crispijn smiled. 'I hear he's got something planned at the Spaniard's Lame Horse, a musico on the far end of the Warmoesstraat. He'll be there tonight, I heard, but not too late. And if I know Hendrick, which I do more than I'd like, he'll be in and out quickly. You'll want to be there no later than when the tower strikes seven, I think. Then

412

maybe you'll be able to catch him, though maybe it were better that you didn't.'

Miguel muttered his thanks and headed out, wishing it were not already too late to visit the Exchange. He despised the feeling of a day of business entirely lost. Damn the East India Company, he cursed silently. Was there not another ship for them to have rerouted rather than his? His coffee would be on its way and therefore he would not have struck Joachim.

With no business to conduct, Miguel wanted to avoid being seen, particularly by Joachim. He visited a bookseller and purchased, on credit, a few pamphlets – and, on a whim, a simple book in the most elementary Portuguese on the basics of holy Law. He would give it as a gift to Hannah. She could not read, but perhaps she might learn sometime.

After passing the day in taverns, reading his lurid tales of crime, he took Crispijn's advice and travelled to the Spaniard's Lame Horse. Miguel generally avoided musicos of this nature, catering to low sorts of fellows. A band of three string musicians played simple tunes while the whores drifted from table to table, seeking business. Miguel suspected there were rooms in the back, and he briefly considered inspecting them with one buxom beauty with dark hair and fetching black eyes, but his business was with Hendrick and he considered it no good bargain to miss his opportunity while gaining the clap.

413

Within an hour the whores knew they would get nowhere with him, and they kept their distance, ignoring him except to administer the occasional scowl. Miguel drank quickly and ordered repeatedly. He reasoned that he would have to pay for his seat in beer or the owner might toss him out.

After nearly two hours of steady drinking, Hendrick had not yet shown himself. Sleepy with beer, Miguel wondered if he might not be better off abandoning his station; this was no place for a man to fall asleep unless he wanted to awaken stripped of all his goods.

He lifted his tankard and set it down again. A loud conversation a few tables over began to distract him. Something about cargo, ruin, a lost ship called the *Bountiful Providence* carrying slaves in the Africa trade.

Then something happened. A drunk fellow rose to his feet and turned towards the sailors. 'The *Bountiful Providence*!' Saliva flew from his mouth. 'Are you certain?'

'Aye,' one of the sailors said. 'She's been taken by pirates all right. Vicious Spanish pirates, too. Bloodthirsty bastards. The very worst of the lot. My brother was a seaman aboard her and barely escaped with his life. Do you know the ship, friend, or have kin upon her?'

'I know her.' He put his face in his hands. 'I owned stock in her. Good God, I'll be ruined. I have sunk my fortune in a ship now sunk!'

Miguel stared. Even in the murkiness of beer he knew the scene was far too familiar. It reminded him not only of his recent misfortune with the coffee but of something else, from many months before. It was like watching his own life played on stage before him.

'You might not be entirely ruined,' said one of the sailor's companions in a voice full of hope, such as one might use with a frightened child. 'You see, the news has not yet reached the Exchange, and that might work in your favour.'

The stockholder turned to the new speaker. He alone of the party did not look like a sailor. Not exactly a man of substance, he yet had something more to him than his companions.

'What do you say?' the stockholder asked.

'That you may take advantage of the ignorance still to be found upon the Exchange. Or at least someone could. I would be willing to take those shares from you, sir, for fifty per cent of their value. That should be far more lucrative than if you lose it all.'

'And sell them at a discount at the Exchange tomorrow?' the stockholder said, rolling the words about on his tongue. 'Why should I not do that as well as you?'

'You are welcome to try, friend, but then you assume the risk. And when the world learns that you have unloaded your stock only hours before news of the loss becomes general, you will become mistrusted. I, on the other hand, do not spend

415

much time upon the Exchange and can escape from such an adventure entirely unscathed.'

The man said nothing, but Miguel could see that he stood on the precipice of acquiescing.

'I might also add,' the prospective buyer told him, 'that not every man might sell spoiled goods with an honest look in his eye. You might find yourself ready to sell and with no one to buy because you cannot conduct yourself like a man who has nothing to hide.'

'You, however, do a mighty good job of looking like an honest man,' a new voice, a heroic voice announced, 'though as sure as I am standing here, I know you to be a scoundrel.'

And there was Hendrick, dressed in black like a man of business. He stood behind the prospective buyer with his arms crossed, and he appeared nothing if not heroic.

'I know you, Jan van der Dijt,' Hendrick announced, 'and you are a liar and a knave.' He turned to the shareholder. 'Nothing has befallen your ship, sir. These men are tricksters, who prey upon the fear of investors. They seek to rob you of your shares at half their value and then reap the rewards when the cargo arrives safely.'

The sailors and their companion rose from their seats and hurried out the door. The shareholder stiffened and looked as though he prepared himself to sprint after the cheats, but Hendrick put his arm around the man's shoulders and held him back.

'Let the villains run,' he said soothingly. 'You've

undone their scheme, and you can't defeat so large a group. Come.' He led the man to a table and applied pressure upon his shoulder so he would sit.

Miguel had just witnessed the precise events that had transpired when he had met Geertruid and become her friend. But their friendship was a sham and everything had been false. The men who had offered to buy his shares hadn't been exposed by Geertruid, they had been in her employ. It had been no more than a trick to gain Miguel's trust.

Making sure the fellow's back was towards him, Miguel quickly paid his reckoning – indeed, he overpaid, that he might get out quickly and with little conversation. He then found the door and slipped out unseen.

Out in the cool night, he lit his lantern, which barely penetrated the thick fog off the IJ. What did it mean? How could he explain it?

In an instant, all became clear. Geertruid had laid some scheme that involved gaining his trust not for a single night at a single moment but over a period of days or weeks. Then Miguel had lost almost everything when sugar collapsed. Surely that explained why Hendrick appeared so uneasy around him – the man did not understand what Geertruid wanted with this Jew who had now become penniless and of no value to them.

So Geertruid had created value. She had hatched this coffee scheme in order to – to do what? What plot had she constructed? It could not be that

Geertruid planned to take anything from Miguel. She had provided money, money that, by her own admission, did not truly belong to her.

Perhaps it did not belong to her late husband's children either. That story, Miguel realised, had the hollow ring of a lie. How could he have not seen it sooner? He, who made his livelihood by distinguishing truth from falseness, though it was but a scurvy livelihood now. And coffee, which was to save him from his ruin, was now revealed to be but another disaster. But why? Why would Geertruid advance money, why would anyone advance money, to dupe a ruined man into ruining himself further?

There could only be one answer. There could only be one person willing to expend capital on Miguel's destruction. Geertruid, he concluded with perfect clarity, served Solomon Parido.

CHAPTER 27

The idea that one might see things more clearly upon a new day, or that matters of importance could be worked out during sleep, seemed to Miguel foolishness. His restless sleep offered him no answers the next day, nor the day thereafter, the Sabbath. On the following morning, however, he did wake up with one important detail on his mind: standing outside the Singing Carp, Joachim had spoken suggestively about Geertruid. He could remember the precise smell in the air – beer and piss and canal stink – as the wretch suggested he knew something.

At the time, Miguel had assumed Joachim had somehow learned about Geertruid's money, but now Miguel thought that unlikely. The business with the husband's children was almost certainly a lie, a plausible deception meant to sound like a dishonest but forgivable means of generating capital. Surely it was more likely that Solomon Parido had provided the money.

But if Geertruid did Parido's work, why did the *parnass* not know the details of Miguel's plans? Would Parido let Miguel and Geertruid obtain their monopoly on coffee and then strike, ruining Miguel for his partnership with Geertruid and splitting the proceeds?

'No,' Miguel said aloud. He sat upon his cupboard bed, throwing the heavy feather duvet aside in the morning heat. None of it made sense, but someone – Geertruid, Hendrick, Parido – someone would make a mistake that would reveal the truth, and he would be ready when they did.

Two days later, Annetje announced that Miguel had a visitor. Her voice quivered slightly, and she could not bring herself to meet Miguel's eye. When he followed her out to the front room, he saw Joachim standing just inside the doorway, a new wide-brimmed cap in his hand, looking about the house with a kind of childlike curiosity: So, *this is where a Jew lives.*

'You've lost your mind,' Miguel said calmly.

Joachim wore new clothes – where had they come from? – and while they were not the finery he had once been used to, he presented himself neatly and with dignity, much like a tradesman in his white shirt, new doublet, and close-fitting woollen jersey. The wound on his face belied any hint of gentility, but it also made him less recognisably a mendicant, and he certainly no longer carried with him the stink of decay.

'I must speak with you,' he said, in an even voice Miguel hardly recognised. Had a bath and new clothes driven out his madness? 'I'm already in your house. To cast me out now would do you no good, particularly if I made a great deal of noise about it. Surely you would be better off if I left quietly when my business is done.' He left the alternative unspoken.

Could not the rascal have had the courtesy to knock upon the kitchen door? Miguel was not about to stand in the front of the house with this fellow, so he stepped aside and led the villain down to his cellar.

Joachim examined his surroundings as he descended the stairs and stood uneasily in the damp room, perhaps surprised that Miguel did not live in luxury. He sat on a stool with uneven legs and let a moment pass while he stared into the flame of the oil lamp upon the table. Finally he took a deep breath and began. 'I have been under the influence of a lunacy that has now passed. I have made demands and issued threats, some of which may have been unreasonable, and for that I apologise. I still think I should be paid the five hundred guilders I lost, but it need not be immediately or all at once. That is to say, I would like to set upon a schedule of repayment, such as one might have if he took a loan. Then I'll no longer bother you.'

'I see.' Miguel spoke slowly, trying to buy himself time to think. Someone had given Joachim money; that much was evident. That someone could only be Parido.

'I'm glad you see, so on to business: I will accept

a gradual repayment of what you owe, though in order for me to feel comfortable, I'll have to know how you plan to make your money. So, you see, that's the bargain. You tell me about this business project in which you plan to make money over the next few months, and, understanding your strategy, I may feel confident that you will repay my five hundred guilders over, shall we say, the next two years.'

It could not have been more simple or more obvious. Parido had engaged Joachim to find out what Miguel had planned. Whatever Parido had done, he appeared to have quite tamed the man. Had money been enough to effect this change? Miguel thought there must be more. Joachim held himself with the uneasy bearing of a man awaiting trial.

Miguel felt a sudden unexpected exhilaration. Things had gone badly in the past few weeks – very badly – but now he knew how to take command. He knew what others were planning and, knowing their plans, he could manipulate them to his advantage.

'How do I know that you won't prey on whatever information I provide?' he asked, stalling for time while he considered his options. 'You have not been so long away from the Exchange that you have forgotten the value of secrecy.'

'I don't want anything to do with the Exchange. Those days are past for me. I only want to provide for my wife and retire into a quiet existence in the countryside.' He winced for a moment. 'If you pay me, I'll buy a plot of land and work it. Or perhaps I'll open a tavern in some village.'

'Very well,' Miguel said carefully, 'I promise to pay you.'

'But you must tell me what I ask,' Joachim said. He ran his fingers through his long hair, recently washed smooth.

Miguel tasted blood. 'Must I? What will you do if I don't tell you?'

'I only want assurance that I shall not be ill-used.'

'Then you have my assurance.' Miguel smiled.

'That won't be enough.' Joachim shifted uneasily. 'We have had our differences, yes, but you see now that I come to you somewhat humbled. I am ready to admit my wrongs. I only want a little thing from you, and yet you withhold it.'

What could he give Parido that would satisfy him and also buy Miguel some time? The answer came to him in a sudden burst of inspiration: fear. He would give the man cause to tremble, to doubt his allies, to look upon the unknown and the future as his enemies.

Miguel nodded slowly in an effort to look thoughtful. 'Unfortunately, I can give you no details of my business because there are other men involved, and I haven't the right to say on my own something that may affect the well-being of the combination.'

'You have joined with a trading combination?' he asked eagerly, diving for the scraps.

'A combination of sorts. We have joined together that we may better engage in a rather momentous piece of business. Each of us has a particular skill or contribution, making the whole stronger than the sum of its parts.' Miguel felt a twinge of sadness. That had been the case with his partnership with Geertruid – at least until he learned that Geertruid had betrayed him.

'What will this combination be doing?'

'I can't tell you that – not without breaking a vow I made to the others. Please understand that no matter how much you may make your case, I can't give you those details.'

'I must have some information.' Joachim was nearly pleading. 'Surely you can see that.'

For the first time, Miguel began to wonder if Joachim was Parido's servant or his slave. He appeared to be genuinely afraid of leaving without information for his master. With what could Parido have threatened Joachim?

'Without betraying confidences, I can tell you there's a great deal of money to be made. You no longer follow the affairs of the Exchange, so I will confide in you if you promise not to repeat it to another soul. Do you solemnly promise, Joachim?'

Inexplicably, Joachim hesitated and swallowed in discomfort. 'I promise,' he said.

'Do you swear by your own Jesus Christ?' Miguel asked, twisting the knife.

'I don't make such oaths lightly,' Joachim said. 'Despite all that has happened, I hope I shall do nothing blasphemous.'

'I ask nothing blasphemous,' Miguel explained with a broad smile. 'Only to swear a holy oath to do what you have already promised to do. I suppose you could break your word. Any man who would threaten to take another's life, surely among the most serious of sins, could break a vow made to his God. But if you make the vow, it will offer me some small comfort.'

'Very well,' Joachim said, examining the light that filtered in through one of the small windows. 'I swear by Jesus Christ not to repeat what you tell me.'

Miguel smiled. 'What more could I ask for? Know then that with this scheme we plan to make a great deal of money, an amount so large that the thousand you ask for will seem as nothing. Men will talk about it ten years hence. It will be the very model to which young upstarts on the Exchange aspire.'

Joachim's eyes widened. He straightened himself in his chair. 'Can you say no more? Can you not tell me if you deal in a particular commodity or route or stock scheme?'

'I can't answer that question without violating my own vows,' Miguel lied. 'There are other Jews of importance involved in this business, and in order to protect ourselves we have all taken vows of silence.'

'Other Jews of importance?' Joachim asked. He had been in Parido's service long enough, apparently, to know when he had hit upon something of note.

'Yes,' Miguel told him. His little deception was so sinister he could hardly contain his pleasure. 'I have thrown my lot in with several members of the community of the highest standing. That's why I never feared your bringing our history to the Ma'amad; I only wished to avoid being embarrassed before my partners. I have an enemy on that board, but I also have very powerful friends.' He paused to lean forward and assume the hunched pose of a teller of secrets. 'You see, one of the members of the council is part of my combination, and another has invested heavily in our enterprise.'

Joachim nodded and appeared to visibly relax. It would seem that he now had enough information to return to his master and not fear his dissatisfaction. He had the glimmering jewel he had sought.

'Does that satisfy your curiosity, Joachim?'

'For now,' Joachim said. 'Though I believe I may have more questions later.'

'When you think of them, you mean.'

'Yes, I might think of more.'

'You always were a curious fellow. I suppose there's nothing to be done about that.'

Miguel ushered him up the stairs and saw him out of the kitchen door. When he closed it, he barked out a laugh. Miguel need no longer fear the Ma'amad. Surely Parido would never agree now to have Miguel questioned. He had too much to lose.

CHAPTER 28

O ne week later, Miguel received a note from Geertruid. She had returned from her trip, all was well, and she wished to meet later that day at the Singing Carp.

When he arrived, Miguel thought she looked uncommonly beautiful in a gown of bright red with a blue bodice and a matching blue-trimmed red cap. Her lips were deep red, as though she had been biting them.

'It's good to be back,' she said, kissing him on his cheek. 'My ailing aunt in Friesland has made a complete recovery – so complete I wonder if she was ever truly sick at all. And now' – she took Miguel's hand – 'tell me what news, my handsome partner.'

Miguel wished he could have doubted his own eyes, but he had seen what he had seen. Geertruid had tricked Miguel into their friendship, and Miguel still did not know why.

'I'm happy your aunt is well.'

Miguel had spent some time thinking about this problem, and he had come to a comforting conclusion: if Geertruid worked for Parido, she would provide any reasonable amount he asked for;

otherwise whatever scheme the *parnass* hatched would fail. Miguel would get the money he needed to cover his own investments, and then he would show Parido how foolish it was to attempt to outwit a man who was well read in the stories of Charming Pieter. But after days of thought, he was still unsure how to make his request.

'Well, then,' Geertruid said. She took a long drink of beer. 'Any news of our shipment? Any news upon the Exchange? I am feverish with the desire to press forward.'

'There has been some news,' Miguel began, 'though not as good as I would like. You must understand that these arrangements almost never happen as smoothly as planned, and as a merchant runs along, he must always do his best to avoid hidden dangers.'

Geertruid licked her lips. 'Hidden dangers?'

'You see, the price of a commodity is subject to any of a variety of changes over a period of time. No one can truly predict its movements – that is, unless one has a monopoly, as we plan to do – though we do not have one yet.'

'The price of coffee has risen?' she asked flatly.

'It has, and somewhat more than I could have predicted. Then there is the matter of the shipping costs, which have turned out to be significantly more than I had been led to believe. And secrecy – that costs money too. A palm greased here and a palm greased there – a man looks down and his purse is empty.'

'I begin to suspect where this conversation is taking me.'

'I thought you might. You see, I think we must have more money to make this thing certain. For just a little bit more, we can remove any element of doubt.'

'A little bit more?'

'Fifteen hundred guilders,' he told her breezily, though when he saw the look on her face he realized he might have been too ambitious. 'Although a thousand might do our business.'

'You must think me a far greater woman than I am,' she said. 'I told you how difficult it was to raise the three thousand. Now you casually ask me for half again as much.'

'Is this money to gratify my own needs, madam? No, it is to assure our wealth. You asked me to work with you because you trusted that I knew how to order matters of business. I do know how, and I tell you we need this money if we want to depend on victory.'

Miguel had expected her to be sulky and chastising but also amused. Instead, she glared at him in anger. 'When we began I asked you how much you required, and you told me three thousand guilders. I committed that money to you. If you had told me forty-five hundred, I would have said the thing could not be done. Will not the three thousand I gave you carry this? Is the money lost?'

'Not lost,' he told her hurriedly. 'I promise you

that. The worst danger we face is that we make not so much as we wished, and that you return your investment whence you got it. I only thought that if more money was to be had, it would serve us well.'

'More money is not to be had,' Geertruid said, 'and I need you to speak truthfully to me. I know the truth comes hard to a man who has been a Secret Jew.'

'That is unkind,' Miguel protested.

'You've told me so yourself. You told me that out of necessity you were schooled in the arts of deception. I want no deception now, however. I want the truth.'

'Just because a man knows how to deceive doesn't mean that he has forgotten how to be truthful. I would not lie to you, just as I know you would not lie to me.' He probably should not have said it, but he felt sure that his face betrayed nothing of the irony. 'Your money is safe, and though more money would have made my task far easier, I believe I can still order everything.'

'Better to do it, then,' she said. 'You cannot eat the same rabbit twice, Miguel. You've got all there is to get from me.'

'Then I will have to make do,' he said, with an easy grin.

Geertruid said nothing for a moment. She took a deep drink of her beer and stared past Miguel. 'I believe you,' she said. 'I know you are my friend, and I know you would not hurt me. But if there is something I must know, you had better tell me, because if you do hurt me – if it even appears to unschooled eyes that you have hurt me – you must understand that Hendrick will kill you, and I won't be able to stop him.'

Miguel affected a laugh. 'He'll have no cause to resent me when all is done, and neither will you. Now, if things are to be this way, I had better go and make certain all is in order.'

'When will the shipment be in port?' she asked.

His speculations on coffee came due in three weeks' time. He had planned originally that the coffee be in port some two weeks later. It would not happen, but no one need know that. Not for what he had in mind.

'A month,' he said. 'Maybe less.'

The meeting left a sour taste in his mouth, but that could not be helped. As he crossed the Warmoesstraat, Miguel saw a pair of men who pretended that they did not keep their eyes upon him – surely Ma'amad spies. It was no matter. There was no crime in being on the street. Still, he felt compelled to lose them, and ducked into a side alley that led to a back street. He took another alley and then another side street, which took him back again to the main road.

He turned around, and the spies were still behind him. Perhaps they had never turned in the alleys, knowing Miguel would come back to where he started. He picked up a flat stone and tossed it into the canal to make it skip, but it sank the instant it hit the murky water.

Miguel lifted up the sack of coffee berries. It was light, light enough to toss from hand to hand. He would have to start being careful how he used it or he would soon have none left. Perhaps the people at the Turkish coffee tavern would allow him to buy for his own use.

Having taken an inventory of the problems before him, Miguel now saw what he faced: his coffee scheme was on the brink of foundering, owing to late shipments and insufficient funds; his partner, Geertruid, was not what she seemed, perhaps in league with Parido, perhaps not; Joachim was certainly in league with Parido, but that made Miguel's life easier, not harder, since Parido's money seemed to have returned the fellow's sanity; Miguel could not pay his debt to Isaiah Nunes because he had used the funds to pay off his brother and to pay his Muscovy agent; the money he'd earned from his brilliant whale oil trade was unavailable because the broker Ricardo would not pay Miguel or reveal the name of his client; Miguel could do nothing about Ricardo's treachery since using the Dutch courts would bring upon him the anger of the Ma'amad, and going before Ma'amad was too risky because of Parido.

Rather, it *had* been too risky.

Miguel swallowed the last of the coffee in his

bowl. There was at least one thing he could resolve, he realised, and he could do so at once.

After searching a half-dozen taverns, Miguel called on Ricardo at his home. The broker was notorious for hiring the cheapest servants he could find, and the creature who opened the door must have been a rare bargain: well into her last years in life, she was hunched and trembling. Her eyes were mere slits, and she had trouble propelling herself forwards.

'What is it?' she asked Miguel in Dutch. 'You here for the Jew's supper?'

Miguel smiled brightly. 'Certainly.'

'Come in then. The rest are already eating. The Jew doesn't like for the people he invites to be late.'

'Has it occurred to you,' Miguel asked, as he followed her along at her shuffling pace, 'that as you speak of the "the Jew", you are speaking to yet another Jew?'

'Take that up with him,' she said. 'It's none of my business.'

The woman led him down a long, brightly tiled hallway and into a spacious room, furnished with hardly more than a large table. The walls, however, were thick with paintings: portraits, landscapes, biblical scenes. Miguel recognised one portrait, a painting of Samson, as being in the style of that curious fellow who had lived in the Vlooyenburg and was in the habit of paying poor Jews to model for him.

The models, however, were the only poor Jews who graced the inside of this house; surrounding the table, which seemed to Miguel to have relatively little food on it, were some of the wealthiest men of the Portuguese Nation, including Solomon Parido. From the volume of the conversation, Miguel guessed that Ricardo had been more liberal with his wine than with his food.

The broker, who had been laughing at something, now looked up and saw Miguel standing with the old servant.

'It's another Jew for you,' she announced.

'Lienzo.' Ricardo spat. 'Surely I didn't invite you here.'

'You told me to come and join you and your friends for a merry feast, so here I am.'

Parido raised his glass. 'Let us toast Lienzo, then. Amsterdam's most uncanny trader.'

Ricardo pushed himself to his feet. 'Walk into my private chambers for a moment.' He lurched forward, stumbling briefly, and then, after taking a breath, seemed to regain his balance. Miguel bowed at the guests and followed.

Ricardo let him up a narrow half-flight of stairs to a smallish room, furnished with a writing table, a few chairs, and piles of papers that rested on the floor. The windows had been pulled shut, and the room was nearly entirely dark. The broker opened one of the shutters so there was just enough light for them to see each other, but hardly more than that.

'I'm beginning to suspect,' Miguel said, 'that you drink more wine than is healthy for one of our nation. The Dutch are bottomless vessels, but you seem to have reached your limit.'

'And I think,' Ricardo said, 'that you may be more of a rascal than I had first suspected. What do you mean coming here while I am entertaining my friends, a category, I might point out, that certainly does not include you?'

'I had no idea you had friends here. I was merely looking for you in some obvious places. Had you not hired your serving girl out of the graveyard she might screen your visitors a little more thoroughly.'

Ricardo lowered himself into a chair. 'Well, what is it you want? Speak quickly, but if it is about that cursed money again, I will have to tell you what I've told you before: you'll get what you have coming in due time and not before.'

Miguel chose not to sit but, instead, paced back and forth in the room like an advocate making a speech before the burgomasters. 'I have thought about what you've said and found it wanting. You see, I am owed money, and if I cannot have it I am entitled at the very least to know who is my debtor.'

Ricardo's moustaches twitched with superior amusement. 'You may think so, but we both know there is nothing you can do about it.'

'So you say. You believe I won't risk the anger of the Ma'amad by going to the Dutch courts, and

I won't go to the Ma'amad because one of its members might lead the council against me. That, at any rate, is what you think. I suppose you also know about my recent encounter with the council and my day-long banishment, but because those proceedings are held in secret, you don't know what was revealed. So let me tell you this: my enemy on that council betrayed himself and revealed his antipathy for me to the other *parnassim*. That man would be unable to lead the council against me.'

Ricardo made a hissing noise like a snake. 'Very well. If you want to take that chance, you may bring your complaint forward. We will see what happens.'

Miguel nodded. 'I thank you for your courtesy. I am sure the council will find this case very interesting. As it will find it interesting when it learns that you have hidden behind that man's protection in order to avoid giving me my due. That will be very embarrassing for him, and I'm sure he will resent your having put him in so awkward a position. But,' Miguel said, 'then again, he may not resent it at all. As you say, we'll see what happens.'

Ricardo pulled himself to his feet. 'Are you threatening me, senhor?'

Miguel belched out a laugh. 'Of course I am. I am threatening you with the very thing you have challenged me to do. Not much of a threat, really, but it does seem to have you agitated.'

Ricardo nodded rapidly, as though discussing

something with himself. 'You don't want to bring this before the Ma'amad,' he said.

'No, I don't, but if you give me no choice, I will do it, and watching you and Parido squirm will prove more than ample compensation for my trouble. I have nothing to lose in this, Ricardo, but you do. You can pay me, you can give me the name of your client, or you can allow the Ma'amad to compel you to do both while embarrassing you and making Solomon Parido your enemy. It is your choice, but I intend to request a hearing first thing in the morning. You might want to make your decision soon.'

Miguel turned to leave, not that he thought Ricardo would let him but his statement required a pretended exit.

'Wait,' Ricardo said. He slowly lowered himself back into his chair. 'Wait. Wait, wait, wait.'

'I'm waiting. I've been doing a great deal of it.'

'I understand.' He held up a hand in a stay-your-tongue gesture. 'Here is what I will offer you. I will tell you the name of my client, and you may pursue your debt yourself, but you must not tell him I was the one who betrayed him. And you must not say anything to Parido. He doesn't know I've used his name in this, and I would have him continue not to know.'

Miguel swallowed hard. At last this money would be his. And he had won – something that happened far too infrequently of late. 'I agree,' he said.

Ricardo sighed. 'Very well. Understand that my

client instructed me very clearly to keep this information a secret. It was not my choice or my doing.'

'Just give me the name.'

'I said I would. The name,' he said, 'is Daniel Lienzo.' He let out a squealing little laugh. 'It is rather funny, when you think about it. He put the squeeze on you for the thousand you had borrowed of him, but all the while he owed you more than twice that. He has been lording it over you because you are in his debt, but these past weeks he has been your debtor and you did not even know it. Do you find that as amusing as I do?'

Miguel picked up a stack of papers and threw them at Ricardo, scattering his notes and ledgers and correspondence all over the room. By doing so he hoped to indicate that he did not, in fact, find it as amusing as Ricardo did.

CHAPTER 29

Miguel had known that Daniel's finances were in trouble, but he had not known to what extent. All his sneering, all his grumblings about Miguel's dealing in mischief when he was making mischief of his own – Miguel could forgive that; he could forgive the superiority and the judgmental glares. He could not forgive Daniel for taking money – for stealing money – when he knew his brother needed it.

But even with his resentment, Miguel did not dare to speak of it. He did not dare to complain, because until he resolved this coffee matter one way or another, he could not risk moving from his brother's house, a move that would attract far too much notice.

Some days later, Annetje came again to Miguel's study with an announcement that would have been far more shocking if it had been unprecedented. Joachim Waagenaar was at the door and wished to meet with him.

Joachim climbed down the narrow stairs using one hand to steady himself, the other to clutch his hat. He stumbled when he reached the floor, teetering like a drunkard.

'Well, now, senhor, I see things have come full circle. As the saying goes, a bird always returns to the place of its nest.'

Joachim was not so drunk as he had first seemed. An idea came into his head: Joachim had drunk just enough to give himself courage. But courage for what? Once more, Miguel looked for anything that could be used to protect himself.

'Is this your nest?' Miguel asked. 'I hardly think so.'

'I disagree.' Joachim sat without being asked. 'I feel like this very room is where I was born – the me I have become. And what I have become – even I hardly know that now.'

'Is that what you came to say?'

'No. Only that I've been thinking, and in a strange way I've decided you may be the greatest friend I have right now. Strange, isn't it? Once we were – well, not friends really, but friendly-like. Then we were enemies. I'll take most of the blame for that, though my anger was justified; I'm sure you know that. And now we are friends at last. True friends, I mean. The kind who must look after each other.'

'How do you come to such an unusual conclusion?'

'Very simple, senhor. I have information you want. I have information from which you can make a great deal of money. In fact, I have information

441

that will save you from ruin. I cannot help but fear you may be too much of a fool to take it, but just the same I have it and I am willing to share it.'

'And for this information you want the five hundred guilders of which I've heard so much?'

The Dutchman laughed. 'I want instead a piece of your profit. You see the joke, I hope. I want my success, my fortune, once again to be bound with yours.'

'I see.' Miguel took a deep breath. He hardly even recognised his own life any more. Here he sat, in his cellar, negotiating with Joachim Waagenaar. Were he to be caught doing so, in all likelihood Solomon Parido would argue to the Ma'amad that the crime should be forgiven. The world had become an unknown wilderness.

Joachim shook his head. 'You don't see, Lienzo, but you will. Here is what I propose: I agree to give you information from which you will make wondrous profits. If I'm right, you give me ten per cent of what you make because of that information – a broker's fee, shall we call it? If I am wrong, you owe me nothing, and you'll never hear from me again.'

'Aren't you overlooking an important detail?'

'What detail is that?'

Miguel swallowed. 'That you are a madman, and nothing you say can be trusted.'

Joachim nodded, as though Miguel had made a sage point of law. 'I'll ask you to trust me now. I've never been a madman, only a ruined man. Can you say what would become of you, senhor, if you lost everything – if you had no money, no home, no food? Can you say that you would not fall victim to the lunacy of desperation?'

Miguel said nothing.

'I've never wanted revenge,' Joachim continued, 'only what's mine, and I'll not sit by and watch one man destroy another for the pleasure of it. I've no love for you. I suppose you know that, but I've learned what ruin is. I'll not bring it on another.'

Joachim now had Miguel's full attention. 'I'm listening.'

'You'll have to do more than listen. You'll have to agree.'

'Suppose I listen to what you have to say and don't believe you?'

'That's well and good, but if you decide that you do believe me, and you act on that information, you'll have to give me ten per cent of what you make.'

'Or?'

'There's no *or*,' Joachim said. 'There can be no more threats between us. I'll not make you sign a contract; I know you risk ruin if you put something on paper with one of us. I will leave it to your own sense of what a gentleman should do.'

Miguel took a gulp of his wine. Joachim no longer spoke like a madman. Would Parido's coin be enough to drive the evil vapours from his brain, or could only Joachim's own clarity and determination do that? 'I'll listen.'

Joachim breathed in deeply. 'You have any of that wine for me? Or maybe some beer?'

'I'm not your host, Joachim. Speak or get out.'

'There's no need to be so unfriendly, senhor. You'll be serving me drinks aplenty when you listen to what I have to say.' He paused again. 'All right, then. You see, last time I came to you, I was not entirely honest about what I wanted. As it happens, I fell in with this man who sent me here to do his bidding.'

'Solomon Parido,' Miguel said. 'You might as easily have brought him with you for all that I was fooled.'

'I suspected you knew, but I didn't say a word to him. I was already thinking about what might come of our sad partnership, and I figured you told me what you did because you wanted him to believe it. I had already begun to hate him more than I hate you, so I held my tongue.'

'Let's take this path more slowly. How did you find yourself in Parido's employ?'

'He's a tricky one. He came to me, said he knew I'd been following you through the town, and said he knew why. He said maybe we could do some business together. He was very kind to me. He even gave me ten guilders and told me he would come to see me in a week's time. A week goes by, and he wants me to start coming to talk to you. I tell him I won't do such a thing, that things have taken a turn for the worse between us. I admit I only wanted to hear what he might offer me. But he offers me nothing. He tells me that if I feel that way, he would just as soon I repaid that loan and its interest, and that would be all between us. I told him I couldn't repay the loan, and he began to threaten me with the Rasphuis. He knows men on the City Council, he says, who will lock me away without cause or regret, and perhaps raise some questions about how I had been released so quick after my previous detention. I had no desire to return to that dungeon, I can tell you.'

'Go on.'

'So I do what he tells me for a while, but all the time I'm thinking about what I might do for myself, which, as it turns out, has a lot to do with what I might do for you. I liked the little trick you tried to play, by the way, but he didn't believe it. When I told him what you had said to me, he said that of all the Conversos he knew, you were the one best made to be a liar.'

Miguel said nothing.

Joachim rubbed his sleeve against his nose. 'In any case, I managed to fit a few things together. You know someone named Nunes, a trader in goods from the East Indies?'

Miguel nodded, for the first time really believing that Joachim might have some information of importance.

'This Nunes works for Parido. There's something to do with a shipment of coffee, a drink I had once, by the way, and very much despised for its piss-like taste.'

Nunes working for Parido? How could that be? Why would his friend betray him?

'What about the shipment?' Miguel spoke so quietly he could hardly hear himself.

'Nunes lied to you – told you a shipment is late, never obtained, or such nonsense that he concocted – but it's all false. They changed the ship, so it's on something called the *Sea Lily*, which near as I can tell is to come in next week. I don't know much more than that, except that Parido doesn't want you to learn this and he wants to do something with the prices.'

Miguel began to pace about the room, only vaguely aware that Joachim stared at him. Parido and Nunes together! He would not have thought Nunes such a traitor, but it explained a great deal. If Nunes was Parido's creature, he would have reported Miguel's sale. Parido would then have begun conspiring to find ways to ruin Miguel while simultaneously making money himself. But Parido knew only about the coffee itself and how Miguel had gambled on its price falling. Perhaps he did not know about the plan to establish a monopoly. The shape of the scheme eluded him, but Miguel knew he had to assume one thing: if Geertruid did work for Parido also, she had not told Parido all she knew.

'You mentioned Geertruid Damhuis to me before. Does she work for Parido?' Miguel asked, hoping he might resolve the question forever.

'You'd be wise to keep clear of that one.'

'What do you know of her?'

'Only that she's a thief and a trickster, she and her companion both.'

'That much I already know. What does Parido have to do with her?'

He narrowed his eyes. 'Nothing that I am aware. Two such jackals could never run in the same pack. I've only heard him say he knows you have some business with her.'

Miguel returned to his seat. If Geertruid did not work for Parido, what was her plan and why had it been necessary for her to deceive him into a friendship? Perhaps Joachim did not know all of Parido's secrets. He might have hired her and then realised she had been deceiving him as well as Miguel. He could make no sense of it, but it seemed likely that Parido had only a murky idea at best of his plans with Geertruid. 'What about my brother?' Miguel asked at last, blurting out the words before he had fully realised his intentions.

'Your brother?'

'Yes. What do you know of his relationship with Parido? Have you heard him speak the name of Daniel Lienzo?'

Joachim shook his head. 'What a sad affair when a man cannot even trust his own brother. I suppose it has ever been thus among your people. Only look at Cain and Abel.'

'Cain and Abel were not Jews,' Miguel said testily, 'they were merely the sons of Adam and, as such, your ancestors as much as mine.'

'I'll be careful not to quote you scripture again. But as for your brother, I can tell you nothing. I know he spends a great deal of time with Parido, but you know that yourself. You want to know if he acts against your interests, but I can't tell you.'

'And the pig's head? Parido's doing or yours?'

Joachim's lips parted just a little. 'Both,' he said.

Miguel paused for a moment to feel justified. Daniel had thought Miguel the villain for bringing down such horrors on his house, but the *parnass* was the villain all along. 'How is it that Parido was so foolish as to speak of all of this in front of you? He may well have sent you to me with this information.'

'He may have,' Joachim said. 'I'd wonder the same thing if I were you. But I don't see what he would have to gain by giving you this information. Once the *Sea Lily* docks it will be easy enough to pay a sailor to crack open a barrel and tell you what is inside.'

'You haven't answered my first question. Why would he reveal all this to you?'

'He wouldn't,' Joachim said. 'At least he wouldn't intend to. After all, who would suspect a half-mad Dutchman of understanding the language of Portuguese Jews?'

Miguel laughed in spite of himself. 'In a city like Amsterdam,' he said, repeating what Joachim once told him, 'one must never assume that a man does not understand the language you speak.'

'It's still good advice,' Joachim agreed.

'I'll have to think very carefully about what you have told me.' It could all be a lie, he told himself. Another of Parido's tricks. But what trick? What trick would be worth revealing to Miguel this web of deception? He could bring Nunes before the courts now if he chose; no one would blame Miguel for not trusting this matter to the Ma'amad. Would Parido have knowingly given Joachim such powerful information?

Miguel looked at Joachim, who now appeared for all the world his old self – twitchy and uneasy, but no madman. It must be true, he told himself. A sane man could fake madness, but a madman could never trick the world into thinking him sensible. Money had brought Joachim back to his senses.

'You think, then,' Joachim said. 'But I ask you to give me your word. If you choose to act on what I've told you, and these acts turn to profit, will you give me ten per cent of what you make?'

'If I find you have told me the truth and acted with honour, I'll do so gladly.'

'Then I am content.' He stood. He looked at Miguel for a moment.

Miguel opened his purse and handed him a few guilders. 'Don't spend it all at the taverns,' he said.

'What I do with it is my concern,' Joachim said defiantly. He stopped halfway up the stairs. 'And you may take it out of the ten per cent if you like.'

Having concluded his business, Joachim bade Miguel a good afternoon, but Miguel followed him up the stairs for no reason other than that he did not like the idea of Joachim wandering around the house unescorted. At the top of the stairs, Miguel heard the swish of skirts before he saw Hannah as she hurried away. The panic that burst in his chest dissipated almost immediately. Hannah spoke not a word of Dutch; she might listen all she liked, but it would hardly tell her anything.

After Miguel had seen Joachim out, however, Hannah awaited his return in the hallway. 'That man,' she said softly. 'He was the one who attacked us on the street.'

'He didn't attack you,' Miguel said wearily, half staring at the swell of her belly, 'but yes, it's the same man.'

'What business can you have with such a devil?' she asked.

'Sadly,' he told her, 'a devilish business.'

'I don't understand.' She spoke softly, but she held herself with a new confidence. 'Do you think because you know my secret you may intrude upon my good sense?'

Miguel took a step forward, just enough to suggest an intimacy. 'Oh, no, senhora. I would never behave thus to you. I know it appears unusual, but the world' – he let out a sigh – 'the world is a more complicated place than you realise.'

'Don't talk to me so,' she said, her voice growing

450

a bit louder. 'I'm not a child who must be told tales. I know what the world is.'

How this woman had changed. His coffee had turned her Dutch. 'I don't mean to belittle you. The world is more complicated than even I realised until recent events. My enemies have become my allies, my allies untrustworthy. This strange and bitter man has oddly put himself in a position where he can aid me, and he chooses to do so. I must let him.'

'You must promise me never to let him in my home again.'

'I promise you, senhora. I did not ask him to come, nor plan that things should end as they have. And I'll do everything in my power to protect you,' he said, with a force that he had not intended, 'even at the cost of my own life.' The boast of a hidalgo came easily to him, but he saw at once that he had said too much, for it was the boast a man makes to his lover, not to his brother's wife.

Miguel could not take it back. In an instant he had committed himself to becoming her lover, so that was what he would be. 'Senhora, I have a gift for you.'

'A gift?' His sudden change in tone broke the spell.

'Yes. I'll return with it in a moment.' Miguel hurried down to the cellar and found the book he had bought for her: the Portuguese listing of the commandments. It would do her little good without instruction, but he hoped she might like it all the same.

He hurried into the parlour, where she stood looking fretful, as though Miguel might present her with a great diamond necklace she could neither refuse nor wear. The gift he did hold out was almost as precious and almost as dangerous.

'A book?' She took the octavo in her hand, running her fingers along the rough leather binding. It occurred to Miguel that she might not even know to cut the pages. 'Do you mock me, senhor? You know I can't read.'

Miguel smiled. 'Maybe I shall tutor you. I have no doubt you will make a fine student.'

He saw it then in her eyes; she was his for the asking. He could lead her down to the cellar and there, in the cramped cupboard bed, he could take his brother's wife. No, it was a defilement to think of her as Daniel's wife. She was her own woman, and he would think of her as such. What held him back, propriety? Did not Daniel deserve to be betrayed after the way he had taken Miguel's money?

He was ready to reach out for her, to take her hand and lead her to the cellar. But something happened first.

'What is this?' Annetje's voice fell hard, startling them. She stood at the doorway to the drawing room, arms folded, a wicked smile on her lips. She glanced at Miguel and then looked at Hannah and rolled her eyes. 'I think the senhora is bothering you.' Annetje walked forward and placed a hand on Hannah's shoulder. 'And what have you here?' She took the book from Hannah's hands. 'You know you are too foolish for books, dear senhora. No doubt she's being tiresome, Senhor Lienzo. I'll make certain it does not happen again.'

'Return that to your mistress,' he said. 'You forget yourself, girl.'

Annetje shrugged and handed the volume back to Hannah, who slipped it in the pocket of her apron. 'Senhor, I am sure you do not mean to raise your voice to me. After all' – she smiled slyly – 'you are not the master here, and your brother may not like the tales he hears if someone should speak them. You might think upon these things while I remove the senhora to where she will trouble you no more.' She tugged roughly on Hannah's arm.

'Let me go,' Hannah said in Portuguese, her voice loud, almost a shout. She pulled herself loose of the maid's grip and then spun around to face her. 'Don't touch me!'

'Please, senhora. Let me just take you to your room before you shame yourself.'

'Who are you to speak of shame?' she answered.

Miguel could not begin to understand this display. Why did the maid think she could speak to Hannah with such cruelty? He hardly ever thought of her as speaking at all, just some pretty thing fit only for the occasional romp. Now he saw there were intrigues – plots and schemes he could not have imagined. He opened his mouth, prepared to speak once more, but Daniel appeared at the door.

'What goes on here?'

Daniel looked at the two women, too close for any casual business. Hannah's face had turned red by now, and Annetje's had hardened into a mask of rage. They flashed cold stares at each other, but upon hearing his voice, they turned and shrank into themselves like guilty children, caught at dangerous play.

'What goes on here, I say?' Daniel repeated, now to Miguel. 'Is she touching my wife?'

Miguel tried to think of what lies might serve best Hannah, but nothing came to mind. If he accused the maid, she might betray her mistress, but if he said nothing, how could Hannah explain this abuse? 'Servants don't behave so,' he said haplessly.

'I know these Dutch have no sense of propriety,' Daniel shouted, 'but I have seen too much. I have indulged my wife with this impudent strumpet long enough, and I'll not listen to her pleas any longer. The girl must go.'

Miguel strained to find some words to cool everyone's tempers, but Annetje spoke first. She took a step toward Daniel and sneered at him full in the face. 'You think I don't understand your Portuguese palaver?' she asked him in Dutch. 'I'll touch your wife when I please. Your wife,' she laughed. 'You don't even know your wife, who

454

takes gifts of love from your brother and then hides them in her apron. And her lust is not the least of her crimes. Your wife, mighty senhor, is a Catholic, as Catholic as the Pope, and she goes as regularly as she can to church. She gives confession, and she drinks the blood of Christ and eats his body. She does things that would horrify your devilish Jew soul. And I won't stay in this house a moment longer. There's more work to be had, and with Christian folk too, so I take my leave of you.'

Annetje spun and swished her skirts as she had seen actresses do upon the stage. She held her chin high as she walked, pausing a moment at the threshold. 'I'll send a boy for my wages,' she said, and paused, waiting to see Daniel's response.

They stood there, still and silent. Hannah clenched her body, hardly daring to breathe, until her lungs became hot and desperate and she sucked in air like a woman who had been under water. Miguel bit his lip. Daniel remained as still as a figure in a painting.

Here was trepidation, hot, itching trepidation of the kind Miguel had known only a few times in his life: once in Lisbon when he had been warned that the Inquisition sought him for questioning; then again in Amsterdam when he knew his investments in sugar had ruined him.

He thought of all the steps that had led to this moment: the sly glances, the secret conversations, the drinks of coffee. He had held her hand, he had spoken to her as a lover, he had given her a present. If only he could have known what there was between the girl and Hannah. But he could not erase the past. There could be no duplicity now. A man can live his life through trickery, but there are moments, there must always be moments, when the trickery is exposed.

Annetje basked in the silence. Each awkward second excited her as she dared Daniel to speak, but he only stared at her in utter astonishment.

'You have nothing to say, cuckold?' she spat at him. 'You are a fool, and I leave you to your own wickedness.' With that she forced her way past Daniel and out of the room.

Daniel stared at his wife, cocking his head slightly. He glanced at Miguel, who would not meet his gaze. He removed his hat and scratched his head thoughtfully. 'Can anyone understand a word that slut speaks?' he asked, carefully replacing the hat. 'Her Dutch is the most garbled thing I know, and it is as well for her, for the look on her face was of such impudence, I'm sure I should have struck her if I'd comprehended her rudeness.'

Miguel cast a look at Hannah, who stared at the floor, trying, he suspected, not to weep with the force of relief. 'She said she is leaving your service,' he ventured cautiously, still not certain Hannah had escaped. 'She tires of working for Jews; she might prefer a Dutch mistress – a widow.'

'Good riddance to her. I hope,' Daniel said to Hannah, 'she has not upset you too greatly. There are other girls in the world, and better ones too, I'd venture. You'll not miss her.'

'I'll not miss her. Perhaps,' she suggested, 'you will let me select the servant next time.'

Later that day Miguel received a message from Geertruid expressing concern that they had not spoken for some time and requesting a meeting as soon as possible. To find some reason for delay, Miguel wrote to his partner that he could not possibly think of meeting until after the Sabbath. His words were so jumbled as to hardly make sense, even to their author, and Miguel moved to tear up his note. Then he thought better of it, deciding he might gain something by being incoherent. Without rereading what he had written, he sent the note.

From

The Factual and Revealing Memoirs of Alonzo Alferonda

There are, of course, a hundred such homes in the Jordaan – hastily built things of three or four storeys, cramped rooms, narrow windows, too little light and too much smoke. This one is owned, as they all seem to be owned, by a pinch-faced widow who sees nothing and judges all. This particular pinch-faced widow had recently rented rooms to a young girl. There were two rooms – one more than the girl had ever paid for on her own, but then she was now being paid better than she had ever been in the past. She had new clothes and some treats too – apples and pears and dried dates.

She had been enjoying these dainties along with the scent of her civet perfume and her new linens and ribbons, when the pinch-faced widow informed her that there was a man – a merchant, it seemed – there to see her. The widow did not like that the girl said to send him up, for she did not enjoy being a woman who allowed young women to receive men in their rooms, but she could hardly prevent that sort of thing, and since some folks will be Christian and some will not, there was not much to be done for it. She sent the man up.

A knock on the door, and the girl answered, wearing a new blue gown, cut just so. Most enticing, I promise you, showing off her shape to full advantage. What man could resist this beauty in that dress? She smiled at her visitor. 'Hello, senhor,' she said. 'Have you missed me?'

I doubt he smiled back, and he had most likely not missed her. 'I want a moment of your time, Annetje.'

He stepped in and closed the door behind him, but he kept his distance from her. Here was a man who knew the dangers of a blue dress.

'What?' she asked. 'No kiss for your old friend?'

'I have something to enquire of you.'

'Of course. You may ask me anything you wish.'

'I wish to know if, while you were in my brother's employ, you were paid by anyone to observe the doings of our household.'

The girl let out a loud titter. 'You want to know if I was a spy?'

'If you like, yes.'

'Why should I tell you?' she asked saucily, as she swished her skirts around the room like a little girl at play. Perhaps she enjoyed teasing her visitor. Perhaps she wished him to see what she thought of as her finery: her furniture, her ribbons, scattered about the room as though she had a hundred such things; her ample fruit. She could eat an apple or a pear anytime she liked. She could eat another one. There seemed to be no end to the supply. She lived in these two rooms – two of them! – in the newest part of town, while some folks lived in wet basements on a soggy island in the midst of a foul canal.

'You should tell me,' he answered, his voice hardening, 'because I asked it of you, and for no other reason. But if you like, I can pay you for your answers since they seem to require considerable effort.'

'If you pay me,' she observed, 'then I might give any answer I think would please you so you will think your coin well spent. I do like to please those who give me money.' She certainly spoke the truth there.

'Then tell me what I ask because I have always been kind to you in the past.'

'Such kindness.' She laughed again. 'Such kindness as that may be found in the breeches of any man in this city, but that's all one, I suppose. You want to know if anyone paid me to spy on you. I will tell you that someone did. It is no betrayal for me to say so – at least I don't think it is, for I have not been paid as I was promised, and if I am not to have my money then at least I will have my revenge.'

'Who was it that paid you?'

'Why, it was your widow friend,' she said. 'The lovely Madame Damhuis. She promised me ten guilders if I but kept an eye on you and that wilful bitch, the senhora. Have you been kind to her too?'

The visitor would not be baited. 'What did she pay you to do?'

'Only to see how she was discussed in the house. I was to discourage the senhora from speaking of her encounters with madam. She said you were not to suspect anything, but that you would not – so long as I showed you my favours. Then, she said, you would be as stupid as a cow being led to its slaughter.'

'What are her ends?' he asked. 'Why did she want you to do these things?'

Annetje shrugged with an exaggerated flair of the shoulders that opened the neck of her gown deliciously. 'I could not say, senhor. She never told me. She only gave me a few guilders

461

and promised me more, but those promises have all been lies. In my opinion, the woman is inclined to lies. You ought to be cautious.'

Annetje offered her visitor the bowl of dates. 'Would you like to eat one of my dainties?'

The merchant declined. He only thanked the girl and took his leave.

Thus went the final conversation between Miguel Lienzo and his brother's former servant. It is sad how badly these matters can end. He and the girl knew a fond intimacy for many months, but there was never any real tenderness there. He wanted only her flesh, and she his coin. A sad foundation for any congress between man and woman.

And how does Alferonda know all of this? How can he write of the private words spoken in an obscure boardinghouse in the Jordaan? Alferonda knows because he heard it all – he was in the next room, lying on the girl's rough mattress.

Not so long ago I had been enjoying some of the dainties she had offered to Miguel. She had told her visitor exactly what I had instructed her to say, in case he came calling. Madame Damhuis, of course, had never paid the girl a stiver, nor had she ever promised to do so.

She had never spoken a word to the girl but once, when she had stopped the senhora on the Hoogstraat.

Annetje had been in my employ at the time, and it had been my design that Senhora Lienzo should not speak of the widow to Miguel. That she had, in the end, done so would prove immaterial.

CHAPTER 30

Miguel had been ignoring notes from Isaiah Nunes for weeks, and had been doing so self-righteously since he learned that Nunes was in league with Parido. But then Nunes' notes began to talk of the Ma'amad, and Miguel wondered if he ought not take these threats more seriously. In all likelihood, Nunes only meant to add verisimilitude to his ruse, but it was also possible that Parido might want to see Miguel brought before the board. It would be difficult to prove the trickery, Miguel suspected, and he could not begin to do so without revealing his connection to Geertruid.

Miguel had come to believe there was only one way to obtain the money he needed. He therefore dashed off a quick note and three hours later found himself in the coffee tavern meeting with Alonzo Alferonda.

'I'll be direct with you,' Miguel said. 'I would like to borrow some money.'

His companion's eyes narrowed. 'Borrowing from Alferonda is a dangerous business.'

'I'm prepared to take the risk.'

Alferonda laughed. 'Very bold of you. How much did you have in mind?'

Miguel swallowed a gulp of Turkish coffee. 'Fifteen hundred guilders.'

'I am a kind man with a generous heart, but you must think me a fool. With all the difficulties you face, why would I give you such a sum?'

'Because,' Miguel said, 'by doing so you will help me ruin Solomon Parido's plans.'

Alferonda ran a hand across his beard. 'I don't know that there could have been another answer quite so effective.'

Miguel smiled. 'Then you'll do it?'

'Tell me what you have in mind.'

Miguel, who had not bothered to formulate a plan fully, began to talk, but what came out was greatly to Alferonda's liking.

Miguel sat in the Three Dirty Dogs awaiting Geertruid. Like all the Dutch, she thrived on punctuality, but not this time. Perhaps she had found out that Miguel knew of her deception. Miguel tried to think of the ways that might possibly happen. It seemed unlikely that Joachim and Geertruid would have any contact, and he felt fairly certain that Alferonda could not have betrayed him. Had Hendrick seen Miguel observing him in the tavern that night? What if he had, and then he had held off telling Geertruid for some reason of his own? Or perhaps Geertruid had waited to see how Miguel would respond to that knowledge.

When she showed up she appeared disordered and out of breath. He had never seen her so shaken. Lowering herself down, she explained what had happened. A man had fallen and broken his leg in front of her on the Rozengracht, she said, and she and a gentleman who happened to be there had helped to take him to a surgeon. It was shocking stuff, she said. The man had screamed with agony the whole time. She called at once for a beer.

'It makes you think about the preciousness of life,' she said, while awaiting her drink. 'A man is going about his business, and the next thing he falls and has a broken leg. Will he survive its repair but walk for the rest of his life with a cane? Will he have to have it off? Will it heal and be as it once was? No one can say what God has in store.'

'That much is certain,' Miguel agreed, without much enthusiasm. 'Life is full of unexpected turns.'

'By Jesus, I am glad we're doing this thing.' She squeezed his hand. The serving girl put the beer down, and Geertruid drank down half the contents at once. 'I'm glad. We'll make our fortunes and live in luxury. Perhaps we'll die next day or next year, no one knows. But I'll have my fortune first, and we'll laugh while my husband looks on from hell.'

'Then we must go ahead,' Miguel began humourlessly. 'We must send the letters at once. We can't delay any longer. The time must be set. Eleven in the morning, three weeks from today.'

'Three weeks from today? The ship has not yet made port.'

'It must be three weeks from this day,' he insisted, looking away. She had betrayed him. He knew it was true, but his own act of betrayal tasted bitter in his mouth.

'Senhor, have you decided to get forceful with me?' She reached out and began to run a finger lightly along Miguel's hand. 'If you're going to thrust something upon me, I should like to know what I shall be receiving.'

'You shall be receiving a great deal of money,' he told her, 'if you do what I say.'

'I should always like to do what you say,' she told him. 'But I must know why.'

'I have been assured the shipment will be here by that time. I have reason to believe there are others who take an interest in coffee, and if we wait too long, they may make it more difficult for us to manipulate the prices as we planned.'

Geertruid considered this for a moment. 'Who are these people?'

'Men of the Exchange. What does it matter who they are?'

'I only wonder why, at this time, they take an interest in something that hardly anyone has taken an interest in before.'

'Why did *you* take an interest in it?' Miguel asked. 'Things happen all at once. I've seen it countless times. Men from all over the city, from all over Europe, will suddenly decide this is the time to buy timber or cotton or tobacco. Maybe it's the stars. All I know is that this may be coffee's moment, and we may be but one party to have recognised it. If we are to do what we planned, then we had better act decisively.'

Geertruid remained quiet for a moment. 'You say you've been given assurances about the shipment, but those assurances cannot predict pirates or storms or any of a thousand things that can make a ship late. What if the shipment is not yet in port when our agents begin?'

Miguel shook his head. 'It won't matter. I have been on the Exchange too long to let it matter. I know it as though it were my own body, and I can make it do what I want, just as I move my arms and legs.'

Geertruid smiled. 'You speak with such confidence.'

'I only speak the truth. Our only enemy now is timidity.'

'I love to hear you talk so' – she leaned forward and touched his beard – 'but you can't risk putting yourself in a position in which you must sell what you do not have.'

'You needn't worry about that. I'll not be caught unprepared.'

'What do you plan?'

Miguel smiled and leaned back. 'It's very simple. If need be, I'll cover my own losses as the price drops and therefore simultaneously acquire the very goods I will promise to sell, only I'll buy when the price dips below the price at which I have promised to sell, so I might profit on the sales while lowering the value. It is something I would not have known how to do before, but now I believe I can order it effectively.'

This plan was nonsense. Miguel would never have attempted anything so foolish, but he doubted Geertruid had sufficient business sense to know it.

She didn't say anything, so Miguel pushed harder. 'You asked me to join you because you needed someone who understood the madness of the Exchange, someone who can navigate its peculiarities. I am doing the very thing you sought me out to do.'

She let out a sigh. 'I don't like taking this risk, but you're right: I did ask you to order these things, and I'll have to trust you. But,' she added with a grin, 'when we are rich, I'll expect you to obey me in all things and treat me as your mistress.'

'It will be my pleasure to do so,' Miguel assured her.

'I understand you must be cautious, but there is no need for you to be so grim. Have you no laughter to spare until you are rich?'

'Very little,' Miguel said. 'From now until all this is settled, you will find me to be a man of business and very little else. You've done your part; now it is time for me to do mine.'

'Very well,' Geertruid said, after a moment. 'I admire and appreciate your dedication. In the meantime, I'll have to seek out Hendrick, who has nothing to lose by being jolly. We'll make merry on your behalf.'

'Please do,' he said sadly. He had once thought Geertruid the jolliest woman in the world, but he had just made her complicit in his plans to destroy her.

Perhaps they should have gone to the coffee tavern in the Plantage. It would have been more appropriate, and it would surely have made it easier for Joachim to concentrate. But they'd let him pick the tavern, and here they were, all three – two of them marked by their beards as Jews – in a tiny room full of drunken Dutchmen who stared and pointed. One even came over and examined Miguel's head by gingerly lifting his hat and then, when he was done, politely replacing it.

Joachim's months of hardship now compelled him to drink all the beer that someone else was willing to buy, so only an hour after the meeting began, he was already slurring his words and having some difficulty remaining on his splintered bench.

What surprised Miguel was how much Joachim did not irritate him. Now that he, as Joachim had phrased it, was no longer mad, he had demonstrated an endearing warmth Miguel had never seen in him before. He laughed at Alferonda's jokes and nodded approvingly at Miguel's suggestions. He raised his tankard to toast the two of them, 'and Jews everywhere,' and did so without irony in his voice. He treated Miguel and Alferonda like men who had pulled him aboard their vessels when he had believed himself left to drown.

Now they sat together in planning, all of them having had too much to drink. It would not be long now, only a few weeks, and they were equal to the task. It would tax them and torment them, but it could be done.

'I understand,' Joachim said, 'how it is we are to buy and sell what it is that no one wants to buy and sell. What I do not understand is how we are to sell what we do not have. If this Nunes has sold your fruit to Parido, how can we affect the price though sales?'

Miguel had wanted to avoid speaking of this, for it was the hardest thing. He would have to do something he had vowed he would never do on the Exchange – a practice that, no matter how desperate he became, would always be the height of madness.

'By a *windhandel*,' Alferonda explained, using the Dutch word.

'I was told they were dangerous,' Joachim said. 'That only a fool would attempt such a thing.'

'True on both counts,' Miguel said. 'That is why we will succeed.'

Windhandel: the wind trade. A colourful term for something dangerous and illegal, it was when a man sold what he did not have. The burghers had outlawed the practice, since it added chaos to the Exchange. It was said that any man who engaged in a *windhandel* might just as readily throw

471

his money into the Amstel, for these sales could easily be voided if the buyer provided proof. The seller would then have worse than nothing for his pains. But in their coffee trade, they would have an advantage – the buyer would be guilty of too many tricks of his own, and he would not dare to contest the sale.

Later, when they had concluded their business, Alferonda excused himself and Miguel and Joachim remained alone at the table. Here he was, Miguel thought, drinking with a man he would gladly have strangled only a few weeks before.

Joachim must have read the look on Miguel's face. 'You're not scheming something, are you?'

'Of course we are,' Miguel answered.

'I mean against me.'

Miguel let out a laugh. 'Do you really think that all this – these meetings, these plans – are a trick against you? That we have so much invested in your destruction that we would play these games? Are you certain you've left your madness behind?'

Joachim shook his head. 'I don't think these schemes are about me. Of course not. But I wonder if I am to be sacrificed on the altar of your vengeance.'

'No,' Miguel said softly. 'We are not out to trick you. We have thrown in our lot with yours and so have more to fear from your treachery than you do from ours. I cannot even imagine how we might sacrifice you, as you say.'

'I can think of a few ways,' Joachim said, 'but I will keep them to myself.'

When Miguel walked into the entrance hall, he knew Daniel could not be at home. The house had turned shadowy in the dusk, and the inviting scent of cinnamon filled the air. Hannah stood ready to greet him at the far end of the hall, the single candle she held in her hand reflecting off the black-and-white tiles of the floor.

It was not the way she was dressed, for she wore her usual scarf and shapeless black gown, revealing the now undeniable swell of the child growing inside her. There was, however, something in the intensity of her face, the way her dark eyes shone in the candlelight and her jaw jutted forward. She stood unusually still, with her chest pressed out as if to accentuate the heaviness of her breasts, and in his drunkenness he felt dizzy with desire.

'It seems as though it has been weeks since we've talked, senhor,' she said.

'I am attempting something on the Exchange. It takes much of my time.'

'It will make you rich, yes?'

He laughed. 'I most fervently hope so.'

She looked at the floor for what felt like minutes. 'May I speak with you, senhor?'

With her arm holding the candle outwards, as though she were a spirit in a woodcut, she led Miguel into the drawing room and set the candle down in one of the sconces. Only one other candle was lit, and the room shimmered with flickering light.

'We must hire another girl soon,' she said, as she sat.

'You are clearly too busy to light candles,' Miguel observed, as he took a seat across from her.

She let out a burst of air, a half laugh. 'You make sport with me, senhor?'

'Yes, I do, senhora.'

'And why do you make sport with me?'

'Because you and I are friends,' he said.

Miguel could not see her face clearly, but he detected something of a smile. It was so hard to tell. What did she want of him in this poorly lit room? What if Daniel were to walk through the door now and find them, scrambling to light candles together, brushing off their clothes as though they had been rolling together in sawdust?

He almost laughed aloud. If he were to make a success of himself at this late stage in his life, he had to stop planning for what could never happen. He had outlived the time when he could gamble away guilders he did not have or invest in commodities because of an inexplicable urge. I am a grown man, he told himself, and this is my brother's wife. There is nothing more to it.

'You wished to speak to me about something,' he said.

Her voice cracked as she tried to talk. 'I wish to speak to you about your brother.'

'What about my brother?' His eyes shifted momentarily to her belly.

A moment of hesitation. 'He is out of the house,' she said.

When he was a boy, he and his friends had a favorite rock from which they would leap into the waters of the Tagus. They fell five times the length of a man. Who could say how far it was now, but in the thrill of childish excitement it seemed halfway to eternity. Miguel remembered the twisting and terrifying feeling of freedom, like dying and soaring at once.

Without moving he now felt the same terror and excitement. His guts twisted, his humours rushed to his brain. 'Senhora,' he said. He rose, planning to escape as quickly as he could, but she must have misunderstood. She stood as well and walked to him until she was only a few inches away. He could smell the sweet perfume of her musk, feel the heat of her breath. Her eyes locked upon him, and with one hand she reached up and pulled the scarf from her head, letting her thick hair fall around her shoulders and down her back.

Miguel heard himself suck in his breath. The urges of his body would betray him. He had been so resolved only an instant before. This beautiful, eager woman could not, he reminded himself, be made any more pregnant that she was already. Her body emitted its own heat and closed in on him. Miguel knew he need only lift his hand and put it upon her arm, or run it along her face, or touch her hair, and nothing else would matter. He would be lost in the mindless revel of senses. All his determination would be for nothing.

And why should he not give in? he asked himself. Had his brother treated him so well that he should not pluck this illicit fruit of his hospitality? Adultery was surely a great sin, but he understood that such sins were born of the need to maintain order in households. It was not bedding another man's wife that was the sin; it was getting her with child. Since that could not happen, it would be no sin to take her here upon the floor of the drawing room.

And so he leaned in to kiss her, to finally feel the press of her lips. And in the instant he thought to pull her closer to him, he felt something much darker. He knew with perfect clarity what would happen if he kissed her. Would she be able to return to her husband's bed without revealing what had happened? This poor, abused girl – she would, in a thousand silent ways, betray him before a day had passed.

He took a step backwards. 'Senhora,' he whispered, 'it cannot be.'

She bit her lip and looked down at her hands, which were twisting her scarf so hard as to almost destroy it. 'What cannot be?' she asked.

Let us pretend then, Miguel silently agreed. 'I beg your pardon,' he told her, as he took another step back. 'I seem to have misunderstood something. Please forgive me.' He hurried out of the room and into the dark hall to feel his blundering way to the cellar.

There, in the damp and the dark, he sat mutely, listening for some sign of her anguish or her relief, but he heard nothing, not even the creaking of floorboards. For all he knew she remained motionless, her hair exposed to the empty space. And strangely, Miguel felt the heat of tears on his own face. Do I love her so much? Perhaps he did, but he did not cry out of love.

He wept not for her sadness, or even for his own, but for the knowledge that he had been cruel, that he had led her to believe what he had always known must be impossible. He had acted out the fancies of his imagination upon her without thinking that for her to abandon those fancies might crush her. He had been cruel to a sad woman who had done nothing worse than be kind to him. He wondered if he had indeed played his hand so badly in all other spheres.

CHAPTER 31

Just before noon, outside the Exchange, excitement was building upon the Dam. Two weeks had passed since Miguel's conversation with Geetruid. Today was reckoning day on the Exchange, and today Miguel's investments came due. He stood in the crowd, awaiting the opening of the great gates, and scanned the faces about him: hard and intense stares into the distance. Dutchman, Jew, and foreigner alike all clenched their teeth and maintained a martial watchfulness. Any man who had spent enough time on the Exchange could sense it, like the smell of coming rain. Great schemes were ready to be unleashed that would affect everyone who traded. Every reckoning day was charged, but today something more than the usual would happen. Everyone knew it.

As he had made himself ready that morning, Miguel felt a troubling peace. His stomach had been in a twist for weeks, but now he felt the calmness of resolve, like a man walking to the gallows. He had slept surprisingly soundly but still drank four large bowls of coffee. He wanted to be wild with coffee. He wanted coffee to rule his passions.

He could not have been more ready, but he knew some things were beyond him. Five men, knowingly or not, were his creatures, and he depended on them to act their parts. It was all so fragile. This enormous edifice could in an instant crumble into dust.

And so he prepared himself as best he could. He cleansed himself before Shabbat at the *mikvah* and dedicated himself to prayer on the holy day. The next day he continued in prayer, and he fasted from sunrise to sunset.

He could not survive two ruins. The world might blink at the first one, forgive it as bad luck. Two ruins would crush him for ever. No substantial merchant would ever entrust such a failure with his daughter. No man of business would ever offer Miguel a partnership. To fail today would mean he would have to abandon the life of a merchant.

With his teeth gritty from ground coffee berry, Miguel had stepped outside and breathed in the early morning air. He felt more like a conquistador than a trader. Only a few wisps of clouds drifted across the sky, and a light breeze came rolling in from the waters. A superstitious Dutchman might see clear skies as a good omen, but Miguel knew the skies were clear for Parido too.

Outside the Dam, Miguel waited in the unusually silent crowd. No arguments or bursts of laughter. Nowhere did the sound of early trading set off a ripple of exchanges. When men spoke, they spoke in whispers.

Parido's calls, like Miguel's puts, were to come due at the close of the day. That meant Parido needed to keep the price high, and the higher it went the more he would profit, just as the lower it went, the more Miguel would earn. If Miguel did nothing, Parido would gain on his investment and Miguel would lose. As Parido held the coffee shipment that was meant to be Miguel's, he would hold on to his goods until after tomorrow. He might then slowly sell what he had at the inflated price.

'If you were Parido,' Alferonda had reasoned, 'you would want to use your trading combination. You could spread the rumour that his combination was planning to dump holdings which would bring down the price. But you don't have that kind of power. Parido does.'

'Why does he not simply spread the rumour that his combination will be buying, thus causing the price to rise even higher?'

'The rumour game is a delicate one. If a combination overuses it, no one will believe rumours associated with that combination any more, and it has lost a valuable tool. This business with the coffee is Parido's, not his combination's. The other members would be unwilling to expend the capital of rumour on his behalf here, not unless the promise of wealth were sufficiently compelling. But there are other ways he can use his combination.'

'He can instruct his men not to respond to me.'

'Precisely. Parido will assume that you will try to sell such coffee as you have acquired, and make it seem as though you have more than you do, thus causing a fall in the price. Alternatively, you will sell what you don't have. Now, he knows this is tricky, because if you can set off a selling frenzy, you can then buy cheap what others unload, and if anyone challenges the sale you can produce what you have promised. But he will surely have instructed his combination to spread the rumour that you will not have what you pretend to sell, and no one will buy off you.'

Miguel smiled. 'Can it be as simple as that?'

'Parido is a very powerful man,' Alferonda said. 'He has made his money not by being overly clever but by seeing to the simple things. You've demonstrated in the past that you work alone, you work without much strategy, and you tend to follow your instincts rather than clear business plans. I see you are insulted, but you cannot deny it is true. You've made mistakes, Miguel, but those mistakes will serve you very well when you step forth on to the Exchange this time. Parido will be expecting a very different opponent from the man he finds.'

The clock upon the tower of the great Town Hall struck noon, and the gates to the Exchange opened in a burst of shouting that echoed across the Dam. Miguel pushed his way in, along with the hundreds of other traders, and slowly made his way towards the East India corner of the courtyard, ignoring the traders who called out to him with their goods.

A larger crowd than was usual milled around

the East India traders. Many of the men were of Parido's combination. They wore the bright colours and feathered hats of the Portuguese, and they held themselves like imperious hidalgos. They were there as a favour to their friend. It would cost them nothing to monitor the trade in coffee, to sell nothing themselves, and to muscle out anyone who might respond to Miguel's efforts. It was all as he and Alferonda had speculated.

Off to the side, talking with some traders Miguel recognised, stood Isaiah Nunes. He nodded at Miguel. Miguel nodded back. There would be time for accusations later, but for now he put forth his best face. What would Nunes expect to see from Miguel? Disappointment, of course. He knew about the puts. Still, he had to make a certain show of determination.

In the open courtyard where the Hamburg merchants did their business, Alferonda conferred with the few Tudescos on the Exchange. These long-bearded Jews nodded their sage heads as the usurer explained something at great, probably needless, length.

Miguel looked up and saw Parido in front of him. 'This day has a familiar feel to it. Does it not remind you of the day the price of sugar fell?'

'No.' Miguel smiled back. 'As a matter of fact, this day feels utterly new.'

'Surely you don't think you can orchestrate a downturn in coffee prices. You were warned to keep away from the coffee trade, but you would do things your own way. That is how it must be. I've anticipated your moves, and I've taken steps to prevent their success. The kindliest advice I can give you is to walk away. Accept your losses at the day's end. At least you'll be spared a public humiliation.'

'I appreciate your advice. But you might wish to keep in mind that you will be pressing your lips to my arse before the day ends.'

'You forget to whom you speak. I am only trying to spare what remains of your reputation. A lesser man than I would have held his tongue.'

'There is no lesser man than you, senhor.'

Parido clucked his tongue. 'Do you really believe you can outmanoeuvre me?'

'I have my business well in hand.' Miguel did not like the wavering of his own voice. Parido seemed too confident. What if he knew the details of Miguel's plans? What if he had taken steps to prevent Alferonda's clever scheme to circumvent Parido's influence? What if Joachim had betrayed him?

'How in hand do you truly have it?' Parido asked.

'I don't understand your question.'

'It's quite simple. Do you believe so firmly that you can prevail today and bring down the price that you are willing to make a wager?'

Miguel locked his eyes upon his enemy's. 'Name it.' Parido was foolish to offer a wager. Miguel had already gambled everything.

'The price of coffee now stands at seven-tenths of a guilder per pound, which means I have raised it to forty-two guilders per barrel. I only need keep it above thirty-eight guilders to make my money. You need it to fall to below thirty-seven to make any profit from your puts. At thirty-seven or greater, you make nothing, and your brother answers for your bad investment.'

Miguel felt himself redden.

'You thought no one knew of your reckless use of his name? You thought you could keep secrets from me on this bourse? And now you think you can outmanoeuvre me when I am determined not to be outmanoeuvred? I admire your optimism.'

It meant nothing, Miguel told himself. He might have learned of Miguel's trick from his broker. It did not mean Parido knew everything. 'You're doing nothing but boasting, senhor.'

'Very well, I'll do more than boast. If you can bring the price to thirty guilders a barrel or below, I'll allow you to buy ninety barrels from me at twenty guilders each.'

Miguel attempted to appear sceptical. 'Where would you hope to get ninety barrels of coffee? Can the warehouses of Amsterdam have so much?'

'The warehouses of Amsterdam contain surprises that men such as you cannot imagine.'

'Your wager seems one-sided. What do you get if I cannot defeat you?'

'Well, you'll be ruined, so I'm not sure you'll have anything to give me but your person. So let us say this: if you lose, then you will confess to the Ma'amad that you lied about your relationship with Joachim Waagenaar. You will tell the *parnassim* that you are guilty of deceiving that council, and you will take the punishment that so grave a deception deserves.'

Cherem. It seemed like madness to agree to such a thing, but if he lost he would have to leave Amsterdam regardless. The banishment would make no difference.

'I agree. Let us draw up a paper to that effect, though what it is that I've agreed to will have to be kept between us, lest that paper later fall into the wrong hands. But I would like a surety of some kind. You see, I'd hate to win my wager only to discover you guilty of a *windhandel* – of not having the ninety barrels you promised.'

'What are you suggesting?'

'Only this. I'll take your wager, and we'll put it all to paper. And if, by some chance, you can't supply the coffee at the price you mention, you will instead pay me what those barrels are, at this moment, worth. That would be' – he took a moment to calculate – 'thirty-eight hundred guilders. What say you?'

'It is an empty bet, for I never sell what I do not have.'

'Then you agree?'

'Of course not. Why should I agree to a foolish wager that includes the possibility of my paying almost four thousand guilders?'

Miguel shrugged. 'I won't accept otherwise.'

Parido let out a sigh. 'Very well, I'll agree to your silly conditions.'

He quickly drew up the contract, insisting on writing out both copies himself. Miguel therefore had to waste more time reading it over, making certain his rival had not inserted any trickery into the language. But all appeared well, and the contract was witnessed by one of Parido's friends who stood close by. Each man now had his copy in his pocket. The clock tower told him he had lost a quarter of an hour. It was time to begin.

Miguel took a step backwards and called out in Latin, 'Coffee! Selling twenty barrels of coffee at forty guilders each.' The price hardly mattered, as Miguel had none of it himself. This, after all, was a *windhandel*. He had to make the price low enough to attract attention, but not so low that his call would arouse suspicion. 'I have coffee at forty,' he called again. He then repeated the call in Dutch and again in Portuguese.

No one replied. Parido's men began to move in, menacing Miguel like a pack of dogs. A minor trader from the Vlooyenburg glanced over at Miguel and appeared on the verge of taking the sale, but Parido locked eyes with him and the merchant turned away, muttering. It was clear that no Portuguese Jew would want to incur Parido's anger by breaking the blockade.

Casting his eyes about the Exchange, Miguel saw Daniel hovering on the perimeter of their little crowd. He had dressed in his best trading suit today – not bright enough to wear on Shabbat but a handsome ensemble: matching crimson doublet and hat with a blue shirt beneath, black breeches, and shiny red shoes with enormous silver buckles. He looked at Parido's men and at Miguel and then down at the ground.

Silence had descended over their little section of the Exchange. In the near distance he could hear the shouts of other transactions, but no one among the East India traders said a word. The battle had begun, and it surely appeared to the spectators that Miguel was already defeated. Parido smiled and whispered something in the ear of a member of his combination, who answered with a hoarse laugh.

Miguel called out his price again. A few Dutchman looked on curiously but, seeing the crowd of menacing Jews, kept their distance. Miguel had nothing to offer that was sweet enough either to entice the Portuguese Jews to defy Parido or draw the Christians to trouble themselves with what was so obviously a duel among aliens. Standing alone in the midst of a circle, Miguel looked like a lost child.

Miguel called out once more. Again, no reply. Parido locked eyes with his and smiled. His lips moved silently. *You've lost.*

Then Miguel heard the call in poor Latin. 'I'll buy twenty at thirty-nine.'

Alferonda had worked his contacts among the Tudescos. One of that nation, a man whose usual

487

trade was in the discounting of bank notes, stood forth and repeated his call. He wore black robes, and his white beard swayed as he shouted out his bid. 'Twenty barrels at thirty-nine!'

'Sold!' Miguel shouted. He could not help but smile. It was not the usual trader who hoped his buyers would keep lowering his price. But his business today was to sell cheap.

'I'll buy twenty-five at thirty-eight and a half,' cried another Tudesco, whom Miguel recognised as a dealer in unminted gold.

Miguel pushed his way through the wall of Parido's men to acknowledge him. 'Twenty-five barrels at thirty-eight and a half, sold!'

The blockade had loosened. A sell-off had begun, and Parido knew he could not stop Miguel merely by keeping his men near him.

'Thirty barrels of coffee to buy,' Parido shouted in return, 'at forty guilders.'

The Tudescos would be fools not to turn around and sell for an immediate profit. They had never agreed to act as Miguel's combination, only to break the blockade, motivated by the promise that their assistance would yield its own profitable opportunities. Miguel could see that they considered selling, which would stabilise the price for Parido. Portuguese Jews stood by and waited to see which way the prices went, which faction had command. The odds surely favoured Parido. The only thing he could not counter would be a general sell-off. If too many men moved to sell, he could not stem the tide alone, and the men in his combination would not sacrifice their own money for him.

Here was the pivotal moment for the coffee scheme, and the whole of the Exchange sensed it.

Miguel looked up and, unexpectedly, locked eyes with his brother. Daniel stood at the far reaches of the circle of spectators, his lips moving silently as he calculated the odds against a general sell-off. Miguel would not release Daniel from his gaze. He wanted to see that his brother understood. He wanted to see it in his brother's eyes.

And Daniel did understand. He knew that if he chose, at that moment, to join sides with Miguel, to throw himself in with his brother, to call out a sale of cheap coffee, the scheme would succeed. The momentum from Daniel's participation would tip the scales in Miguel's favour. Here was the time at last in which family might rise above petty interests. Daniel might say that yes, Parido was his friend, and friendship should be honoured, but family was another matter and he could not stand by while his brother faced ruin, permanent ruin – not while he had the power in his hands to prevent it.

They both knew it. Miguel could see that his brother knew it. He had asked Daniel once if he would choose his brother or his friend, and Daniel had not answered, but he would answer now. One way or another. Miguel could see from the look on his brother's face that Daniel, too, recalled that conversation. He could see the look of shame on

Daniel's face as he turned away and allowed this coffee business to unfold without him.

A strange quiet fell within the walls. Certainly not what would have passed for quiet in any other part of the world, but for the Exchange the noise reduced to a mere din. Traders moved in close as though they watched a cockfight or a brawl.

They would get good sport, Miguel told himself. When Parido had moved to buy, he had himself given the signal for Miguel's next move, one the *parnass* could not have anticipated.

'Selling coffee! Fifty barrels at thirty-six!' Joachim shouted.

Parido stared in disbelief. He had not seen Joachim arrive upon the Exchange, or perhaps he had not noticed him. Having lost his peasant's attire, he was once more dressed like a man of means, looking every bit the Dutch trader in his black suit and hat. No one who did not know him would have guessed that a month ago he had been less than a beggar. Now he was surrounded by a crowd of buyers whose eager calls he engaged with one at a time, calm as any seasoned merchant upon any bourse in Europe.

This move had been Alferonda's inspiration. Parido could easily assert his influence over the traders of the Portuguese Nation. Every man knew of his rivalry with Miguel, and few would willingly cross a vengeful man with a seat on the Ma'amad. Alferonda knew he would be able to encourage a few foreign Tudescos to begin the trading, but there were not enough of them to sustain the sell-off, and most would be unwilling to invest heavily in so unknown a commodity or do too much to irritate Parido. But Joachim could entice the Dutch market into seeing that this conflict was a matter of business, not some internal Portuguese contest. He could bring in the Dutch traders willing to make a profit off this new product. They might be sheepish about jumping into a fray where Jew battled Jew over a commodity hardly anyone had ever heard of, but once they saw one of their own intrepid countrymen joining in, they would fall in line lest they lose the chance to profit.

Another Dutchman called out to sell. Miguel had never seen him before. He was only some unfortunate trader who had taken a chance on coffee and now found himself caught in the crossfire. Desperate to get rid of his goods before the price dipped even further, he let his fifteen barrels go at thirty-five. Miguel was now only two guilders per barrel away from the price he needed to survive, five guilders from what he needed to defeat Parido. But even if he brought the price to thirty, he would have to keep the price stable until two o'clock, the end of the trading day.

A new man shouted out in Dutch, but his accent sounded French. Then another, this one Danish. Thirty-five. Thirty-four. Miguel need only look on and monitor. He had sold eighty barrels that he did not own. It was no matter. Far more barrels had already changed hands than the warehouses of Amsterdam could hope to house.

Now Miguel would have to wait to see how low the price went and then buy enough to protect himself. If a buyer chose, he might file an appeal so that he would not have to buy his coffee at the now-high prices of thirty-eight and thirty-nine, but that hardly mattered to Miguel. Let them keep their money. Only the price of the barrels mattered now.

Parido looked on, his face blank. He had stopped shouting orders, for one man could not buy everything, not without ruining himself. He had artificially raised the price himself, and he knew that if he bought back enough barrels at a price to bring coffee back to thirty-nine, he would surely lose a great deal of money, even if he factored in the profit of his put.

The price began to stabilise, so Miguel bought at thirty-one and then sold at once for thirty. The loss was nothing, and it set off another frenzy of selling.

Miguel smiled at Parido, who turned away in disgust. But Miguel would not let him walk away. He pushed through the crowd. He heard sales at twenty-nine and twenty-eight. He looked at the clock on the church tower. Half past one. Only thirty minutes remaining.

'I believe the day is mine,' Miguel called.

Parido spun around. 'Not yet, Lienzo. There's still time.'

'There may be time, but I don't believe you have any more options.'

Parido shook his head. 'You think your little tricks will save you? Relish this moment, Lienzo. I think you'll find you are not nearly so clever as you think.'

'No, probably not. But I have the distinct pleasure this day of being cleverer than you. I wish to take possession of those barrels of coffee you promised me by this time tomorrow.'

'You haven't the money to pay for them,' he spat. 'If you look at your copy of our contract, you will note it specifies the exchange must take place within seventy-two hours of the end of market today. I frankly don't believe you will be able to raise the money. Indeed, in seventy-two hours in the eyes of the Ma'amad you may no longer be a Jew.'

So Parido planned to use the council to avoid his debts. The council would never stand for it. 'You may believe what you wish, but I'll transfer the amount to your account by this time tomorrow. I expect you to transfer ownership with a similar punctuality, or you will have to honour the contract and pay me an additional thirty-eight hundred.'

Miguel stepped away and glanced towards the crowd of buyers and sellers. The price appeared now to have stabilised at a remarkable twenty-six, with very little time left to trade. If the price only stayed there, he would earn a profit of almost seven hundred guilders from his puts alone, another two thousand from the futures. Now, too anxious to simply stand and observe, he thought to take care of one last bit of business.

Isaiah Nunes had been speaking quietly with some acquaintances, attempting to ignore the selling frenzy. Miguel smiled and asked Nunes to walk with him a moment privately. The two stepped away behind a pillar.

Miguel allowed his face to brighten into his best merchant guise. 'I would like you to transfer ownership of the coffee I contracted with you to deliver. I would like ownership papers in my hands no later than tomorrow morning.'

Nunes straightened his posture, as though making some effort to align himself perfectly with the earth, and then took a step forward. 'I'm sorry you find yourself in a difficult situation, Miguel, but I can't help you. I told you the shipment never arrived, and your needs cannot undo what has been done. And if I may be so bold, you are hardly a man to demand prompt action in any regard. Getting you to pay what you owed me has been no easy task, and I feel that you've abused my friendship unforgivably.'

'An odd comment from a man who sold my contracted goods to Solomon Parido.'

Nunes tried to show no expression. 'I cannot understand you. You are talking like a madman, and I'll not be insulted.'

'You're overplaying your part, senhor. You should appear confused, not horrified.'

'Nothing you say may horrify me.' He took a step forward. 'I once looked upon you as a friend, but I see you are only a cheat and I'll discuss nothing further with you.'

'You'll discuss it with me, or you will discuss it in the courts,' Miguel answered. He saw at once that he had Nunes' attention. 'You took the coffee I had contracted for and delivered it to Solomon Parido. You then lied and told me my shipment had never been acquired. I presume you then arranged for another shipment, but I know the cargo that belongs to me by legal right came in on a ship called the *Sea Lily*. I have witnesses who will testify to hearing Parido discuss the matter. If you refuse to comply, my only question will be whether to bring you before a Dutch court or the Ma'amad, or both, and force you to provide not only the coffee but pay such damages that result of my not having the original shipment.' Miguel showed Nunes the contract he had made with Parido. 'If I lose money on this contract, I'll be able to sue you for the losses, for if you had not deceived me I should surely have won. And you may wager that once this matter goes to court, your reputation as a trustworthy merchant will be utterly dashed.'

Nunes flushed. 'If I withhold the coffee from Parido, he will make me an enemy. What of my reputation then?'

'Surely you can't expect me to care. You'll transfer ownership to me by morning, or I'll see you ruined.'

'If I give you what you ask, you'll say nothing? You'll not tell the world of this?'

'I ought not to keep quiet, but I'll do so out of memory of our friendship. I never would have expected this from you.'

Nunes shook his head. 'You must understand how difficult it is to resist Parido when he wants something. I dared not say no to him. I have a family, and I could not afford to put myself at risk by protecting you.'

'I understand his influence and power,' Miguel said, 'and I have resisted him just the same. And he did not ask you to refrain from protecting me, he asked you to lie to me and cheat me, and you agreed. I never thought you a particularly brave man, Isaiah, but I was still shocked to learn the extent of your cowardice.'

As he walked away he heard the clock tower strike two. He asked a man standing near him how coffee had closed: 25.5 guilders per barrel.

Miguel would look at once into renting a splendid house on the shores of the Houtgracht. He would contact his debtors to offer some small payment to the most anxious. Everything would be different now.

And there was his brother. He turned around. Daniel stood no more than an arm's length away. Daniel looked at his brother, tried to lock eyes with him, but Miguel could not bring himself to say anything. The time for reconciliation was over; there could be no forgiveness. Daniel had bet his own future against his brother's, and he had lost.

Miguel moved away. Crowds of men swarmed around him. Word had begun to spread; already every man upon the Exchange understood he had had a great victory. Even if they did not know what he had won or whom he had defeated, these traders knew they stood in the presence of a trader in his glory. Strangers whose names he barely knew clapped him on the shoulder or pumped his hand or promised they would call upon him soon to speak of a project whose value he could scarce believe.

And then, through the thickness of the traders, he saw a haggard Dutchman in fine clothes grin widely at him. Joachim. Miguel turned away from a triumvirate of Italian Jews who wanted to speak to him about figs, uttering some polite excuse and promising to call on them at a tavern whose name he forgot the moment the men spoke it. He pushed on until he stood facing Joachim, who appeared both greater and smaller than he had in his impoverished madness. His grin appeared not so much triumphant as sad. Miguel returned it with a smile of his own.

'I told you I would make things right,' he said, 'if you would but trust me.'

'If I had done no more than trust you,' Joachim replied with equal cheer, 'I would still be a poor man. It is only because I hated you and hounded you that you have won this victory. There is a great

497

lesson to be learned here, but I shall burn in hell if I know what it may be.'

Miguel let out a bark of a laugh and stepped forward to embrace this man who, not so long ago, he had wished dead with all his heart. For all he knew, he might wish him dead again, and soon. For the moment, however, he did not care what Joachim had done or would do, and he did not care who knew of their hatred and their friendship. He cared only that he had righted his own wrongs and unmade his ruin in the process. Miguel would have hugged the devil himself.

CHAPTER 32

The new girl spoke no Portuguese but made herself content with a rough exchange of signs. Catryn had a dour face, closer to plain than homely, but unpleasant enough to suit her mistress. It hardly mattered. Miguel was out of the house now, and the prettiness or plainness of the maid meant nothing to anyone.

In the mornings, Daniel left the house almost before she was awake, and Hannah was left to her breakfast with the girl hovering over her. Catryn gestured towards the decanter of wine on the table. She seemed to believe that a woman with child could never take too much wine, and Hannah had been disordered with drink every morning for a week before she had found the will to say no. Now she just shook her head. When she drank so much the baby quieted down inside her, and she liked to feel it kicking and squirming. When it lay still, even if just for a few minutes, Hannah feared the worst. If the baby died, what would Daniel do? What would he do *to her*?

She sent Catryn to the market outside the Dam to buy coffee and had the girl prepare it for her each afternoon. One day Daniel came home early and grew so enraged when he saw her drinking it that he struck her until she cried out for the well-being of their child. Now she only drank it during Exchange hours when she knew Daniel would not be there.

Sometimes she saw Miguel on the street, dressed as he was now in his fine new suits, walking in his familiar way with the great merchants of the Vlooyenburg. He looked content, youthful in his triumph. Hannah didn't dare look too long. If she went to his house, if she told him she wanted to leave her husband and be with him, what would he say? He would tell her to be gone. Maybe if he had failed in his mighty scheme and had nothing more to lose, maybe then he might have taken her, but not now.

After Catryn cleared away the breakfast things, she and Hannah went out to the markets. The girl could not cook half so well as Annetje, and she knew less about picking meats and produce. Hannah had a better eye than the girl, but she didn't speak her mind. Let her pick bad vegetables and turning beef. What did it matter to her if their meals were bland or sour?

This was her life now, pale carrots and rotten fish. These things were her only pleasures. She had her husband and she would have her daughter, whom she prayed would be born healthy and fit. Those things would have to be enough. They would have to be enough, because there could be nothing else.

*   *   *

Moving from his brother's house was sweet. Miguel had rented a fine home across the canal, and though it was smaller than his brother's, he thought it far more elegant and perfectly suited for his needs. He hardly even knew what he would do with the space he had, though he hoped soon enough to fill it with a wife and children. The marriage brokers had already begun to pound on his door.

The day after his victory on the Exchange, his last in his brother's house, he had climbed up from the cellar and walked through the kitchen and then up again to the main level, where he saw Daniel sitting in the front room, pretending to look at letters. Daniel said nothing to him. Not a word of kindness. Miguel had told him that morning that he would be moving out and had thanked Daniel for his hospitality. Daniel had merely nodded and advised Miguel to be certain not to take anything that was not his.

There was still one order of business, and Miguel wanted it put to rest before he left. He cleared his throat and waited while Daniel slowly raised his head.

'Is there something?' he asked.

'I wanted to talk to you about a matter of money,' he said. 'It is an awkward thing, and I would not have you think me over-eager. Right now my affairs are quite healthy, thank the Holy One, blessed be He, but I am told that you owe me some money.'

501

Daniel rose to his feet. '*I* owe *you*? What nonsense is that? After I sheltered you for the past six months, you would say that I owe you?'

'Your shelter has been very generous, Daniel, but such generosity is not worth two thousand guilders. Ricardo has explained everything to me.'

'I cannot believe you would fly in my face with this!' he shouted. 'I lent you money when no one else would, when your name was a byword for failure. I took you in and gave you shelter when you had nowhere to turn. And now you dare tell me I owe you.'

'I have not said when you must pay me. I know your finances to be in disorder.'

'Who told you such a lie? Now that you have a few coins jingling in your pocket you think yourself the finest man in Amsterdam. I must tell you, brother, it does not work thus. Because you are now solvent does not mean I must be ruined.'

'I had not thought it worked that way,' Miguel said quietly.

'And I will tell you something else. That little scheme of yours on the Exchange would never have worked had you not taken my name and done with it as you ought not to, promising my money to back your ventures. I suppose you thought yourself too clever to be discovered.'

'I thought it only fair,' Miguel said, 'considering you had the effrontery to demand that I pay you what you lent me when you knew yourself to be my debtor.'

'Well, I won't forgive you,' Daniel said. 'The money you claim I owe you was made by stamping upon Senhor Parido's plans, plans in which I was also invested. While you profited from whale oil, I lost – but I never chastised you for your trickery. And while you profited from your little scheme with coffee, you have cost Senhor Parido a great deal of money. Can you only profit, Miguel, by tricks and schemes that injure others?'

'How can you speak of tricks and schemes when all this time Parido's interest in coffee was based on nothing but revenge? That is no kind of way to do business, I assure you. It would have been far better had he looked to making money rather than to making me lose it.'

Daniel shook his head. 'I had always thought you lax and undisciplined, too free with drink and women, but I had never before thought you a villain.'

'Tell yourself what lies you like,' Miguel said bitterly. 'I won't take you before the Ma'amad. I leave it your own sense of right and wrong to act as you see fit.'

The letters had gone out to all the agents Miguel had hired: agents in London, Paris, Marseilles, Antwerp, Hamburg and half a dozen other exchanges. He had not contacted those agents to whom Geertruid was responsible, those secured in Iberia with the aid of her lawyer. Geertruid handled those herself, and she had no idea her own letters contained something very different from Miguel's.

On the day that Miguel had indicated, Geertruid's agents in Lisbon, Madrid and Oporto were to buy as much coffee as they could. Word of the Amsterdam sell-off would have trickled to the foreign exchanges already. Prices would have dipped after Miguel's manoeuvre, and Geertruid's agents would be prepared to pounce on the low price.

Geertruid arrived at the Amsterdam Exchange at midday. She was not the only woman to set foot there, but her sex was still rare and she attracted some small attention as she strolled across the courtyard in her flowing red skirts, imperious as a queen. During the early stages of their planning, Miguel had suggested that she come to the Exchange to watch the buying take place and witness the birth of their wealth. Miguel had never repeated the suggestion, but Geertruid had not forgotten it.

She beamed, tilting her head just slightly in the way that drove Miguel mad. There was Miguel, her partner, her friend, her puppet. She had sent him out to do her bidding, and he had done it.

Except she now saw he did something else entirely. Her partner was selling. He stood amid a crowd of traders who called out their price. Miguel sold off his ninety barrels piecemeal – ten to this merchant, five to that. Since the recent upheaval, coffee had come to be regarded as a risky venture and no one bought in any great quantity.

'What are you doing?' She rushed over as soon as Miguel had finished the transaction. 'Have you gone mad? Why aren't you buying?'

Miguel smiled. 'With a little manipulation and a carefully placed rumour here and there, I've managed to raise the price of coffee to thirty-seven guilders to the barrel, so I'm unloading the barrels I bought from Nunes. I'll make a tidy profit, which will enhance the wealth I acquired from my puts. After the events of last closing day, I bought some short-term futures, and I believe I should profit quite nicely from those as well.'

'A profit? Your puts and short-term futures? You've been gazing at the moon. When the other markets learn that Amsterdam has not gone down, we'll lose money across Europe.'

'Oh, I'm not worried. The agents will buy nothing. I've dismissed them.'

Geertruid stared at him. She began to speak but choked on her words. She tried again. 'Miguel, what game are you playing? Please tell me what is happening.'

'What is happening,' Miguel said calmly, 'is that I have changed the scheme to my advantage, and I have left you to muddle through as best you can.'

Geertruid opened her mouth but nothing came out, so she turned away for a moment to master herself. 'Why would you do such a thing to me?' Her eyes blinked and she stared into nothingness. 'Why would you do this?'

Miguel smiled. 'Because you deceived me and

betrayed me. You thought, even now, that I would never have learned that our chance meeting was no accident. You have manipulated me since the day we met, but now I have manipulated you. You sought to use this coffee scheme to ruin me, but I have found you out and made a handsome profit. It is not the profit I dreamed of, I grant you, but it is certainly enough to restore my reputation, resolve my debts, and give me the freedom to trade as I like. You, on the other hand, have committed yourself to your agents in Iberia, and I believe they will turn to you to repay them.'

This time Geertruid could not find her voice at all.

'Of course, I shall return your capital. Though you sought my ruin, I'll not steal from you. The money should go a little way towards repaying your agents for their purchases.'

'I am undone,' Geertruid whispered. She took hold of his arm, as though he were a witness to her ruin and not its architect.

'Perhaps your master will rescue you. Surely it is his responsibility to do so. I suspect the three thousand guilders you laid out were his to begin with. Of course, this incident has not left Parido untouched, and he may not find himself as generous as he once was. But that is no concern of mine.'

Geertruid still said nothing but only stared ahead in disbelief. Miguel, who had more coffee to unload, turned away.

CHAPTER 33

Maybe she had wanted it to happen. When she thought back on it, that was how it seemed. She hadn't hidden the book particularly well, setting it in the pocket of an apron, with one corner sticking out, or under a pile of scarves, its sharp corner jabbing through the fabric.

She took it out often, leafing through its uncut pages, peeking at the images hidden in pages that were still attached. She knew she ought to separate them – it was her book and she might do as she pleased – but she did not know how and she was afraid of damaging it.

The words meant nothing to her. She could not tell one letter from another, but the woodcuts were pretty and they suggested to her a world beyond what she knew. Delicately drawn fruit, a fish, a boat, a little boy at play. Some of them were silly, like the cow with the almost human face, smiling out at her with maddening cheer.

She and the new girl, Catryn, had been washing the floors before Shabbat when Daniel entered the hallway and trod along the clean floors with his muddy shoes. His face was blank, hardly even changing as he slipped and had to grab on to the doorjamb to keep from tumbling. Catryn muttered under her breath but didn't look up.

'Come with me,' Daniel said to Hannah.

She raised herself and followed him to the bedroom. The book had been set out on the bed. She had known it would happen. She had been waiting for it. Even so, her stomach wrenched so hard she feared for her child. She took deep breaths and willed herself calm.

'Explain this,' Daniel said, jabbing a bony finger in the direction of the book.

Hannah stared at it but said nothing.

'Do you not hear me, wife?'

'I hear you,' she said.

'Then you will answer me. By Christ, I've not often raised a hand to you, but I will do so now if you continue to be obstinate. Has someone been teaching you to read?'

She shook her head. 'No.'

'Then where did the book come from?'

There was no point keeping it a secret. Daniel could no longer do him any harm. She suspected that Miguel would want her to tell him, that he would get some pleasure from her doing so. 'It came from Senhor Lienzo, your brother,' she said. 'He gave it to me.'

Daniel could not have turned any more red if he had held his breath. 'Miguel,' he said softly. 'What business had he giving you things?'

508

She shook her head. 'I told him I wished I knew how to read, and so he gave it to me.'

Daniel sucked in his breath. He rubbed his jaw and then stuck his thumb and index finger into his mouth and began to root around. After a moment he stopped. 'Did he give you anything else?' he asked bitterly.

She had not known she was going to say it. She could not have willed herself to do it. The courage would have eluded her. And it was hardly a choice she felt entitled to make herself. There could hardly be anything more selfish than to entangle another person in her lies, and yet she did it. The words slipped out.

'This child,' she said, both hands on her belly. 'He gave me this child.'

She felt so cold she could hardly keep her teeth from chattering. She became dizzy, her vision blurred. What had she done? What horrible step had she taken? She nearly threw herself at Daniel's feet and told him she had spoken those words out of spite and that of course she had never defiled her marriage bed. But though it would be the truth, the words would sound like lies. That was why she had spoken them. Once uttered, they could never be retrieved.

Her husband remained still, with his arms hanging limply by his sides. She had expected him to rush at her, to beat her with his hands or with whatever he could grab. She was prepared to protect her baby, come what may.

He might have simply walked out of the room or he might have cursed her. He did none of those things, and Hannah now had cause to regret her words, not for what they might mean for her or even for Miguel, but for what they might mean for her husband. She had imagined him enraged, furious, murderous, but not broken and defeated.

'I have nothing, then,' he said softly. 'Everything has been lost. I will have to sell the house. And now I won't even have my son.'

'She's a daughter,' Hannah said softly. 'I dreamed it.'

Daniel seemed not to hear her. 'I've lost everything,' he said again. 'And to my brother. I'll not stay here.'

'Where will you go?' she asked, as though she were speaking to a grieving friend.

'Venice. London, perhaps. You will go to Miguel?'

'I don't know that he will have me.' Those few words, spoken out of malice towards Daniel, had changed Miguel's life for ever. How could she have done something so cruel? Yet, if she could take them back, she wouldn't.

'He will have you. He has honour enough. I will have the Ma'amad grant a divorce, and I will be gone.'

She thought to step forward and take his hand and offer some kind word – but she would be doing it for herself, only to lessen her guilt. And she dared not break the spell. 'I'll leave now,' she told him.

'That would be best.'

*　　*　　*

As she walked through the Vlooyenburg, the terror slipped away drop by drop. She had imagined Miguel turning her away, cursing her, slamming his door in her face. What would she do? She would have no home and no money, and a child to look after. She might find a convent to take her in, but she did not even know if there were convents in the United Provinces. She might have to go south, perhaps to Antwerp, to find one. How would she get there? She had only a few coins to her name.

But she would not torment herself with these fears. Miguel would never turn her away. At the very least, now that he was a great merchant again, he would give her something with which to support herself. She too could go somewhere and start afresh, perhaps pass herself off as a widow. It would not be an ideal life, but neither would it be a miserable one. The world was all before her, and if it was not for her to choose her place of rest, she believed anything would be better than the place from which she had emerged.

Miguel had not yet hired a servant for his new home, so he answered the door himself. He stared at her for a moment, not certain what to do, and then invited her in.

'I told your brother that the child is yours,' Hannah said, as soon as she heard the door click shut.

He turned and looked at her, his expression inscrutable. 'Will he give you a divorce?'

She nodded.

Miguel said nothing. His jaw clenched and his eyes half closed as he indulged in a long, a cruelly long, inscrutable silence.

Too many shutters in the house remained closed, she thought, and the hallways remained dark and murky, the whiteness of the tiles appearing as a dull grey. Miguel now lived here, but he had not made the place his own. No paintings hung on the walls. A dusty mirror leaned against the floor. In the distance, Hannah could smell the burning of an oil lamp, and she could see the faint dance of light from another room. Somewhere in the house a clock chimed.

'If I take you as my wife,' he said at last, 'will you agree to obey me in all things?'

'No,' she said. She bit her lip to fight back both tears and a grin.

'Not even a little?' he asked.

'Very well. I will obey you a little.'

'Good. A little is all I require,' he said, and reached out for her.

CHAPTER 34

With a belly full of slightly cured herring, served with turnips and leeks, Miguel leaned back to survey the Flyboat. The moment was his. All the men of the Portuguese Nation spoke of his wondrous though still largely incomprehensible manipulation of the coffee market, a market so insignificant that most men had never given it more than a passing glance. Lienzo had shown himself a man of substance, they said. Parido had set out to destroy him, but Lienzo had turned the villainy back on itself. Brilliant. Ingenious. This man who had once seemed no more than a foolish gambler now showed himself to be a great man of commerce.

Half a dozen traders of the highest order sat at Miguel's table, drinking their fill of the good wine for which he had paid. Eager fellows had crowded around him the moment he had walked into the room the door, and Miguel had found it difficult to force his way through to his new friends. Older senhors who had once looked at Miguel with contempt now wished to do business. Would Senhor Lienzo be interested in considering a matter of ginger? Would Senhor Lienzo be interested in hearing of the opportunities arising on the London Exchange?

Senhor Lienzo had a great deal of interest in these matters, and he had an even greater interest in the fact that these men now sought his business. But, he thought, men of commerce were best treated like Dutch sluts. If they were put off a bit now, they would only be more anxious later. Let them wait. Miguel still had no firm ideas about what he wished to do with his new-found solvency. He was not as wealthy as he had hoped to be by now, but he had wealth enough, and he would soon have a wife and – sooner than expected – a child.

He could not help but laugh at the irony. The Ma'amad would expel from the community a right-eous man who dared to cast a few coins to an unsanctioned beggar, but Miguel could steal his brother's wife so long as he did so legally. She would have her divorce, and then she would be his. In the meantime, he had rented some rooms for her in a neat little house in the Vlooyenburg. She had hired a girl of her own choosing, she drank coffee, she entertained friends she never knew she had, women who flocked to her parlour now that she was the subject of so delicious and neatly resolved a scandal. And she had been to visit Miguel in his new house. Of course she had. There was no reason to wait for the legal sanction of marriage.

Miguel drank heavily with these new friends and retold the story of his triumph. The look of surprise on Parido's face when Joachim began to sell. The delight when the Tudesco merchants sent the price falling. The surprising interest of those strangers from the Levant. Was that truly an East Indian who had bought fifty barrels of coffee from the Frenchman?

They might have continued this celebration for hours, or at least for as long as Miguel bought wine, but Solomon Parido entered and silenced their conversation. Miguel felt a strange mixture of fear and delight. He had expected Parido to be there. A man such as he, so invested in his power, could not hide from defeat. He would show his face publicly, demonstrate to the nation that his little losses were nothing to him.

Parido leaned forward and spoke to some friends with particular warmth. Miguel expected the *parnass* to remain among these men, turn his back on his enemy, and make nothing of his presence, but such was not Parido's plan. After speaking with his fellows, he came over to Miguel's table. Those who had just moments ago been laughing at the stories of Parido's failure now climbed over one another to show their respect for him, but the *parnass* had no interest in their display.

'A word,' he said to Miguel.

He smiled at his companions and followed Parido to a quiet corner. All eyes were upon them, and Miguel had the uncomfortable feeling that now he was the subject of merriment.

Parido stopped and leaned in towards him.

'Because I am a kind man,' he said quietly, 'I gave you these weeks to revel in your glory. I thought it cruel to crush you too soon.'

'Who among the children of Israel is as wise and good as you?'

'You may be flippant, but you and I both know that I have never done anything but in the service of the nation, and nothing I did deserved the schemes you hatched against me. And what of your poor brother? He protected you and lent you money when you were friendless, and you repay him by undoing his finances, cuckolding him and stealing his wife.'

Miguel could not correct the world's belief that he had cuckolded Daniel, not without betraying Hannah, so he let the world think what it liked. 'You and my brother are of a piece. You plot against me and seek my ruin, but when your methods fail you blame me as though *I* had acted against *you*. This surely is a madness worthy of the Inquisition itself.'

'How can you look me in the face and say it was I who plotted against you? Did you not seek to ruin my whale oil scheme for your own profit?'

'I sought to ruin nothing, merely to profit from your own manipulations. Nothing more than any man does on the Exchange each day.'

'You knew full well your interference would cost me money, even while I interceded on your behalf with your brandy futures.'

'An intercession,' Miguel pointed out, 'that cost me money.'

'You don't seem to understand that I did not act against you. I had bet on the price of brandy going down, and my machinations in that field threatened to turn your futures into debt, so I did what I could to rescue you. I was as surprised as anyone when the price of brandy rose at the last minute. Unlike you, who made a small profit, I lost by my efforts.'

'I am certain you had nothing but the best of intentions in plotting against my coffee trade as well.'

'How can you speak to me thus? It is you who trod upon my coffee trade – you and your heretic friend.'

Miguel let out a laugh. 'You may call yourself the injured person if you like, but that will not change what is.'

'I have a great deal of power to effect changes, you forget, and when I bring this case before the council, we will see how smug you look then.'

'And for what reason am I to stand before the Ma'amad? For making you look a fool or for refusing to be ruined by your scheme?'

'For conducting unseemly business with a gentile,' he announced. 'You deployed that man, Joachim Waagenaar, intentionally to create a drop in the price of coffee. I happen to know he is the very same Dutchman you ruined by brokering for him and forcing upon him your foolish sugar scheme. Clearly he found it hard to get enough of you, but I think you will find the Ma'amad feels somewhat differently. You have violated the law of Amsterdam and so put your people at risk.'

Miguel studied Parido's face. He wanted to savour the moment as long as he could, because it might be, he knew, the most satisfying of his life. Then, knowing he could not wait too long, he spoke. 'When I am called before the Ma'amad,' he began, 'shall I mention that I only asked Joachim to work with me after he came to me and confessed that you had attempted to force him into discovering the nature of my business arrangements? You, in other words, deployed a gentile as a spy, not even for Ma'amad matters but in the hopes of ruining a fellow Jew against whom you harbour a vendetta. I wonder what the other *parnassim* will think of that information. Should I also mention that you conspired with Nunes, a merchant with whom I had placed an order, and that you used your position as a *parnass* to force him into betraying me so you might prevail over me? This should make for a very interesting session.'

Parido chewed upon his lower lip for a moment. 'Very well,' he said.

But Miguel was not finished. 'I might add that there is the matter of Geertruid Damhuis, a Dutchwoman you employed with the single purpose of ruining me. How long was she your creature, senhor? The better part of a year, I think.'

'Geertruid Damhuis,' Parido repeated, suddenly

looking a bit more cheerful. 'I heard something of this. She was your partner in your schemes, but then you betrayed her.'

'I merely did not allow her to ruin me. What I have never fully understood, however, is why you needed Joachim if you already had Geertruid. Was she not telling you all? Was she hoping to turn this treachery into a little profit for herself, and you could not live with the knowledge that you could not control your own creature?'

Parido let out a laugh. 'You are correct about one thing. I cannot bring you before the Ma'amad. You have won on that score. I admit here between the two of us that I did ask that foul Dutchman to find out information about you. But you must know I had nothing to do with that whore you ruined. As near as I can tell, she was a perfectly honest slut who wanted nothing more than to aid you. And you destroyed her.'

'You are a liar,' Miguel said.

'I don't think so. There is one thing I do admire about you, Lienzo. Some men are cold in matters of business. They harden their hearts against those they hurt. But you are a man with a conscience, and I know you will truly suffer for what you did to your honest partner.'

Miguel found Geertruid in the Three Dirty Dogs, where she was so drunk that no one would sit with her. One of the other patrons warned him to be careful. She had already bitten the cheek, to the point of drawing blood, of a man who had attempted to feel her bosoms. But she had clearly drunk herself past the point of anger, because when she saw Miguel she made a sloppy effort to stand and then held out her arms as though ready to envelop her former partner.

'It's Miguel Lienzo,' she slurred. 'The man who ruined me. I had hoped to see you here, and now you are here. Where I hoped to see you. Will you sit with me?'

Miguel sat himself down very carefully, as though afraid the bench might break. He looked across the table at Geertruid. 'Who were you working for? I must know. I promise you I'll take no action on the information. I need to know for myself. Was it Parido?'

'Parido?' Geertruid repeated. 'I never worked for Parido. I would never even have heard of Parido if it had not been for you.' She laughed and pointed at him. 'I *knew* that's what you thought. The moment you told me you had undone me, I knew you thought I was Parido's agent. If I were Parido's agent,' she explained, 'I would have deserved to be crushed.'

Miguel swallowed hard. He had hoped to hear something very different. 'You tricked me into trusting you. Why?'

'Because I wanted to be wealthy,' Geertruid said, slamming her hand upon the table. 'And a respectable woman. That's all. I was not working for anyone. I had no plan to destroy you. I only wanted to go into business with a man of influence who would help me make my fortune. And when you lost your money, I stuck by you because I liked you. I never meant to trick you. All I am is a thief, Miguel. I'm a thief, but I am no villain.'

'A thief?' he repeated. 'Then you stole that money, the three thousand guilders?'

She shook her head, and doing so let it drop so low that Miguel feared she might bang it upon the table. 'I borrowed that money. From a money-lender. A very nasty moneylender. So nasty even the Jews won't have him.'

Miguel closed his eyes. 'Alferonda,' he said.

'Yes. He was the only man I could find who was willing to lend me what I needed. He knew what I wanted it for, and he knew who I was.'

'Why did he not tell me so?' Miguel demanded aloud. 'He played the two of us against each other. Why would he do such a thing?'

'He's not a kind man,' she said sadly.

'Oh, Geertruid.' He took her hand. 'Why did you not tell me the truth? How could you let me ruin you?'

She let out a little laugh. 'You know, Miguel, sweet Miguel, I don't blame you at all. What could you have done? Confronted me? Asked of my scheme? You knew already I was a deceiver, and you wished to make your money as best you could. I can't blame you. But I could not have told you the truth either, for you would never have continued to trust me. You feared that council of yours over a matter of merely doing business with a Dutchwoman. Would you have convinced yourself that any good can come with doing business with a Dutch *outlaw*? Particularly one such as me.'

'One such as you?'

'I must leave the city, Miguel. I must leave tonight. Alferonda has been searching for me, and he won't go easy with me. There are tales of his wrath, you know.'

'Why should Alferonda care? Can you not simply give him the money I transferred to your account? I have repaid the three thousand I borrowed of you.'

'I owe him another eight hundred in interest.'

'Eight hundred,' Miguel blurted out. 'Does he know no shame?'

'He is a usurer,' she said sadly.

'Let me speak to him. He is my friend, and I am certain we can come to an understanding. He needn't charge you so much interest as that. We will reach a more reasonable fee, and I will help you pay him.'

She squeezed his hand. 'Poor sweet Miguel. You are too good to me. I can't let you do that, for you would be throwing away your money, and nothing would be gained but your ruin. Alferonda may be your friend, but he is not mine, and he won't let his reputation suffer by a kindness. And how good a friend is he, deceiving you as he has done? Even if you could stay his hand, there is the money I owe the agents in Iberia. They have my name, not yours, and they will come looking for Geertruid Damhuis in Amsterdam. If I stay, it will be only a matter of time before I am undone. I must leave tonight, so I will give you no more than you deserve by telling you the truth at last.'

'There is more?'

'Oh, yes. There is more.' Through the fog of her drunkenness, she managed a smile such as never failed to fell him. 'You asked what I meant when I said a thief such as me. I'll now tell you.' She leaned in closer. 'I am no ordinary thief, you must understand. I don't pick pockets or cut purses or break into shops. You've wondered often about my journeys to the countryside and, poor foolish man, you have read all the tales, and you have read them because I introduced you to them, imp that I am.'

Miguel reminded himself to continue breathing. 'What are you saying? That you and Hendrick . . . ?' He could not quite finish.

'Yes,' Geertruid said quietly. 'We are Charming Pieter and his Goodwife Mary. As to which of us is which, I cannot say.' She let out a laugh. 'Poor Hendrick is more the fool than you, I'm afraid, but he always did as he was told, and he let the world believe that he was behind Pieter's heroic robberies. It hardly mattered. I had come to believe that, in this age of stories and adventures, if we could make people believe in Charming Pieter as a hero, no one would turn him in, and the legend would only confound the efforts to catch him. Little did we know how well the plan would work. I expected to hear stories of our adventures, but I never expected to see these tales in print. Half the stories you read are false and the other half wild exaggerations, but they have served us well.'

'Where is Hendrick now?'

'Fled.' She sighed. 'He is a silly man, but not so silly as not to know what it means to be unable to pay a cruel usurer. I have not seen him since the loss upon the Exchange. He was never at peace with my dealings with Alferonda and my plans to make our fortune through trade. He could not understand how it all worked, and he thought it doomed. I fear that any way this ended, Charming Pieter's adventures were destined to reach their conclusion.'

'How could I have done this to you?' he said. He put his face in his hands.

'It is my doing. I put you at risk. And that poor girl, your brother's wife – please tell her I am sorry to have had to frighten her.'

'She is to be my wife soon,' Miguel said, feeling somehow the need to be honest.

'Is she now? Well, I can't say I understand the ways of the Israelites, but they are not mine to understand.'

'What is it that Hannah saw? She did not even know.'

Geertruid laughed. 'She did not even know. How very amusing. She saw me speaking with Alferonda, and I was afraid that if you were to learn of it you would grow suspicious. But,' she said, pushing herself to her feet, 'enough chatter, senhor. I must be on my way.'

'You are too drunk, madam, to leave town tonight. Let me take you home.'

She laughed, holding on to his arm for support. 'Oh, Miguel, still trying to find your way to my bed!'

'I only want to see you safely—'

'Shh.' She pressed a finger to his lips. 'There's no need to tell stories. Not any more. I must go, and it must be tonight, and my being drunk shall only make things easier, not harder.' Yet she did not move. 'Do you remember, senhor, the night you tried to kiss me?'

He thought about lying, to pretend it had been no matter to him and he had not bothered to remember. But he did not lie. 'Yes, I remember.'

'I longed to kiss you back,' she said, 'and more, too. I never let you, not because I did not want to but because I knew you would be more pliable if I never gave you more than enough to whet your appetite. A woman such as I am must know how to use her quim, even if it means not using it.'

'Let me take you home,' Miguel said again.

'No,' she said, pushing herself off with unexpected sobriety. 'I said I must go, and so I must. Let us part quickly, or we'll never part at all.' And so she left, out of the door and into the night. Without a lantern. If ever a woman lived who could outwit the thieves and the Night Watch, it was Geertruid Damhuis.

He remained still for a long time. He simply stared into the distance until a pretty girl came over and asked him if he required anything. 'Wine,' he whispered. 'A great deal of wine.' When he drank it, when he had so much wine in him that he could no longer tell what was right and what was wrong – that was when he would go in search of Alferonda.

From

The Factual and Revealing Memoirs of Alonzo Alferonda

I had hardly thought that after Miguel Lienzo's victory on the Exchange all would be done with. I had won, Parido had lost, and the victory tasted sweet, but there was still Miguel. I had trod upon him, and he would not take it kindly. I had thought to fool him when he came to see me, to dazzle his eyes with tricks and illusions until he doubted that there even was such a man as Alonzo Alferonda, let alone one who had used him ill. But I had always liked Miguel, and I owed him a debt. I had begun with no intention of hurting him or his friends but rather using him as an instrument that would facilitate what I wanted and at the same time allowing him to make a guilder or two.

There would have been no harm done, surely. If some lies were told, if some coins were palmed and made to magically appear, what wrong can there be in that? All men love trickery and tricksters. That is why half-starving peasants surrender their hard-earned wages when mountebanks and gypsies come through their towns. All the world loves to be deceived – but only when it consents to the deception.

I sat in my rooms one night reading the Holy Torah – I speak the truth, for the cherem had not diminished my love of learning one jot – when there was a loud banging on the door below. In a few moments my serving man, old Roland (for, despite the Dutch fashions, I like a manservant and will not allow a nation of cheese-eaters to tell me whom to employ), tapped upon the door to my closet and told me there was 'a very drunk Hebrew of the Portuguese kind' come calling and, when asked his business, stated that it was to kill the man who lived here.

I carefully marked my place in the volume and closed it reverently. 'By all means,' I said, 'show the fellow in.'

Soon enough a besotted Miguel Lienzo stood before me, teetering this way and that. I asked Roland to bring us some wine. I doubted Miguel wanted any more than he had already enjoyed, but I could still hope this encounter might end with his falling asleep. With the servant gone, I offered my visitor a chair and told him I awaited his words.

He awkwardly lowered himself into the hard seat, for in this room I only received visitors whom I did not wish to stay long.

'Why did you not tell me you lent money to Geertruid Damhuis?' he asked, his words a thick mumble.

'I lend to so many people,' I said, 'I cannot be expected to keep track of every one.'

This bit of obfuscation was not meant to trick him. In fact, I'm not sure what it was meant to accomplish. I can say what it did do: it angered him greatly.

'Damn you,' he shouted, half rising from his chair, 'if you play games, I will kill you.'

I began to believe him, though he had no weapon in sight, and I did not anticipate any great difficulty in eluding his drunken pursuit, should things so degenerate. Nevertheless, I held up my hand in a staying gesture and waited for him to settle back into his chair. 'You are right. I did not tell you because it suited me for you to think she was in league with Parido. You must know by now that I could not be more delighted that your scheme has burnt Parido, but the truth of it is I had more of a hand in this than you could have imagined.'

Miguel nodded as though recollecting something. 'Parido was invested in coffee before I decided to begin my venture, wasn't he? He was not the man who sought to undo my scheme. I was the man who sought to undo his. Is that right?'

'Yes,' I admitted. 'Parido entered the coffee trade a few months before you. It was a bit of a trick keeping it from you, but I had my man at the coffee tavern refuse to admit you if Parido was there. A simple precaution. Parido, you understand, had nothing so elaborate as your monopoly scheme in mind. He only wanted to play in calls and puts, and when you started buying up coffee as you did, you threatened his investments, the way you had done in whale oil.'

Miguel shook his head. 'So you had Geertruid lure me into the coffee trade for the single purpose of damaging Parido, and you then turned around and betrayed her?'

'I am flattered you think me so ingenious, but my involvement was something less than that. Your Madame Damhuis discovered coffee on her own and enticed you into the trade because she thought you would make a good partner. When I learned of your interest, I admit I encouraged it because I knew it would be bad for Parido, and I fed you a hint here and there about how Parido plotted against you. But I did no more than that.'

'How is it that Geertruid came to you for her loan?'

'I don't know if you are familiar with that woman's story, but you must know she is a thief, and I am the man thieves come to when they need large sums. I doubt she could have borrowed three thousand guilders from any- one else.'

'You'll not see that money. She has fled the city.'

I shrugged, having expected something of that sort. 'We'll see. I have agents in such places as she might go. I have not given up hope on those guilders, but if they are gone it is a price I am willing to pay for harming Parido. He has not only lost a great deal of money, he looks like a fool before the community. He'll never again be elected to the Ma'amad, and his days of power are over. Is that not worth inconveniencing a thief like Geertruid Damhuis?'

'She is my friend,' he said sadly. 'You could have told me what you knew. You need only have told me all and I could have avoided all of this.'

'And what else would you have avoided? Had you known that Parido's overtures of friendship were genuine, that he had come to coffee first and that you threatened his investments, would you have gone ahead? Would you still have sought to best him in that contest, or would you have backed down? I think we both know the truth, Miguel. You are a schemer, but not so much of a schemer as to do what needed to be done.'

'It did not need to be done,' he said softly.

'It did!' I slammed my hand on the desk. 'That wretch Parido had me cast out of the community because he did not like me. He used flimsy excuses to justify himself, but he was no more than a petty despot who relished what little power he had to make himself feel great. So what if he reached out to you, the brother of a partner, to make amends? Does that excuse the evil he has already done and the evil he would continue to perpetuate? I've done our people a great service, Miguel, by knocking him down.'

'And it hardly matters that Geertruid, who was my friend, gets destroyed?'

'Oh, she's not destroyed, Miguel. She's a thief and a trickstress. I know the kind. I am the kind, and I can tell you she will always do well for herself. She is a wily woman with yet an ample share of beauty. This time next year she'll be the wife of a burgher in Antwerp or the mistress of an Italian prince. You needn't worry about her. I'm the one who has lost three thousand guilders, after all. She might have repaid me something.'

Miguel merely shook his head.

'You're angry about something else, I suppose. You've made some money. You've extricated yourself from debt, you have a tidy profit besides, and you are the most popular merchant in the Vlooyenburg – at least for the moment. But you are angry that you are not on your way to opulence, as you had hoped.'

He stared. Perhaps he was ashamed to admit that he was indeed angry not to have earned so much as he believed he might.

'The two of you might have captured the coffee market in Europe,' I said, 'but I don't think so. This plan of yours was too ambitious, the East India Company would never have allowed it. I had every intention of rescuing you before you overreached yourself. Had I not done so, you would have been destroyed again in a half year's time. Instead, you have done quite well. You think because your scheme with Geertruid Damhuis failed that you can have nothing more to do with coffee? Nonsense. You have made that commodity famous, Miguel, and now the city looks to you. There is still a great fortune to be made. You wanted a trade that would put all your scheming to an end, but instead you have one that presents only a beginning. Use it wisely, and you'll have your opulence in due time.'

'You had no right to trick me as you did.'

I shrugged. 'Perhaps not, but you are the better for it. You have your money, and, I now hear, you are to be married soon as well. Many congratulations to you and the beautiful bride. You have said you wanted a wife and family, and now you shall have those things because of me. I may not have been your most honest friend, but I have always been your best one.'

Miguel rose from his chair. 'A man must make his own fortune, not be played like a chess piece. I'll never forgive you,' he said.

Given that he came to my home with the intention of killing me, I considered never being forgiven a considerable victory.

'Someday you'll forgive me,' I said, 'and even thank me.' But he was already gone – down the stairs at a hurried pace that came just short of a tumble and off to find his own way to the door. Drunk as he was, it took him a few minutes. I heard some bottles break and a piece of furniture topple, but that meant little to me. Once he was gone I had Roland tell the girl,

Annetje, that she could come out of hiding. She was much more beautiful, now that she had me to take care of her. I knew it was for the best that Miguel not see her in my home, for her radiant face gave unmistakable testimony that I was a superior lover, and that was information from which his fragile feelings were best protected at this tender time.

CHAPTER 35

Miguel hardly knew the layout of his furniture, and there were trunks of clothes and boxes of newly bought goods scattered about the rooms. The knock came at his door early in the morning, before the sun had only just burned off dusk, and he sensed that his serving woman had already left for the morning milk and bread. His head ached and the nagging sense of something terrible, something he dare not recall, haunted the outer reaches of his thoughts.

Geertruid. He had destroyed Geertruid for nothing – for Alferonda's petty revenge against a man who had truly wanted to make things right and be Miguel's friend. Parido had been but a merchant looking to preserve his investments. Miguel had been the villain.

Better to go back to sleep and think of it no more, if only for a few hours.

The pounding at the door would not let him be. He rolled out of his bed – for the first time since he moved in not relishing the comfort of a full-sized bed instead of one of those cupboard monstrosities

– and quickly wrapped himself in a dressing coat and found a pair of wooden slippers. The house was a maze of trunks and misplaced furniture, and he tripped twice before reaching the back door in the kitchen. He had only been in the place a fortnight and hardly even knew where the kitchen was; the serving woman, after all, looked after these things for him.

At last he made his way to the kitchen and opened the top portion of the door. The pleasant odours of the early morning – fish and beer and freshly baked bread – burst in upon him so strongly his stomach turned forcibly, and he had to close his eyes to keep from vomiting. When he looked again, there to greet him was the haggard face of Hendrick. He had lost his hat, and his hair hung filthily around his face. He had a cut just below his eye that had clotted nastily, and blood smeared his shirt. Miguel somehow knew at once that the blood was not Hendrick's.

'I haven't the luxury of time,' he said, 'so I won't make you ask me in.'

'What do you want?' Miguel had begun his new life, and he did not want to be seen having a conversation with one such as this. And the distant memory of a conversation echoed on the fringes of his consciousness. Hadn't Hendrick promised to kill Miguel if he betrayed Geertruid?

But it seemed Hendrick had not come for murder. 'I've come for my fifty guilders,' he said, smoothing some dirt out of his moustache.

'I don't understand you.'

'We had a contract, you and I. A deal. You offered me the money, and I took you up on it. Last night. I found the fellow, and I did the business.'

Joachim. He had beaten up Joachim. 'But I never told you to carry on with that. I merely asked you about it.'

'Well, it's too late for quibbling back and forth, arguing over this detail or that. The deed is done, and I need the money. There you have it.' He let out a throaty half laugh that turned into a cough. 'The fellow is beaten, and I'd best leave town as quick as I can before the constable's men catch up with me.'

'I won't give you a thing,' Miguel said. 'I never asked for this.'

The violence that always lurked in Hendrick now rose to the surface. His face reddened and his eyes grew wide. 'Listen to me, Jew Man. You'll give it to me, or there will be more trouble than you reckoned on. If they do catch up with me, I'll not hesitate to say you were the one to set me upon the task, so you had better think about that, and think about it quickly. I know you don't want me to be seen here, so let's just have this over with.'

Miguel knew it was well worth fifty guilders to make him disappear, so he excused himself and found the money in metal, presuming Hendrick would not care for a banknote.

'How badly did you hurt him?' he asked, as he handed over the purse.

'That's the thing,' Hendrick said. He patted at the cut on his face with his sleeve. 'More than I intended. I don't suppose he needed both eyes, though, did he? One will do quite nicely.'

Miguel swallowed. 'You took out an eye?'

'I didn't take it out,' Hendrick corrected him. 'It came out on its own. These things happen from time to time, and there isn't much point lamenting what can't be undone.'

'Get out of here,' Miguel said quietly.

'He didn't know what was going on, why I should just grab him and throw him down and kick him in his face. He kept asking me *why, why, why* – like a little girl being fucked for the first time. But I believe in honesty. I told him to ask the Jew Man. The Jew Man would tell him why, since the Jew Man paid for it.'

Miguel closed his eyes and looked away. After a moment – too long a silence, he thought – he turned back to the wretch. 'Why would you do such a thing? Why did you tell him that?'

'Because Madame Damhuis made me promise not to hurt you, despite your treatment of her. So I decided it was well enough: I would not hurt you, but I would have my own way with something. And there it is.'

'Get out of here,' Miguel said again.

'Oh, that I'll have no trouble doing, you can depend on it. Best to you, Jew Man.' Hendrick pretended to tip the hat he had lost and then took off in a happy skip along the canal side. Miguel stood at the door and watched him go, and even after he had been long gone, he stood by the door watching the space where he had disappeared.

Later on he could not say how long he stood there in cheerless and nauseated silence. He finally looked behind him and saw his servant woman cooking in the kitchen, ignoring him out of fear and confusion, pretending that men always stood by the open door in their bedclothes, staring out into the morning. Later that day, he looked up and saw himself doing business on the Exchange and wondered how he had come to be there, what trades he had made already, and if in such a state he traded with more prudence than when his wits were about him. How could he think of business? His friend Geertruid, ruined and exiled for ever. Joachim beaten and perhaps in danger of dying. His brother ruined and humiliated.

He waited for the Watch to come and question him about his role in the beating, but they never came. When he went in search of Joachim a few days later, to bring him gifts, to make certain he had the best surgeon, he found that he and his wife had left town, scurrying away with their share of the coffee scheme money before Miguel could, as he surely now suspected, find some way of taking it back. He had left believing, as always, that these gestures of friendship were but a prelude to treachery.

The thought weighed him down, a dourness that no triumph on the Exchange could extinguish. But in a few weeks' time, when Hannah was free of Daniel, he took her for his wife and vowed he would be dour no more. In the comfort of married life, he found it easy to forget Joachim and Geertruid by turns and to once more take pleasure in his business. He put a hand to his temple. Alferonda had surely been right about one thing: it would be madness for him to let coffee go. Already, buoyed by the fame of Miguel's duel against Parido on the Exchange, the drink's fame had begun to spread. Already he saw jittery merchants, animated by the wondrous fruit, shouting out their business maniacally. At taverns all over the city, traders had begun to demand the brew in place of beer or wine. Miguel might make his fortune yet.

Though Hannah found, after the baby was born, she had no time to learn to read as she had planned, she did not complain, not even in her heart. Miguel knew she had wanted a girl, but she loved the boy, Samuel, all the same. They discussed the problem of hiding from Daniel that the boy was his, but there was no way to undo what had been done. And Miguel loved the boy as though he were his own. But later, when they had their second son, whom they named for his true father, Miguel found himself favouring this child. At times it sat ill with him that he repeated the arbitrary preferences with which he found such fault in his own father, but what could he do? Some things, he had come to conclude, were merely in a person's nature.

HISTORICAL NOTE

If business and commerce in the Dutch golden age conjure up any image for most people today, it is that of the trade in paintings, which were regarded mostly as aesthetically pleasing commodities rather than objects of art, or of the tulipomania, the crazed tulip market of the 1630s, which was so recently mirrored in our own dotcom bubble. I was drawn to business in the period, however, because of its sheer innovation. If it would be overstating the case to say that business as we know it came into being in the Netherlands in the seventeenth century, it would be fair to propose that *modern* business saw its origins in that time and place. The Dutch developed new methods of trade – the joint stock company, commodities markets, futures, stocks and other forms of speculative trading – mostly because they had to. Coming out of a bitter and protracted war of independence against Spain, the Dutch of the seventeenth century found themselves with very little of any particular value other than their business sense, and with this commercial drive they transformed their nation into one of the most powerful in Europe.

I was also drawn to the period because of the unusual tolerance of the Dutch people. Having vanquished the Catholic Spanish, they offered Catholics an unusual amount of freedom in comparison to other Protestant countries. Jews also found that many cities in the United Provinces offered freedoms unimaginable in the rest of Europe. The Spanish and Portuguese Jews who settled in Amsterdam found their international connections prized by local businessmen.

I began this novel with the idea that I would write about an attempt to control a commodity just as it was emerging. I briefly flirted with the idea of making the novel about chocolate, in part because the seventeenth-century documents about chocolate are much more colourful than those concerning coffee, but coffee and business go so naturally that the switch was inevitable. As I suggest in the novel, coffee was only just catching on in Europe in the middle years of the seventeenth century. By the end of the century, it would be well established as a vital part of public culture in nearly every major capital on the continent.

My efforts to recreate the world of the Dutch, the Dutch Jews, and the coffee trade involved a great deal of research. In the interest of full disclosure, I have provided a list of my reading.

WORKS CONSULTED

Allen, Stewart Lee. *The Devil's Cup: Coffee, the Driving Force in History*. New York: Soho Press, 1999.

Barbour, Violet. *Capitalism in Amsterdam in the 17th Century*. Ann Arbor: University of Michigan Press, 1950.

Bloom, Herbert I. *The Economic Activities of the Jews of Amsterdam in the Seventeenth and Eighteenth Centuries*. Williamsport, Penn.: Bayard Press, 1937.

Bodian, Miriam. *Hebrews of the Portuguese Nation: Conversos and Community in Early Modern Amsterdam*. Bloomington; Indiana University Press, 1997.

Boxer, C. R. *The Dutch Seaborne Empire, 1600–1800*. New York: Alfred A. Knopf, 1965.

Braudel, Ferdinand. *Civilization and Capitalism, 15th–18th century*. 3 vols. Trans. Sian Reynolds. Berkeley: University of California Press, 1981–84.

Chancellor, Edward. *Devil Take the Hindmost: A History of Financial Speculation*. New York: Farrar, Straus & Giroux, 1999.

Van Deursen, A. T. *Plain Lives in a Golden Age: Popular Culture, Religion and Society in Seventeenth– Century Holland.* Trans. Maarten Ultee. Cambridge, England: Cambridge University Press, 1991.

Gitlitz, David M. *Secrecy and Deceit: The Religion of the Crypto-Jews.* Philadelphia: Jewish Publication Society, 1996.

Gluckel of Hameln. *The Memoirs of Gluckel of Hameln.* Trans. Marvin Lowenthal. New York: Schocken Books, 1977.

Gullan-Whur, Margaret. *Within Reason: A Life of Spinoza.* New York: St. Martin's Press, 1998.

Israel, Jonathan I. 'An Amsterdam Jewish Merchant of the Golden Age: Jeronimo Nunes Da Costa (1620–1697), Agent of Portugal in the Dutch Republic.' *Studia Rosenthaliana* 18.1 (1984): 21–40.

Israel, Jonathan I. 'The Changing Role of the Dutch Sephardim in International Trade, 1595–1715.' In *Dutch Jewish History: Proceedings of the Symposium on the History of the Jews in the Netherlands, November 28–December 3, 1982, Tel-Aviv, Jerusalem,* ed. Jozeph Michman, 31–50. Tel-Aviv: Hebrew University of Jerusalem, 1984.

——. *Dutch Primacy in World Trade, 1585–1740.* Oxford, England: Clarendon Press, 1989.

——. *European Jewry in the Age of Mercantilism, 1550-1750.* 3d ed. London: Littman Library of Jewish Civilization, 1998.

Jacob, Heinrich Eduard. *Coffee: The Epic of a*

Commodity. Trans. Eden and Cedar Paul. New York: Viking Press, 1935.

Jardine, Lisa. *Worldly Goods: A New History of the Renaissance*. New York: W. W. Norton, 1996.

Mak, Geert. *Amsterdam: A Brief Life of the City*. Trans. Philipp Blom. London: Harvill Press, 1999.

Nadler, Steven. *Spinoza: A Life*. Cambridge, England: Cambridge University Press, 1999.

Netanyahu, B. *The Marranos of Spain: From the Late 14th to the Early 16th Century, According to Contemporary Hebrew Sources*. 3rd ed. Ithaca, New York: Cornell University Press, 1999.

North, Michael. *Art and Commerce in the Dutch Golden Age*. Trans. Caroline Hill. New Haven: Yale University Press, 1997.

Pendergrast, Mark. *Uncommon Grounds: The History of Coffee and How It Transformed Our World*. New York: Basic Books, 1999.

Regin, Deric. *Traders, Artists, Burghers: A Cultural History of Amsterdam in the 17th Century*. Amsterdam: Van Gorcum, 1976.

Roth, Cecil. *A Life of Menasseh Ben Israel: Rabbi, Printer, and Diplomat*. Philadelphia: The Jewish Publication Society of America, 1934.

Safley, Thomas Max. *Matheus Miller's Memoir: A Merchant's Life in the Seventeenth Century*. New York: St. Martin's Press, 2000.

Schama, Simon. *The Embarrassment of Riches: An Interpretation of Dutch Culture in the Golden Age*. New York: Vintage Books, 1987.

Schivelbusch, Wolfgang. *Tastes of Paradise: A Social*

History of Spices, Stimulants, and Intoxicants. Trans. David Jacobson. New York: Pantheon, 1992.

Swetschinski, Daniel Maurice. *The Portuguese Jewish Merchants of Seventeenth-Century Amsterdam: A Social Profile.* Ph.D. diss., Brandeis University. Ann Arbor: UMI Dissertation Services, 1980.

Temple, Sir William. 'Observations upon the United Provinces of the Netherlands.' *The Works of Sir William Temple, Bart.* Vol 1, 31–203. London, 1814; Greenwood Press repr., 1968.

Vega, Joseph de la. *Confusion de Confusiones: Portions Descriptive of the Amsterdam Stock Exchange.* 1688. Trans. and ed. Hermann Kellenbenz. Boston: Baker Library, 1957.

de Vries, Jan, and Ad van der Woude. *The First Modern Economy: Success, Failure and Perseverance of the Dutch Economy, 1500–1815.* Cambridge, England: Cambridge University Press, 1997.

Westermann, Mariët. *A Worldly Art: The Dutch Republic, 1585–1718.* New York, Harry N. Abrams, 1996.

Zumthor, Paul. *Daily Life in Rembrandt's Holland.* Trans. Simon Watson Taylor. Stanford, Calif.: Stanford University Press, 1994.

ACKNOWLEDGMENTS

Novels are by no means solitary pursuits, and this book could never have happened without the help of many wonderful people.

My first and heartiest thanks go to those who offered me their time and knowledge. J. W. Smit, Deby Abram, Henk Reitsma, Harko Keijzer, and the staff of the Jewish Historical Museum of Amsterdam. I cannot sufficiently thank Rienk Tychon, Thille Dop, and everyone at the offices of Uitgeverij Luitingh-Sijthoff, who made my research in the Netherlands infinitely more productive and enjoyable. Samantha Heller and Sue Laizik read early versions of the novel, and their suggestions were invaluable.

Once again, I am in debt to the people at Random House, particularly Dennis Ambrose, Robbin Schiff, and, of course, my editor Jonathan Karp, whose guidance, enthusiasm, and superhuman editing make my work so much more manageable. And I am eternally grateful to my agent, Liz Darhansoff, and everyone at Darhansoff, Verrill and Feldman for their ceaseless efforts.

It would be impossible to catalogue the reasons I am indebted to my friends and family – the support, the enthusiasm and, perhaps most importantly, the willingness to listen while I thought out loud. Still, I must point out that this book owes a great deal to the kindness, patience, as well as the sometimes smarting honesty of my wife, Claudia Stokes. Thanks for making me do that rewrite. Our daughter, Eleanor, provided unceasing inspiration with her silliness and inexhaustible supply of good cheer. She motivated me in a thousand ways on a thousand occasions. And I'm grateful to Tiki, the orange foundling, for showing up at just the right time.